The Leader and the Damned

In eighteen years Colin Forbes has written eighteen novels. He is translated into twenty languages.

He wrote his first book in 1965 and for two years worked a ninety-hour week – forty-five hours in business in London and another forty-five writing at home to establish himself as a novelist. He achieved this phenomenal work pattern by sleeping four hours a night. For the past sixteen years he has earned his living solely from his writing.

Avalanche Express, starring Lee Marvin and Robert Shaw, was filmed with a $12,000,000 budget. Film rights have also been sold for *Tramp in Armour*, *The Heights of Zervos*, *The Palermo Ambush*, *Year of the Golden Ape*, and *The Stone Leopard* – all of which, with *Target Five*, *The Stockholm Syndicate* and *Double Jeopardy*, are available in Pan.

He now lives in Surrey 'where there are still more trees than houses, although the battle continues'. Married to a Scots-Canadian, he has one daughter, and his safety valve from work is 'to travel abroad fast and always to new places'.

COLIN FORBES

The Leader and the Damned

Pan Books
in association with Collins

First published 1983 by William Collins Sons & Co. Ltd
This edition published 1984 by Pan Books Ltd,
Cavaye Place, London SW10 9PG
in association with William Collins Sons & Co. Ltd
© Colin Forbes 1983
9
ISBN 0 330 28367 7
Printed and bound in Great Britain by
Cox & Wyman Ltd, Reading

FOR JANE, FOR MARJORY
who made it happen . . .

ACKNOWLEDGEMENTS

The Author and Publishers gratefully acknowledge permission to quote from the following:

The Last Days Of Hitler by Hugh Trevor-Roper: reproduced by kind permission of Macmillan Publishers Limited.

Hitler, A Study in Tyranny by Alan Bullock: reproduced by kind permission of The Hamlyn Publishing Group Limited. Originally published by Odhams Press Limited.

The Craft Of Intelligence by Allen Dulles: reproduced by kind permission of George Weidenfeld & Nicolson Limited.

During the night (if we are to believe the report of Hanna Reitsch) Hitler called his court round him, and in this macabre conclave all rehearsed their plans for suicide. . .

That is all that is known about the disposal of the remnants of Hitler's and Eva Braun's bodies . . . 180 litres of petrol, burning slowly on a sandy bed, would char the flesh and dissipate the moisture of the bodies . . . but the bones would withstand the heat. *Those bones have never been found. . .*

. . . the fate of Martin Bormann remains a mystery.

Extracts from *The Last Days of Hitler* by H. R. Trevor-Roper (italics are author's).

In the last years of his life Hitler deliberately refused to exercise the extraordinary powers he had once displayed as a mass orator.

Extract from *Hitler, A Study In Tyranny* by Alan Bullock.

. . . the Soviets developed a fantastic source located in Switzerland, a certain Rudolf Roessler (code name 'Lucy'). By means which have not been ascertained to this day, Roessler in Switzerland was able to get intelligence from the German High Command. . .

Extract from *The Craft Of Intelligence* by Allen Dulles.

CONTENTS

PART ONE

MIRROR MAN:
Der Führer

Chapter One

13 March 1943. The time bomb which was to kill Adolf Hitler, Führer and Commander-in-Chief of the German Armed Forces, was assembled at Smolensk with great care.

The terrible Russian winter was still persisting. Temperatures were far below zero as Hitler conferred with Field Marshal von Kluge on the next planned offensive against the Red Army. Wearing his military great-coat and the peaked cap decorated with a gold eagle clutching the swastika in its claws, Hitler's mood was buoyant and aggressive.

'We shall smash the Russians by attacking earlier than they expect,' he told von Kluge and his staff officers. 'We shall annihilate them with one hammerblow – because we shall outnumber them, out-tank them, out-gun them . . .'

'*Mein Führer,*' von Kluge intervened respectfully, 'I feel it my duty to point out that at the moment Stalin's troops outnumber ours. . .'

'At the moment.'

Hitler paused, glanced round the half-ruined concrete building inside which the conference was being held, and stalked away to stare out through a broken window only half-protected by a canvas flap. The flap whipped in the wind which moaned in the brief silence. It was a typical dramatic gesture, the trick of a superb actor – to grip his audience in suspense before he made his sensational announcement.

Staring out of the window Hitler watched the endless line of Soviet prisoners trudging through the snow and guarded by Wehrmacht soldiers. The white hell of Russia faded into the distance, masked by falling snow. Beyond the line of prisoners stood another half-ruined building, its roof almost collapsed. Even Hitler's extraordinary intuition did not warn him of what was going on inside the relic.

He turned away, returned to the table and smashed his clenched fist on the map of the Eastern Front spread over its surface. His voice rose to a manic shriek.

'At the moment,' he repeated. 'What you do not know, what I have come here to tell you is that soon you will have at your disposal another forty divisions – including ten Panzers! Now tell me that you cannot wipe the Red Army off the face of the earth within two months!'

Numbed with the cold despite the oil-heaters placed round the table – the building reeked with the stench of oil fumes – von Kluge, like every man on his staff, was astounded. The Field Marshal was the first to recover his wits. Cautiously, he posed his question.

'*Mein Führer*, may I ask where these divisions, this truly massive reinforcement, is coming from?'

'From the West, of course!' Hitler shouted. 'The order will be given immediately I return to my headquarters. With these fresh troops and tanks you will be in Moscow by May! Once Moscow – the hub of the Soviet rail network – falls, Stalin is finished!'

'But the West will be left defenceless,' von Kluge persisted. 'It will be wide open to an Anglo-American landing. . .'

'Your memory is short, my dear von Kluge,' Hitler snapped. 'I have conducted the same manoeuvre successfully when we overran Poland in 1939. The western frontiers of the Reich were defenceless then. At that time the British and French armies were on the Continent. Did they attack? No! All went as I predicted.'

'But when Churchill is informed of the withdrawal. . .'

Hitler was deliberately working himself up into a mood of contempt and rage.

'You think I have overlooked that? Dummy encampments and mock tank laagers are already prepared! When the enemy's reconnaissance planes photograph France and Belgium they will bring back evidence that the forty divisions are still there! It will be a military master-stroke! And once Moscow falls, it will take a mere handful of troops to wipe out the rabble remaining of Stalin's forces. You will have the

16

whole summer to do that at your leisure. Then one hundred and twenty divisions will be transferred back to the West to face Mr Churchill and his American masters. I may put you in command, von Kluge,' he added casually.

Alone inside the other concrete building Hitler had gazed out at, General Henning von Tresckow, GSO1 of von Kluge's Army Group Centre had just completed the fabrication of the bomb and was fixing the timing device. At the doorway his accomplice, Lieutenant Schlabrendorff, stood anxiously on guard. Many years younger than the General, he was a bundle of nerves, half-frozen and his mind occupied with everything that could go wrong with the plot.

'How can we be sure when he will board the plane?' he asked. 'That affects your fixing of the clock. The bomb must explode while he is in mid-air – or we are finished . . .'

'Calm yourself,' von Tresckow reassured him without looking up from the device he was attending to. 'As soon as the conference is over the Führer is returning to the Wolf's Lair in East Prussia, a flight of eight hundred kilometres. That gives plenty of margin to time the detonation . . .'

'Unless he decides to stay overnight.'

'That he will not do. He never likes to spend a moment longer than is necessary from his power base. He trusts no one – he never has.'

And hence Hitler's unique capacity for self-preservation, von Tresckow was thinking. But this time he had slipped up; in Berlin certain generals were only waiting for news of the Führer's death to seize power. Satisfied that the time-bomb was ready, he took two bottles of brandy, placed them on a table, inserted the bomb inside an open package and shoved the bottles on top of it. Then, without hesitating, he walked out of the building followed by his aide and made for the airstrip where the Condor waiting to take Hitler back to Germany stood.

As he approached the machine Otto Reiter, an SS officer, stopped him and demanded to know what he was doing. General von Tresckow stood stiffly, his manner cold and overbearing as he stared back at the white-faced SS man with skeletal cheekbones. After a few seconds Reiter's eyes dropped from the chilly stare and looked at the package which the General shoved at him.

'A little present for a friend at the Wolf's Lair which I am about to place aboard the plane. Now, do I walk through you and over you or will you get out of the bloody way? Alternatively, I can ask the Führer himself – explaining that you have exceeded your rank and a spell at the front might teach you discipline.'

Reiter, his mind half-paralysed with the cold, shivered at the threat and stood aside. Climbing up inside the Condor, von Tresckow walked along between the special seats which had been fitted into the aircraft, peered through a frosted-up window to see the silhouettes of Reiter engaged in conversation with Schlabrendorff, and jammed the package under one of the seats. Straightening his cap, he left the aircraft, sneezing violently as he passed Reiter, and returned to his quarters a short distance from the conference building.

The General would normally have attended the conference but at the last moment he had pleaded an attack of influenza to his chief, von Kluge, and now – away from his aide's presence – his outwardly calm demeanour changed. Sinking onto the mattress of his trestle bed he was wracked with anxiety. So many things could go wrong and his head was now well and truly on the block.

Would that swine of an SS officer, Reiter, decide to board the plane for a last-minute check? He *seemed* to have been satisfied with his glimpse of the two necks of the brandy bottles protruding from the package. Would the Führer – as he had so often in the past – change his schedule at the last moment? The man seemed to have an uncanny instinct for danger. He had so far survived six different attempts on his life. There was even a rumour von Tresckow had once heard that he had possessed a double – someone who could pass for Hitler himself in appearance. Was it indeed Adolf Hitler who at this moment was haranguing von Kluge's staff?

'Damnit, I used not to be so full of doubts,' he said to

himself. It must be this accursed Russian cold which ate its way into the system and numbed all logical thought. He looked up, the door opened and Schlabrendorff appeared.

'He is just leaving! He is about to board the plane!'

'What did I tell you?'

The General stood up and pressed his palm against the ice-cold glass of the window. His own room was also filled with the stench of fumes from the oil-heater. He was not sure which he hated most: that ghastly stink which kept you alive or the dreaded cold which made it hard to think, an effort to move. Resolutely he held his hand against the numbing glass until they could just see through the outline of his palm-print the blurred figure of the Führer.

'You understand, von Kluge,' Hitler repeated, 'one giant hammerblow with massed tanks and men. With the huge force under your command – larger than any general has directed in this war – you will drive on and on! Non-stop until you reach Moscow! Not one chance for the enemy to recover from the initial shock! Ignore taking prisoners . . .' His hypnotic eyes fixed von Kluge. 'As in France in 1940 you keep up the momentum – roll over the swine! On and on until you have the domes of St Basil in your artillery sights!'

'I understand, *mein Führer*! With the new forces you are sending it shall be done . . .'

Deliberately lingering in the terrible cold as an example, Hitler gripped von Kluge's arm and softened his voice. 'You are about to make history, my friend. A hundred years from now the historians will still be writing about the Second Battle of Moscow which finally destroyed Stalin and burned the Communist plague from the face of the globe!'

He turned away and behind him von Kluge, one of the shrewdest and most experienced of Hitler's commanders, felt a sensation of excitement rising inside him. The unique power of Hitler to inspire men was working again. He saluted as the Führer walked slowly towards the waiting Condor.

Reiter's heavily armed SS guard was ready for his departure, drawn up in two lines as Hitler walked very slowly

19

between them, staring into each face. The cold seemed not to affect him at all; long ago as a pauper during his youth in Vienna he had learned to ignore the elements, to summon up his unique willpower to withstand all discomfort. Then, at the foot of the staircase leading up to the aircraft he paused. Something was wrong.

His intuitive sixth sense told him something was wrong. What could it be? As the snow fell softly he looked round for a clue. Von Kluge's GSO1, General von Tresckow, had been absent from the war council. Something to do with suffering a bout of influenza. Why had that thought come into his mind? He remained motionless, indifferent to the insidious wind from the East freezing his face. The double column of SS guards stood equally motionless, their right arms raised in the Hitler salute. In the far distance the Führer could hear a sound like muted thunder, the rumble of gunfire at the front carried all the way to Smolensk by the wind.

Inside his quarters General von Tresckow watched the scene through the de-frosted shape of his palm-print which was rapidly misting up. He dared not apply his frozen hand again; the movement might be seen – even by the Führer who seemed to miss nothing.

'He's hesitating – he's suspicious. . .'

In the tension of the moment Schlabrendorff found himself whispering with fear. His legs felt like jelly and he was cursing inwardly. How could they have performed such an insane act?

'Yes,' von Tresckow agreed sombrely, 'that blasted sixth sense is at work. It's uncanny.'

Already he could picture himself standing in front of a firing squad; erect, stripped of all his medals; the order given; the line of rifle barrels levelled at him; the brief command. 'Fire!' Then oblivion. With an effort of will, worthy of the Führer himself, he maintained an outward air of composure and waited.

Hitler had still not boarded the plane. The raised arms of the SS guard were almost frozen rigid in their posture. Field

Marshal von Kluge and his staff stood a few yards away at attention. Von Kluge was still experiencing a sensation of exhilaration. Before Hitler's arrival he had been despondent; the more Russians you killed the more of them appeared. It had been a nightmare.

Now he was turning over in his mind the new plan. The more he thought about it the more sure he was it would work. It had done so in Poland and in Russia it would succeed. But this time the victory would be colossal, earth-shaking. The whole Red Army would be annihilated in one shattering onslaught. Only a man with Hitler's mesmeric powers could have changed the mind of so calculating a commander as von Kluge in one short conference.

Suddenly Hitler raised his own arm and the cry '*Heil Hitler*' echoed round the bleak, snowbound encampment of broken buildings. Without a word the Führer turned, mounted the steps to the plane, disappeared inside. The door was closed as the pilot fired his engines, the steps were hauled away and the machine began to move bumpily over the freshly cleared airstrip.

Inside the plane Hitler took off his cap and coat, handed it to an aide who shook it free from snow, and walked rapidly along the corridor. He chose the seat in front of the one under which von Tresckow had placed the time-bomb and called for his briefcase. He needed something to occupy his mind: he detested flying as much as he loved being driven at high speed in a car.

The stern expression he had adopted when facing the SS guard disappeared. Despite his dislike of planes his face relaxed into a smile, the smile which had charmed – and disarmed – so many Western leaders. As he extracted a folded map of France and the Low Countries showing the locations of the dummy encampments, the plane left the ground.

Von Kluge and his staff still stood in the cold, watching the machine disappear into the murky overcast, the machine carrying the greatest political and military genius since Napoleon and Julius Caesar. Evil he might be in many of his methods, but his predecessors had not been saints. And he

21

had not had any of their advantages in upbringing and professional training.

He had risen from the gutter, his only weapons his extraordinary powers of speech and supreme willpower and belief in his own destiny. Alone he had done it: had dragged a nation of eighty million from the depths of degradation and despair to become the most feared and mighty power in the world.

But two other hidden men also watched the tiny blur of the plane disappear into the sky. Von Tresckow and Schlabrendorff turned away from the window and the latter wiped beads of sweat from his forehead. Even the strong-willed von Tresckow sank on to a chair.

'We've done it!' Schlabrendorff said jubilantly.

'The bomb still has to detonate,' his superior reminded him. He roused himself from the feeling of torpor which was a reaction to the strain they had undergone. 'And I must send the signal to Berlin to warn Olbricht . . .'

Leaving his quarters, he strode briskly through the snow to the signals building which housed the direct line to Berlin. Inside he told the operator to leave him alone. 'I am sending a highly confidential message,' he remarked curtly. Waiting until the door was closed, he rang Berlin and asked to be put through at once to General Olbricht, Chief of the Home Army who commanded the troops in the capital.

'Von Tresckow here,' he informed Olbricht when the General came on the line. 'The present I promised you has been delivered . . .

He cut the connection the moment he had spoken the key words; these days no one knew when the bloody Gestapo was monitoring calls. Now everything was ready: as soon as the news of Hitler's death reached Berlin, Olbricht would move, using his garrison troops to seize all major control points in Berlin – the War Ministry, the radio stations, the Ministry of Propaganda and Enlightenment and so on.

He walked out of the signals building and stared briefly in the direction where Hitler's plane had disappeared on its long flight to the Wolf's Lair in East Prussia. Everything now hung on one thing. The explosion of the bomb.

Chapter Two

13 March 1943. At the airfield several kilometres from the Wolfsschanze – the Wolf's Lair, Hitler's secret headquarters in East Prussia – Martin Bormann, head of the Party Chancery, stood outside the control tower waiting for his master's plane to arrive.

By his side stood Alois Vogel, chief of the SS security guard. A tall man with a thin face and a tight mouth, Vogel was clad in his black uniform with the SS lightning flashes on his collar. While he stamped his frozen feet, crunching the rutted snow, Vogel glanced impatiently at his watch. He used his gloved thumb to remove the film of ice which had formed on the glass casing.

'He should arrive soon now,' he remarked. 'I wish this accursed fog would lift . . .'

'It is normal,' Bormann replied calmly, 'and the Führer's pilot is an expert.'

It was indeed normal. For half the year this dreary part of Germany was smothered in a white mist and covered with snow. It was an eery, hushed atmosphere. The mist rolled in drifts like a sea-fog, occasionally parting to expose vague silhouettes of the stands of endless pine forest. Unlike the SS officer, Bormann stood quite motionless, always patient, his hands clasped behind his back.

One of the most puzzling figures in recent history, Bormann was a short, heavily-built man with a Slav face. He had a strong nose, a mole-like head and rarely showed any emotion. It was impossible ever to know what he was thinking: on the surface he appeared to be no more than Hitler's faithful secretary who transmitted the Führer's orders and ensured their immediate execution. But to more perceptive observers there was something sinister in his chameleon-like personality. 'He is Hitler's shadow,' one general had observed. 'And the shadow is darker than the man who casts it.'

'Here he comes,' said Vogel.

He left Bormann's side and issued orders to the twenty armed SS men who formed the Führer's personal bodyguard. Bormann turned his head slightly. Vogel was right: the sound of an approaching plane's engines had broken the silence of the rolling mist. Still no more than a distant mutter, the sound was growing louder. Bormann went inside a building and emerged with an Alsatian he held on a chain. After his long flight from Smolensk the Führer would be pleased to see Blondi, the dog Bormann himself had found for Hitler to comfort him after the defeat at Stalingrad.

It was by little considerate acts such as this that Bormann had cemented his position as Hitler's personal secretary; the man who passed on most of the Führer's orders to everyone. Bormann had even changed his sleep pattern to accord with the Führer's. In this way he was never absent from Hitler's side at the Wolf's Lair. The fact that he was hated by Goering, Himmler and all the other Nazi chiefs disturbed him not at all. Bormann's ambition was to be what he was, Hitler's shadow, ever present when decisions were made.

'He's coming in to land,' Vogel called out. 'Shall I inform headquarters?'

'No. Leave that to me.'

Bormann remained where he was, scanning the heavy overcast for his first sight of the plane which was very close now. Luckily the mist was briefly dissolving as a light wind blew up, exposing the runway on which the machine would land.

Hitler's luck again, Bormann said to himself wryly. For the whole day the airfield had been blotted out and now it was going to be an easy task for the pilot to bring his plane down safely. As though sensing the arrival of his master, the Alsatian tugged at his lead. 'Stay still!' Bormann snapped, his cold eyes searching for the machine.

Aboard the Condor Adolf Hitler had donned his military greatcoat and peaked cap. His expression was severe and arrogant, the face of a world-conqueror ready to be greeted by the waiting SS guard. Yet only half an hour earlier he had reduced his small group of aides to hysterical laughter as he paraded up and down the corridor mimicking Prime Minister Chamberlain when the Englishman had visited him at the pre-war Munich conference. He peered out of the window for his first sight of the ground.

No one with him inside the plane could have guessed that he was a bundle of nerves at this moment. He hated landing just as much as he hated take-off. I shall never fly again, he promised himself. But he knew that, if he had to, he would do the same thing all over again. His blue glaucous eyes flickered. He had caught sight of a glimpse of pine trees.

On the airfield below Bormann had seen the machine descending. It appeared and then disappeared again as the pilot turned for the final run-in. Glancing round the airfield where Vogel had drawn up his troops ready for the Führer's arrival, Bormann sensed the normal atmosphere of tension and excitement which always surrounded these occasions.

What news would Hitler bring back from the Eastern front? A few minutes before his departure he had taken the Chancery Leader aside and hinted at his plans – which was most unusual. It was Hitler's invariable rule to keep to himself all major strategic decisions until the moment of announcement.

'Bormann', he had confided, 'we are on the eve of a massive manoeuvre which will tip the whole balance of the war in our favour – a manoeuvre so audacious it is worthy of Napoleon or Frederick the Great . . .'

'I will await your return eagerly,' Bormann had replied.

The plane came into view again, much lower now and no more than one kilometre from the airfield. It was descending rapidly when it again vanished in the overcast. As Bormann stood there he saw a blinding flash which dissipated the mist. He actually glimpsed the machine breaking up in mid-air followed by a muffled detonation. Then the mist rolled in again and the hush of the fog-bound forest descended. Silence.

Stunned, he didn't move for several seconds, but the Alsatian did. With a low, moaning howl it leaped forward, freeing itself from his grip, running off in the direction of the explosion. The dog's flight jerked Bormann into action. He shouted towards Vogel.

'Send two men to the control tower! Close down all communications! Ring the airfield with troops! No one is allowed in or out! Then come with me.'

Vogel reacted instantly, issuing the instructions before running to join Bormann who had hurried over to where a Kübelwagen stood. The strange vehicle – with wheels at the front and caterpillar tracks at the rear – was for negotiating difficult terrain. Bormann was behind the wheel as Vogel arrived with his warning.

'They may have heard the explosion at headquarters . . .'

Bormann thought for a moment, idling the engine as Vogel got into the passenger seat beside him. 'Kempner,' he called out to Vogel's second-in-command. He studied the SS man who stood at attention below him. No sign of panic. He took another quick decision.

'Kempner. Drive back to headquarters. Inform them that the Führer's plane has been delayed by bad weather – that it has put down at another airfield. Tell them he has cancelled tomorrow's conference at noon. And if anyone mentions hearing an explosion, say it was caused by a fox running over a mine . . .'

It was only too plausible an explanation. The Wolf's Lair was ringed by minefields and there had been many a false alarm when foxes had detonated a mine. Leaving Kempner running for a car, Bormann set the Kübelwagen in motion, beckoning for several SS men to climb aboard.

Soon he was driving along a track through the pine forests, the airfield lost from view as the mist swirled amid the trees in a sinister fashion. He did not have to drive far. Suddenly they came to a clearing where pine trunks were blasted stumps projecting at awkward angles like mutilated limbs. As he stopped the vehicle the scene they gazed at was appalling, horrific.

Bits of the plane were scattered everywhere. It must have been close to tree-top level when the detonation occurred – and the blast had gone downwards. Fragments of bodies were caught in the branches of trees. It was like a slaughter-house where a maniac with a meat-axe had run berserk. A stench of petrol mingling with burnt flesh hung in the mist. Blondi, the Alsatian, was sniffing around the charnel house. Bormann and Vogel climbed out, followed by the SS men.

'He could not have survived this,' Bormann said slowly.

'What do we do?' asked Vogel.

'Wait a minute while I think . . .'

Bormann had risen to the position of being Hitler's right-hand man because of his powers of meticulous administration and planning. The Führer hated the donkey work of routine and had come to rely on the quiet, stocky deputy to deal with all details. He would issue an order and Bormann would process it – to such an extent that he could send out any instruction, ending it with the words no one dare question: 'By order of the Führer!'

At this moment he held the fate of Germany in his hands and he showed what he was made of. As he stood in the snow with the mist drifting among the encircling pines, surveying the carnage with the stench of death in his nostrils, his mind was racing.

'Vogel, cordon off the entire area. Shoot anyone who tries to approach it. Bring in trucks and clear up the mess. Miss nothing. Every remnant of corpses – bits of the plane – go aboard the trucks which will be driven to a remote spot. Empty the mess out and burn it – then bury it . . .'

He was interrupted by a nearby sound of someone retching. An SS man came stumbling through the mist, so shaken he omitted to salute Bormann. He had difficulty speaking.

'What is it?' Bormann snapped. 'Get a grip on yourself.'

'Karl has just found the pilot's head in his helmet – just his head. . .'

27

'First item to go aboard the trucks,' Bormann told Vogel brutally.

'There is something else,' the SS man stammered. He showed them what he had been hiding behind his back. A briefcase with the relic of a hand still clutching the handle tightly. 'It is the Führer's . . .'

Without a sign of squeamishness Bormann took the briefcase, holding its sides before he ripped it open. The hand fell to the ground, still clutching the handle which had broken off.

Bormann examined the contents of the scorched briefcase. Yes, it was the Führer's – he recognised the maps of Western Europe he had personally inserted inside the case before Hitler's departure for Smolensk. He returned the briefcase to Vogel.

'Put that with the rest of the relics ready for the trucks.' He gestured to the grisly object on the ground. 'That goes with all the other remnants . . .'

Vogel was appalled. 'But surely he must have a decent burial – a state funeral.'

Bormann stared bleakly at Vogel. 'Do you think that a man like the Führer did not foresee this contingency – that he might one day be assassinated? Do you really think he did not leave a contingency plan for just such a situation as we face now?' he lied.

'My apologies . . .' Vogel stammered.

'Your apologies are not accepted – yet,' Bormann told him coldly. 'Your entire future depends on your carrying out my instructions. By order of the Führer,' he added.

'I will start at once . . .'

'When the trucks have been emptied, when their contents have been burned,' Bormann continued, 'you will drive the trucks to the nearest lake and sink them.'

'There will still be all this.' Vogel gestured towards the broken tree stumps, the charred pines, their branches hanging like limp limbs in the drifting mist.

'Bring a mine and detonate it – that will explain the wreckage.'

Turning his back on the SS man, Bormann climbed up

behind the wheel of the Kübelwagen and drove away from the scene of carnage.

It was still 13 March 1943. Adolf Hitler was dead – over two years before the end of the war.

Chapter Three

Martin Bormann sat at the nerve centre of the huge power apparatus which controlled the movement of millions of armed men, vast fleets of planes and columns of tanks and guns – one of the greatest war machines assembled in history.

He sat inside the *Lagebaracke*, a single-storey wooden building which housed the room where Hitler held his twice-daily military conferences at noon and midnight; the telephone system which relayed the Führer's orders throughout his huge empire; a cloakroom, a washroom and an entrance hall.

The *Lagebaracke* was located at the heart of Security Ring A, the heavily cordoned off Wolf's Lair protected by three separate barbed wire fences and a minefield. Elite SS troops patrolled the area and admittance through three checkpoints was strictly controlled by special passes issued by Himmler's chief of security.

Bormann sat alone with the telephone on the table, thinking carefully before he picked up the receiver and gave the orders on which the fate of Germany hung. So far his precautions had concealed the catastrophe. Kempner, Vogel's second-in-command, had arrived earlier and spread the story that the Führer's plane – delayed by bad weather – had landed at another airfield.

Returning to the Wolf's Lair, Bormann had met Colonel-General Alfred Jodl, the Führer's Chief of Operations. Jodl had helpfully supplied his own explanation for the delay.

'I suppose this is another of his sudden changes of schedule – to foil any assassination attempt?'

'Possibly,' Bormann had replied.

'And the next conference with the Führer will be noon tomorrow?'

'That is the present intention,' Bormann agreed cautiously.

Now, alone in the *Lagebaracke*, the meticulous Bormann studied the list of names he had written down on a scratch pad. Timing was everything if he was to pull off this coup – timing and the sequence of events which must be fitted together like a cleverly designed jigsaw. He studied the list of names afresh.

Commandant, Berghof
Kuby
Reiter, SS, Smolensk
Schulz, SS, Berlin
Vogel, SS, Wolf's Lair

His decision taken, he picked up the 'phone and asked to be put through immediately to the Commandant at the Berghof, Hitler's mountain retreat at Berchtesgaden on what had once been the frontier between Austria and Germany before the Anschluss incorporated Austria into the Greater German Reich. His conversation with the Commandant was terse and to the point.

' . . . so you have understood your instructions perfectly? Kuby is to be flown here tomorrow in a Condor – it must be a Condor – and the markings on the plane are to be exactly as I have specified. Now, put me on to Kuby himself . . .'

His instructions to Heinz Kuby were equally curt and brief.

'I will meet you personally at the airfield and brief you before we proceed to the Wolf's Lair. You know exactly what you have to do?'

'I have no doubt at all in my mind,' the familiar voice replied. 'The fate of Germany is in my hands . . .'

'Don't overdo it,' Bormann interjected coldly. 'Everything depends on my briefing when you arrive here at the airfield.'

He put down the phone. Despite the rebuke Bormann felt relieved, suddenly realized that for the first time he himself was convinced that it could work. God in heaven, it had to work or he would be dead within days. His next call was the really dangerous one, the call to Otto Reiter, chief of the SS guard at Smolensk. The trick, he decided, was to let Reiter do most of the talking. He ticked off from his list Commandant, the Berghof, and Kuby while he waited for the Smolensk call to come through.

'Bormann here,' he announced when Reiter came on the 'phone, 'I am calling by order of the Führer. You were in charge of the guard which watched over his plane while he conferred with Field Marshal von Kluge?'

'Yes, Reichsleiter. I personally supervised all checks while the machine was on the ground.' There was a hint of pride verging on arrogance in Reiter's voice. Bormann smiled thinly; the idiot was obviously hoping for promotion or even decoration.

'While the plane was waiting did anything unusual happen? Did anyone at all approach or go aboard the aircraft?'

'Reichsleiter, is there something wrong?' The arrogance had been replaced by anxiety.

'Yes – you have not answered my question.'

Words began tumbling across the wire as Reiter explained. 'I can think of nothing unusual. The most strict precautions were taken, I assure you. When General von Tresckow took a package on board I examined it personally. He was not pleased, I can tell you. But I know my duty, Reichsleiter. This package contained two bottles of brandy. I even noticed the make,' he continued. 'It was Courvoisier. No one else boarded the machine until the Führer himself left Smolensk . . .'

'Obviously this has nothing to do with von Tresckow,' Bormann interjected smoothly. 'A map appears to be missing from the Führer's briefcase – but now I am sure we shall find it here.'

'My story can be confirmed by Lieutenant Schlabrendorff who is coming to the Wolf's Lair via Berlin – he is von Tresckow's aide . . .'

Bormann froze. He decided Schlabrendorff's visit must be postponed until after the plane from the Salzburg airstrip arrived. What later happened was that Tresckow's aide was

31

stopped from approaching the aircraft and – to cover his failure – returned to Berlin and reported to his chief he had removed the unexploded bomb, dismantling it on the train and throwing the pieces out of the window. Bormann resumed talking to Reiter.

'No confirmation is necessary. Put me on to Field Marshal von Kluge at once.'

When von Kluge came on the line Bormann explained that with his eye for even the smallest detail the Führer had observed that Otto Reiter had performed sloppily while he was at Smolensk. 'Please arrange for him to be sent to the front to join an SS division today. By order of the Führer!'

Von Kluge, puzzled and a little irritated that Hitler should bother himself with such details, was not entirely surprised. The Führer seemed to miss nothing. He acted at once on the instruction. Reiter never reached the front. On his way a long-range Soviet shell burst within metres of the vehicle he was travelling in and he died instantly. When the news reached Bormann he crossed Reiter's name off the list.

His next call was to Rainer Schulz, commander of a special SS execution team then stationed in Berlin. Again the conversation was brief, but this time Bormann did most of the talking.

' . . . you have been here once before, Schulz . . . we went for a drive in the Kübelwagen, so you know the spot . . . the lake which is little more than a large swamp . . . you remain hidden until they have sunk the trucks . . .'

'It seems an extreme measure,' Schulz ventured cautiously, – 'the killing of twenty men. . .'

'One of whom, as I have already told you, is a spy. Since we cannot detect which one, all must go. Realize – this man, whoever he may be – has access to the Wolf's Lair. Needless to say, you do not come with your men anywhere near Security Ring A. As soon as the job is done you return to Berlin under oath of secrecy. By order of the Führer!'

'*Heil Hitler*, Reichsleiter . . .'

'One more thing. We have uncovered another member of the underground – no less than the Commandant at the

Berghof. As soon as you return to Berlin you will fly to Berchtesgaden alone and deal with him, too. It must be made to look like an accident. Understood?'

'I will begin my preparations at once, Reichsleiter . . .'

During the night of 13 March – 14 March, Alois Vogel, commander of the Wolf's Lair SS guard, drove his men mercilessly in the bitter cold to remove every trace of the plane crash. With the aid of powerful mobile lamps mounted on trucks the area was scoured for every trace of the wrecked plane and the grisly remnants of bodies.

Vogel himself, whose maxim was 'thoroughness', spotted the machine's tail perched at a crazy angle in the fork of a huge pine. By some miracle almost intact, it was added to the human debris piled aboard three trucks. It was close to dawn before he was satisfied they had removed every trace of the disaster.

'Now place the mine and detonate it,' he ordered one of his men as the three trucks rumbled off a safe distance down one of the tracks leading through the forest towards the lake. The mine was buried deep to muffle the explosion. The blast of the explosion smashed and scarred a few more trees – but now there was an explanation for the scene of destruction if anyone wandered into this part of the woods.

'To the lake!' he shouted, jumping aboard the last truck.

By four o'clock in the morning of 14 March Vogel and his twenty men had completed the first part of their task. The contents of the three trucks – the remains of the Condor and its passengers – had been shovelled into the snow by the edge of the swampy lake, petrol had been poured over them, ignited and the shrivelled remnants had been shovelled back inside one of the trucks.

'Now all we have to do is to sink the trucks,' Vogel told his exhausted men. 'The sooner the job is done the sooner we can get back to our warm beds . . .'

The driver of the first truck revved up his engine, pausing to make sure the door by his side was wide open. In the headlights he saw the mist rising from the dank waters of the muddy lake which was little more than a quagmire coated with ice – thin ice beneath which lay a mixture of mud and water. It was not a task he relished: he had to drive the truck forward at speed and jump clear at the last moment. Several of his comrades stood by the edge of the lake waiting to help him. Taking a deep breath, he released the brake and sped forward.

In his eagerness to complete the task properly – Vogel was a man who expected nothing less than perfection – he almost jumped out too late. The truck roared on past him as he landed and felt his legs sinking into the ooze just beneath the ice which crackled and gave way like glass. Two men grabbed his arms and hauled him clear, his boots covered with slime. From a safer distance Vogel watched the truck dive forward, its headlights vanish, followed by the rear light. The vehicle settled, sinking out of sight beneath the surface.

'Come on! Hurry it up!'

He waved the second truck forward which entered the lake a few metres away from the first. The driver, having seen what almost happened to the previous truck's driver, jumped earlier. Then the third truck was driven into the swamp. Now the only evidence of what had just taken place was the shattered ice and it was so cold a fresh film began forming almost at once. Vogel gathered his men round him.

'I think a little liquid refreshment is called for,' he announced and produced a flask of vodka Bormann had given to him earlier. They were standing bunched together, passing round the flask when a dazzle of blinding lights illuminated them.

Earlier, Rainer Schulz, commander of the special ten-man execution team, recently returned from the Russian front, had flown his men to the airfield near the Wolf's Lair in a transport plane. Inside the machine his men huddled together for warmth a short distance from the five motor-cycles with out-rider cars they had loaded aboard the machine in Berlin.

The controller of the airfield had been told by Bormann

himself to expect the new arrivals who would land in the early hours of the morning. He was given the special code signal the pilot of the plane would use when approaching the airfield: '*Dragon*'. The macabre implications of the word totally escaped the controller.

'They have come to replace the present security guard,' Bormann had explained. 'Men grow stale after a while performing the same duties. I do not have to tell you how important it is that the security team remains constantly on the alert . . . by order of the Führer!' he had ended.

By order of the Führer! Time and again these five words, repeated with almost regular monotony, gave Bormann the immense power he wielded on Hitler's behalf. It had reached the pitch where no one throughout the whole of Germany dreamed of questioning such a command.

At three-thirty in the morning, aided by the landing lights briefly switched on, the transport plane landed and cruised to a halt on the runway. Everything went as smoothly as clockwork; Rainer Schulz was a meticulous organizer. Seated now in the sidecar of the first motor-bike, a Schmeisser machine-pistol resting in his lap, he waited while the ramp was lowered before giving the order.

'Go! I will guide you . . .'

The motor-bike and side-car cavalcade, led by Schulz, left the aircraft whose propellers were still spinning and headed for the exit gates which were already open. Turning right, away from the Wolf's Lair, the cavalcade plunged off the road onto a track leading into the forest.

Behind Schulz his other eight men also sat on their machines, and each man in the outrider car was armed with a machine-pistol and several spare magazines. The headlights of Schulz's motorbike shone on the deserted track, showed up a palisade of pines and the drifting mist.

They proceeded at a steady pace, guided by their leader who had a phenomenal memory for geography. He only had to follow a route once and it was engraved on his memory for ever. He had, as a precaution, brought a detailed map of the area, but he did not once refer to it as he led his column over the ice-rutted, bumpy track through the frozen forest, his only guide the beam of the motor-bike's headlight.

'Halt! Dismount! We proceed from here on foot . . .'

Schulz again led the way, holding his machine-pistol loosely. All the lights of the motor-cycles and side-cars had been extinguished. From his neck a pair of night-glasses was slung, but his excellent vision in the dark took him down the broad track without their aid. The aroma of the drifting mist mingled with damp pine foliage scent in his nostrils as he moved silently forward.

Behind him, as previously ordered, six of his men – three in pairs – pushed their machines as the side-cars wobbled over the icy ruts. Their weapons were loaded in the side-cars. The only sound in the eery mistbound forest was the occasional crunch of a wheel as it broke ice in a rut. Padded against the bitter cold in his leather greatcoat, Schulz paused.

'Get those machines off the track onto the grass,' he ordered. 'I want you to make less noise than a column of mice . . .'

Having given the order, he moved ahead of the main body with only one man. They were nearing the lake. Turning a corner of the track, he stopped and raised his night-glasses. The lake was in view, mist like steam rising from its surface. At that moment one of Alois Vogel's men struck a match to light his cigarette, his stomach savouring the warmth of the vodka he had just swallowed. Vogel's team had only recently sent the third truck to its watery oblivion under the ice of the lake.

'Very convenient,' Schulz commented in a whisper to his subordinate. 'They are all bunched together. Place the bikes in position and await my order.'

The three motor-bikes and side-cars were manhandled some distance apart, their headlights aimed to illuminate Vogel and his group of men from different angles. Schulz perched himself with his backside on the seat of one bike, unlooped his machine-pistol and steadied the weapon for firing.

'Everyone is ready,' his subordinate reported to him.

'Proceed,' Schulz ordered.

Synchronization was perfect. The lights came on, their beams illuminating and blinding the targets. The forest silence was shattered briefly by the murderous crossfire of the machine-pistols.

Vogel and his men were slaughtered and so swiftly that not a single individual had time to reach for his weapon. In the glare of the headlight beams they crumpled like matchstick men, falling in grotesque attitudes, often one man toppling on top of his comrade. In less than a minute it was all over. Schulz rammed a fresh magazine into his weapon and walked slowly forward, his grey bleak eyes searching for any sign of survival.

He thought he saw one man twitch and emptied half the magazine into the heap the man lay atop of. He had no particular reaction to what had just happened, no thought as to which of the bodies had been the spy Bormann had spoken of. It was just an order to be carried out, an action his special SS team had accomplished against Soviet guerrillas time and again on the Russian front.

'Proceed to the next phase,' he told his second-in-command.

He waited while his team stripped the corpses of the SS men until they lay naked in the snow, their uniforms and the contents of their pockets neatly stacked in a separate pile. Schulz himself fetched a jerrican filled with petrol, poured it over the pile and set light to it.

By the illumination from the blaze he watched as his men completed their task systematically. A pair would take the body of one of the dead SS men by the shoulders and the ankles, swing the body back and forwards and then hurl it as far as possible out across the lake. The bodies disappeared beneath the freshly-forming ice, following the three trucks they had themselves consigned to the dark waters.

Schulz watched the macabre scene with an expressionless face. He knew the Masurian lakes. The bodies would sink deep into the foul ooze, would lie frozen there until spring. And even then they would not surface. It was never really warm in East Prussia. Embedded in the ooze, they would remain there until they disintegrated.

'Now, the uniforms and the clutter . . .'

Two men with shovels carefully scooped up the red-hot embers of the fire Schulz had lit and cast them into one of the broken areas of the lake where the ice had cracked as a body went through it. There was a sizzle, a brief puff of steam. Only when he was satisfied they had removed every trace did Schulz give his next order.

'Back to the Wolf's Lair airfield – back to Berlin. And hurry it up – I have an appointment . . .'

Mentally to himself Schulz added the words, ' . . . with the Commandant of the Berghof at Berchtesgaden.'

14 March 1943. Almost eight hours later Reichsleiter Bormann was again waiting at the airfield which served the Wolf's Lair, watching a Condor land at the airstrip. As before, he waited alone except for the new team of SS guards which had been flown in earlier from Munich.

As he had mentioned to Colonel-General Jodl, 'The Führer was warned that a spy had been infiltrated into the previous SS team. Which may explain certain mysterious happenings. So, the whole bodyguard has been flown to the Russian front and replaced by a group of fresh men.'

Certain mysterious happenings. Jodl had no need to enquire as the meaning of the phrase. For some time the Russian High Command had always seemed to have advance warning of impending German attacks – as though someone at the Wolf's Lair was transmitting the Führer's plans to Stalin as soon as he made his decisions.

'Rather drastic,' had been Jodl's only comment. 'Sending all the section for the sake of one man . . .'

'It was the only way. By order of the Führer,' Bormann had intoned.

The new Condor cruised to a stop between the landing lights which were immediately switched off. In the gloom Bormann walked forward as the plane door opened, the flight of steps was lowered and the single passenger ran down them at a jaunty pace.

Exchanging a few words with the passenger, Bormann led him to a waiting six-seater Mercedes with a running-board and magnificent headlamps. Bormann opened the rear door, saluted and followed the passenger inside. He slammed the door and no time was wasted. The engine was running and the moment the two men had settled themselves the driver released the brake and headed away from the airfield in the direction of the Wolf's Lair. The Mercedes was preceded by a motor-cycle escort of the fresh SS team while another escort brought up the rear. Bormann handed the new arrival a map marked with the walking-path through the minefields in the forest. 'For when you feel like a little exercise . . .'

During the drive Bormann talked at length with his passenger who merely nodded and stared ahead. This lack of reaction surprised Bormann and was the first time he sensed events were not going to take the course he had planned. A glass partition separated them from the driver who was not able to hear one word of the conversation. The car swept past Checkpoint One and then past Checkpoint Two, pulling up in front of Security Ring A.

Inside the *Lagebaracke* Hitler's military staff waited, poring over a large-scale map of Russia spread out over a table. A feeling of tension pervaded the large room, which was normal on such occasions. Jodl was irked by the fact that the lights were dim and flickered frequently, although he knew the reason. Bormann had explained earlier what was happening.

'There has been an interruption to the power supply – it is probably a technical fault although the possibility of sabotage is being investigated. But for the military conference we have to rely on the emergency generator . . .'

Jodl was occupying himself by commenting on the disposition of the German forces on the Eastern Front to Field Marshal Wilhelm Keitel, a stern-faced man whose immobile expression concealed the fact that he was an orthodox professional soldier of the old school. In other words, like most generals on both sides – with the exception of Guderian, Montgomery and McArthur – he had never had an original thought in his life. He simply did what Hitler told him to.

'He's coming . . .'

Keitel had been the first to hear the car pull up outside. All conversation ceased. All eyes turned to the doorway. The sense of tension increased. What mood would he be in, everyone was wondering nervously? He was so unpredictable – and only the more intelligent Jodl suspected that this was how their chief kept everyone off balance. The door opened.

Adolf Hitler, Führer and Commander-in-Chief of the German Armed Forces, strode into the room. He was wearing his military great-coat, flecked with snowflakes collected during the short walk from the car to the building, and his peaked cap surmounted with the German eagle clutching the swastika in its claws.

He stood in the doorway, his face grim as he surveyed the gathering while Bormann helped him off with his great-coat and cap. The famous forelock drooped on his forehead, his protuberant eyes stared hard at Keitel. 'Christ,' the Field Marshal thought, 'he's in a bad mood.'

Hitler strode to the head of the table and adopted a characteristic gesture, clasping his hands behind his back as he stood in the shadows and glared at the map on the table. For a whole minute he didn't speak and Bormann remained impassive, hiding his intense nervousness. The silence was suddenly broken.

'Give me a full report on the present situation – and in all details.'

He had barked out the command, his accent still showing traces of his Austrian origins which he had never eradicated from his speech. He listened in silence as Jodl spoke, his expression still grim although in the dim lighting his figure was little more than a motionless silhouette. When the General completed his survey the familiar figure looked round the room. His tone was harsh.

'The flight back from Smolensk was tiring. Everyone will be

here for the midday conference tomorrow. I will then announce the details of the new offensive to be launched against the Red Army without delay . . .'

As he marched out of the room Bormann prepared to follow him to his quarters but Hitler brushed him aside. Bormann preserved an impassive countenance but inwardly he was bewildered and disturbed.

To explain the phenomenon which took place at the Wolf's Lair on 14 March 1943 it is necessary to go back four days – and then five years to the golden days of 1938.

Chapter Four

10 March 1943. Outside the Berghof, perched on the Obersalzberg on the fringe of the old frontier of Germany and Austria, the snow lay thick, the temperature was low and an awesome silence which was almost a sound lay over the desolate mountains.

Inside a large room in the Berghof, Hitler's private retreat, it was not so silent. A nightmarish scene was taking place inside the room which was a wilderness of large mirrors. They were positioned at varying angles so that the man performing could judge the effect he was creating all round.

Clad in a military uniform exactly like Hitler's, Heinz Kuby was making a speech, his only audience himself. Shrieking at the top of his voice, increasing the volume, he gestured violently. His right hand shot forward in an emphatic movement. A lock of dark hair fell over his forehead.

'I will no longer tolerate that bloody swine, Benes!' he shouted. 'He is crucifying the Germans in the Sudetenland. I will crucify *him* . . . !'

His small moustache bristled with venom as he raised both fists in a threatening stance. And as he worked himself up, Kuby studied with care the seven Hitlers reflected in the mirror images. He observed right profile, left profile, the twist of his shoulders in the rear view.

In the cinema in the basement of the Berghof he had spent long hours studying films of the Führer making speeches and attending functions – films provided by Martin Bormann.

An actor by profession, he had noted Hitler's every mannerism – down to his occasional odd twitch of the right shoulder accompanied by a slight jerk of the left. There were two Adolf Hitlers he had observed. The modest, retiring man who smiled shyly and displayed great charm and consideration. And the incredible demon of energy he was now imitating as he hypnotized an audience of thousands.

Kuby had spent equally long hours listening to records of the Führer's voice, playing them over and over again so he was familiar with every intonation of speech. Staring now into the weird ring of mirrors, he raised right arm and head at the same moment – a well-known gesture as the Führer reached the climax of a speech.

The images gyrated, the voice climbed to a manic scream. The nightmare was reaching its peak. *'Benes is a bloody murderer! He is knee-deep in the blood of our German brothers and . . .'*

A second image appeared in the mirrors, the image of a fair-haired attractive girl. The many reflections emphasized that, although attractive, she was not overburdened with brains. Confined to the Berghof while the Führer was at the Wolf's Lair, she had grown bored, bored – *bored*!

She liked dancing but read nothing more mentally demanding than the pages of women's fashion magazines. Now she waved her hand as Kuby frowned and broke off his speech. Knowing interruptions annoyed him – the two men *were* rather alike in character as well as the astonishing duplication of appearance – she coaxed.

'Heinz, enough is enough. Come to bed . . .'

'Mein Führer!' he corrected her. 'How many times do I have to tell you . . .'

'Mein Führer,' she began submissively, 'let's go to bed . . .'

He was in a daze and clasped the extended hand automatically as she led him upstairs out of the mirror room. Eva Braun was a girl who liked male attention and the Führer seldom provided it. And there was something gloriously erotic about climbing into bed with the Führer's twin. Besides, Kuby was a more vigorous lover.

An adjutant at the Berghof had told Martin Bormann about Heinz Kuby in October 1938 some months after Germany had merged with Austria. Bormann's original intention on hearing about Kuby had been to arrest him on some trumped-up charge so he would disappear for ever inside a concentration camp.

'This Heinz Kuby,' the adjutant had informed Bormann, 'performs in a small private night club in Salzburg. He imitates the Führer – makes fun of him . . .'

'In Saltzburg!' Bormann was more scandalized by the creature's brazen impertinence, insulting the Führer on his own doorstep. He was taken to the club in the back streets of the Old Town by the adjutant that same evening.

The earlier acts were charades recalling the wild days of the pre-1930s' Berlin. There was even a tall, slim-legged girl in long black stockings rather like Marlene Dietrich. Bormann watched as she stretched her right leg full-length.

'Disgusting!' he murmured to the adjutant, his eyes glued to the suggestive movements of the leg. The adjutant kept a poker face. At the Berghof it was well-known no secretary was safe from advances from Martin Bormann, who also kept his wife permanently pregnant.

But nothing the adjutant had said prepared Bormann for Heinz Kuby.

'The likeness is incredible,' he whispered. 'I thought you said he made fun of the Führer . . .'

'Well, doing that on a stage . . .'

The adjutant was lost for words. He had also lost Bormann who was staring fixedly as Kuby proceeded with his act. He noticed the uneasy hush which had descended on the small audience, uncomfortably seated at the closely packed tables.

Heinz Kuby was *not* caricaturing the Führer – he was giving an impersonation of the German leader which was so life-like it was quite uncanny. Had he not known, had the surroundings not been so unsuitable, Bormann would have been convinced he was staring at the Führer himself. He was very thoughtful as Kuby completed his performance.

'We'll go backstage and see him at once,' he announced.

'We arrest him, of course. The charge will be . . .'

'Perhaps you will remember it is I who give the orders,' Bormann snapped.

His interview with Kuby in a cramped room hardly larger than two 'phone kiosks and smelling of stale face powder and grease paint was brief. He had been born in Linz, quite close to Hitler's birth-place – which accounted for the Austrian accent so uncannily like that of the Führer.

'Any relatives?' Bormann demanded.

'No, sir . . .' Kuby was frightened, recognizing his visitor who had not taken the trouble to introduce himself. 'Both my parents died in a car crash when I was . . .'

'How old are you?'

'Forty-seven. . .'

More and more remarkable. Kuby was only two years younger than the Führer. The manager of the club opened the flimsy plywood door and peered inside, gazing at Bormann in disbelief.

'Is anything wrong? We can always cancel Kuby's act . . .'

'Already cancelled,' the small fat Nazi told him. 'And if you value your life you have never seen me. Heinz Kuby is leaving with us. Now, get out of my way . . .'

'Will he be coming back?' the manager enquired. 'The playbill for next week has to be prepared . . .'

'You will never see him again.'

One week later when Hitler arrived at the Berghof from Berlin his secretary, Bormann, was careful to choose the right moment to raise the subject. It was ten o'clock at night. The Führer had finished his evening meal of spaghetti and apple rind tea and was settling himself in front of a great blazing log fire made up of small tree trunks. Bormann began tentatively.

'I am always searching for new methods to protect you from the attack of a madman . . .'

'Very commendable,' Hitler agreed affably, staring into the leaping flames. He seemed to find some comfort in the destruction of the massive trunks.

'I found someone in Salzburg the other day who could provide a novel form of protection. May I bring him in?'

'By all means, my dear Bormann . . .'

With a dramatic flourish he opened a door and ushered in Heinz Kuby who was now wearing a suit of the Führer's – earlier Bormann had been astonished to find it was a perfect fit – with an armband carrying the swastika symbol. Hitler rose slowly to his feet, staring at the apparition, his face expressionless.

'*What* is this?' hs asked after staring for a whole minute.

'Your double, *mein Führer* . . .' He hurried on, sensing that something very serious had gone wrong. 'On occasions when you have to expose your presence when there might be danger we could instead substitute . . .'

Bormann got no further. Still gazing at Heinz Kuby as though he were afflicted with some loathsome disease Hitler pronounced his verdict.

'T-a-k-e- *i-t* a-w-a-y. Never let me see *it* again. *You hear*!'

The last words were spoken in a shriek. Bormann hastily took the terrified Kuby to another room and equally hastily returned to try and repair the damage. As he came into the room Hitler was walking up and down in a characteristic pose, hands clasped behind his back. He gave Bormann no chance to speak first.

'Where did you find that hideous freak? No one else has seen it, I hope? Thank God for that. You must get rid of it. You think I want someone just like me hanging round the place? The next thing we know General von Brauchitsch will arrive, see *it*, and mistake *it* for me!'

'We all have our doubles somewhere, *mein Führer* . . .'

'I am *unique*!'

Ten minutes later Bormann had a brainwave. He felt sure the idea would appeal to the Führer's devious mind.

'There is one advantage in keeping him in a back cupboard – if you want to appear to be in one place while secretly you are in another. Kuby would have been useful during the Röhm crisis . . .'

'Bormann, you are right!' Hitler, who revelled in tricks, was delighted. He had just one observation – inside which back cupboard should the 'dummy' be kept?

'Why, here at the Berghof,' Bormann replied confidently. 'I will allocate him quarters and personally guarantee he never leaves them when you or anyone from the outside world is here.'

'In any case he must never leave Berchtesgaden, I insist.'

'That, also, I will guarantee. The only other problem is the adjutant who found him. I suggest we post him immediately to a minor post at a Far East embassy . . .'

'Excellent! He can stay there forever – until his skin turns yellow!'

Bormann inwardly heaved a sigh of relief. The crisis was over. The Führer had even switched from referring to Kuby as *it* in favour of *he*. He really wished he'd never brought the blasted actor anywhere near the place, but now Hitler had agreed, Kuby must be kept in a 'back cupboard'.

In October 1938 Bormann can never have foreseen the earthquake-making proportions of the minor episode which was now forgotten as Hitler, settled again in front of the log fire, welcomed Eva Braun as she came into the room, and began one of his endless monologues on the story of his youth in the bad old days.

Chapter Five

12 March 1943. The pilot of the British Mosquito, wearing the German uniform of a colonel in the SS, swept across the Obersalzberg. He saw the jagged tip of a snow-covered mountain sheer up immediately ahead, climbed and missed the tip by feet.

The timing of Wing Commander Ian Lindsay's long flight had been perfect. Dawn was now spreading an eery light over summits which stood like sentinels guarding the Führer's refuge at the Berghof. He turned the aircraft – made of wood to boost speed – in a wide circle, searching for a suitable drop point.

He was crammed into the small cockpit, his parachute attached to his back, making movement difficult. Then he saw his objective far below. The rooftops of the Berghof heavy with snow. The tracks of a vehicle which had recently made its way up the curving road to the refuge showed up clearly.

Ian Lindsay had taken off from Malta – after being flown to the island from Algiers in a Dakota – in the early hours. His course had taken him up the centre of the Adriatic Sea, across a small area of northern Italy where he had then turned north-east over the Alps.

Even up to the last minute, permission to undertake his mission had been in doubt. The argument had gone as high as General Alexander who had asked to see Lindsay personally at Allied Force Headquarters in Algiers. Inside his villa the General had returned Lindsay's salute casually and asked him to sit down.

'What is all this pother about – your flying to meet Hitler?' he asked amiably.

'Just how many people *do* know about this mission?' demanded the Wing Commander. 'Two in London and one here who flew out with me to arrange liaison was supposed to be the limit . . .'

'And now you get me babbling on about it?'

Alexander pulled at his trim moustache, his expression amused. He heard that Ian Lindsay ranked high in the field of insubordination and clearly he was not intimidated by a mere Deputy Commander-in-Chief of Allied Forces. Alexander rather liked that as he studied the man on the other side of the simple trestle table.

Twenty-six years old, Lindsay had thick blond hair, a nose

like that seen on coins of Roman emperors, a good jaw and firm mouth. Five feet nine inches tall, he exuded an aura of strength of character. His expression was mobile – like an actor's. He had, in fact, toured with a repertory company before the war.

'Babbling is what worries me,' Lindsay replied. 'Sir,' he added as an afterthought.

'I have worries, too,' Alexander drawled, leaning back in his chair. 'Keeping the peace between Eisenhower and Monty. Planning the final attack on the Germans in northern Tunisia. Little things like that. And Telford, your liaison officer told me your own plans in confidence. I compelled him to – no info, no cooperation . . .'

'Surely you had a signal?' Lindsay rapped back. Was this general with his casual air any damned good?

'Read it for yourself, Lindsay . . .' Alexander pushed a slip of paper across the table. 'And I like to know *everything* that is going on in my command.'

Lindsay revised his opinion. There had been a snap in the general's eye as well as in his voice as he sat and waited while his visitor digested the decoded signal.

Please extend all facilities to Wing Commander Lindsay who is engaged on special rear area duties. Brooke.

'Suitably camouflaged – the wording – I trust you will agree,' Alexander suggested in an ironic tone. 'And apart from myself no one else in Africa even knows you're here. Good luck on your suicide mission. A sort of Hess in reverse, wouldn't you say?'

Manoeuvring the Mosquito in ascending circles high above the Obersalzberg, Lindsay recalled the Alexander conversation while he tried to watch for a host of perils through his goggles. A German fighter plane sent up on a visual spotting? Another of those bloody peaks appearing out of nowhere in the isolated mist patches? Above all, the dreaded down draught which could suck a machine into the abyss before the pilot was aware of it happening.

He decided he had used up his portion of luck in the air and that it was time to leave the comforting confines of his cockpit. He took a deep breath and ejected. Exposed to the bitter elements of icy space, he had a brief glimpse of a snowbound world far below.

He seemed to descend with extraordinary slowness, to *float* in space – which they had warned him was a danger sign. He could lose consciousness in seconds. He took a firm grip on the parachute ring and gave it a hard tug. Nothing happened. He continued to drift in nothingness. They had warned him about this, too, but the sensation was no less terrifying.

He looked up and a cloud had appeared from nowhere. God! A storm was blowing up . . . The straps jerked at his shoulders. The 'cloud' was the huge umbrella of his opened 'chute. And he was conscious of the return of a sense of *purpose* – of control. He looked down and saw the Berghof in the distance.

Lindsay became aware of a breeze carrying him straight towards the vertical rock face of a mountain wall. He tugged at the lefthand strap, held on and now he was descending diagonally on a course which should carry him close to the Berghof. Then he saw something he had forgotten about – the shaft of his abandoned Mosquito.

No more than a rapidly-falling spear, it was heading for another mountain. Subconsciously he felt it hit – his last link with a world he might never see again. A flaring flash as the fuel tank detonated, a distant thump which he could have imagined, then a shower of fragments fluttering into the valley.

He was engulfed by an eery silence, a lack of sound characteristic of the desolation of the winter-bound mountains. He had never felt more alone.

Lindsay concentrated on guiding the parachute away from those vicious precipices which reared to north and south. Was the Führer at the Berghof, he wondered? He hoped to God he was and that if so he would remember their pre-war meeting at the Chancellery in Berlin. Hitler had taken a distinct liking to the young Englishman who spoke fluent German and who

49

was sympathetic to Nazi aims. For over four hours they had talked together alone.

The hard, snow-crusted ground of the valley was very close now – and he was going to land near the curving road which led up to the Berghof. What was it General Alexander had said? *A Hess in reverse.*

On Saturday 10 May 1941, Rudolf Hess, the Führer's Deputy, had flown on his own to Scotland to meet the Duke of Hamilton on a 'peace mission' to Britain. On 12 March 1943, Ian Lindsay, nephew of the Duke of Dunkeith and a pre-war member of the Anglo-German Fellowship flew to Bavaria on a 'peace mission' to Bavaria.

A Hess in reverse?

Chapter Six

'Take me to the Berghof! Immediately! *Heil Hitler*!' Lindsay rasped.

His right arm shot out in the Nazi salute as he stared arrogantly at the SS officer who had alighted from the military truck which had come racing and skidding down the road from the Berghof. Four other SS men armed with machine pistols had emerged from the rear of the vehicle and they gazed curiously at the German parachute billowing in the breeze on the slope below.

Lindsay noticed with satisfaction that he out-ranked the office who automatically returned his salute and showed signs of hesitation. It was the first thirty seconds when you appeared on stage which counted – the Englishman had learned that from his pre-war experience in repertory, and he had learned a great deal more. He followed up his verbal offensive.

'What the hell are you standing about for? I'm frozen. Get me to the Berghof, I said . . .'

'Why did you not land at the airstrip?' the SS officer enquired. He was a slim, thin-faced man with full lips more appropriate for a girl.

'For Christ's sake!' Lindsay stormed. 'Do you think I enjoyed parachuting in weather like this? My engine stalled, of course, you bloody fool . . .'

The question told him one thing for which he was much relieved. They had *not* observed the Mosquito until after it had exploded into pieces against the mountain wall. In due course a team would go to that remote area and identify the machine but by then he hoped to be grappling with other problems – breaking through security to see the Führer, for example. He just hoped to God he *was* at the Berghof. He waited for the final question and it came.

'My name is Kranz,' the officer continued. 'There has been no notification to expect you. So, may I ask who you are and what is the purpose of your visit?'

'You may find yourself posted to the Russian front if you keep me hanging around here in this beastly cold,' Lindsay threatened. 'A signal was sent informing the Commandant of my arrival . . .'

'From the Wolfsschanze?' Kranz asked tentatively.

'Of course! Has the damned system not worked again? As to who I am, that is my business. As to the purpose of my visit that is top secret and I do not propose to discuss it in front of your men who, incidentally, are annoying me with their goggling . . .'

Kranz reacted at once, ordering his men back inside the vehicle, and Lindsay knew he had won the first round. The idiot had not even demanded identification papers – which Lindsay could have produced if requested. But it was important to dominate the man from the first moment – like gripping an audience when you walk on to the stage – and showing him papers would have been a concession.

'You can sit with me in front with the driver,' Kranz suggested.

They had to drive downhill some distance before they came to a point where they could reverse and take the truck back on the long climb to the Berghof. As the wipers swept back and forth to clear the film of ice which kept forming on the windscreen Lindsay stared straight ahead without looking at Kranz. He was intrigued.

The Wolfsschanze. The Wolf's Lair – or Fort Wolf. He had never heard of the place and he was sure neither had anyone else in the Allied High Command or the intelligence services. The location of the Führer's headquarters, the nerve centre of military operations, was a secret no one had penetrated.

Close to the Berghof they came to a checkpoint and the pole was raised as the truck arrived. Lousy security. Why, Lindsay wondered, did one always assume the enemy were supermen and only your own people were mental deficients? He took off his gloves and blew on his hands.

Out of the corner of his eye he saw Kranz glance at the ring on the fourth finger of his right hand, the ring embossed with the swastika. It seemed the right psychological moment to rush Kranz into a fresh decision which would delay discovery of his identity.

'When we get there give me a decent room where I can clean up and prepare myself before I see the Führer. And it must have a safe where I can store secret papers . . .'

'But the Führer is at the Wolfsschanze,' Kranz replied.

Lindsay swore inwardly as he sensed the twist of Kranz's head and heard the note of suspicion in his voice. First blunder – unavoidable but an unguarded remark which could betray him now. He responded instantly, still staring ahead, growling his reply.

'Kranz! Security – there is a driver with us in case you have overlooked that little fact . . .'

'I don't understand . . .'

Suspicion was giving way to bewilderment and Lindsay pressed his advantage home. He dropped his voice, without a glance towards Kranz, his expression bleak.

'He is *expected*,' he whispered. 'You know he never gives out advance warning of his intended movements – to foil any assassination attempt. Really, Kranz, I hardly like to hazard his reaction if I reported this conversation to him . . .'

'You have my full cooperation . . .'

Lindsay was unyielding. 'You are between the devil and the Lord none of us believes in. Russia or promotion stares you in the face. Don't forget that private room I asked for. Not a word to the Commandant concerning my arrival. And, preferably, not another word from you until I have rested.'

They could see the famous and vast picture window behind the terrace which had so impressed pre-war visitors to the Berghof. It was misted over with condensation which pleased Lindsay. Inside the place there would be terrible danger – but there would, also, thank God, be *warmth*. He was chilled to the bone – with the fatigue from the flight, lack of sleep, and, he admitted to himself, the most appalling drain on his nerves from the situation he had faced since landing in enemy territory.

Lindsay opened the door leading from his room inside the Berghof quietly after first checking the door frame. No alarm system to warn when the door opened. He peered out into an empty corridor. No guard outside. He had – by force of personality – frightened Kranz into accepting his presence.

How long that state of affairs would last was anyone's guess and he needed to explore the layout of the place before the inevitable unmasking of his true identity. Closing the door behind him, he padded silently along the polished woodblock floor. At the end a staircase led down to the next floor. He paused.

The whole place seemed deserted – not at all what he had anticipated. Then he heard the faint sound of a voice, a familiar voice. He moved down the carpeted staircase a step at a time. In the hall below a heavy wooden door was almost closed. The voice came from inside the room beyond.

As he approached the hall the voice became more distinct. Lindsay, puzzled, paused again. Kranz had quite positively told him the Führer was at the Wolfsschanze and the Englishman was certain he had spoken the truth. So what – *who* – was behind that door?

The lower hallway was equally deserted, the heavy door

open only a few inches – as though someone had omitted to close it properly. He recognized the voice now – there was only one man in the world who ranted and thundered in German in that fashion.

Cautiously, he gripped the handle and very slowly opened it a few more inches. He froze, stupefied at the spectacle inside. An assortment of large cheval mirrors stood arranged in a large circle. Inside the circle Adolf Hitler stood gesticulating, his forelock of hair drooped as he went on practising his speech and staring into the mirrors.

Lindsay watched, fascinated, then a wrinkle of doubt appeared on his ample forehead. His memory for people was encyclopaedic and highly visual, a memory finely honed by his experience as an actor. There was something horrific and yet unreal about the six Hitlers he could see from various angles.

Not daring to risk a second movement of the door he left it at the point he had pushed it open and, light-footed, skipped back up the staircase. The girl appeared as he was re-entering his room.

'I'm Eva Braun. And who might you be?'

The girl patted her fair hair and studied Lindsay frankly. It occurred to him that she was a bit of a flirt. He had performed another stage trick – swivelling on his heel in the doorway to his room as though just *leaving* rather than re-entering it. Not too intelligent, he summed her up, but possessed of a certain native shrewdness where men were concerned.

'I'm the Magic Man,' he responded humorously. 'I've just flown in to see the Führer . . .'

'He's away at that awful place, the Wolf's Lair. Come and keep me company.' She led the way down the corridor in the opposite direction from the staircase and into a comfortably furnished living room, chattering all the time. 'I get so bored here while he's at Rastenburg – sit down on this sofa with me. I've just made some coffee – it's the real thing . . .'

Rastenburg? That was in East Prussia. Had he found the location of Hitler's secret headquarters? And there was something strange going on. Kranz might just have been unaware of the Führer's presence at the Berghof – but Eva Braun, rumoured to be the Führer's mistress, was bound to know his whereabouts. So who was the man pirouetting downstairs surrounded by mirrors? Lindsay was confused as Eva brought two cups, placed them on a low table and joined him on the sofa.

'I haven't seen you before, Magic Man,' she remarked, enjoying his little game. Intuitively he had sensed this rather childish approach would appeal to her. She was a girl who liked constant amusement. 'Does your crystal ball tell you the Führer is coming here soon. . ?'

Lindsay never replied. The door was flung open and slammed back against the wall. The room was filled with SS armed with Schmeisser machine-pistols. Seven of them led by a Colonel in ordinary army uniform. Kranz hovered in the doorway.

'Excuse us, Fräulein,' the army Colonel said deferentially, 'I think this man is suspect.' His tone changed as he addressed Lindsay. 'Now who are you and where have you come from? 'I'm Müller, Commandant of the Berghof. We received no signals about you . . .'

Müller was a far more dangerous man than Kranz. Lindsay stood up slowly and studied the erect, stern-faced German from head to foot. His tone was quiet, almost offhand when he replied.

'I cannot see you remaining Commandant much longer – I am here on a special mission which concerns the Führer and no one else . . .'

Müller took three quick paces forward, grabbed Lindsay's SS uniform by the collar and ripped it open. The RAF uniform beneath was exposed. The commandant placed his hands on his hips.

'I thought there was something wrong about you. A session in the cellars should prove rewarding . . .'

'Hardly for you – once the Führer arrives . . .'

Outraged at this insolence, an SS man hefted his machine-pistol and lunged with the butt, striking Lindsay on the jaw. The Englishman fell backwards and hit the wall and slithered to a sitting position as Eva ran from the room. He wiped blood from his mouth. At the last second he had moved; the butt had only grazed his jaw.

'I hope the wound is still visible when the Führer sees me,' he commented.

A flicker of uncertainty crossed Müller's eyes. His prisoner's calm reaction worried him. Behind the Commandant, Kranz took a few tentative steps into the room, speaking hesitantly.

'There is a safe in his room. I gave him the key – he spoke of secret papers . . .'

'I am Wing Commander Ian Lindsay,' the Englishman said quickly. 'Nephew of the Duke of Dunkeith. I knew the Führer before the war. Those documents are for his eyes only – I stole a plane and flew here from Algiers. You think I wanted to commit suicide? I was a member of the Anglo-German Fellowship. And that's all I'm going to tell you until I see the Führer. If you value your cushy job here you'd better signal the Wolf's Lair informing them of my arrival. Meantime, I'd like to go back to my room . . .'

He was escorted back and, inside his room, Müller watched while he was searched. They found nothing of interest, except the key to the wall-safe and his RAF identity papers. Müller looked at the papers, returned them to their owner and balanced the safe-key in the palm of his hand as though trying to come to a decision. Lindsay, getting himself dressed again, began needling Müller to help him make up his mind.

'Go on! Do it! Open that safe! Open the package inside so you're privy to what it contains. Once the Führer realizes you have seen its contents you'll be standing in front of a firing squad within the hour . . .'

Lindsay was gambling on his assessment of Müller's character. An old war-horse put out to grass, stolid and unimaginative and serving out his time, waiting for his army pension. The SS man who had hit him earlier lifted his machine-pistol. Müller barked the order.

'Klaus! I give orders here! You have already assaulted the prisoner once without my permission . . .'

And Lindsay knew he had won his gamble. Müller was already disassociating himself from Klaus's impetuous action – and until Hitler arrived the last thing he would do would be to open the safe. He pocketed the key and Lindsay spoke again.

'If you keep that key I must remain in this room . . .'

'God in Heaven! Why?'

'For your own sake, dumbhead! That is the only way I will be able to assure the Führer no one else has seen the contents of the package – by telling him I was here all the time! And that means I shall need meals sent up to me – three hot cooked meals a day. I eat breakfast at . . .'

Müller was beaten. After Lindsay finished speaking the Commandant and his unit left the room. The Englishman heard someone lock the door on the outside. He wiped the moisture off his palms onto his trousers. He was now gambling on something he had carefully not brought up during the confrontation.

The Commandant would worry about his presence, would be terribly anxious to pass on to the Wolf's Lair the responsibility for what action should be taken next. Once the signal about his arrival reached Rastenburg the Führer would be curious about this strange development. And Lindsay was gambling everything on Hitler's reputed fabulous memory – that he would recall his meeting with the young pro-Nazi Englishman in Berlin before the war.

As he sat in a chair and felt waves of fatigue – reaction – sweeping over him, he began to worry about something else. His stay at AFHQ – Allied Forces Headquarters in the Central Mediterranean – had been brief and General Alexander had seemed a man who was the soul of discretion.

But there was a Russian military liaison mission with AFHQ and whatever other disaster might lie ahead one thing was vital. The Soviets must never catch a whisper of his existence, let alone the purpose of his mission.

Commandant Müller slept on the decision as to whether or not to inform the Wolf's Lair about the Berghof's enigmatic visitor. So it was near midday on 13 March when he personally 'phoned the HQ in East Prussia and asked to speak to the Führer. As usual, Martin Bormann intercepted the call and insisted that Müller speak to him.

'You think this Englishman might have flown to see the Führer on a peace mission?' Bormann asked after a few minutes.

'I can't be sure of anything, Reichsleiter,' Müller covered himself quickly. 'I felt you should know of his presence . . .'

'Quite right! A good decision, Müller – to inform me. I like to know all that is going on – so I can keep the Führer himself informed when the matter merits his attention. Continue to keep Lindsay under close guard. *Heil Hitler!*'

Inside the signals office at the Wolf's Lair Bormann replaced the receiver and took a quick decision. The Führer was visiting Field Marshal von Kluge's front at Smolensk. A signal must be sent telling him about the Englishman.

Bormann composed the signal himself. This extraordinary event could have incalculable possibilities. The nephew of the Duke of Dunkeith! He could be bringing peace proposals – if he delayed reporting Lindsay's landing the Führer would never forgive him.

After despatching the signal to Smolensk Borman mentioned the news to Jodl who immediately told Keitel. Within hours the Wolfsschanze was buzzing with rumours and it was the main topic of conversation.

Hitler's response arrived almost by return. It was terse and to the point. Clearly he had remembered his pre-war meeting with the Englishman and knew exactly who he was.

Arrange immediately for Wing Commander Lindsay to fly direct to Wolfsschanze in the afternoon. Will interview him several hours after my return.

The Führer was already airborne, flying back from Smolensk.

Chapter Seven

13 March 1943.   During most of 1943, Section V (counter-espionage) of the SIS occupied two country houses – Prae Wood and Glenalmond – outside St Albans. Twenty-nine-year-old Tim Whelby was stationed at Prae Wood.

Whelby always seemed older than his years, a quiet, generally popular man with his colleagues. They found his company relaxing, which encouraged tense men to talk to him, especially after a few drinks at the local village pub in the evenings. His dress was as casual as his manner – flannels and an old tweed jacket with elbow patches. He smoked a pipe, which seemed to add to his reputation for reliability.

On the evening of the 13th he was leaving the country house on his way to the pub when a Morris Minor pulled up in the drive with a jarring clash of gears. Behind the wheel sat Maurice Telford, a lean-faced man of forty. Whelby approached the vehicle and saw by the faint light from the dashboard that Telford looked positively haggard. He had also noted the gear clash. Normally Telford was a first-rate driver.

'Back from a trip, old chap?' Whelby enquired. 'Haven't seen you around for days . . .'

'You can say that again! I'm bloody all in . . .'

'Join me for a drink at the local? Do you good before you get to bed.'

'That's all I want – to flop into bed.' Telford hesitated. He was strung-up after the long flight back from Algiers. Tim Whelby waited patiently, pipe stuck out of the corner of his mouth. He never *pushed*.

'Yes, I could do with a noggin. And some blotting paper. You wouldn't believe when I last ate . . .'

'Good man.' Whelby climbed into the front passenger seat and sagged. 'I could do with a bit of company . . .'

Telford was left with the impression he was conferring a favour on Whelby by agreeing to accompany him. There was no further conversation between the two men until Whelby led the way inside the deserted bar of The Stag's Head and gestured towards a seat in an oak-beamed corner.

'I'll get the drinks – the inglenook looks comfortable.'

Telford settled himself on the banquette. He stared when Whelby placed a glass before him. 'What's that?' he asked.

'Double Scotch – no point in doing things by halves. And eat up those sandwiches – they only had cheese. Here's to no more trips abroad. Cheers!'

'Who said anything about my going abroad?' asked Telford and then swallowed half the contents of the glass.

'Someone did. Can't remember who. Does it matter?'

'I suppose not.' Reeling with fatigue, Telford drank the rest of his Scotch. Its warming glow relaxed him. 'All the way to North Africa in a freezing bloody Liberator bomber – no seats, nothing except the floor and a sleeping-bag. I'm bruised all over. And all to nanny that lunatic Wing Commander, Ian Lindsay, now en route to meet the Führer, for Christ's sake.'

'Sounds a bit stupid – couldn't he make it out there under his own steam?'

Whelby's manner was offhand as though making polite small talk. He summoned the barman and ordered another couple of rounds. Telford protested. 'My round, this one . . .'

'Then you shall pay, old chap. We'll both end up drunk – what else is there to do in this benighted neck of the woods?'

'I wasn't really his escort,' Telford explained. 'AFHQ had a secret report which they wanted delivered door-to-door. When I got back earlier this evening I dropped it off at Ryder Street before driving out here. I was cover for Lindsay – two people landing at Algiers attract less attention than an individual . . .'

He sipped cautiously at his Scotch, swallowing more with care. Whelby stood up to divest himself of his overcoat, took out his pipe and sucked at the stem without lighting it. They sat in silence for several minutes, soaking up the warmth from the crackling log fire. Telford had devoured his sandwiches. What with the food, the drink and the comfort he was nearly falling asleep.

'You're jo-jo-joking, of course,' Whelby said eventually. 'About this RAF type flying to see Hit-Hit-Hitler?'

He had an unfortunate habit of stuttering. Muddled though he was with alcohol and fatigue, Telford remembered that people who stuttered were often caught by their affliction in moments of tension. The fact seemed important – significant . . . Seconds later he found he couldn't recall what fact was – or might be – important. Then he remembered what Whelby had just said and he felt indignant. He spoke with great deliberation.

'Wing Commander Ian Lindsay of the RAF flew on to Malta for the express purpose of flying on alone to Germany to see the Führer. And don't ask me why – *because I don't know!*'

'Anyway you're just damned glad to be back home so let's have one for the road. My treat. Double Scotch for both of us . . .'

Telford waited for the barman to bring the fresh drinks and go away. He had experienced one of those rare and brief flashes of clear insight which can break through an alcoholic haze. People were coming into the bar so he lowered his voice. Whelby bent his head to catch what he was saying.

'I shouldn't really have told you any of this, Tim. I trust you, but one word and I'm out – maybe something even worse . . .'

'Official Secrets Act, old chap,' Whelby confided with a lack of tact which startled Telford. 'We both signed it,' Whelby continued, 'so we're both locked into the same gallows. Neither of us remembers a word and no one puts a noose round our necks . . .'

'Ghoulish, aren't we? Let's go home . . .'

Whelby went over to the bar to pay while Telford made a careful way to the door and the waiting car outside. The landlord noticed Whelby seemed remarkably sober – he counted out the coins exactly.

Two days later Tim Whelby went on a forty-eight hour visit to Ryder Street in London to discuss with his chief a problem of an overseas agent he suspected was feeding them with rubbish to justify his existence. At ten o'clock at night he was strolling down Jermyn Street alone.

The advantage of Jermyn Street is that it runs straight from end to end. This makes it difficult to follow a man secretly, especially at ten o'clock at night in wartime when there are few people about. Earlier Whelby had made a brief call from a telephone kiosk in Piccadilly underground station.

He paused to light his pipe, pretending to peer inside a shop window while he checked the street behind him. The shadowed canyon was deserted.

He resumed his stroll, drew alongside an entrance setback to another shop. With a swift sideways movement he stepped inside. One moment he was on the street; the next moment he vanished. Josef Savitsky, a short, heavy-set man wearing a dark overcoat and a soft hat spoke first.

'These emergency meetings are dangerous. I do hope what you have brought justifies this risk . . .'

'Calm down. Either you have confidence in me or you don't . . .'

'Well, I am here . . .'

'So listen!' Whelby's normally diffident manner had changed. He stood more erect and there was an authoritative air about him as he spoke crisply and without a stutter. 'On 10 March a Wing Commander Ian Lindsay was flown to Allied Headquarters in Algiers. From there he was flying on alone to Germany to meet the Führer . . .'

'You are certain of this?' There was an appalled note in the stocky man's voice as he spoke English with an accent. Whelby became even more abrupt.

'I'm not in the habit of giving reports I'm uncertain about. And don't ask me my source – which is totally reliable.'

'It is a peace mission, is it not?' the small, pudgy-faced man stated rather than queried.

'Don't play those tricks on me.' Whelby's tone became even sharper as he checked again the illuminated second hand of his watch. 'I have no idea why Lindsay has been sent. Better add to your report that he is the nephew of the Duke of Dunkeith. The Duke was one of the leading lights in the Anglo-German Fellowship before the war. I should know – I was a member, too. Time's up. I'm going . . .'

Before Savitsky could respond Whelby had strolled out and resumed his walk along the street, both hands thrust inside his overcoat pockets. At the nearby intersection he turned down Duke of York Street and walked rapidly into St James's Square. *If* anyone was following they would now hurry to find out his destination – which was Ryder Street. Whelby was circling an elaborate block.

Josef Savitsky remained quite still in the deep shadow of the doorway. The arrangement was he should give Whelby five minutes' grace before he emerged on to the street. When the time interval elapsed he began his marathon walk – a walk which took him across many open spaces where no one could shadow him without being seen. It was midnight before he arrived back at the Soviet Embassy.

The Russian – his official position was commercial attaché – went straight to his office where he locked the door, switched on the shaded desk light and then extracted the one-time codebook from a wall-safe. He was sweating as he composed his signal – although in March at that time of night the office was chilly.

Satisfied with the result – it had to be just right considering its destination – he proceeded to encode the terse message. He then personally took the signal to the signals clerk on night duty in the basement. He even waited while the signal was transmitted. Savitsky was a careful man. His signal was addressed to 'Cossack' – the codeword for Stalin.

Chapter Eight

'Wing Commander Lindsay, you are to fly immediately to the Wolfsschanze to meet the Führer. *Heil Hitler*!'

Commandant Müller of the Berghof security detachment shot out his arm in the Nazi salute as he stood in front of the Englishman in his room where he had been confined overnight. The Commandant's manner had changed entirely from the domineering attitude of his first encounter with the unexpected arrival. It was now one of respect.

'I can fly myself there,' Lindsay responded with typical audacity. 'Supply me with a flight plan.' He stood up and returned the salute. '*Heil Hitler*!'

'One of the Führer's personal pilots, Bauer, has just arrived at the airstrip. He will pilot you there. It is an honour . . .'

'It is, indeed.' Lindsay, who had just finished a meal, gazed at a girl dressed as a nurse who entered the room and waited for instructions. She was dark-haired and attractive. 'Do I get her as well as the pilot, Müller?'

The Commandant laughed coarsely. Lindsay had struck exactly the right note to appeal to the Commandant, who shook his head. 'She will attend to your face wound. Please sit down so she may attend to you. Meantime . . .' He produced a flask from his hip pocket and unscrewed the cap. 'A drink of schnapps? Very difficult to obtain these days in Germany . . .'

'Thank you . . .'

Lindsay sat down in a leather arm chair and took a generous swig from the flask – so generous he caught a flicker of alarm across Müller's face. The Englishman was greatly amused, holding firmly on to the flask as the girl knelt by the arm of his chair, gently removed the sticking-plaster which had been roughly applied to his jaw earlier. Using a piece of gauze soaked in some disinfectant liquid she skilfully removed the ugly scab which had formed over the wound. There must be no traces of ill-treatment when he met the Führer. From now on he was to be coddled as a very important person – until the confrontation at the Wolfsschanze took place.

Lindsay recognized the Junkers 52 transport plane when the Mercedes in which he had been driven arrived at the airstrip. It was a reliable workhorse and should reach East Prussia in a few hours – even though it had to fly the full breadth of the Third Reich before they reached their destination.

As he opened the door and put a foot on the ice-encrusted running board he felt the bulk of the sealed envelope Müller had permitted him to take from the wall-safe. True, a bomb-disposal expert had tested the package – Müller certainly knew his job – but the actual contents remained secret.

'Bauer? I'm Ian Lindsay. From the look of you I shouldn't have any worries on this flight . . .'

Lindsay held out his hand to the man in a pilot's helmet who had come forward from his machine. His step was firm and his face was creased into a pleasant grin as they shook hands. The Englishman knew exactly what had been in the pilot's mind. 'Another bloody God Almighty . . .' He would have been told his passenger was a Wing Commander who considerably out-ranked him. He would further have been impressed on hearing Lindsay knew the Führer. But above all else – discounting difference in rank – there is a camaraderie among fliers, regardless of which nation they represent.

Bauer was surprised and pleased at Lindsay's friendly informality. He also noted that Lindsay paused to thank his driver for getting him to the airstrip safely. Commandant Müller had apologized for not accompanying the Englishman.

'I have to do every ruddy thing myself,' he had explained back at the Berghof. 'I must stay here in case that creep, Bormann . . .' He stopped and winked at Lindsay. 'You went deaf suddenly, didn't you?'

'As a matter of fact, yes. You were saying?'

'Happy landings . . .'

Lindsay was about to climb into the passenger seat of the Junkers 52 when he asked Bauer the question, hoping to catch him in a relaxed mood. He gestured towards fresh plane ruts in the snow, tracks made by a heavy machine.

'Somebody else took off earlier today?'

'Very hush-hush.' Bauer looked resentful. 'The SS hustled me away into a hut – but not before I saw the Condor land. It was a bit weird.'

'Weird?'

'It looked just like the Führer's plane. Same markings, a twin of the Condor he always uses. Then there was the convoy of cars from the Berghof which arrived at the same moment.'

'Something funny about them, too?'

By his complete lack of side Lindsay had already established an excellent rapport with the amiable Bauer.

'Couldn't see who was inside any of them,' the pilot chattered on, taking final drags on his cigarette. 'Curtains all drawn. The odd thing is the Führer is at this moment at the Wolf's Lair.'

'I hope so,' Lindsay replied, carefully not probing any further. 'I'm supposed to be on my way to meet him.'

'Then we'd better get cracking . . .'

Bauer ground out the cigarette under the heel of his boot and within minutes the machine was airborne. It gained height swiftly on a north-easterly course. When Lindsay glanced back through his goggles the Obersalzberg had disappeared.

'Commandant Müller! You are to delay Wing Commander Lindsay's departure from the Berghof until further notice.' Bormann barked the order over the telephone from the signals office at the Wolf's Lair. Müller's reply came back to him with horrible clarity.

'Reichsleiter, I am afraid he took off half an hour ago as per your previous order . . .'

'Recall him, for God's sake! Radio the pilot . . .'

'I cannot do that,' Müller informed him. 'Control at the airstrip have lost radio contact with the pilot. There is a storm north of Salzburg – and the mountains don't help . . .'

'Are you telling me you cannot reach the plane before it lands at the Wolf's Lair?' Bormann demanded.

'Quite possibly, yes!' Müller snapped with some satisfaction.

'In that case,' Bormann said more calmly, 'put me through to SS Colonel Jaeger. On the private line . . .'

He waited, his mind in a turmoil. He had not slept for twenty-four hours, the Führer was dead, killed on his way back from Smolensk. The local SS team had cleared up all traces of the catastrophe, the second team from Berlin, the execution squad under the command of Rainer Schulz, had arrived and liquidated the local team when it had completed its grisly task.

Bormann had been so absorbed in attending to the details, the extraordinary arrival of Wing Commander Lindsay had slipped his memory until this moment. And the second 'Führer', Heinz Kuby, was due to land at the Wolf's Lair shortly. He would decide how to deal with the unwanted Englishman later. The fresh priority was solving the problem of Müller, the only man at the Berghof aware of Kuby's existence. A confident voice came on the line.

'Colonel Jaeger speaking. You wanted something?'

No respectful reference to Bormann's title of Reichsleiter. At the Wolf's Lair Bormann pursed his lips: he disliked Jaeger and his independence intensely. He would have to handle this bastard.

'You are sure this line is safe?' Bormann demanded.

'Unless the Gestapo is tapping the line.' Jaeger sounded very much as though he didn't care one way or the other.

'Colonel Jaeger! You are the commander of the special Waffen SS unit charged with security at the Berghof . . .'

'I'm not a communications expert . . .' Jaeger now sounded thoroughly bored. 'As for being in control of security here that's a laugh. There's a whole area of the Berghof sealed off from my inspection . . .'

'Don't let's go into that,' Bormann said hastily. He became more conciliatory. 'I'm phoning to warn you of the imminent arrival by plane from Berlin of SS Lieutenant Rainer Schulz. I have arranged for Schulz to come straight to your barracks. On no account let the Commandant know he is coming.'

'If you say so . . .'

Jaeger replaced the receiver and swore. A tall, well-built man of forty, bluff in manner with thick, dark eyebrows, a neat moustache and a firm jaw, he hated his present assignment. A veteran of all the major campaigns so far, Hitler had taken a liking to him and had personally selected him to command his private bodyguard.

The Waffen SS later became smeared by being lumped together with other – less savoury – SS organizations. In fact it was an honourable body of elite soldiers comparable with any Guards regiment in the British Army. Its allegiance was strictly confined to the Führer and the Reich – not to Himmler. Its structure was unusually democratic, there being little difference between the officers and other ranks. Jaeger, champing at the bit for more active service, was a typical Waffen SS officer.

'Schulz, why *have* you come here?' Müller asked. There was a note of exasperation in his voice.

The Commandant was in the front passenger seat of the Mercedes which Lieutenant Schulz was driving up the winding road leading to the famous Eagle's Nest at the top of the Kehlstein. This unique engineering feat built before the war under the direction of Martin Bormann at a cost of thirty million marks had, ironically, not been used by Hitler for years. He had become bored with his teahouse in the sky and had complained of vertigo. It was to this deserted eyrie the two men in the car were going.

'We have a problem . . .' The pallid, bony-faced Schulz paused while he negotiated another dangerous bend. He spoke slowly, as though stringing words together was akin to handling sticks of gelignite. 'It is so delicate we have to be sure no one could overhear our conversation. By order of the Führer, the Reichsleiter said . . .'

Müller was uneasy and relapsed into silence. Characteristically, Colonel Jaeger had ignored Bormann's orders and had 'phoned the Commandant warning him Schulz was on his way from the barracks to the Berghof.

'. . . a very welcome type of visitor he is. A walking bloody death-mask . . .'

At the end of the ice-bound drive to the Kehlstein they left the car at the base of the mountain. They continued on foot inside the underground passage which had been blasted out of the peak. Müller found himself growing more and more nervous.

Still in silence the two men stepped inside the copper-lined elevator and Schulz, staring straight ahead, pressed the button. The elevator began its 400-foot ascent up the vertical shaft excavated out of solid rock. Müller pulled at his collar with his finger. The elevator stopped, the doors opened.

'Where are the guards?' Müller asked sharply. 'It's a good job I came up here – they're getting slack. Disciplinary action will be taken . . .'

Schulz had not replied. He led the way through a gallery of Roman pillars, across an immense, circular, glassed-in room and out onto the open terrace. The surface was covered with snow which had an icy, treacherous sheen. Müller noted that Schulz walked firm-footed to the wall bordering the terrace, a wall as high as an average-sized man's thighs. The man had no nerves.

Still with his back to the Commandant, Schulz placed both his gloved hands on the snow-crusted wall and gazed out across the incredible panorama of mountains. Below, the Kehlstein dropped a sheer four hundred feet. Müller joined him, careful not to look down. He also suffered from vertigo.

'Well,' he snapped, determined to put an end to this nonsense, 'now you have dragged me all this way it had better be good . . .'

'But it is good . . .' Schulz purred. For the first time he looked at Müller. 'We have located a traitor actually inside the Berghof . . .'

Müller was stunned. Thoughts raced through his mind, all of them frightening. He was responsible for overall security. There would be an official enquiry. He glanced down and shuddered – whether at the sight of the abyss or the news he had just been given he wasn't sure. He placed both hands on the wall to steady himself.

'Who is the traitor?' he asked eventually.

'The traitor is yourself . . .'

Schulz moved while he was speaking. His right hand grasped the back of Müller's overcoat belt. His left hand struck the Commandant a hard blow beneath his cap and above his collar, hitting a nerve centre. The SS man employed all his strength to heave Müller up and forwards. His victim's feet slithered on the ice, increasing the momentum.

The Commandant grabbed at the wall-top but there was no purchase. He dived into space like a swimmer leaving the high board at the side of a pool. His scream came back through the clear mountain air. Schulz saw the falling figure become tiny as it descended four hundred feet. The heavy mountain silence returned.

Schulz went down in the elevator, walked slowly along the passage and headed for the waiting car without going anywhere near the crumpled body. As a matter of interest, he observed the Commandant had hit the ground a surprising distance from the base of the Kehlstein. He started up the motor and drove back to the Berghof to report the accident'.

'Most unfortunate,' Bormann commented in reply to Schulz's call telling him of the incident. 'You will return to Berlin at once. Inform Colonel Jaeger that he is to take over the post of temporary commandant at the Berghof. By order of the Führer . . . !'

Bormann replaced the receiver and took out his notebook, turning to the page where he had written down the list of problems to be attended to. He put his pen through two words, cancelling out another task successfully dealt with: *Commandant, Berghof*.

When Rainer Schulz arrived back in Berlin he found his marching orders waiting for him. He had been posted to the Leningrad front. Three days after his arrival he was killed by a rocket fired by the Russian defenders.

It is approximately six hundred miles as a Junkers 52 flies from the Berghof's airstrip to Rastenburg in East Prussia. Bauer's course involved flying over Czechoslovakia, on over Poland and, on the last lap, into East Prussia. The two men chatted about how to fly a Junkers and there was not the slightest hint of tension between them. They were in the same business. Flying.

It was during the late morning of March 14 when the plane was approaching the Wolf's Lair. In the co-pilot's seat Lindsay tried to flog his cold-numbed brain into some kind of alertness ready for the ordeal when he confronted the Führer. Below they were passing over a desert, a plain of snow which went on forever. Above loomed another desert – a low ceiling of dense, dirty-grey cloud which threatened further snow. Lindsay's mind went back to the interview in Ryder Street where this crazy scheme he had volunteered to undertake had begun.

Colonel Dick Browne, who briefed him, was not his favourite person. He recalled thinking this when he had sat on the far side of the desk as Browne continued in his clipped voice.

'If you reach Germany . . .'

'*When* I reach Germany,' Lindsay corrected him.

'When,' Browne said reluctantly as though it were the most unlikely outcome. 'Your first task is to locate the Führer's headquarters. As your pre-war attitude was known to be pro-Nazi – above all, since you visited Hitler personally – you might just receive a warm welcome . . .' He extended his hand, offering his pack. 'Have a cigarette, Lindsay.'

He made it sound as though he were granting a condemned

man his last request. Lindsay took the cigarette and used the German lighter he was accustoming himself to. He said nothing so Browne, who had hoped for some reaction, was compelled to go on.

'*When* you arrive at the Führer's secret headquarters, your second task is to discover whether Hitler himself is personally directing military operations – or whether some field-marshal is the real brain. If so, what is the identity of this man?'

'From some of the phraseology this sounds to come from pretty high up,' Lindsay observed.

'The origin of the directive is top secret. Having obtained this information – I gather the second bit is what they're really after – you then make your way back behind Allied lines by whatever means possible, report your presence to us via the local commander-in-chief. We fly you home . . .'

'A piece of cake.'

'Really, Lindsay, I do hope you are not going to treat this mission in a flippant manner . . .'

'For Christ's sake, Browne, you expect me to sit here shaking like a bloody road drill?'

'My rank is that of Colonel . . .'

'And mine is that of Wing Commander . . .'

'Which will prove helpful,' Brown said quickly, changing tack as he realized this RAF type might put in a complaint higher up than he dared to contemplate. 'They're bound to check up on you, put you under the microscope. The Allied order of battle documents you'll be taking may bolster your cover . . .'

'They're fake, I assume?' Lindsay queried as he eyed the package Brown had produced from a locked drawer. 'The Germans should have at least some information about General Alexander's troops.'

'Do let me put you completely in the picture, there's a good chap,' the Colonel said smugly. 'These documents . . .' he laid a fond hand on the package, 'list Alexander's present order of battle in Tunisia. You'll be perfectly safe.'

'You reassure me mightily,' Lindsay responded. 'That bit about being perfectly safe where I'm going. And won't I be popular with Alexander – flying into enemy territory with that package in my hip pocket.'

Browne looked even smugger, if that were possible. 'That is the beauty of the whole plan.' He leaned back in his chair and smarmed his thinning hair with the palm of his lean hand. 'If they check with German HQ in Tunis they'll get confirmation that *was* our order of battle when you flew off to Germany. As soon as you fly off into the wild blue yonder Alex changes his troop dispositions. With a bit of luck Jerry will attack on the basis of what's inside this package – and come a real cropper.'

'So Alexander . . .'

'Is only too pleased to cooperate with us. That's how we got his go-ahead. Pretty neat, eh?'

'It would appear so.'

'To recap,' Browne concluded. 'Find out where Adolf is holed up, check on whether he's running the show himself – and if not, who is his pet commander. Also the peace mission business. Then use the underground, who'll be waiting, and dash for Switzerland.'

'A piece of cake,' Lindsay repeated drily.

The Englishman jerked himself into the present as he felt the machine change angle into a gentle descent. They were coming in to land at Rangsdorf, the airfield closest to the Wolf's Lair. Where, he wondered, peering down, the hell was it? Below was a sea of dense pine forest, the branches encrusted with snow, a forest dimly seen beneath a lake of white mist and nowhere was there a sign of human habitation. Bauer's voice spoke in his earphones.

'Five minutes and we'll be down.'

'Not in that lot, I trust?' Lindsay responded with a touch of grim humour, holding the headset microphone close to his mouth.

He heard the pilot's amused chuckle followed by his response. 'The radio works – none of those damned Bavarian Alps round here. I've contacted the airstrip and we're cleared to land. Watch my smoke!'

The airstrip appeared suddenly in a large clearing which seemed bereft of buildings, which struck Lindsay as strange. Where was the f-ff'ing control tower? It was a beautiful landing – Lindsay's professional expertise gave the German ten out of ten. The landing wheels kissed the earth and they glided along the runway.

Only at ground level did the buildings become visible. Their rooftops were camouflaged with netting entwined with creeper. Several even had plants growing on top. It was little wonder no one had so far spotted the Wolf's Lair from the air. Lindsay climbed out as soon as the plane was stationary – he had felt glued to his seat, petrified. First night nerves.

He thanked Bauer, shaking his hand warmly and genuinely as he congratulated him on his performance. The German had a self-deprecatory gesture but Lindsay could tell he was pleased.

'See you around.' Bauer grinned. 'How about a trip over the Russian front some time?'

'*Some* time . . .'

Lindsay turned his attention to the large Mercedes which had driven almost alongside the aircraft. A tall, good-looking man in army uniform greeted him, shooting out his right arm. 'Wing Commander Lindsay? I am Guensche, the Führer's Adjutant. I am instructed to escort you immediately to meet the Führer who has just arrived from the Eastern Front. *Heil Hitler!*'

The news of his coming had preceded him, Lindsay realized at once. He noticed that all round the hidden airstrip men had stopped their work to stare at him. A Luftwaffe officer checking a Condor – the plane which had flown in the Führer from the Eastern Front? The twin of the machine Bauer had described as taking off earlier from the airstrip near the Berghof? A mechanic holding a cloth also paused to stare at him and inside the small control tower someone was using binoculars to study him. He was the star turn!

'Thank you, Guensche. Do you mind if I ride in front. Sitting alone in the back I'd feel like the King!'

'But certainly, Wing Commander!' Guensche closed the

74

rear door he had opened and led him to the front passenger seat. 'You know,' he continued after getting in behind the wheel and starting up the motor, 'whenever the Führer is driven anywhere he, too, always insists on sitting next to the driver. He is truly a man of the people. Like youself, sir, if I may say so. . .'

Lindsay reflected it was all so different from what he had feared. He was making friends hand over fist, a feat a certain Colonel Dick Browne of Ryder Street, London, would have found difficult to emulate. The Adjutant drove with skill along tracks between walls of gloomy pines as he continued to talk, providing interesting information.

'At the moment there is much activity, comings and goings, alarms and excursions . . .'

'Nothing serious, I hope?' Lindsay enquired.

'In the end, no! I'm thinking of yesterday – there was a loud explosion. Like a bomb dropping. Then we realized it was the usual thing – a fox setting off a mine. Although this must have been several of them setting off two or three mines – the detonation was so loud. Wing Commander, you must not wander about without a guide. The Wolf's Lair is heavily guarded by minefields. I see the first checkpoint coming up. Don't worry – there are two more before we are inside the Wolf's Lair . . .' Ian Lindsay was not worried. He was petrified.

Chapter Nine

Adjutant Guensche had escorted Lindsay through three different checkpoints. Before getting into the Mercedes the Englishman had stripped off his flying jacket and was wearing his RAF uniform. He was intrigued that there were no signs of hostility from the various guards who stared at him with curiosity. He also noted that even Guensche, who must be known to all of them, had to show his pass which carried his photograph.

'The security is very good,' he commented as the German switched off his engine after the third vetting.

'Even Keitel and Jodl have to show their special passes before they're allowed through,' Guensche told him. 'The only exception is the Führer himself . . .'

The journey from the airstrip had been depressing – everywhere the pine forest dripping with moisture, indicating a rise in temperature, had closed round them. The coils of drifting mist slipping between the trees like a ghost army added to the atmosphere of oppressive desolation. Now that they had arrived at the Wolf's Lair Lindsay was even more surprised at his primitive surroundings.

Beyond the wire they passed through was a jumbled collection of single-storey buildings which gave the impression they had been thrown up overnight. It reminded Lindsay of an army transit camp. The greatest attention seemed to have been paid to concealment.

As at Rangsdorf airstrip, the rooftops were covered skilfully with camouflage netting overlaid with creeper. The walls were painted in brown and green. Guensche turned and indicated a building they were approaching.

'The *Lagebaracke* – all military conferences are held either in there or in the Führer's bunker. That building over there belongs to Field Marshal Keitel, that one is Jodl's. Martin Bormann's is outside. Speak of the devil . . .'

A short, overweight man in Nazi uniform had emerged through the doorway and stood respectfully to one side. Another man appeared, also in uniform. Lindsay could not prevent a brief stiffening of his muscles, then he forced himself to relax. The short man took up a position alongside his master and Lindsay was surprised to observe Bormann barely came up to Hitler's shoulder.

Bormann had seen Lindsay and said something to the Führer, indicating the Englishman as the couple came closer to Guensche and his companion. He's telling him who I am, which is curious, Lindsay was thinking. Then, like the Adjutant, he shot out his right arm and held it at a motionless angle. His greeting coincided with Guensche's.

'*Heil Hitler!*'

The Führer acknowledged the salute, his expression grim. Then the expression underwent a remarkable transformation. Lindsay – with his experience as an actor – was particularly well-equipped to appreciate the phenomenon.

The forbidding personality melted as Hitler held out his hand and shook Lindsay's. His smile was engaging, there was not a hint of affectation or condescension and he spoke as though addressing an old friend he was especially fond of.

'Welcome to my simple headquarters, Wing Commander. I look forward to our enjoying a long talk together. Before the war you were one of the few Englishmen who really understood what I was trying to do. Will you excuse me? I have had a tiring time and must rest . . .'

Then he was gone and two more men, both in military uniform, followed their leader out of the *Lagebaracke*. Guensche hardly moved his lips.

'The first one is Field Marshal Keitel. Very formal. The man behind is Colonel-General Alfred Jodl.'

Keitel was tall, heavily built, held his head high and had a trim moustache. He paused briefly, his manner arrogant and overbearing. Guensche had stiffened to attention.

'You are the English defector from the Berghof. You will hold yourself in readiness until the Führer grants you a short interview.'

Having issued his *diktat*, Keitel marched off. Colonel-General Jodl was a very different man. He wore his peaked cap at a jaunty angle and there was an ironic expression in his eyes verging on amusement as he stopped and studied Lindsay. Lean-faced and clean-shaven, his manner was crisp but polite.

'Who do you think is winning this war?'

'God alone knows at the present stage . . .'

'I wish you had brought God with you then – so we could consult him,' Jodl commented. He nodded to Guensche. 'Today's conference never got off the ground. Probably just

as well – the generator is playing up. It was so dim in there
you'd think it was night.' He turned back to Lindsay and again
surprised him. 'Anything interesting in that packet you are
hugging as though it contained the British Crown Jewels?'

'The Allied order of battle on the North African front.'

'In two hours come to see me! No one else has asked you
about it? Not even the Führer? Curious – he rarely misses a
trick. You really should have brought God . . .'

Lindsay's mind was a whirlpool of conflicting impressions.
He had a vivid picture of his brief meeting with Hitler.
Recalling their long encounter before the war he had the
oddest feeling – as though the Führer was exaggerating his
earlier personality . . .

Jodl left them with an expression of cynical disgust. Lindsay
turned to check which were his quarters as Guensche spoke.
'He would be the one to notice that packet – except that I too
would have expected the Führer to ask the same question
first. Ah, here we have someone more to your taste, I expect.'

A slim, dark-haired girl with an excellent figure had come
out of the *Lagebaracke* exit and was walking towards them
slowly as though to give herself time to observe Lindsay. She
swung her right arm; under her left she clutched a notebook.

'Christa Lundt, the Führer's top secretary,' Guensche
whispered. 'She was asking about you. I think you intrigued
her.' He sighed. 'You should be so lucky.'

They sat facing each other across a table in the canteen and
Christa Lundt immediately threw Ian Lindsay off balance.
She had been sipping coffee when she asked the question.

'Are you really pro-Nazi, Wing Commander?'

She had asked the question in excellent *English*. Up to this
moment they had conversed in German. Introduced to her by
his escort, Guensche, Lindsay had been surprised when she
suggested he should accompany her to the canteen inside
which they were now sitting alone, apart from the waiter
behind the bar who was too far away to overhear them.

'I was a member of the Anglo-German Fellowship before

the war,' he replied and left the ball in her court as he drank more of his indifferent coffee.

He studied her, noted the strong nose, the firm chin and her large, slow-moving blue eyes. A tiny alarm bell was ringing at the back of his mind. All his defences were up, although nothing in his casual manner indicated his wariness.

'But that was before the war, as you say,' she continued in his native language. 'A lot of water has flowed under many bridges since those days . . .'

'And where did you learn to speak English so well, may I ask?' he enquired.

'Thus he evaded my question.' She smiled, a slow smile like the warming glow of a fire. 'I was eighteen when I spent time with a nice family in Guildford, Middlesex . . .'

'Guildford is in Surrey,' he said quickly.

'So, you are English – not a German posing as an Englishman.'

'And why should I do that in the name of sanity?'

She smiled again. He told himself to watch it. That smile of hers could undo a man. She even had a plausible reply for his fresh question.

'Because your German is so good and, if you won't think me impossibly rude, with your fair hair you look so Teutonic . . .'

'A worthy member of the master race?'

He was practising what he had been trained to do: carrying on a conversation with one part of his brain while the other part acted independently on a different channel – this talented and attractive creature was grilling him, carrying out an interrogation. Had Bormann put her up to it? That didn't quite fit – he could not have said why. He was deeply puzzled.

'A worthy member of the Anglo-German Fellowship,' she replied, her eyes holding his own. 'There's something odd about you, Wing Commander – just as odd things have been happening here before you landed at the end of the world.'

'What sort of odd things?'

He sounded uninterested, making conversation, but he had the uncomfortable sensation he was not fooling Christa

Lundt. She had small, finely-wrought hands. Every movement was graceful. Her voice was soft and soothing. She lowered it even though the man behind the counter had moved even further away and was reading a newspaper.

'For one thing, there was a very loud explosion yesterday just before the Führer was expected back from Russia. We were told foxes had blundered into the minefield. Now that has happened before, but this explosion was very loud and to me – I have good hearing – it sounded to come from *above* the forest. As it turned out, the Führer's plane was delayed.'

'Doesn't sound to amount to much,' Lindsay replied.

'There was a lot of activity beyond the perimeter later that afternoon. I'm sure I heard tracked vehicles moving into the forest. Today the Führer does arrive for his normal midday conference – and then curtails it. Something was wrong with the generator – the lights went dim and stayed that way. With the cloud overcast we could hardly see each other inside the *Lagebaracke*.'

'So, the power goes on the blink. There's a war on, in case you'd forgotten. . .'

'I'm not a complete fool, Wing Commander!'

'I'm an informal type. Call me Ian. May I call you Christa?'

'All right, Ian – but only when we're alone. Otherwise it must be Fräulein Lundt. Martin Bormann has tried to get me into bed a dozen times – he's succeeded with most of the other secretaries. You don't want to upset him – he's the most dangerous man at the Wolf's Lair. And he's in charge of all admin – including operation of the power supply.'

'He's the only one – who knows about the generator?'

'Well, no. Keitel and Jodl are both technically-minded and poke their noses into everything. Like most of us, they get so bored in this oasis of hell.' Her eyes held his. 'And we've got spy fever! The Führer is convinced there's a Soviet agent inside the Wolf's Lair.' Her face went passive. 'Bormann has just arrived. He's coming to see you. I'm leaving . . .'

Lindsay lay on the bunk, arms folded behind his head, staring up at the heavily-reinforced roof and not seeing it. Bormann had shown him to his quarters, a small hut in the cantonment inside Perimeter Two where Keitel and Jodl had their own private abodes – neither of which looked any more luxurious than the primitive place allocated to the Englishman.

He was amazed at the whole layout which reminded him vividly of descriptions he had read of prisoner-of-war camps. But he was recalling every word of his conversation with Christa Lundt. Could he trust one word she had said?

First there was the mysterious explosion which – according to Christa – had taken place *overhead*. Second, the business about the power dimming at the military conference was odd. Third there was something unreal about his brief meeting with Hitler. Then he remembered Christa's tale of a Soviet agent inside the Wolf's Lair. That really did destroy her whole credibility.

The heavily-muffled figure passed through the outermost checkpoint and vanished inside the mist-bound forest. It trod with almost feminine light-footedness, making hardly a sound on the crusted snow.

In the distance there was a sound like a rifle shot. The unreal silhouette didn't even pause. An ice-cased branch had snapped from a tree. It was a frequent occurrence. The figure moved on confidently along the path through the minefields. Half a kilometre from the checkpoint it stopped inside a clump of trees and bent down.

The radio transmitter was concealed in what looked like a hide for an animal, a pile of logs – of which there were many – half-covered with snow-covered undergrowth. Extracting a notebook from a pocket, the figure turned to the page with the already encoded message.

Sensitive fingers began tapping out the signal, fingers which first extended the telescopic aerial of the high-powered device. Nothing was hurried. Once the message had been sent, logs were replaced in position. A hand reached up and shook a branch above the 'hide', bringing down a fresh fall of snow to conceal all signs of disturbance.

The muffled figure then began its slow return to the checkpoint, taking its time. A number of personnel inside the Wolf's Lair were in the habit of taking walks beyond the perimeter – anything to escape for a short time the claustrophobic atmosphere which pervaded the headquarters.

Half an hour later Ian Lindsay put on a military great-coat Guensche had loaned him and left his hut to stretch his legs. The mist – it was almost dark – had invaded the Wolf's Lair and dirty grey swirls drifted past his face. Without warning a muffled figure loomed in front of him.

Field Marshal Keitel raised his baton in a weary gesture and walked on across the compound to his quarters. He had not exchanged a word. It was the kind of evening when no one liked the world.

PART TWO

THE LUCY RING:
Roessler

Chapter Ten

Lucerne, Switzerland. It was a crisp, cold night in the ancient Swiss town. Few people walked the snowbound cobbled streets in the dark silence. Closeted in his apartment on the top floor of an old building, Rudolf Roessler took off his headphones and gazed at the pad recording the coded signal he had just received from Germany. He sat half inside a cupboard in front of a lowered panel which concealed his powerful transceiver.

Middle-aged, a man you could pass on the street a hundred times without realizing you had passed anyone, he peered through thick-lensed spectacles at the signal he would shortly re-transmit to Moscow. Even in its present form – Swiss cryptographers had long ago broken the code – he knew he was looking at the current order of battle of the German Army on the Eastern Front.

The mystery – the solution to which Roessler could never even have guessed – was the identity of Woodpecker, the agent so close to the summit of the Nazi hierarchy he could supply regularly the German order of battle. Roessler never ceased to wonder about this incredible source.

Roessler himself had mysterious aspects. For one thing he was a German. Prior to 1933 he had been a theatrical publisher in Berlin and the editor of an anti-Nazi paper. During those abandoned days when the German capital was the fleshpot of Europe he had built up the contacts which – years later – led to the founding of the most successful spy network of World War Two. The Lucy Ring.

'Anna, I could do with a cup of hot coffee before I re-transmit to Moscow . . .'

He turned in his swivel chair and his wife smiled and nodded as she reached for the container of coffee. An attractive, dark-haired woman of forty, she was slim and brisk and enormously efficient. She talked as she bent over the stove.

'You work too hard, you know. All this work we do must put a tremendous strain on you . . .'

'Anna, we may well be making history. We could even change the whole course of the war – if only they will, please God, in Moscow, *listen* to us!'

'Either they will or they won't,' Anna replied. 'You can only do your best. Come and sit down at the table while you drink your coffee,' she scolded. 'Life is complicated enough as it is . . .'

It was indeed complicated. In 1933 Roessler fled to Switzerland, one jump ahead of arrest when Hitler came to power. As war came close he struck a bargain with Nachrichten-Dienst, the Swiss Military Information Service. In return for being allowed to operate his transceiver he would supply the Swiss with the signals obtained from his old contacts in Berlin.

One of these men had approached Roessler just before he left Germany. Roessler never knew the identity of this particular contact, although he had felt sure he was talking to a Communist.

'There will be a war,' the man had said. 'When it comes you'll receive radio signals from Woodpecker. He is so high up you would never believe it. A powerful transceiver will be smuggled across the Swiss border to you. I shall see you are given all the codes and technical data re radio transmission. And the name of a Swiss who will train you in the operation of the set . . .'

In 1943, the mild-mannered Roessler, who a decade earlier looked forward to a life spent as a theatrical publisher, found himself the controller of the world's most important spy network. The original contact in Berlin had given him one more instruction.

'You need a code-name to protect your real identity. We have decided to call you Lucy . . .'

In his office inside the Kremlin, Stalin was holding a decoded message in his hand as he stood by his desk. Two other men stood in front of him, respectfully silent.

One was Lavrenti Beria, a pallid-faced man wearing pince-nez, the head of the NKVD, the Ministry of State Security, later to become the KGB. The other visitor was General Zhukov, wide-shouldered and with a large, muscular body. Stalin handed the signal first to Beria, retired behind his desk, leaned back in his chair and lit his pipe which had a bent stem. From beneath bushy brows his yellowish eyes watched Beria as he spoke in his Georgian accent.

'That is another message which just came in from Lucy.'

'Who is this Lucy?' Zhukov asked with a hint of impatience.

'That is not your concern. The signal originates from Woodpecker, an important contact inside Hitlerite Germany. May I assume General . . .' he paused as though the rank might be of a temporary nature, ' . . . Zhukov that you send out regular patrols on the battlefront?'

Zhukov stiffened. The question was a near insult. He forced himself to conceal his indignation – to reply as though it were the most natural of questions.

'Generalissimo, I make it a point personally to ensure there are both daily and nightly patrols. They are told they need not return unless they bring in prisoners for interrogation . . .'

'Then tell me,' Stalin requested in his soft-spoken voice, 'do you believe that signal giving the German order of battle is to be trusted?'

They waited. The purse-lipped Beria, who had learned never to speak unless asked a direct question by Stalin, had handed the signal to Zhukov. There was something sinister in the sheer immobility of the NKVD chief. Zhukov spoke, gazing at Stalin.

'From the latest information I have, this signal – as regards the forward areas – is correct . . .'

'But the Germans could have planted a thin screen of unit in those forward areas to correspond with the signal,' sai Stalin.

Zhukov sighed. He hated these insidious military conferences, any summons to the Kremlin. But he was careful to suppress the sigh. It was all so typical of Stalin – *trust no one*! Was there the same atmosphere of intrigue at Hitler's headquarters – wherever that might be – he wondered? He refused to knuckle under completely.

'That is so,' he agreed. 'But Woodpecker's previous signals have proved astonishingly accurate – as though they were sent by someone in the Führer's immediate entourage. As a soldier, you get a sixth sense about these things. . .'

'We will wait a little longer – see a few more of these signals before we base any operation on them.'

Stalin lowered his eyes and knocked out his pipe in a large ash tray on his desk. The embers in the crystal bowl glowed redly in the dimly-lit room. Power was still rationed in Moscow. And General Zhukov realized he had been dismissed.

As soon as he was alone with his secret police chief Stalin produced a second signal and handed it to him. He did not look at Beria when he commented.

'That message came in from London. An English air force officer, Lindsay, has flown from North Africa to see Hitler. Churchill is up to his old tricks again, I suspect.'

'Do you mean negotiating a separate peace with the Germans?' Beria suggested cautiously after scanning the signal.

'I didn't say that, did I? We will await developments.'

It was a favourite phrase of Stalin's, expressing an attitude he always adopted until he saw which way the cat jumped. He had used the same words when in June 1941 warnings had poured into the Kremlin from all quarters forecasting an imminent German attack.

'And if it should prove to be the case?' Beria ventured.

'Then we may have to take drastic steps, may we not?'

Two hours earlier in Lucerne, Rudolf Roessler had completed his transmission of the signal to Moscow, closed the flap concealing the transceiver, and shut the door to the cupboard inside which he stored his only reason for existence.

88

Even when the long-distance aerial had first been installed he had practised caution. A Swiss civilian technician had strung the wire all round the room along the top of the picture ledge. Roessler had his casual explanation ready.

'I want to listen to the British BBC overseas transmissions clearly,' he had remarked.

His wife, Anna, stood waiting for him in the doorway. She had heard the familiar slap when he had shut the cupboard door.

'I'll stay up for Masson's courier,' she suggested. 'You get to bed and try to sleep. I've made a copy of the signal. It's in this envelope. I phoned the Villa Stutz while you transmitted.'

'What should I do without you?' Roessler wondered.

'Starve!'

'It's all so crazy, this war,' Roessler continued. 'I am German. I receive signals from the anti-Nazi underground. I transmit them to Moscow. I make sure Swiss Intelligence has a copy of these signals – in accordance with our agreement for permission to operate in their country. It is crazy, is it not?'

'If you say so. . .'

'I receive the signals from someone right at the top, someone I feel sure I never knew – but who must be taking a terrible risk. I then transmit them from this unknown Woodpecker to the equally unknown Cossack. Is anybody out there listening? The Russians are not winning. . .'

'We'll know when Moscow is listening,' Anna told him.

'How, I ask you. . . ?'

'When – if – the Red Army begins to sweep across Europe. Now, for the last time, Rudolf Roessler – go to bed!'

Chapter Eleven

Heinz Kuby, the Führer's double, had summoned Martin Bormann to his quarters after resting. He received his visitor dressed in Hitler's wartime uniform, dark trousers and a military-style jacket. As Bormann entered and closed the door Kuby was pacing up and down, hands clasped behind his back.

Bormann studied his creation carefully and was astounded. He *felt* he was in the presence of the real Führer. The one-time actor's opening remark was typical of Hitler, too typical for the liking of Bormann who had been waiting for the opportunity to 'instruct' Kuby.

'The first conference went well, Bormann. You understood, of course, my tactics? I said very little and made the others report the present military situation on the Eastern Front. Now, at the next meeting, I shall begin to issue orders. . .'

'That would be terribly dangerous. . .' Bormann protested. He glanced nervously round the simply-furnished room. 'I trust we are alone. . .'

'Of course! You imagine I did not take precautions before I summoned you here?'

Summoned. Bormann stiffened at the phraseology. He had assumed Kuby would lean heavily on him for advice in every field. Instead the man who was now Adolf Hitler already was addressing him with an air of supreme authority. Hitler continued speaking.

'The main point is I have to grasp in detail the existing military dispositions – then I can exercise supreme control. . .'

'Supreme control?' Bormann was stupefied. 'You have not the knowledge to direct operations involving millions of men. . .'

'Interrupt me once more and you will leave the room,' Hitler threatened. 'While at the Berghof I have spent all my life preparing for just this moment.' He began to wave his hands, his gestures savage to punctuate his words. 'I have studied Clausewitz, von Moltke – all the military literature I found in the library, all the books my predecessor read I have soaked up so I could repeat them backwards. You forget, Bormann, I have a most excellent memory for facts. . .'

'And if I do not support you?'

'*Mein Führer!*' the apparition hissed. 'That is how you address me in private as well as in public. You think you can denounce me? You who were responsible for bringing me to the Wolf's Lair? How long do you think *you* would last? Answer me that!'

'Is not someone bound to see through the impersonation?' Bormann suggested. 'Keitel? Jodl? We have successfully surmounted the first hurdle because I tampered with the generator – so it was impossible for anyone to see you clearly in the conference room. Then there are the men who visit us – Goebbels, Goering. . .'

'You are a fool, Bormann!'

Hitler sat down in an arm chair, his hands clutching the arms, his forelock draped over his forehead as he stared at the other man. 'The generals who oppose *my* policy are just waiting for an opportunity to replace me – and those who have supported me, including Keitel and Jodl. Their positions – maybe their lives – depend on my continued existence. Your own certainly does. And so do the lives of all who, as you put it, visit us here. So – if anyone suspects he will be careful to keep his mouth shut!'

'I am sure you are right. *Mein Führer*,' Bormann added.

'You *are* a fool,' Hitler continued thoughtfully, his bulging eyes gripping Bormann's attention. 'The whole of our success has been based on propaganda – which in itself is based on my original concept of The Big Lie! I have said – and proved – it time and again. A small lie people may question. An enormous lie so staggers them, they begin to believe it must be true. You see how it works in reverse?'

'Perhaps you would explain that to me?'

Bormann was still standing. But the Führer had not suggested that he sit down. His mind was a whirl, fogged in a kind of hynotic daze as the Führer pressed on.

'The Big Lie. Who would ever dream that a man who looks just like the Führer, who acts just like the Führer, who *speaks* just like the Führer can be anyone *but the Führer*?'

Hitler jumped up suddenly in a characteristic burst of energy and again began pacing the room. His harsh tone mellowed and he became the soul of amiability.

'Bormann, I need your help. I want you always by my side. I can count on you, can I not?'

'Of course, *mein Führer! Always!*'

The small, stocky Bormann found himself stiffening to attention. He gave the Nazi salute. Hitler stopped pacing and grasped him fondly by the arm. He smiled again and there was a film of moistness in his prominent eyes.

'May I mention the problem of the dog?' Bormann suggested.

'There is no problem – I made friends with Blondi during his visits to the Berghof. He trusts me – I have a rapport with dogs.'

'The only other problem,' Bormann began hesitantly, 'would appear to be insoluble – if you ever visit the Berghof again. I refer to Eva Braun. . .'

'The lady is one problem you do not have to worry your head about,' Hitler assured him, a humorous glint in his eyes. 'And I shall certainly visit the Berghof. Considering my life was confined there for so many years that is where I feel most at home. . .' He paused. 'I am glad you brought that up, Bormann. Until people get used to me, a change of scene should throw them off-balance. So, in the near future we *will* all go to the Berghof – I need a rest from my arduous months of labour at the Wolf's Lair. I think that is all for now. . .'

Bormann returned to his own quarters, trudging slowly through the snow, in a state of turmoil. The past few days had been the busiest of his life. He had taken decision after decision, his mind too full of the present to look into the future.

Vaguely he had assumed that Heinz Kuby would be putty in his hands, to be moulded in any shape he wished. Now the 'robot' he had created was taking on a life and will of its own – and there was nothing he could do about it.

From the outbreak of World War Two, Adolf Hitler had demonstrated he was a military genius – fit to rank with Caesar, Frederick the Great and Wellington. In half-a-dozen crises he had proved his enormously superior flair.

April 1940. It was Hitler who had enthusiastically approved and backed the audacious invasion of Denmark and Norway. While his generals wrung their hands and predicted disaster, Hitler had ordered that the plans devised by Admiral Raeder should proceed.

Norway! A thousand miles of open sea and coastline from its southern tip of North Cape – with the British Navy based at near-by Scapa Flow. Madness! Hitler had contemptuously waved aside all objections. Go ahead! Invade, General Falkenhorst! The plan had succeeded.

France! It was Hitler who put all his authority behind one general's crazy operation – Guderian's fantastic panzer drive through the 'impassable' roads of the Ardennes, bursting out into the open country beyond, thundering across the Meuse bridges at Sedan. On and on towards the Channel while, again, his general staff shivered in their shoes and repeated their forecasts of disaster!

That was, until the British were driven back across the water inside their inland fortress – and France fell within weeks. It was such brilliant successes which had cowed the High Command, which had led to Hitler being able to appoint his own tame men, Keitel and Jodl, to the peak of the command structure.

All this passed through Bormann's mind as, bleak-faced, he walked alone on that fateful afternoon under lowering skies in March 1943. What did the future hold? This was what obsessed him.

The plans of the Allied Military dispositions in North Africa lay spread out on Colonel-General Jodl's desk. They had been delivered to him two hours earlier at his request by Ian Lindsay. Now the Englishman sat waiting and wondering as he struggled to conceal the tension inside him.

Jodl had had time to communicate with the German High Command in Tunis – whose forces faced those of General Alexander. What would the verdict be? The Englishman was becoming aware there was something devious in Alfred Jodl's expression and nature. It would take an agile mind to survive the domestic warfare of the Wolf's Lair.

'I have communicated the contents of these plans to Tunis. I have further had their reaction to what you say purports to be the Allied order of battle. . .'

Jodl paused, tapping a pencil gently on his desk. A naked bulb shed a harsh light over the military documents. It was early in the evening, as black as pitch in the compound outside, where dense mist blotted out the masked lights. Jodl was playing with him – Lindsay could sense it as he was careful to resist the overwhelming temptation to say something – anything – to break the loaded silence.

'In a way these documents are a clue as to your *bona fides* – is that not so?' Jodl enquired eventually.

Lindsay shrugged, a gesture of complete indifference. 'That is for others to decide. I simply await my interview with the Führer. . .'

'You may have to wait a long time,' the German said sharply.

Lindsay's stomach revolved. God, something was wrong with the bloody documents. He wanted to reach for the pack of cigarettes in his pocket. Again he resisted temptation since Jodl, he felt certain, was waiting for the slightest sign of nerves.

The pencil continued tapping its tattoo. Lindsay could have wrenched it out of Jodl's hands and snapped the thing in two. Instead, he leaned back further in his chair and clasped his hands lightly in his lap.

'You may have to wait a long time,' Jodl repeated. 'You

see, I happen to know the Führer has a list of appointments as long as your arm.'

Lindsay nodded, no particular expression showing in his reaction as he concealed the shock of relief. Jodl's manner, his choice of words, had convinced him he was about to be arrested and interrogated.

'Tunis,' Jodl said suddenly, still staring hard at Lindsay, 'tells me all the present data as to the Allied dispositions on the African front coincides with the documents you brought us. . .'

For the second time the Englishman forced himself to hide his relief. This really was a tricky bastard – he was convinced Jodl had been testing him. He watched while the German arranged the documents tidily, returned them to the thick envelope and pushed the package across the desk.

'Your passport to the Wolf's Lair. Guard them well.'

His expression was ironic and even when he left the hut Lindsay was uncertain whether he had gained the man's confidence – or at least his neutrality. An enigmatic personality, Colonel-General Alfred Jodl.

He closed the door behind him and stopped. Dense fog was rolling into the compound, an icy fog which penetrated his great-coat and reached for his bones. The leaden silence – no, it was the complete absence of sound – bothered him.

Then he realized it was not the atmosphere which had alerted him. A shoe or boot had squeaked nearby. Standing quite still in the grey blanket of vapour he knew he was not alone. A hand grasped his arm.

'Don't make a sound!'

It was the soft, sleepy voice of Christa Lundt – he had already guessed her identity from the smallness of the hand which gripped his arm.

'I want to talk to you,' she went on, 'but we must not be seen. You know you are being watched? Don't let's go into that now – just concentrate on not making a noise. We'll go to my quarters.'

Still holding on to him, she led the way across the compound. Lindsay was disturbed by the way she drifted through the fog like a wraith. Only a professional could move so silently. Who was Christa Lundt?'

'We're here. Wait while I open the door. . .'

He listened and watched. Not a hint of a sound as she inserted a key inside the lock, turned and withdrew it. Recently she must have oiled the lock for it to operate so noiselessly. She gently pulled him inside the darkness of the interior and asked him to stay still.

Again the door was closed with great skill, the lock turned, a light switched on. They were standing in a narrow corridor. No carpet on the bare floorboards. She ushered him inside a room, switched on another light and went immediately to check the curtain drawn over the window.

'Coffee?'

'Maybe later, thank you.' He sat in an arm chair she indicated with a graceful gesture. 'You said something about my being watched. . .'

'Martin Bormann. It would be, of course. He has allocated an SS man to follow you and report all your movements. I met the SS chap – who'd lost you.' She sounded amused as she sat close to him, crossed her shapely legs and used both hands to loosen her glossy hair. 'He was in a bit of a panic. I told him I was sure I'd seen you going to see Keitel. So now he's freezing outside our respected Field Marshal's hut. With a bit of luck he should be there all night. . .'

'Why would it be Bormann who set the dogs on me? "Of course", I think you said. . .'

'Because he's suspicious of everyone.' She grinned. 'Sometimes I think he wonders about himself. He thinks you're a British spy – he's furious that the Führer has agreed to see you.' She had gone to the kitchen area. She was boiling water for the coffee on a stove. As she spoke she glanced at Lindsay as though to assess his reaction. He turned the direction of the conversation away from himself.

'There certainly seems to be a case of spy mania,' Lindsay observed. 'I recall you said there was a Soviet agent inside the Wolf's Lair. . .'

'I said the *Führer* is convinced a Soviet agent has penetrated the security system,' she corrected him. 'Someone at the very top. . .'

'You get that sort of thing in wartime.'

The Englishman introduced a hint of disbelief into his assertion and it provoked a reaction. She began straining the coffee as she replied.

'He does have grounds for thinking that way. Every time the Wehrmacht launches an offensive the Russians have troops ready to meet it. The curious thing is they don't launch offensives themselves. If they did know our order of battle, you'd think they would take us by surprise. Here you are – real coffee. Not that acorn muck we drank in the canteen. . .'

'Who exactly does know the order of battle?'

She perched on the arm of a chair and sipped at her coffee as though she hadn't heard the question. Had he probed too far? The girl puzzled him and he was irked that he couldn't weigh her up. The obvious explanation was that she had been instructed to find out all she could about him and then report back to. . . Bormann? The Führer himself? She surprised him again by replying.

'Only a very few people know the daily order of battle – the Führer himself, of course, since he takes all the major operational decisions. Field Marshal Keitel is another. Martin Bormann is present at every conference. Then there's Colonel-General Jodl. . .' The latter seemed to be an afterthought. 'That's about it.'

'The short list of suspects is a trio, then. Bormann, Keitel and Jodl.' Lindsay leaned his head against the back of the arm chair and appeared to relax completely as he stretched out his legs and crossed his ankles. 'This coffee is very good.'

'And your trio is ridiculous. All of them are so high up they are above suspicion. . .'

'The most successful spies in history have always been so high they had access to really vital information – and were, as you say, above suspicion. In the old Austro-Hungarian

97

Empire their chief of counter-espionage, Colonel Raedl, was eventually caught passing secrets to the other side by the trainload.'

'Why have you flown to Germany, Ian?'

'I like to travel. I was getting a hemmed-in feeling back in Britain. . .'

'Oh, you flew direct from Britain to Africa and then on to the Berghof?'

He didn't reply to the question. He was beginning to change his mind about Christa being a pawn sent to find out all she could and then report back her findings to Bormann or someone else. He sensed that she was in a nervy, jumpy mood, that she was deeply concerned about her own safety.

Christa Lundt attended all the military conferences. Christa Lundt recorded all the Führer's instructions – she had said so earlier in the canteen. She was the ideal person to provide the answer to the second question which had brought him to Germany. He decided to take the gamble.

'One thing intrigues me,' he began. 'Is the Führer really the military genius he poses as? Or is there some brilliant general directing the armies? Keitel? Jodl?'

'You're joking, I assume.' Her tone was full of contempt. 'I thought you would have spotted those two are Hitler's obedient satellites. The Führer alone is in command. Throughout the war so far he has taken all the crucial decisions which brought us so many victories. He is his own mastermind. . .'

'You admire him?' he suggested.

'We all do. And not only for his genius. He's considerate – especially with women. He can be very gentle and understanding. And it's fascinating to watch the way he manipulates his generals, all of whom are highly educated while he rose from the bottom. . .'

Lindsay was still leaning back in his chair when he threw the question at her. 'What are you so nervous about? Don't deny it – you crept about like a phantom on the way back here from Jodl's quarters. You kidded me it was all for my sake – it was for your *own*. You weren't scared someone would spot me – you were scared someone would spot *you*! Why?'

She stood up and began walking round the room slowly, interlacing her fingers, kneading them restlessly. She gave the impression of a woman struggling to take a major decision. She stopped in front of Lindsay and looked down at him through her lashes.

'Bormann is going to make me his scapegoat. I know it! The Führer keeps on and on about this hidden traitor at the Wolf's Lair – Bormann always provides the Führer with what he wants – that's how he got where he is. He's going to denounce me as the Soviet spy. It's just a question of when. I need an escape route.'

'You know something?' Lindsay adopted her own tactic of talking very slowly. 'You're good – you're very good, indeed. I'll give you that. . .'

'What the hell do you mean?'

Her face was white with anger. She clenched her knuckles and he sensed she was on the verge of attacking him. He remained still, silent. She couldn't stand the silence.

'I said what the hell do you mean?'

'That stuff about Bormann making you a scapegoat is a load of rubbish. He'd need evidence. And you know it. But the second part intrigues me – the escape route bit, that you feel you're going to need. And soon. Why?'

Christa Lundt had cracked up. She sat on the sofa shuddering. It was an unnerving, pathetic sight. She sat very erect, staring in front of her, like a person under hypnosis. From her hips upward her body quivered like a sick person with the fever. In her lap she clenched her hands tightly, the knuckles white and bloodless. For a whole minute she uttered no sound.

At the other end of the sofa Lindsay sat without reacting, his face expressionless. He watched her closely. He could hear Colonel Browne giving the warning in faraway Ryder Street.

'It may all go wrong. You may never reach the Führer. Then you will be subjected to every trick in the book – and they have a very big book. Torture cannot be ruled out. But they can be more subtle. *They may use a woman to undermine your defences. . .*'

Still gazing fixedly ahead, she gripped her graceful hands as though fighting for control. A tear appeared at the corner of her right eye, rolled down her cheek. He waited for the handkerchief to appear. She opened her trembling lips, closed them and then the words came through teeth clenched as tightly as the fingers.

'Bormann, Jodl, Keitel – they know they have to be suspects. *I take down the Führer's bloody minutes for his military directives.* I'm made to order for the scapegoat. I have to get away from this place, for Christ's sake. . .'

'Why consult me?'

Her voice was low, little more than a whisper. So quiet he had to lean an arm across the top of the sofa and bend closer to hear her next words.

'Because I'm convinced you've come here to find out something. When you've found it out you'll leave. Oh, yes, you'll escape. You're that sort of man, I can sense it. . .'

For the first time since the paroxysm had begun she looked at him. She had spoken the last sentence calmly. The fever of fear – if that was what it had been – passed as swiftly as it had appeared. She produced a handkerchief from somewhere – he was too intent on studying her to notice from where – and wiped her face. That was when someone tapped gently on the outer door.

'I am Major Gustav Hartmann of the Abwehr. May I come inside. The weather is rather inclement tonight. . .'

Lindsay froze. A whole chain of events had been stage-managed. First, Christa Lundt had waited for him outside Jodl's hut to coax him back to her own quarters. She had then tried to trap him – to throw him off balance by creating an extreme, emotional atmosphere. He had not reacted to that. Now the Abwehr had arrived.

Lindsay was certain that someone was desperate to discredit him before he ever talked to the Führer. The question he needed an answer to was the identity of the stage-manager of the series of events he was being subjected to. Bormann, Keitel – or Jodl?

Hartmann was a large man. Over six feet tall, well-built, he wore a military great-coat with wide lapels. In his late thirties, he had a well-shaped head, a small, trim moustache, strong features and watchful eyes. He removed his peaked cap, still waiting in the open doorway. The aroma of fog mingled with damp pinewoods lingered about him.

'You want to see me, Major?' Christa demanded.

'I have a routine mission – to interrogate your guest. . .'

'You have papers? And how did you know he was here?'

She was giving a convincing demonstration that she had never met Hartmann before. The Abwehr man produced a folder, showed it to her while he studied the Englishman. She returned the folder after checking it.

'You'd better come in. You do understand security is tight at the Wolf's Lair?'

'I have found that out since I flew in from Berlin.' There was an ironical note in the German's voice. 'I was informed that the Englishman was being interviewed by Colonel-General Jodl. . .'

'You followed us here and then waited,' the girl said sharply.

'It seemed discourteous to intrude immediately,' Hartmann replied smoothly. 'I went to the canteen and then came back. . . .'

Hartmann was unbuttoning his great-coat when Lindsay decided he had had enough. This charade between Lundt and Hartmann – with the girl pretending the Abwehr officer was a stranger – had to be blown sky-high. He stood up.

'You can keep your coat on, Hartmann. No one is interrogating me until I've seen the Führer. And who the hell gave you authority to ask me questions first?'

'I am not at liberty to reveal the identity of my superior,' the German said stiffly, but he stopped taking off his coat.

'Then I'm not at liberty to tell you anything. If you persist I shall go straight to the top and complain. . .'

Lindsay's manner was brusque, almost arrogant. He stood

erect and outwardly confident as he waited to see whether his bluff had worked. Once caught up in the coils of the lower echelons there was a great danger he would never reach the Führer.

'The interrogation has to be purely voluntary,' Hartmann said quietly, his dark eyes still studying the Englishman. 'So. . .'

He buttoned up his coat again slowly. Christa had closed the outer door and Hartmann held his peaked cap in his hand as he took a few steps closer to both of them, his voice confidential.

'It is very much in Wing Commander Lindsay's interest – even his safety could be involved – if neither of you say a word about my visiting you.' He bowed to Christa, put on his cap and said, 'I repeat, my presence here should remain a secret between us. Should anyone confront you with the fact of my visit you simply deny all knowledge of it. . .'

'I don't understand you. . .' Christa began.

'Which is my intention. Good night. . .'

Lindsay waited until Christa had closed the door again and they were alone. She leaned back against the door, her brow furrowed.

'He's Section Three of the Abwehr – counter-espionage. Creepy.'

'I thought you'd never seen him before,' Lindsay rapped. 'How do you know what section he's attached to?'

'Because I examined his paper, idiot!' She folded her arms and walked slowly towards the coffee pot. 'They're all around us, Wing Commander – and closing in. . .'

Chapter Twelve

'Who the devil are you?'

'Major Hartmann. Abwehr. . .'

The question had been arrogant, overbearing in tone. Hartmann's reply was brusque, abrupt. On leaving Fräulein Lundt's quarters he had moved across the fog-bound compound and was passing under a high overhead light beamed downwards when accosted.

Field Marshal Keitel gripped his baton more tightly as he summoned a nearby guard to join him. The uniformed soldier came running, his rifle held ready for action in both hands. The powerful light was blurred in the swirling grey vapour as the three men faced one another, the soldier staring at the Field Marshal as he waited for the next instruction.

'Are you carrying a weapon?' Keitel demanded.

'Only a 9-mm. Luger,' Hartmann replied. 'And before you ask, yes, the weapon is fully loaded. An empty pistol is rather pointless, would you not agree?'

Keitel was almost speechless with fury. No more than the mouthpiece of the Führer – 'the ventriloquist's solid wooden dummy' as one battle-weary general commented after a visit to Rastenburg, he compensated by bullying all those of inferior rank or influence.

'Disarm him!' Keitel ordered.

Hartmann's movement would have seemed like a conjuror's sleight of hand in broad daylight; in the murk of the night beneath the dim lamp it seemed little short of miraculous. Before the soldier had even begun to react, the Luger appeared in Hartmann's hand. It was aimed point-blank at the soldier's chest.

'Drop the rifle!'

In the soundless compound there was a clatter as the

weapon left the soldier's nerveless fingers and fell to the ground. There had been a grim urgency in Hartmann's voice which made his action a reflex. Keitel, astounded, made several attempts before he managed coherent speech.

'Do you realize whom you are addressing?'

'No.' A pause. 'In this benighted fog how the hell could anyone? I have identified myself. Kindly repay the compliment before I lower this pistol. You could be bluffing – it's the oldest trick in the world to assume an autocratic tone. And I have come here because this place is crawling with treachery. . .'

'Field Marshal Keitel! I am Keitel. . .'

'You look like anyone in this lousy light. If we are to talk, may I suggest you dismiss this soldier – who, incidentally, does not handle his weapon very impressively. Security here appears lax. . .'

'You can go!' Keitel snapped at the guard. 'Don't forget your weapon – not that the bloody thing is any use.' He turned to the Abwehr officer. 'Kindly accompany me to my hut. I want to talk to you. . .'

Walking slowly behind the ramrod back, Hartmann smiled to himself as he extracted a pipe after returning the Luger to its holster. Without lighting it, he clenched the much-used pipe between his teeth.

'No smoking in here!'

Keitel issued the edict when they were inside his office and he turned and saw Hartmann's pipe. The Abwehr officer kept it in his mouth and removed his cap as he spoke.

'I hardly ever light it. The pure atmosphere inside here will remain unpolluted. But it helps my concentration. That, I feel sure, you can hardly object to.'

It was a statement, not a question. From the first few seconds of their encounter in the compound the Abwehr man had recognized Keitel – but he spent half his life using his considerable skill as a psychologist to establish respect, however grudging, for his position. Keitel was the schoolboy bully, the head boy who sucked up to the headmaster and made life hell for the rest of the pupils. Oh God, he had met the type before – times without number. The trick was to throw them off balance instantly.

'Under whose authority were you permitted to enter the Security Zone?' Keitel barked.

After removing his cap and outer coat he had sat down behind a large desk. The chair was large – needed to be to accommodate his bulk – and he sat erect. He had overlooked the courtesy of suggesting that Hartmann sat down. The Abwehr officer paused to give his statement maximum shock effect.

'By order of the Führer.' He took the pipe from his mouth and examined the bowl, then replaced it in its original position as he continued. 'There are serious rumours – too serious to ignore any longer – that a Soviet spy is operating inside the Wolf's Lair. My job is to identify him.' He extracted a folded piece of paper from his wallet and placed it on the desk. 'There is my movement order. . .' Again, the enigmatic pause. 'It gives me full power to question everyone regardless of rank. . .'

Keitel's face had changed, like the lowering of a shutter as he checked the order. Hartmann was intrigued. Was Keitel really the obstinate automaton he was reputed to be? Or did the bluster conceal something quite different? More deadly?

'May I sit down? That is kind of you. My thanks. . .'

Hartmann hung cap and coat on the wall-rack next to Keitel's and seated himself in the chair facing the Field Marshal across the wide expanse of desk. Keitel had not replied. He re-folded the document slowly, pushed it across the desk surface, staring at Hartmann. The atmosphere inside the hut had subtly changed. Hartmann sensed tension, unease.

'That document gives you plenipotentiary powers,' Keitel observed slowly.

'That's right!' Hartmann responded cheerfully. He crossed his legs and leaned back in the chair, the soul of relaxation. 'The right of interrogation, summary powers of arrest. Regard me as the agent of the Führer. . .'

The Abwehr. . . No one liked them – because everyone

feared them. It was unclear where their authority began and ended. That was the style of Admiral Canaris, their chief, Keitel was thinking. It gave the old fox infinite room for manoeuvre. He decided to test the Abwehr man, his manner now bluff and amiable.

'Of course it goes without saying that your brief does not extend to the upper echelons of the High Command. Colonel-General Jodl, for example. . .'

'Or yourself?' Hartmann broke in agreeably.

'Well, naturally. . .'

'Perhaps you had better read the movement order again,' Hartmann suggested jovially. "Regardless of rank". . . Is that phrase not included? Doubtless inserted at the Führer's specific wish – since he himself signed the order.'

Keitel's mouth tightened. He would have liked to explode – was only holding himself in check with a supreme effort of will, the Abwehr Major noted. Again the Field Marshal glanced at the document still lying on his desk but made no move to re-read it. He went off at a tangent.

'Do you have to keep that beastly pipe in your mouth when you're addressing me?'

'As I said, it helps the concentration. We all need something. I notice this interview is something of a strain for yourself – you have not stopped fiddling with that baton since you sat down. . .'

Keitel stopped himself looking at his own hands but could not stop himself gripping more tightly the baton he had been revolving on the surface of his desk. Hartmann waited, amused. Keitel was unsure whether to push the baton away – which would have been some kind of concession to this bloody Abwehr creep – or whether to continue as before. Such tiny incidents were everyday stock-in-trade to Hartmann, who excelled in interrogation techniques.

'I find you insolent,' Keitel responded eventually.

'Others have found the same. It must be something in my manner – or in the job I have to do. . .'

Hartmann took out a notebook and pencil, perched the notebook at an angle so Keitel could not see what he wrote, his manner respectful and businesslike. His action created the impression there was no doubt that Keitel would cooperate. He asked his questions in rapid succession, concealing what he did not know – the normal technique for keeping a witness off-balance.

'The Führer takes all military decisions himself at the twice-daily conferences. You then see that these are carried out?'

'Of course. There is also Colonel-General Alfred Jodl. . .'

'Who again is privy to all decisions?'

'That is so. . .' Keitel paused and perched the tip of his baton beneath his jaw. Hartmann waited, guessing something important was coming. Keitel was *not* the complete wooden dummy of repute – he was capable of verbal fencing. Which Hartmann found interesting.

'You should know that someone else is always present – *always* – at these military conferences. Martin Bormann. . .'

'But for years he has acted as the Führer's secretary,' Hartmann interjected as though he saw nothing significant in this comment.

While he spoke the Abwehr officer's pencil was apparently making notes. Keitel would have been startled had he been able to see the pencil jottings – which were nothing more than caricature doodles of himself. Hartmann was blessed with total recall of any conversation he participated in.

'So,' Hartmann continued, 'we have yourself, Jodl and Bormann as the three men who always know the present – and *near-future* – order of battle of the Wehrmacht?'

'You have not included the other secretary,' Keitel remarked in a remote voice. Once again Hartmann had the strong sensation of shutters closing down, masking Keitel's real thoughts. It was a reaction he had not expected. He knew exactly who Keitel was switching his attention to.

'The other secretary?' he queried.

'I use the word *secretary* in a different sense, I am referring to Christa Lundt who personally notes down the Führer's orders. . .'

'How old would Fräulein Lundt be?' Hartmann asked.

107

'Her early twenties, I suppose.' Keitel looked irritated and puzzled. 'What significance is there in her age?'

'Too young!'

The Abwehr officer closed his book after making a slashing motion as though deleting a name. In fact he had crossed out a doodle of Keitel decorated with a monocle. He put away the notebook and extracted his pipe again.

'I don't follow your reasoning,' Keitel protested. 'What has age to do with tracking down a hypothetical Soviet spy?'

'Hypothetical?' Hartmann enquired sharply.

'You have no proof of his – or her – existence. . .'

'You are challenging the Führer's unalterable conviction – I use his very words – that there is a Soviet spy passing details of our order of battle to the Red Army?'

Hartmann could not have been more genial as he stirred his bulk in the chair as though soon to leave. He could not have said anything more likely to throw Keitel on the defensive – the oblique suggestion that he was questioning the Führer's judgement. Hartmann held his dead pipe and moved his fingers round the bowl while he watched his victim.

'I said nothing which could possibly be construed to have meant what you so outrageously suggested. . .' Keitel protested.

'Words are strange things, Field Marshal, especially when reported second-hand to a third party. I should know – I am a professional interrogator. Was it not Richelieu who said, give me six lines any man has written and I will hang him?'

'You were pointing the finger at Fräulein Lundt,' Keitel snapped.

'No – with respect, *you* first mentioned the girl. As to her age, my organization is convinced any Soviet spy who has penetrated this far must be much older – someone planted by the Soviet underground years ago in the hope that one day they would reach the dizzy heights. You suffer from vertigo, Field Marshal?'

'Certainly not, and this interview. . .'

'Is now at an end,' Hartmann broke in quickly as he stood up and collected cap and coat from the wall-rack. 'I shall, of course, in due course inform the Führer of our interview. May I bid you good night?'

It was the perfect note on which to take his leave, Hartmann reflected as he walked into the clammy cold of the compound outside and closed the door behind him. Keitel would remember most vividly the Abwehr man's last enigmatic remark – a remark calculated to disturb any man with a guilty conscience.

'*Mein Führer*,' said Bormann, 'your predecessor had made arrangements for an Abwehr officer to be brought in from outside to check security here. The officer has arrived, a Major Hartmann. He is now prowling round the encampment. . .'

'Security *here* needs checking?' demanded Hitler.

'I suggest we have this Hartmann flown straight back to Berlin,' Bormann said. 'He could be dangerous to you – he is the Abwehr's cleverest agent. . .'

It was one o'clock in the morning and the second Hitler paced back and forth inside his room listening without commenting – a favourite technique of the Führer's until his guest ran out of words. He would then deliver his own views in a non-stop monologue.

'There have been rumours of a Soviet agent infiltrating the Wolf's Lair,' Bormann continued. 'Your predecessor intuitively sensed that something was wrong. . .'

'So! You suggest we send this Hartmann back as soon as he arrives? You further suggest I turn the Englishman, Lindsay, over to the Gestapo? I cancel two major decisions the Führer took within hours of my landing – thus creating a hotbed of gossip and rumour just when we are fighting to make everything appear normal?'

Bormann was appalled and amazed. Appalled at his own lack of foresight. Amazed at Heinz Kuby's reaction – which would have been the same mental process followed by the Führer who had recently died during the explosion of the plane from Smolensk. Kuby continued pacing as he built up his monologue.

'We shall do the exact opposite of what you suggest. Lindsay is to remain here – treated with all due consideration – until I am ready to interview him. Before that – possibly tomorrow afternoon when I have taken my nap – I want to see Hartmann. Meantime, he is to continue his investigation. . .'

'The Führer armed him with a document which confers plenipotentiary powers. He can question anyone – even men like Jodl. . .'

'Better and better! I must urge him to pursue his interrogations at length and with the utmost vigour! Don't you see, Bormann, this is a further distraction which will keep people occupied until they accept me for ever! No more argument! I have spoken. By order of the Führer!'

'I will see to it at once. . .'

'If he has plenipotentiary powers, Bormann. . .' A half-smile on Hitler's face held a touch of malice as he glanced at the small, plump man – an expression which further startled Bormann since it was so characteristic of the Führer in a certain mood when no one was safe from his victims. '. . . then,' Hitler continued, 'Hartmann can, if he is so minded, question you.'

'As the repository of your secrets, that I would resist. . .'

'The document specifically excludes you then from this security investigation?'

'Well, no. . .'

'Let us hope he does not end up by arresting you!'

Bormann subsided, stupefied by the way Hitler was exploiting all possible circumstances to mask his own impersonation.

Chapter Thirteen

Locate the secret headquarters of the Führer. . .
Identify who is directing the German military machine. . .
This was the scenario Lindsay had been given before he left

the haven of Ryder Street, London, by Colonel Browne of the SIS. Lindsay found himself using the word scenario in his thinking because the whole atmosphere at the Wolf's Lair was so theatrical – all the chief characters seemed to be playing a part.

A fortnight after his arrival he had positive answers to the two questions London was so anxious to know. The Wolf's Lair was hidden in the horrific pinewoods of East Prussia where the mist never seemed to lift, turning day into night.

From his conversations with Guensche, the Führer's Adjutant; the mysterious Christa Lundt; from remarks dropped by Martin Bormann and his own observations of the submissive attitudes of Keitel and Jodl – from all these indications the Englishman now knew Hitler himself personally took every major decision.

'When you have obtained this information,' Browne had informed him blandly, 'you make your way to Munich and contact our agent. You go to the front of the Frauenkirche at exactly eleven o'clock in the morning on a Monday. You light a cigarette and put it in your mouth with your *left* hand. After a few puffs you throw it away and crush out the stub with your *left* foot. The agent will introduce his presence – or her presence – by telling you his name, Paco. You reply, "When in Rome". You will then be under the control of Paco who will pass you across the Swiss border. . .'

'And supposing I have been taken there by the Gestapo?' Lindsay had queried.

Browne had fiddled with objects on his desk before replying. It was a contingency he had not overlooked, but Browne preferred to wrap up unpleasant topics in oblique language. He had never been in the field.

'That possibility has been catered for,' he said, not looking at Lindsay. Browne was conscious of the fact that, however long the war lasted, he, personally, would never be sent 'over the top' – would never be dropped behind enemy lines and maybe end his life tortured to extinction slowly in some filthy Gestapo cell; which was the prospect facing the man who sat opposite him. He cleared his throat and continued.

'If it came to that – and you have revealed the existence of our agent, Paco – they might take you to the Frauenkirche to keep the rendezvous. You would simply light the cigarette with your *right* hand. After all, you are right-handed. You take a few puffs and then crush it under your *right* foot. The use of the wrong hand and foot will alert Paco. Our agent would remain under cover. . .'

'Rather clever.' Lindsay automatically reached for a cigarette and inserted it in his mouth with his right hand. Suddenly conscious of his action he paused in the act of lighting up and looked at Browne. The Colonel was staring at the cigarette as though hypnotized.

'Paco,' Lindsay went on, lighting the cigarette, 'is a man – or a woman?'

'Better you do not have that information,' Browne said tersely.

Lying sprawled on his bunk inside the hut allocated to him at the Wolf's Lair, Lindsay recalled with great clarity Browne's petrified expression over the cigarette incident.

God, how straightforward it had all seemed in the cosy environs of Ryder Street! Lindsay would fly – as he had done – to the area of the Berghof and make his parachute drop. With skill and luck he would obtain the information needed at the very top – Downing Street, he suspected – and make his escape to Munich.

He had spent hours studying the rail maps and street plans prior to his departure. There was a direct main-line rail route from Salzburg – close to Berchtesgaden – to Munich, which, in normal times took something over an hour. He carried the whole street plan of Munich in his head. Arriving in Munich he would keep the rendezvous with Paco at the earliest possible moment. Then via the underground to Switzerland. . .

Now he was over six hundred miles north-east of Munich – lost in the bleak wastelands of East Prussia. How the hell he was going to reach Munich, Paco, Switzerland, he had no idea. And in a few hours – after a fourteen day nerve-racking wait – he was supposed to meet the Führer. He was still remembering Ryder Street when the door was opened quietly, Christa Lundt slipped inside, closed the door and leaned against it, her well-shaped breasts heaving.

'What's wrong now?'

He was away from the bunk in seconds, watching her closely as he walked towards her. Christa's face was bloodless, but when she spoke her voice was low and controlled.

'Why do you say *now* – as though I'm neurotic?'

'Get to the point. . .'

'As if you – we – hadn't enough trouble with that Abwehr man, Hartmann, sniffing all over the place and asking endless questions. He's been here two weeks, you know. . .'

'Get to the point,' he repeated.

'The Gestapo have arrived. They're enquiring about you. . .'

All thoughts of Ryder Street were wiped from his mind.

In wartime the turn of great events often hinge on the most minor of incidents. The same night Colonel Browne came within an ace of being killed.

It was nine o'clock at night. Still March, but only just. Browne was returning to his Ryder Street office and to reach his destination he had to cross Piccadilly, a wide thoroughfare. He had had a tricky time making his way down Dover Street. A heavy mist had drifted up from the river – almost a fog.

He could see his hand in front of his face – but it was a blurred hand. Moisture settled on his skin and the dank atmosphere chilled. There seemed to be no one else about. It was very silent – the dense grey vapour muffled all sound. Browne plodded on, feeling his way. It was too damnably easy to drift off the pavement and find yourself in the middle of the road without knowing it.

There were no street lights. The blackout was total. Even if a badly-drawn curtain had exposed a shaft of light from a window the mist would have masked it. He became aware of the squelch of his damp shoes, a gentle slushing sound. Then he realized that his own shoes were not in the least water-logged. *The sound was being made by another pair of shoes. . .*

Behind him. Don't panic! Instinctively his hand touched his breast pocket under his raincoat. He shouldn't be carrying the papers he had brought away from the meeting. But he wanted to study them again in the quiet of his own office.

He wished he had asked Tim Whelby, his assistant from Prae Wood, to join him for a drink. Whelby was proving to be a great asset. Quiet and attentive, he devoured a mountain of work. Often, while at Ryder Street, he stayed all hours at the office, going on long after everyone else had gone home. . .

Browne stopped suddenly and listened carefully. The slush of the faintly-heard footsteps behind him had stopped. It was his imagination. Bloody nerves! He was getting old and over-cautious. He stiffened his back and walked on. Where the hell was Piccadilly?

The footsteps – treading his own deliberate pace – had resumed. He was certain of it now. Browne wished he was carrying the .38 revolver locked away in his desk. The devil of a lot of use the weapon was lying in a blasted drawer. . .

The shape like a leviathan loomed in the mist and – too late – he heard the slow chug of its engine. He walked into the side of the crawling double-decker bus, slammed his head into its bulk. His vision spun. He fell backwards, caught his foot on something upraised, regained his balance and reached forward with fumbling hands.

There was blood on his forehead, he was certain. Nothing seemed where it should be. The thought that he was suffering from concussion flashed through his mind and then he was staggering. God! He had been walking straight across Picca-dilly without realizing it! A hand from nowhere grasped his right arm firmly.

'Are you all right? You just walked into a bus. . .'

The voice expressed genuine concern, the voice of Tim Whelby.

'Do you think I should be drinking?' Colonel Browne wondered aloud.

'One brandy can do no harm,' Whelby replied in his gentle voice.

They were sitting in a corner at The Red Lion, a pub just off Jermyn Street. Whelby had escorted his chief back to Ryder Street where the Colonel, despite the fact that he felt shaken up, had immediately locked the papers he was carrying in his safe. It was Whelby who had suggested they walked the short distance to the pub.

Browne sipped at his brandy and looked round to check who else was present. It was an old-fashioned place, a solid polished bar counter, the barman at the far end polishing glasses out of earshot. An American soldier stood near the barman absorbed in conversation with a girl who looked like a high-class street-walker.

The smooth liquid warmed and soothed his rattled nerves. His head ached and was bruised where he had connected with the bus. Browne was trying to reach a difficult decision. By his side Whelby sensed this and kept quiet while he drank his Scotch. His presence was relaxing, Browne was thinking. They had chosen the right sort of chap for Prae Wood. Whelby was in charge of counter-espionage operations in Spain and Portugal. He drank rather a lot – but so did the others marooned out at St Albans.

'I could have got myself killed back there,' Browne observed. His speech was slightly slurred. 'Something I'm carrying in my head – nothing written down anywhere – would have perished with me. . .'

'It will never happen again,' Whelby reassured him. He showed no interest in Browne's reference to a secret inside his head. 'I'm going for a refill. Why don't you just stay with the one you've got. . .'

Despite his headache, Browne's mind was still sharp. Any suspicion that Whelby was trying to get him drunk was dispelled by what had just been said. If anything, it reinforced his feeling of confidence in his assistant.

'Cheers!' Whelby had returned with another large Scotch. 'Let me know when you want to go home. . .'

'I like it here. You can think without being disturbed by a call from Downing Street.'

He sipped more brandy and felt even more well-disposed towards Whelby. A sound chap who could keep a secret and not blab it in some club all over London. Browne had seen enough of that. *Careless Talk Costs Lives.* He turned and looked straight at Whelby who returned the appraisal with a diffident smile.

'You should be with us for quite a while,' Browne ruminated.

'Depends on how I handle the job. . .'

'Depends on me. Getting your teeth into Jerry down there in Franco's backyard? Spent time in Spain before the war, I understand.'

'Early days yet,' Whelby replied and left it at that.

Browne finished off the brandy and sat up erect. He'd decided. A bad mistake that – not sharing Operation Eagle's Nest with anyone. He revolved his empty glass in slow circles.

'We've sent a chap called Lindsay to meet the Führer. Knew him before the war, Lindsay did. . .' He paused. No point in going into details as to how Lindsay had made his way inside the Third Reich. 'Point is we had to give Lindsay an escape route when he completed his mission. He has to get to Munich – the rendezvous point is that great ugly cathedral with twin onion domes. . .'

'The Frauenkirche,' Whelby murmured, staring across the room. The American soldier was leaving with the girl.

'You visited Germany?' Browne queried.

'Briefly,' Whelby replied and relapsed into silence, not looking at his companion.

'The Frauenkirche it is. When were you in Germany?'

Browne was more alert than at any moment since his near-fatal encounter with the bus. He was on the verge of probing Whelby's background. The latter sensed Browne's mood of revelation drifting away. He must say something.

'I was a member of the Anglo-German Fellowship. Keeping tabs on the Nazis. It's all on file. . .'

'Quite so, quite so.' Browne felt he had overstepped the mark. Better get it off his chest – show Whelby he regarded him as one of his crowd. 'We have an agent, Paco – pretty silly code-name. The agent will rendezvous with Lindsay at 1100 hours – wait there for him every Monday. Get him over the border into Switzerland. Someone else should know – in case I meet another bus!'

Browne left it like that, ending with a joke which made Whelby smile again. Shortly afterwards they left the pub. Brown refused a helping hand even though he stumbled on the step leaving. Mentally he was relieved: Lindsay now had back-up. Physically he felt terrible. Splitting headache. All he wanted to do was to fall into bed.

Four days later inside the Kremlin, Beria was again summoned to Stalin's office. The Generalissimo with the down-turned moustache, hooked nose and restless eyes handed to his NKVD chief the decoded signal addressed to Cossack from the Soviet Embassy in London.

'As I always said, the British are putting out feelers to make a separate peace with Hitler. This Wing Commander Ian Lindsay is Churchill's emissary.'

'We could have him killed,' was Beria's immediate suggestion. For Beria this was the everyday solution whatever the problem – liquidate the person creating the problem. It tidied up tricky situations. Stalin shook his shaggy head and grinned maliciously.

'Not yet! Am I the only man in the Soviet Union who looks more than one move ahead in the game? At the right moment I may hold Lindsay's mission over Churchill's head to blackmail him. And we have an alternative now. You note that signal details a possible escape route for Lindsay via Munich?'

'So?' Beria encouraged his master.

'Should the need arise we may arrange for the Germans to kill him for us!'

117

Chapter Fourteen

Karl Gruber of the Gestapo was short, plump, pallid – like a man who rarely enjoys fresh air, who spends most of his life cooped up inside offices. As he walked across the compound towards Bormann's quarters he wore the regulation belted leather raincoat, the soft hat pulled well down over his broad forehead.

Behind a curtained window Bormann watched him coming without any enthusiasm. Anyone connected with Himmler was his enemy. And he had taken an intense dislike to this new intruder from his personal appearance. Hands thrust inside his coat pockets, Gruber's lizard-like eyes swept over the compound, cataloguing data for his report.

The location of the various buildings inside the cantonment was familiar – he had earlier studied and memorized a map of the layout of the place before leaving the Prinz Albrecht-strasse in Berlin. Arriving at the door he was taken by surprise when it opened suddenly and Martin Bormann stood in the entrance.

'Yes?' Bormann demanded.

'Gestapo. Karl Gruber at your service. . .'

'Come inside! Shut the door behind you!'

Bormann led the way into his office, walked behind his desk, sat down and indicated a hard-backed chair chosen for its extreme discomfort. Gruber sat down carefully, as though unsure whether it would bear his weight. His small eyes shifted to left and right, noting the furnishings as he produced a folder with a sheet of paper inside. A careful man, Gruber – careful to observe all the formalities in the holy of holies.

'My identification, Reichsleiter,' he said in a hoarse voice. 'The separate document is my authority to check all aspects of security at the Wolf's Lair. . .'

'I *can* read for myself,' Bormann interjected. 'You'll have to be careful not to get in the way. . .' He paused maliciously, holding back the information which would throw the Gestapo officer off balance – and Gruber walked into the trap.

'I shall maintain a low profile,' Gruber assured him. 'I am, of course, here by order of the Führer. . .'

'God in Heaven, I know that! I myself despatched the command to Berlin which brought you here.' Bormann stared hard at Gruber who had completed his shifty examination of the room, an action which had not escaped its occupant. Bormann threw the papers back across the desk and launched his bombshell.

'The Abwehr got here first. Major Hartmann has already spent some time checking the same problem – security. . .'

'*The Abwehr. . . !*'

'That's what I said. Anything wrong with your hearing?'

It gave Bormann satisfaction to watch the consternation on this fat pig's face, but that satisfaction was marred by his anxiety. Martin Bormann had found himself in an impossible position when the plane from Smolensk crashed. So far he had manoeuvred with a considerable degree of success. The problem was caused by what occurred before the Führer boarded his plane for Russsia.

Intuitively Hitler had sensed the presence of a traitor inside the Wolf's Lair. What had eluded him was the source of this treason.

'Bormann,' he had said at one o'clock in the middle of the night after ending a military conference, 'there is a Soviet spy who is operating behind my shoulder – I *know* he is there. We must launch a full-scale check on security at once.'

'The perimeter defences should be strengthened?' Bormann had suggested. He got no further.

'He is here all the time!' Hitler had thundered. 'He is one of us – some swine who is passing to the Red Army our fresh dispositions as I issue instructions! You do understand me! He must be found, this bloody swine – and strung up. No one is to be exempt from the investigation. No one!'

119

'I understand,' had replied Bormann, who did not. He was swiftly enlightened.

'Find the top Abwehr officer in the whole Reich. The one with the best record. Draft a document – which I shall sign – giving him full powers to locate the traitor. No one – no one – is to be immune from this investigation! If he wants to cross-examine Keitel he may!'

Hitler had hammered his clenched fist on a table. Then he turned to look at his deputy, suddenly relaxing and smiling. Bormann responded quickly.

'It shall be done, *Mein Führer*. . .'

'And you, my dear Bormann, must allow yourself to be questioned if necessary. A show of favouritism could bring on you the dislike of the others. . .'

'Understood!'

'I have not finished!' Hitler's mood changed again. 'You will further request Berlin to send a top Gestapo officer to conduct his own investigation at the same time – and with the same total powers. . .'

The Abwehr and the Gestapo were sworn enemies. The two representatives from the different organizations would compete ferociously to be the first to identify any Soviet spy. It was a typical ploy of Hitler's to exploit rival organizations and individuals to gain results.

As Bormann waited for Gruber's reaction to his insulting question he remembered his own dilemma when the plane from Smolensk exploded and the fate of the whole Nazi regime lay in Bormann's hands. Should he – among his other major decisions – send signals to Berlin cancelling the investigations?

In the end he had done nothing. The last thing he wanted was any suspicion aroused in the capital that something was wrong at the Wolf's Lair. And the conspiratorial Bormann had realized it could be an advantage to throw the whole headquarters into turmoil. The investigators would provide the perfect distraction to prevent anyone studying the substitute Führer too closely. A man worried about his own position has no time for independent thought.

'I would have preferred,' Karl Gruber replied cautiously, 'to have known about the Abwehr before I came. . .'

'You imagine the Führer gives a damn about your preferences?' Bormann sneered. 'When you have completed your findings you report direct to me – not to Berlin. Now you may go!'

Gruber received the order with relief. The heating was turned up high inside the hut and he was sweating profusely. To show the necessary respect he had removed his hat but he was still sitting clad in his heavy leather overcoat. The belt felt tight round his ample stomach and he thought he could smell his sweat-soaked socks.

Standing upright, he gave the Nazi salute, retrieved his hat and went out into the raw damp cold of the compound.

'Herr Gruber, it is quite impossible to permit you to enter the precincts of the Signals Office. I have my instructions. . .'

The SS officer barring Gruber's way was polite but firm. He was also tall and looked down on the short, bulky Gestapo official in a patronizing manner. Gruber's pale face coloured and he was in a state of cold fury.

'I have my authority here. Stand aside before I have you put under arrest. . .'

'I have been informed by the highest authority of your powers,' the SS officer replied loftily. 'They do not include access to the Signals Office. As to your placing me under arrest, I fear it is the other way round. If you take one step more forward I shall be compelled to place you under arrest. . .'

The SS officer glanced across the compound and Gruber swivelled to follow the direction of his gaze. The doorway to the hut he had just left was open. Framed in the doorway stood the compact figure of Martin Bormann. Was it Gruber's imagination or could he see a bleak smile on the Reichsleiter's face?

He walked away, full of rage. *You report direct to me – not to Berlin.* So Bormann had said – and so Bormann had acted to ensure Gruber was isolated inside the Wolf's Lair. Some-one would pay for his humiliation.

Mentally he went over the list of names compiled in his notebook before leaving Berlin – the list of personnel in this benighted swampland. Christa Lundt, secretary to the Führer. Yes, he would start there. He would give her hell. . .

'Ah, Karl Gruber. Welcome to the seats of the Mighty.'

The Gestapo man swung round, his expression dark. Even though the ground was covered with crusted snow he had heard no one coming and that disturbed him. His temper was not improved when he saw who was addressing him.

'Hartmann! And how long have you been creeping around here, may I ask?'

'Long enough to give me a head start, Karl.' The Abwehr officer watched him as he stood and lit his pipe, 'You look unhappy. Won't they give you access to the teleprinter?'

'There is something wrong here, don't you sense it?' suggested Gruber, switching tack, trying to draw out his opponent.

'It's the mist which clings to the forest,' Hartmann responded amiably. 'Creates a depressing atmosphere and makes you imagine the end of the world is nigh. . .'

'You think we are losing the war?' Gruber interjected cunningly. *Just one phrase* – one defeatist-sounding phrase – from Hartmann and he would have him.

'You said that – I didn't. . .'

'Really, we two should cooperate, combine our forces – and share the credit when we have completed our mission.'

Gruber was switching tack again, hoping to milk any information Hartmann might have obtained by his earlier arrival. Because he was the best – Hartmann. Gruber, no fool, was only too conscious of the calibre of this quiet, grey-eyed man.

'I gather we have to work independently.' Hartmann sounded regretful. 'Bad luck with the signals people. . .'

He turned on his heel and walked away. His final remark left Gruber in a storming rage – as it was intended to. A man in a fury commits tactical errors. With his hand on the canteen door, Hartmann glanced over his shoulder. The Gestapo officer was entering Fräulein Lundt's hut.

'What the hell do you think you're doing . . . God! You're hurting. Stop it. . .'

Christa Lundt, clad in only a dressing gown open down the front, stared up at Gruber who was twisting her arm viciously. He had thrown her down on to the sofa after marching inside the hut without knocking. She had been about to take a shower and had snapped at him the moment he entered.

'Address your betters respectfully,' Gruber rasped as he gave her arm a further twist behind her back. 'You are the cow who attends all the Führer's military conferences. Is that not so? *Answer me*!'

'Yes,' she gasped. One moment life had been normal – now this fat slug with the shrewd, lecherous eyes was staring at the open gap in her gown. She felt humiliated. Her breasts heaved as she winced with pain and the small eyes continued gazing at them with deep interest.

'So,' Gruber continued, still holding her helpless, 'what do you do with your notebook after you have typed out the signals and handed them in for encodement and transmission. . . ?'

'It's kept locked in a drawer. . .'

'Which locked drawer? Where do you keep the key? Can anyone else read your shorthand. . . ?'

'I don't know. . .'

'I think that's the wrong approach.' The voice came from behind Gruber. He swung round, released his grip on Christa, his stubby hand moving towards the gun under his armpit. The hand froze in mid-air. Hartmann stood facing him, pipe clenched in his mouth, his great-coat unbuttoned.

'That's better,' the Abwehr man observed mildly. 'I'd have put a bullet through you before your fingers touched the butt. . .'

'You threaten an officer of the Gestapo?'

'I thought you were threatening me.' The same calm tone. 'And I have a witness. . .' Hartmann turned to Christa Lundt

123

who had crossed her arms, closing the opened gown and massaging her arm which was badly bruised. 'We have an appointment, as you know, Fräulein. . .' His eyes conveyed a message. 'First, perhaps you'd like to retire and put on some clothes.'

He waited until the girl had left the room, closing the bedroom door. The mildness of manner changed. He stepped close to the Gestapo officer, his tone low and grim.

'You stupid little toad. . .'

'How did you get in here? What is all this crap about you have an appointment?' croaked Gruber.

The outer door leading to the compound was shut. Hartmann had opened the door, slipped inside and closed it again without making a sound. Gruber was livid at the interruption, shaken by Hartmann's incredible ability to move like a ghost.

'The first question – I entered the same way you did. The second question – Fräulein Lundt and I have an appointment so I can begin my interrogation. Your methods are quite stupid – you scare her so her answers are likely to be confused. Beating people with a rubber truncheon may be your only normal resource – but it won't work here. . .'

'I shall report you to the Reichsleiter for interference in my duties. . .'

'Supposing I report you for attempted rape. . .'

'A charge which I shall certainly corroborate,' called out Christa from the bedroom doorway. She had dressed hastily in a blouse and skirt and was finishing combing her long black hair. 'You caught him in the act, is that not so, Major Hartmann? The Führer is most considerate to his staff, so what is the outcome likely to be?'

Hartmann possessed a splendid sense of timing. He knew exactly when to say nothing, when silence alone can break a man's nerve. Gruber's expression was a study in many emotions. He glanced from the Abwehr man to the girl with tilted head and contemptuous eyes and back again to Hartmann.

'You both know this is ridiculous,' he blustered. 'I was merely trying to shake some sense into her. . .'

'When she was naked except for her dressing gown? A

moment ago I hear her turn off a shower – which she was obviously about to take when you burst in on her. I find her pinned down on a sofa with you leaning over her. . .' Hartmann shrugged. 'For the moment I will record the events I witnessed, ask Fräulein Lundt to sign as a witness, and keep the report on file. Do I make myself very clear?'

Gruber picked up his hat from the table where he had tossed it on entering the hut. Hartmann noticed his hand was moist, that he had beads of sweat on his forehead. He left the building without another word, closing the door quietly. Christa came across the room.

'I am indeed in your debt, Major. Thank you seems a feeble reaction to what you saved me from. He is a lecherous brute. . .'

'No gratitude, please. . .' Hartmann raised a gloved hand which held the pipe he had courteously removed from his mouth as soon as Gruber had departed. 'But it is true that I must ask you a few questions. Do you feel up to it? If it is of any consolation to your dignity I start with you, then go on to the others – including Bormann, Keitel and Jodl. . .'

'I will tell you anything you wish to know. Now would be a good time. But first, some coffee?'

'That would be most acceptable. . .'

Hartmann removed his great-coat and cap while she was making the coffee out of sight. A less clever man than Hartmann would have refused the coffee and begun his interrogation at once – before Lundt had time to recover her poise. Hartmann preferred people to be at their ease – and his plan had worked far beyond what he had hoped for. *I am, indeed, in your debt. . .*

Earlier outside in the compound Hartmann had manipulated the conversation with Gruber to trigger off his well-known savage temper. The Abwehr man had seen Christa Lundt going inside her hut – had seen Gruber glance in that direction – and had guessed who was probably the Gestapo man's first target.

It was in the nature of a man like Gruber to bully all those he considered his inferiors, especially women. As Hartmann

125

had hoped, the Gestapo officer had gone straight to Christa Lundt's hut in a wild rage detonated by Hartmann's final remark. Things had gone further than the Abwehr man anticipated – owing to a pure chance coincidence that Christa was about to take a shower. Now, for the time being, he had Gruber in an armlock.

But more important, he had attracted Christa's sympathy and cooperation. Things could not have worked out better from his point of view.

'Is the coffee right for you?' Christa asked a few minutes later.

'Excellent! I think I shall apply for your transfer to my office in Berlin. Your job? Coffee-maker!'

To show her confidence in him she had sat down on the sofa beside him. He took out his pencil and a notebook. They were the tools of her profession so they were hardly likely to inhibit her.

'Very efficient, Major!' she said mischievously.

'First question? Ready?' He paused and smiled, then lit up his pipe after obtaining her permission. His gentle eyes watched her closely as he threw his shaft.

'What is your impression of this Wing Commander Lindsay who says he flew to the Berghof solely to meet the Führer?'

It was not the reply she gave he noted; it was the wary look which came into her hitherto friendly eyes.

'Jodl, the situation here ever since the Führer returned from Smolensk has become intolerable! Intolerable! Did you hear me?'

Field Marshal Kietel was striding round his colleague's office, unable to keep still. The foxy-faced Jodl had observed something was wrong from the moment, unannounced, Keitel had stormed into his quarters.

For one thing the Field Marshal's face was flushed with annoyance. For another he kept revolving his baton in his hands and now he threw his cap on a table with a violent gesture.

Jodl, of a calmer temperament, watching his visitor closely, chose his words with care. You always assumed that every word you spoke, even in confidence, would be repeated by Keitel to the Führer if it suited his book.

'Have you isolated the cause?' he enquired.

'Isn't it obvious! We have two obnoxious outsiders poking their noses into everything that is going on. . .'

'You are referring to Hartmann of the Abwehr and Gruber of the Gestapo?'

Always ask questions. Never make statements. Never express an opinion. It was a lesson Jodl had learned long ago.

'Who else?' Keitel blazed. 'I have just had that supercilious bastard, Hartmann, subjecting me to a cross-examination. Me! Chief of the Oberkommando!'

Supercilious? Jodl suppressed a smile. Hartmann – he had already sensed – was by far the cleverer, the more dangerous of the two interrogators. Clearly he had employed the tactic of exploiting Keitel's weakest point – his vanity and consciousness of his rank.

'You protested?' asked Jodl, still cautious. You could never tell with Keitel. He sometimes suspected the Field Marshal of simulating a posture of arrogance and limited intelligence.

'How could I protest?' Keitel raged. 'His authority derives direct from the Führer himself. I suppose Gruber will turn up next. A fat slug!'

'It is not often that these men get the chance to grill those way above them in rank,' Jodl remarked shrewdly. 'They will make the most of it, submit their reports, and go away. We shall not hear from them again. . .'

'All this nonsense about a Soviet spy inside the Wolf's Lair. . .'

'The Führer carries a great burden. . .'

'I never mentioned the Führer!'

Keitel retrieved his cap, gripped his baton more firmly, glared at Jodl and walked out, slamming the door. Jodl's face had remained expressionless at the reference to a Soviet spy. Now he sat slowly tapping the fingers of his right hand like a man tapping out a Morse signal.

What Keitel said was true. The atmosphere within the claustrophobic confines of the Wolf's Lair was tense. It was bad enough to live in this unhealthy climate – there were marshes as well as lakes nearby in the dense enshrouding pine forests. The Godawful, insidious, creeping mist slipping between the trees depressed you. And now they had spy fever!

Jodl had noticed the change in personal relationships since the arrival of Hartmann and Gruber. Mistrust was in the air like the drifting grey mist. Conversations were forced and tentative. Jodl was convinced that Hartmann – the clever one – was deliberately creating this mood to put the spy under intolerable pressure. . .

Intolerable? Odd how that word had popped into his head. It was the same word Keitel had used twice when he had arrived, ranting at the Hartmann grilling. Jodl checked his watch. Time for the midday conference.

He stood up, put on his cap, straightened his jacket, checked his appearance in a wall mirror. The cap was at the normal jaunty angle. Always present the same impression – the Führer disliked departures in others. And today, Jodl suspected, would see a new disposition of the troops on the Eastern Front.

It was the evening of the day when Keitel had visited Jodl. In the depths of the pine forest amid the swirling mist a figure was crouched over the 'hide'.

The logs concealing the entrance had been removed, revealing the high-powered transceiver. With the aid of a masked torch – night had fallen and there was no moon – the expert fingers completed tapping out the signal which had been preceded by the word 'Wagner'. This indicated that the signal concerned Army dispositions. 'Olga' would have indicated a signal concerning Luftwaffe movements.

The crouched figure, seen as little more than a ghost in the mistbound night, checked the dial of an illuminated wristwatch and waited. There was rarely a signal in the opposite direction – originating in Switzerland and beamed to East Prussia. But if there should be one, it would be transmitted from Lucerne in the next two minutes. One hundred and twenty seconds passed – an endless-seeming pause. A hand reached out to switch off. The machine began to talk. . .

RAHS. The call-sign from Lucy. A message *was* coming tonight. The torch was tucked under an arm, a notebook and pencil held at the ready for the series of dots and dashes in code. The signal was brief.

The operator switched off the machine, replaced the logs, stood up, grasped a branch and shook snow down to cover all traces of disturbance.

Walking some distance along a track, his feet crackling ice, the operator stopped again by a large tree trunk, reached inside a hole and withdrew a code book protected by a waterproof sachet. Crouching down, the operator used the torch to decode the signal, replaced the code book inside its hiding-place and was lost in the mist. The signal was a death warrant.

Liquidate the Englishman. . .

In his apartment in faraway Lucerne, Rudolf Roessler blinked as he sat in front of the cupboard concealing his transceiver. He had the impression it was misty. He closed the flap, sealing off the machine and turned in his chair as he heard someone behind him.

'Oh, it is you, Anna. . .'

'And who else would it be?' the tall brisk woman asked with a reassuring smile. 'Here is some coffee. And your glasses are steamed up. Give them to me. . .'

He stood up, closed the door of the cupboard, holding a piece of paper in his hand as he followed her into the living room. Still in a daze, he sat down at a baize-covered table and sipped his coffee while Anna vigorously cleaned the spectacles.

'I still marvel at the information Woodpecker sends. Who can he be?' he wondered.

'Far better that we never know his identity – and fortunately we never will know. Here are your glasses – and why are you all sweaty? The night is cold.'

'Moscow sent me a message for Woodpecker. I transmitted it to him after receiving his latest data on the movement of the German Army – which I later re-transmitted to Cossack. The signal for Woodpecker from Cossack is in an unknown code – so I have no idea what I was sending. . .'

Anna frowned. This new development worried her but she must try not to show it. 'This is the first time we have had a signal from Moscow. We thought all the transmissions would be in the opposite direction from Woodpecker to Moscow. . .'

'Provision was made for it when we were in Berlin,' Roessler reminded her. 'Call signs were agreed and so on. But it violates our arrangement with Swiss Military Intelligence. We gave them to understand it would be one-way traffic, so what do I do about this new signal? The Swiss may not like it. . .'

'You mean we should not pass on the message from Cossack to the Bureau Ha?'

'What would you do?' he asked, his manner that of an uncertain spaniel dog.

'Forget it.' she decided. 'Say nothing to the Bureau Ha. . .'

'What would I do without you, Anna?'

'Worry all day long!'

'Where are you going?'

'To phone the Bureau Ha asking them to send a courier for the signal from Woodpecker.' She made a gesture of dismissal before picking up the phone. 'I suggest you are out of the way when the courier arrives. Go get your beauty sleep!'

Snow was falling on the walls of the Kremlin. At two o'clock in the morning there was a hushed atmosphere inside the ancient citadel. Laventri Beria was busily polishing his pince-nez while he waited for the closed door at the end of the gloomy room to open. Beside him, General Zhukov, resplendent in uniform, stood and fidgeted irritably.

'Good evening, gentlemen. Or should it be good morning? It is after midnight and another eventful day lies before us. Let us not waste it. . .'

The speaker, Stalin, emerged from the shadows. It was a habit of the Generalissimo, Beria had observed, to sidle up to people unexpectedly. The small Georgian with the withered left arm and crafty eyes held another of those blasted pieces of paper in his right hand. A Woodpecker signal, Beria guessed. He hated networks over which he had no control.

'Your opinion of the contents, General,' Stalin requested. 'It again concerns the alleged German order of battle. . .'

Beria maintained an expressionless face, blinking behind his pince-nez. Let Zhukov be the target. Stalin was in one of his most dangerous moods. Soft-spoken, a cat-and-mouse approach. Zhukov read the signal and spoke his mind as always.

'This agent knows what he is talking about. The details of the German Army dispositions coincide exactly with my picture of the whole front. The other vital information about reserves is likely to be equally accurate. On the basis of this, I propose an attack before the thaw – we will catch them by surprise. . .'

'You guarantee a great victory?' Stalin queried, pulling at his moustache as he glanced sideways at the Soviet general.

'In war there can be no guarantees. . .'

'Then we wait a little longer – until we are certain of Woodpecker, certain he is not being manipulated. . .'

'It would help me if I knew who in hell this Woodpecker is,' Zhukov burst out. 'And how many years will it take for us to be certain. . . ?'

Beria held his breath. He was careful to look at neither man. Within sixty seconds Stalin might well order the arrest of Zhukov. There was a loaded pause, a pause punctuated by the slow tick of a two hundred year old long-case clock standing against the wall.

'I suggest you return to military headquarters,' Stalin remarked eventually with no emotion in his voice. 'And no attacks to be launched yet. Defensive measures only, as previously agreed.'

He waited until Zhukov had left the room and then invited his police chief to join him at the nearby table. Sitting down, he took out his pipe, lit it with great deliberation, and all the time his eyes studied Beria, who clasped the moist palms of his hands out of sight in his lap.

'One day, Beria, we shall have to cut these generals down to size. In the meantime we need them – to win the war. Increase the surveillance on Zhukov. . .'

In London at Ryder Street Colonel Browne pretended to be thinking aloud to get the reaction of his assistant. Whelby was locking away some files prior to venturing out into the night.

'There are people who wonder whether we should seek an accommodation with the Germans. . .' Browne paused. 'By the way, did you get any encouragement along these lines from the other side when you visited Madrid recently?'

'None whatsoever,' Whelby lied promptly.

'Just an idle thought. . .' Browne trailed off and nodded curtly as Whelby bade him goodnight with a hint of urgency.

It so happened that Whelby had a prearranged meeting with Savitsky for that evening. An agent always likes to have something to report. Whelby elevated Browne's chance remark into a decision of British policy.

'It appears Lindsay is a peace emissary of Churchill's, he said during their brief meeting. 'Browne tested out my reaction to the idea not two hours ago. . .'

Arriving back at the Soviet Embassy, Savitsky again encoded the signal to Cossack personally and took it to the basement cipher room at Kensington Palace Gardens. Three hours later the decoded signal was read by Stalin, who 'consulted' Beria for the second time that night.

'The situation at Hitler's headquarters is getting confused,' Stalin commented as his henchmen read the message.

'Confused?' Beria queried.

'Confused,' emphasized Stalin. 'In the same place we have Woodpecker – who may prove to be our most valuable agent of the war. Then we have this Englishman – another trained spy, I suspect. I think he is pro-Nazi. Supposing that with his experience he detects Woodpecker? That must be prevented at all costs.'

'I agree,' Beria said loftily. 'There is an obvious solution. . .'

'We send Woodpecker a signal. . .'

Which is how the message to Woodpecker via Lucy came to be sent.

Liquidate the Englishman. He has Monday rendezvous with Allied agent at Frauenkirche . . .

Chapter Fifteen

'It is madness! I begged the Führer to let me send guards to escort him at a discreet distance. He insisted on taking this walk alone in the forest with the Englishman!'

Martin Bormann could not keep still as he paced round Christa Lundt's hut. She sat stiffly on the chair nearest the door into the compound. It would be her escape route if the Reichsleiter attempted to engage her in sexual intercourse. Bormann continued his tirade.

'The Führer's only protection is his dog, Blondi. . .' Sweating profusely, he paused and threw out one hand in a gesture of frustration. 'What do you think is going on out there in the forest?'

'The Führer is delivering a monologue. The Wing Commander is listening. Nothing more alarming, I'm sure. . .'

Fifteen minutes earlier she had witnessed an extraordinary scene. Lindsay had been sitting on the sofa while they talked about the worsening atmosphere of tension as Hartmann and Gruber pursued their separate investigations.

The door had been thrown open and the Führer stood motionless, his dog on a leash. Wearing his military great-coat and peaked cap, he had stared hard at them while Lindsay and Christa stood up. He then spoke abruptly.

'Get your coat on, Wing Commander. We must talk. We

will walk in the forest where no one can overhear us . . .'

Stunned, Lindsay had donned his own coat and Russian-style fur hat, provided by Guensche, who seemed to have taken the Englishman under his protection. He followed the Führer across the compound and through the first checkpoint.

Now they had passed through the three checkpoints. They strolled alongside each other across the broad track between the minefields in the depths of the snowbound pine forest. The cold was raw, damp and penetrating. The dense silence of the weird desolation closed round them as the Führer talked.

'You say there is a peace party in London but they cannot overthrow Churchill yet. Is London crazy? What would happen should I fail in my great mission in the East? The Communist hordes would sweep across Europe. Great Britain and America would be confronted by an implacable enemy whose only purpose would be to destroy them. They would never again live in peace – even if the Soviets were compelled for a few years to accept some division of Europe, you would still never have freedom from fear – the fear that sooner or later the barbaric Communist Asiatics would grow so strong they would overwhelm you. Then a new Dark Age would descend on Europe. America would be isolated. It would be only a matter of time before the Communist plague swept east into China and Japan. I alone stand between the West and barbarism. . .'

'There are people in high places in London – and Washington – who see this,' Lindsay replied, his face turned to catch every flicker of expression on his companion's face, every intonation of the flow of words which tumbled out like a torrent.

'Then why, in the name of God, do they not act. . ?'

'As yet,' Lindsay interjected firmly, 'they do not have the power. A great German victory in the East would help. . .'

'That is coming! I tell you, that is coming!!' Hitler's voice rose and was not muffled even by the drifting fog. 'Wait only for the summer!!! The summer of '43 will turn the hinge of history.' His voice and manner changed abruptly. He spoke quietly, amiably. 'The Duke of Dunkeith, your uncle, sent

134

you to me as an emissary of this peace party? I knew it intuitively as soon as I heard of your arrival.'

Hitler had answered his own question. Lindsay was learning rapidly. Volunteer as little as possible. The German leader had his own ideas and required only confirmation. So far, Lindsay had found him remarkably well-informed. Tugging at the leash to control the dog, the Führer continued.

'I have definite peace proposals for you to present to Churchill and your other friends. In return for cessation of all hostilities between us I will withdraw all German troops from France, Belgium, Holland – the whole of occupied Western Europe. Then you leave me to finish off Stalin and his hideous creed. The Americans cannot operate without British help and the use of your island base. . .'

'Churchill himself might be interested in such proposals,' the Englishman replied. 'He himself is beginning to worry about just how far the Red Army might penetrate Europe. . .'

'The proposals must be worked out in full detail. I will leave that to Ribbentrop. It's time he did something to earn his keep,' the Führer commented sardonically. 'It's a pity Lord Halifax was sent off to Washington as Ambassador,' Hitler ruminated. 'He was one of the leaders of the peace faction. Is that not so?'

'And to think,' Lindsay replied cautiously, 'that when Chamberlain was forced to resign, he first offered the premiership to this same Halifax. If you had had him to deal with after Dunkirk. . .'

'Britain and Germany would have joined hands as equal partners in the crusade against Bolshevism. Moscow would no longer exist. My only reason for attacking France was to clear my rear before the great campaign against Stalin. And no one seems to understand why I acted as I did. . .'

Hitler was speechless at the thought. They continued walking in silence for several minutes. In places the track was thick with moss and spongy to the tread – as though they moved on the edge of a swamp. The smell of damp, moisture-laden pines filled their nostrils.

They were about to turn back to return to the compound. Hitler had started speaking again when the sound of the rifle crack came. Lindsay *saw* the bullet embed itself in a tree-trunk well to the right of the track. Snow fell to the ground. Hitler was on his left. The Englishman spoke quickly.

'Führer, please return with all speed to the Wolf's Lair. I will try and locate the assassin. . .'

'The bloody cowardly swine! They can't even shoot straight. . .'

Hitler turned on his heel and walked back the way they had come, shoulders erect like a marionette, not varying his pace. Lindsay waited five minutes after the silhouette of the Führer vanished, standing motionless, listening. Hitler thought he had survived yet a further attempt on his lift. Lindsay knew better. The bullet had been aimed at himself. It had shot past well clear of the German leader.

Arriving back at the first checkpoint he was put under arrest. 'For complicity in the attempted assassination of the Führer. . .'

Christa Lundt approached the hut where Lindsay was confined. An SS guard with a machine-pistol moved in front of the door as she held the tray of covered dishes.

'No admittance. Herr Gruber. . .'

She stared straight at the SS man, her manner cold and contemptuous. Her voice was sharp and cutting.

'This is his lunch. By order of the Führer! You want to find yourself on the Eastern front? You have five seconds to get out of my way. . .'

The guard hesitated. Indecision was written all over his face. Christa began to turn away. The SS man moved swiftly to one side, so shaken by her reference to Russia he forgot to check the contents of the tray. She indicated that he should open the door.

'You have the manners of a pig,' she commented. 'Close the damn thing behind me. . .'

Lindsay was stretched out on the sofa, reading a newspaper. He jumped up and cleared a table for her to put down the tray. She sat down on the sofa, her voice low.

'Start eating while it's still hot. Now, what's all this nonsense about your trying to kill the Führer?'

'That Gestapo bastard.' Lindsay lifted off the covers. Veal with potatoes. He was famished. He ate and talked between mouthfuls. 'Gruber alleges he searched my hut while I was away in the forest. He produced a set of photographic copies of the latest military directives. Says he found them hidden. Underneath the mattress in the bedroom here. What a brilliant hiding-place!'

'The latest directives? I could disprove that. You'd need access to a copying device. . .'

'That isn't all. This veal is good. . .' Lindsay forked more into his mouth. Always eat at every opportunity. Number One instruction in the Ryder Street training manual. 'Gruber alleges I led the Führer into a trap, an assassination attempt. . .'

'The Führer doubts that,' Christa interjected. 'Gruber wanted to fly you straight back to his place in Berlin. The Führer said "No". The furthest he'd allow Gruber to go was to confine you to your hut until the incident has been investigated.'

'That's something.' Lindsay wiped his mouth with the napkin she had brought and looked at her. 'You'd better know – Gruber is trying to tie the two of us into this thing together. He's sent a teleprinter message to Berlin for your complete file.'

'Oh, my God!'

The blood had drained from Christa's face. She wrapped the slender fingers of one hand round the wrist of the other – as though clutching an invisible manacle. Lindsay, still cautious, watched her while he poured coffee from a metal pot. When he spoke his tone was casual.

'Is there something incriminating in that file?'

'Gruber could make it incriminating.' Suddenly she recovered her self-possession. 'It records people I have known in the past, people who have come under suspicion since I was last vetted. My ex-fiancé, Kurt, especially. He was despatch-

137

ed to the Eastern Front. No one knew he was my fiancé – only that he was a close friend.'

'Suspected members of the underground? Kurt, too?'

She nodded. Her calm was almost unnerving. 'Now you know why I might need an escape route. I was last vetted ages ago. . .'

'The situation here is complicated,' Lindsay remarked. 'Complex situations can be exploited. What do you know about Gustav Hartmann? There is something odd about the Abwehr man. As an ally he may be persuaded to neutralize Gruber – the Gestapo detest the Abwehr and the feeling is reciprocated. Also, Hartmann is much cleverer. . .'

'I still do not see how you can get Hartmann to help us.' She sounded irritated, frustrated. Christa Lundt was either one of the world's great actresses, or was telling the truth. 'In any case,' she continued with concern, 'you are in a bad position yourself. . .'

'As the Führer would say in a difficult situation, it is time for a little luck to come to our aid. . .'

She was back again in less than an hour, closing the door carefully, then looking round the room and gesturing a question with both hands as she scanned the other closed doors.

'We are quite alone,' Lindsay told her.

'Then I have the most marvellous news!' Throwing caution to the winds she ran forward and sat close to him on the sofa. Clasping both his hands, she moved her face close to his. 'The Führer has just taken one of his lightning decisions. Everyone, including Bormann, was astounded. He does that – to keep even those closest to him off-balance, and for security reasons. Ian, we are all to leave immediately for Obersalzberg! Hitler is temporarily moving his headquarters to the Berghof!'

'How soon is immediately?' Lindsay asked.

'Within two hours! There is a railway siding. . .'

'I've seen it. . .'

'The train is already there. Oh, Ian, it is so luxurious! And you are to come with us. The Führer regards you as his one possible link with the peace party in England. A little luck – that is what you said we needed!'

As they sat together on the sofa the relationship between them was becoming highly charged. Their tremendous relief at the prospect of leaving the Wolf's Lair was releasing their inhibitions. Lindsay made an effort to keep his mind on practical problems.

'When will your file arrive from Berlin?'

'Tomorrow at the earliest. The girl in charge of records is a friend of mine. She will delay it as long as possible – here. . .'

'When is the earliest that file could reach the Berghof?'

'Five days after we leave the Wolf's Lair. And Gruber is coming with us.' The enthusiasm left her voice. It was, after all, only a short-lived reprieve, Lindsay reflected. He was half-convinced now that Christa was genuine – a link with the anti-Nazi faction.

'I suggest you don't worry,' was as far as he dare go.

She still held his hands. She leaned forward slowly and her lips brushed his own, lightly at first. Then her arms were round him and she pressed her mouth hungrily against his, her well-formed breasts firm against his chest. Slowly, with surprising strength, she bent her back down on to the sofa, pulling him with her. The tempo of the embrace quickened. His left hand located the buttons down the side of her skirt and unfastened them deftly. 'Yes, yes, yes!' she gasped. She held on to him fiercely – as though he were her only contact with safety. Lindsay ended it.

'Any moment someone can walk in on us. . .'

After she had gone he opened the carton of cigarettes she gave him as a parting gift. He thought about a dozen things as he lit one, marshalling his thoughts into some sort of order.

The Berghof . . . by train. That meant their ultimate destination was probably Salzburg – from there a motorcade to the mountainous retreat. Salzburg! On the main line to Munich. . .

Munich! The agreed rendezvous with the mysterious Paco – who had the power to get him across the frontier into Switzerland. All he had to do was to exploit the rivalry between the Gestapo and the Abwehr to hold them both in check. Mere child's play! Like bloody hell. Lindsay's mind churned as he packed the case Christa had brought him.

At least he had discovered answers to the two questions Ryder Street was concerned about. But what had shaken him was his recent walk in the pine forest. He had the overwhelming impression the Führer was acting out a part – that of the Führer.

On the surface Hitler was Hitler, the man he had conversed with at length in Berlin before the war. But every movement of his hands, his way of walking, his changes of expression – all had a certain exaggeration. Like an actor overplaying. Lindsay was trying to absorb a major shock. He was convinced he had been in the presence of a double, a *doppelganger*. . .

Still half in a mental trance, he snapped the catches shut on his case. When someone rapped on the outer door he nearly jumped out of his shoes.

'Who is it?' he called out.

'Hartmann. . .'

'You may come in. . .'

Lindsay's voice and manner were arrogant and confident, anything but that of a prisoner suspected of God knew exactly what. The grey-eyed German came in, closed the door and looked at the suitcase.

'You are ready for the long journey, I see. . .'

'Just how long? And what route do we take, for God's sake – to get from the swamps of East Prussia to the Alps of Bavaria?'

'That is classified information. I wish I knew why you made this hazardous trip. No one really knows, I'm sure. Yet. . .'

'That is *not* classified information,' Lindsay responded while the Abwehr officer perched himself on the sofa. 'I came solely to establish links between the Führer and certain

140

powerful elements in Great Britain who foresee Russia as the real enemy. . .'

The German crossed his legs, took out his pipe and lit it, tamping the tobacco with his index finger. His eyes never left the Englishman's face as he took his time replying. Lindsay sensed he was in the company of one of the most experienced interrogators in the Third Reich.

'And who are these powerful elements you speak of?' he eventually enquired.

'That *is* classified information also. Ask the Führer. . .'

Keep the replies short. Don't elaborate – above all don't get drawn into the trap of conversing freely with Hartmann. On the surface the German seemed a kindly man, more like an intelligent civil servant than a member of one of the most ambiguous organizations in Hitler's Germany.

'This nonsense about your being involved in an assassination attempt. . .' Hartmann paused, giving the Englishman time to make some comment. Lindsay remained silent, lighting another cigarette from the pack supplied by Christa.

'You appear to be on good terms with Christa Lundt,' Hartmann remarked, switching the topic without warning.

'She's curious about me because I'm British, I suppose. . .'

'She has also become very attached to you since your arrival. I have found out she kept very much to herself before that.'

'If you say so.'

Hartmann stood up and smiled. 'We are fencing. I gain the strongest impression you have been trained to resist any form of interrogation. . .'

'Wouldn't you be wary if you had people like Gruber prowling about?' Lindsay flashed back. 'Not that I equate you with the Gestapo. . .' It was the Englishman's turn to study the other man's reaction. Hartmann paused in the act of knocking out his pipe in an ash-tray, looking up at Lindsay from beneath his bushy eyebrows. Some kind of message passed between them, something unfathomable.

'We will talk some more at the Berghof,' Hartmann said,

straightening up and adjusting the belt of his trench coat. 'You knew the Führer before the war?'

'We met in Berlin. . .'

'As an outsider, you sense something peculiar about the atmosphere at the Wolf's Lair?'

'Since you arrived, yes! And Gruber. . .'

'A mood of distrust, people looking over their shoulders at men they have known for years – as though treason stalks the compounds very close to the top?'

'You would know more about that than me. . .'

'Would I!'

On the verge of leaving Harmann turned, his hand on the handle of the outer door. His expression had become stern and he stood very erect as he stared at the Englishman while he spoke rapidly.

'Would I!' he repeated. 'Wing Commander, you are nobody's fool. I have only arrived here for the first time in my life. You have been here over *two weeks*! The Führer has what we call in Germany finger-tip-feeling – the ability to sense something wrong before he has located the source of his unease. I, also, in all modesty, am credited with something of the same ability. Is it really the possible presence of a Soviet spy?' He walked a few paces closer to Lindsay. 'Or is it something quite different I sense – without knowing what I detect? Your plane took you to the Berghof before you were flown here. What is it you have noticed? Help me, Wing Commander. I can be a useful ally. . .'

'I haven't the least idea what you're talking about,' Lindsay replied without hestitation.

'Very well! But I warn you – we will talk again. . .'

The Führer's train, curiously called *Amerika*, travelled at high speed. The icy blast from an open window – or door – funnelled down the corridor as Lindsay peered into the distance and saw the vague silhouette of a slim figure at the end of the coach. He began running. The silhouette looked like Christa.

They were somewhere in the mountains – many hours from

Rastenburg in East Prussia. It was nearly midnight. Because of the wartime blackout the corridor was feebly lit by overhead blue lamps which cast a ghostly glow. All the compartments he passed had the blinds drawn. The occupants were sleeping.

Lindsay had been unable to sleep and so he had seen the familiar figure of a girl slip past his window on the corridor side. Opening the door quietly, he had closed it again. There had been something furtive about the girl's movements which had aroused his curiosity. Now he was alarmed.

The cold chilled his face. There was a feel of snow in the icy air. He suspected they were crossing Czechoslovakia, maybe the Tatra Mountains. The deserted corridor remained empty – except for the silhouette. And it was the *door* at the end of the coach which was open. . .

Christa Lundt was framed in the doorway, one hand clutching a rail, the other holding the door back against the train. She was so absorbed in gazing into the night she never saw him coming. The sight of her poised there scared him.

He reached her. She saw him. She took a step into oblivion. He grabbed her upper arm, hauled her back and threw her to the other side of the coach. Reaching out, he grasped the heavy door, swung it inwards and shut. Confined between the lavatory and the end of the coach she was now pressing down the handle of the door opposite. He grabbed her again roughly, with both hands.

'Christa! You stupid little fool! Are you trying to kill yourself. . ?'

'Ian!' She trembled with relief. 'I thought you were Hartmann. I have to leave the train – before Gruber receives details of that file from Berlin. There are guards at every stop. Only while the train is between stations can I get away. . .'

'Inside here. . .' He opened the lavatory door. 'Guards patrol the corridors at intervals. Bit cramped, but it will have to do.' He closed and locked the door. Beneath them the heavy wheels of the train beat out a steady, hypnotic tattoo. He perched her on the closed lid and by the glow from the blue light brushed flakes of snow from her coat and hat.

She was wearing leather, knee-length boots, a fur coat and a Russian-style fur hat. Warmth from the radiators in the adjoining compartment had percolated into the lavatory and the snow he had brushed on to the floor was already beginning to melt.

'Now,' he demanded, 'what were you really up to? Attempting to commit suicide I'd have thought – with the train moving at this speed. . .'

'It was moving quite slowly when I reached the door and opened it,' she said bitterly. 'Then it suddenly speeded up. When you arrived I was sure it was Hartmann so I decided to risk jumping – it would come to the same thing soon. . .'

Lindsay studied the fine bone structure of her face, the defiant tilt of her head as she stared up at him. This was the girl he had made love to. And what she said was borne out by the facts, he remembered now.

The train *had* been moving very slowly when she passed his window, climbing a steep gradient. He had been standing up, sliding open his compartment door, when the speed had unexpectedly increased. The train had reached the gradient summit and the track had changed to a downward angle. She appeared to read his thoughts as she continued watching him.

'I just got the door open when the damned thing picked up speed. If I'd jumped at once I might have managed it – I'm pretty athletic. . . .'

'I found that out not long ago,' he interjected.

'I'm serious,' she snapped. 'But you know how it is – you're not sure, so you hesitate. At least I did. By then the train was going very fast. I was hoping it would slow down again. We're close to the Austrian border – and since my language is German . . .'

'You're crazy – you do know that? The temperature outside must be sub-zero. You'd do better to wait until we reach the Berghof. How long do you reckon you've got before that file lands up in Gruber's greasy paws?'

'Three days' minimum . . . if they rushed it through.'

'Then we have to be on our way in less than three days . . .'

144

Lindsay prayed. He watched her like a scientist studying a slide under a microscope. He had said it, revealing himself to her. If there was one chance in a hundred he was wrong – that she had been playing him on the end of a string for Gruber – then he had only one option. To throttle her until she was dead. Then throw her corpse from the train while it continued through this isolated corner of Europe.

Lindsay was aware his palms were sweating. They would slip when he tried to get a grip on her slim, lovely neck. He would have to bang the back of her skull against the vertical water-pipe just behind where she sat. Oh God . . .

'You mean I was right about you all the time? You can provide me with an . . .'

Tears of relief, wonderment, exhaustion? Lindsay had no idea – but tears welled in her eyes and then she gritted her teeth as she felt under her coat, found a handkerchief and cleaned herself up. It could still be an act . . .

'Why do you have to use an escape route?' he demanded harshly. 'I need the truth – no more playing with words. The honest-to-God bloody truth . . .'

'They could link me to the anti-Nazi underground. Kurt was suspect. So they sent him to Russia. But no one knew. She was talking in short gasps, still apparently in shock, watching him closely. It was extraordinary, Lindsay reflected, the way women gripped by some powerful emotion could still – presumably with another part of their mind – check the effect they were having on a man. Doubtful about her sincerity again, he probed deeper.

'You say you belong to the anti-Nazi underground. . .'

'I went over after Kurt's death. Not that I've done much so far. . .'

'Just what have you done? Which underground? Communist?'

She looked startled, frightened. 'Christ, no! I'm talking of General Beck's people – the military. Occasionally Beck manages to send one of his people to the Wolf's Lair. They always ask for details of the security system. . .'

'You could be a Soviet spy,' he hammered.

'God! You're a Nazi. You're going to hand me over. . .'

'Shut up a minute while I think. No one is handing you over to anyone.'

Lindsay was faced with the most difficult decision of his life. He could trust her. She could be very useful in helping him to escape from Germany. But two on the run more than doubled the dangers. Once he committed himself he'd feel responsible for her. There would be no turning back.

And Lindsay was a loner. Instinctively he shied away from sharing any tricky situation with another man – or woman. You could never tell how they would Goddamn react at the moment of crisis – and there would be moments of crisis, maybe involving killing, he reminded himself grimly.

'Do you know the rail route from Salzburg?'

Still cautious, he phrased the question carefully. She nodded.

'To Vienna? I know it well,' she said. 'And the other way back to Munich. I lived there before the war. Once we go up to the Berghof we'll never escape. . .'

'We could steal transport,' he suggested.

'It wouldn't work – too many checkpoints. They'd know the road we were using once the alarm was raised – and it would be raised before we got clear. One phone call to a checkpoint we hadn't yet passed. . .'

'It has to be Salzburg then?'

'It has to be Salzburg. That's our last chance. . .'

Chapter Sixteen

The pudgy hand had made a hole in the frost-coated window. The hole framed a picture of the nearby Austrian mountains. Stirring restlessly in his arm chair inside the dining-coach of the Führer train, Martin Bormann stared at the view without seeing it. The rumble of the wheels was slowing: they were approaching Salzburg.

'I want you to carry out this order personally,' Bormann told the man sitting opposite across the table.

'Your wish is my command,' Gruber replied.

With Bormann you laid it on with a trowel. No display of respectful awe was too great. No man, Gruber had observed, was more conscious of his position than the Reichsleiter. They were alone in the luxuriously-appointed coach.

The swivel arm chairs were button-backed and made of leather. The Reichsleiter was almost swallowed up inside his chair. The top of his round head did not reach the tip of the chair back. Seen from behind, the chair appeared empty. Bormann let his mind wander.

They would soon be inside the Berghof where the privacy was far greater than at the benighted Wolf's Lair. Married, with nine children, he had not bedded another girl for several weeks. He craved the haughty, distant Christa Lundt. He couldn't get the girl out of his mind. At the Berghof. . .

'I'm worried about this bloody English Wing Commander,' he told the Gestapo officer. 'And the Führer is still convinced we have a Soviet spy among his entourage gnawing at our vitals. . .'

'I *am* continuing my investigation. . .' Gruber protested.

Bormann shut him up with an impatient gesture. 'I am holding you personally responsible for security at Salzburg when we leave the train and transfer to the motorcade to drive to Berchtesgaden. You will take command – including the SS detachment. . .' He leaned forward and stared at Gruber over the small pink-shaded lamp on the table laid for breakfast. 'You will be watching for anyone trying to leave the train without joining the motorcade. . .'

'With the complete SS detachment under my control I assure you, Reichsleiter, no one will escape. . .'

'Listen to me! I have not finished,' Bormann snapped. 'I want you to arrange it so the SS leave the train the moment it stops. *Discreetly*! They must *conceal* their presence. That way we shall trap anyone who tries to slip away. Understood?'

'Of course.' Gruber rose hesitantly. 'With your permission I would like to begin the preparations at once. . .'

'The SS commander has been instructed. . .'

Bormann dismissed Gruber with a curt gesture, still staring out of the window. He was tired and would normally have been in bed. The Führer had kept him up in his compartment talking before retiring, a routine Bormann had accustomed himself to duplicate.

Major Hartmann appeared in the coach carrying a small case a few minutes later.

'Some manoeuvre is taking place with the SS. It would be helpful if I knew what was going on,' Hartmann observed amiably as he peeled the shell from a hard-boiled egg.

The coach was filling up with passengers arriving for breakfast. Jodl cracked a joke with the Abwehr officer as he passed their table. He was followed by Keitel who marched past stiff-necked without a glance to left or right.

'Please keep your voice down,' Bormann responded irritably and swivelled in his chair. The table behind was unoccupied, as were the tables opposite. Automatically everyone was steering clear of any proximity to Bormann.

'No one can overhear us,' Hartmann remarked. 'I am not a fool and it was patently obvious Gruber was conducting some secret exercise. Luckily no one was about to witness his antics. . .'

'His *antics*,' Bormann reacted sarcastically, 'involve an operation I ordered him to direct. The station at Salzburg is sealed off.'

The train was no longer moving and Hartmann used a napkin to wipe a portion of his own window clear of the opaque film. A deserted platform met his gaze. He made no comment but the lack of even one member of the station staff gave the place an unnatural atmosphere.

'By order of the Führer?' Hartmann enquired very solemnly.

'By *my* order. The Führer is still sleeping. We all have breakfast – we take our time. It still means waking the Führer early but at least he gets some sleep. Which is more than I get. . .'

'Eat your breakfast. It will soothe your nerves.'

Hartmann was looking down at his plate as he spoke so he did not apparently see the expression of fury on Bormann's face. This Abwehr officer was a strange type – far too independent for Bormann's liking. A pity that in his pocket he carried that piece of paper signed by Hitler giving him the same plenipotentiary powers as the Gestapo officer.

Bormann poured coffee from the pot with his left hand and sneaked a glance at his watch. Within an hour they would all start leaving the train. The trap would be sprung.

Lindsay, who had shared a compartment with Hartmann, was careful to keep his eyes closed when the German went along the corridor for breakfast. The wheels were still pounding their rhythm inside his head even though the train had stopped. He guessed they had arrived at Salzburg. The windows were steamed up with moisture which made it impossible to see out.

He had let Hartmann go on his own because at breakfast he wanted to be alone if possible, his attention undistracted by conversation. He was aware of a tightening of his stomach muscles, a sensation of general tension. Soon, Christa and himself would make their escape attempt.

He would have liked to use his sleeve to wipe a hole in the window but that might draw attention to himself if a guard were stationed on the platform. When the Führer train arrived at its destination security would be tight, the slightest incident reported.

Taking his small suitcase from the rack, he went into the corridor and turned in the direction Hartmann had followed. It was strangely quiet and deserted. No sound of activity from the station outside. The compartments he passed were empty.

He walked slowly through several coaches and had the feeling he was moving inside a ghost train. Passing into a new coach, an aroma of freshly-made toast greeted him. This was the galley. Ahead, from an open doorway leading from the galley, a white-coated man emerged with a laden tray and hurried into the distance.

Lindsay paused alongside the doorway, peered inside. The galley was empty. Neatly arrayed inside an open drawer lay a row of sharp knives. He selected a strong, flat-bladed knife, eased up his trouser leg and thrust the knife inside his woollen sock.

Resuming his stroll along the corridor he heard the confused babel of many voices. Impossible yet to distinguish clear sentences. He pushed open a padded door and found himself inside a restaurant car so luxurious it reminded him of pictures of the pre-war Orient Express. Christa Lundt sat by herself at a table at the far end of the coach.

Wearing a pair of glasses, she had papers spread all over the table. Her head tilted up briefly as he entered, then she went on eating with one hand while she scribbled away with the other. Her warning was clear. *Don't join me. . .*

'Ah, Wing Commander, you will have to hurry unless you propose to fast. The Führer is shortly due to leave the train. When he goes, we all go. . .'

The ironic tone would have identified the speaker for Lindsay. Hartmann. The German gestured towards an empty place facing him. The Englishman took a quick decision. Don't make an issue of anything at a critical moment. The trouble was it would place him a good half-car length from Christa. He sat down.

'The seat is warm. You have already had company,' he remarked.

'And for a flier, with no experience of intelligence, you are remarkably observant,' Hartmann commented genially while he concentrated on scooping out egg. He looked up, his grey eyes half-closed. 'Consider yourself honoured – a short time ago my breakfast companion was Reichsleiter Bormann.'

Again Lindsay warned himself this was a very clever German. In his first sentence he had probed. In his second he had expressed subtle irony in his opinion of the whole Nazi regime. Just where the hell did Major Gustav Hartmann stand?

'You must have enjoyed that,' Lindsay said.

'He is such a popular man. I suspect it is his personal charm. Ah, here is your breakfast. Eat up – you haven't much time before we leave the train. . .'

Lindsay ate ravenously, his expression blank while his mind raced. Inwardly he cursed the Abwehr man's invitation to join him. The German had finished his breakfast and sat relaxed in his arm chair. He lit his pipe and puffed quietly, looking round the restaurant car as the passengers collected luggage from the racks and left by the exit behind the English-man.

Lindsay couldn't think of how to get rid of him. The second problem was he sat with his back to Christa, so he couldn't see what she was doing. Now the crucial moment was approaching he was racked with tension. He lifted his coffee cup, his hand steady as the proverbial rock.

He glanced casually over his shoulder as Jodl reached for a well-filled brief-case and moved off down the central corridor. At the far end Christa still sat at her table, but papers were no longer scattered over its surface. Most of them were now stuffed inside her own briefcase while she worked on a single file.

She looked up at the moment he turned round, cupped her chin in her hand and placed her index finger across her mouth. For a fraction of a second she met his gaze and then looked down at the file. She was ready to go.

'The Führer must have gone to his Mercedes,' Hartmann remarked. 'That is why Bormann left so abruptly. He really believes that if he is not with the Führer every waking moment, someone else might gain a little influence. You are going yourself now?'

'I think I'll have a word with Christa Lundt. When I arrived at the Wolf's Lair she was very considerate. . .'

'Of course. . .'

Hartmann half-stood up and bowed, then resumed his seat. Lindsay was enormously relieved. But that had been a pretty feeble excuse. The trouble about fencing with an expert was all your energy went into maintaining an outward composure. The coach was empty except for Christa who slid her file into the case, snapped the catch shut and smiled warmly.

'Good morning, Wing Commander. I'm not sure I forgive you for not joining me for breakfast. . .'

Her voice was loud enough to carry down the coach to Hartmann and she was openly flirting for the Abwehr man's benefit. It was, Lindsay thought ruefully, a better performance than his own. He helped her on with her fur coat. She wasted no time donning her Russian-style fur hat, smiled up at him again and led the way out of the car.

'When we got on the platform follow me,' Christa warned, pausing in the empty corridor. 'Don't hesitate. Confidence is everything.'

He was astounded. Mentally he contrasted the girl he had found earlier in the night hanging out of the open doorway, the girl who had trembled and quivered with terror in his arms. They were about to embark on a course fraught with hazard – and she was as composed as a girl going out for the evening with her boy friend. She was bolstering *his* morale. . .

They passed several doors open on to a deserted platform which Christa ignored. The lack of people. Something began to stir at the back of Lindsay's mind, something unsettling and profoundly disturbing.

She trotted on ahead of him. He noticed her stocking seams were perfectly straight. Absurd observation at a time like this! What *was* bothering him? An omission. The most difficult factor of all to locate. They walked on.

Like a house emptied of furniture, there is nothing more dreary than a long-distance train after arrival at its final destination. The deserted compartments were littered with abandoned newspapers and magazines. Ash-trays were crammed with cigarette stubs. The only sound was the steady click-clack of Christa's footsteps.

They reached the end of yet another coach. Christa glanced at the open door and stopped. She turned and looked up at Lindsay as he gazed at the silent platform. Her free left hand grasped his arm and squeezed it. Her voice was calm.

'This is it. That open door leading out of the station – we go through there. We keep moving. No sign of nerves. Ready?'

'Ready,' said Lindsay.

After being confined for so many hours aboard the train the platform seemed dreadfully exposed. Lindsay was conscious of the freshness of the air – a gentle current drifting down from snowbound peaks. The contrast with the smoke-polluted stuffiness of the train almost made him feely dizzy. He had a sensation of exhilaration. The open door yawned before them.

Christa paused briefly, glancing to her left. Lindsay looked in the same direction and saw an open gate, the rooftops of waiting cars beyond. The main exit. *No sign of any guards*. He sucked in his breath. Christa had taken two steps forward.

'Let me escort you to your transport. . .'

Out of nowhere a hand grasped Christa's elbow and turned her in the direction of the main exit. Lindsay froze. His suitcase was in his left hand, leaving the right free – free to reach for the knife secreted inside his sock. The hand guiding Christa belonged to Hartmann. Cat-like in movement, he had simply materialized.

He smiled at the Englishman and stared hard at him, conveying a plea. Lindsay nodded and the trio walked along the platform to the main exit. *No sign of any guards*. That had been the odd omission the Englishman had registered in his subconscious. Had he been on his own he would have spotted the danger signal earlier. This, he reflected bitterly, was the price of having someone else to think about.

Beyond the main exit a uniformed chauffeur opened the rear door of a grey Mercedes. Hartmann made a gesture for Lindsay to follow Christa inside, the door was closed and the Abwehr officer got into the front passenger seat. By the Englishman's side Christa stared straight ahead, clutching her briefcase in her lap. Her knuckles were white with the strength of her grip.

Lindsay waited until the chauffeur had started the motor

153

and the car was moving, before glancing quickly back through the rear window. Along the whole of the outside of the station was drawn up a file of SS guards, their backs to the wall, each man armed with a machine-pistol. Two stood on either side of the inviting doorway Christa had been heading for when Hartmann had appeared.

Chapter Seventeen

It was a Monday in Salzburg when the Führer's motorcade left the station in a series of cars and headed for the Berghof. The air was crisp and invigorating and no fresh snow had fallen.

On the same Monday in Munich the snow was falling, coating the huge twin domes of the Frauenkirche with a mantle of white. At eleven in the morning precisely a road-sweeper was trudging past the great church, dragging one leg as he pushed in front of him a metal trash-bin mounted in wheels.

The bin wobbled because the original rubber tyres had long ago worn threadbare and even ersatz rubber was at a premium in the blockaded Third Reich. Now it had to trundle over the uneven cobbles on the relics of rusty metal wheels.

As the clock struck eleven, the old road-sweeper paused to rest and the snow continued falling, soft flakes drifting down. Across the open space high up in an attic, the agent called Paco scanned the front of the Frauenkirche with a pair of binoculars.

For a few seconds the lenses focused on the road-sweeper and the hidden watcher was satisfied the apparently lame man was positioned perfectly. The lenses moved on, hovering systematically on the few people who hurried, heads down, past the Frauenkirche.

Paco was watching for any trace of suspicious activity – for any passer-by who could possibly be Gestapo. Men and women – they were all too old. Germany had become a place for the very old and very young. The cream of the nation's manhood was fighting on the Eastern Front, in Africa – or stationed with the troops in the West.

Paco was also watching for a man who lit a cigarette with his left hand, took a few puffs, then stamped it under his left foot. By 11.10 it was clear this was the wrong Monday. Paco left the attic viewing platform. The road-sweeper resumed his trudging walk into a side street.

The trash-bin he pushed was half-full of rubbish. The smoke bombs and grenades were concealed under the layer of garbage.

It was Monday in London when Tim Whelby sat at a table in the foyer of the Regent Palace Hotel just off Piccadilly. He was hidden behind a copy of the *Daily Mail* which he held open at a double-page spread.

From where he sat he could see the revolving entrance doors – an ideal position to observe everyone who came inside. At nine o'clock at night the foyer milled with people at the reception counter. Most of the men were in uniform, a mix of Allied troops including the ubiquitous Americans, many with English girl friends.

Outwardly relaxed, huddled in an old sports jacket, Whelby was feeling tense. His contact, Savitsky, was late. He checked his watch. In three minutes' time he would get up and leave. When he had phoned the usual number the Russian had sounded agitated, as though some urgent crisis had arisen, which was out of character.

At the nearby table, which was unoccupied, he had deliberately spread out his rumpled overcoat across a chair to discourage anyone from sitting down. As always, the rendezvous was different. They never met at the same place twice. Nor at the same time.

What made the Regent Palace ideal was the mêlée of visitors at this hour. And should someone he knew arrive and spot him, he was simply passing an idle half hour in the warmth. His eyes were on the entrance when a hand touched his overcoat, the voice apologetic.

'Is this table occupied?' Savitsky enquired.

'No. Excuse me. . .'

Whelby frowned irritably as he transferred the overcoat to the back of a chair at his own table. He settled down again to read his paper. At the next table Savitsky chose the chair closest to Whelby, unfolded a copy of the *Evening Standard* and, following the Englishman's example, opened it wide.

Where the hell had the Russian materialized from, Whelby wondered? He hoped he hadn't hidden himself in the lavatory cubicle. The police and hotel staff checked that area for undesirable activity. Savitsky appeared to read his mind.

'My apologies for being late. I was in the restaurant. I had to wait for ever for the bill. . .'

Whelby grunted without turning his head. Savitsky was no fool. He spoke English with an accent – but the hotel was full of Poles, French and even a few Dutch. No one was going to find anything odd in the Russian's speech.

'My people are very worried about your Englishman, the RAF Wing Commander. You have news?'

'Nothing more so far,' Whelby murmured, his lips hardly moving.

'We have had a signal – from the top – informing us this Lindsay has spent the last two weeks with the Führer. He has just arrived at Berchtesgaden. . .'

Whelby turned to a fresh page, reached out a hand for his glass of beer and drained the contents. Savisky had shaken him. How the devil could they know Lindsay was at the Berghof? He wiped his mouth with a handkerchief, and spoke from behind it.

'How does this concern me?'

'The geography intrigues us. The nearest friendly territory to Berchtesgaden is Switzerland. When he makes his run we believe he will head for Switzerland – then on to Spain. The Iberian peninsula is your responsibility. . .'

'You expect me to do what?'

'Make sure he never reaches England alive. . .'

Savitsky looked at his watch, stood up hastily as though realizing he was late, donned his own coat and walked rapidly away. Whelby watched him disappear through the revolving doors and checked his own watch. Three minutes' time lapse to let the Russian get well clear of the area and then he could leave himself.

Nothing in his smooth-skinned face or slow-moving eyes gave even a hint of the hammerblow shock Whelby had received. This was way above anything he had bargained for. *Make sure he never reaches England alive. . .*

Modern communications – and their interception – have changed the course of great wars. They have even dictated the ultimate outcome. The eventual success of the Ultra system, operated from a country house at Bletchley in England, allowed the Allies to eavesdrop on vital Nazi signals.

In the First World War, more than anyone else the code-breakers who cracked the Zimmermann telegram decided President Wilson to bring America into the war against Germany. Despatched from the Wilhelmstrasse, the German Foreign Office, to their ambassador in Mexico City, it proved Germany was planning to use Mexico as a hostile base against its great northern neighbour.

The most unusual factor influencing the victory of the Allies in World War Two was the Lucy Ring. The night before *Amerika* – the Führer train – left the siding at the Wolf's Lair for Bavaria, a signal was despatched by Woodpecker from the hidden transmitter to Lucerne.

Couched in an unknown code, this was one of the signals which worried Roessler. He received the message as a series of incomprehensible dots and dashes.

'Another signal for Cossack in that funny code,' he told Anna. 'At least we are now passing them to the Bureau Ha. Is that a stew I can smell? I'm not too hungry. . .'

'Kindly sit down at the table and eat what I have taken trouble to prepare. If you had your own way you'd live off coffee and no sleep. . .'

'I have re-transmitted the signal to Cossack. . .'

157

'I assume that! Now, sit down! Eat!'

The trouble started the following morning when the Swiss brigadier of Intelligence called personally. Even Anna was startled when she answered the persistent ringing and found him on her doorstep.

'Please come in, Brigadier Masson,' she said, as though his visit was the most natural thing in the world. 'You got the latest signal?'

'Yes, Madame. Something is seriously wrong. . .'

'What is happening, Anna? Who is calling. . . ?'

Roessler, stoop-shouldered from crouching over his transmitter – operating it, maintaining it for so many endless months – came into the living room and looped the handles of his glasses behind his large ears. He blinked in astonishment.

'Brigadier Masson. . .'

The Swiss Intelligence officer was a tall man in his forties. Instead of his normal uniform and peaked cap he wore his civilian clothes. Clean-shaven, solemn in expression, he stared hard at Roessler and then sat in the threadbare arm chair Anna indicated.

'You received the latest signal? Your messenger collected it,' Roessler assured him.

'Your friend inside Germany has changed the code again,' Masson informed him. 'Our code-breakers cannot decipher it. . .'

'So you have told me before. . .' Roessler made a helpless movement. 'I also have no idea of what those signals mean. . .'

'I must know the identity of this contact at the top of the Nazi hierarchy. Now!'

Masson, normally the soul of courtesy, was cold and distant in voice and manner. Watching him, Anna had the impression he was labouring under great tension. She intervened, her tone sharp.

'After all we have done we cannot be bullied. Tell us what is worrying you or leave us in peace. . .'

Masson shrugged and reached for his hat. 'The identity of your friend in Germany,' he repeated. 'We sense danger. . .'

'Danger to whom? Anna burst out. 'And Rudolf knows our informant only as The Woodpecker – *Der Specht*! I ask you once more – what is it about this latest signal which worries you?'

'Our code-breakers were not entirely unsuccessful,' Masson told her as he rose to leave. 'It makes a reference to *Switzerland*. . .'

At the beginning of April 1943 the whole world seemed to be *waiting* – waiting without knowing it. The war, involving millions of men, could still go either way. Victory was still within the grasp of the Third Reich. One massive blow against the Red Army could destroy Communism. Would the decisive attack be launched?

In London Tim Whelby, who so far had only dabbled his feet in treachery, was disturbed and irresolute. The instruction given by Savitsky confronted him for the first time with the prospect of personal violence. In short, murder. He waited for the next sign.

In Bavaria at the Berghof Martin Bormann waited – waited with the deepest anxiety to see whether his protégé could successfully seal the success of the greatest impersonation in history. If he did, the Nazis would remain in power. If not, the generals would launch a military coup under the direction of General Beck.

At the Berghof another man waited – waited for the chance to get away. Ian Lindsay still felt handicapped by his relationship with Christa Lundt, still had not solved the problem of *two* people making an escape from the most heavily-guarded establishment in Nazi Germany.

And in the ancient city of Munich Colonel Browne's agent, Paco, also waited – waited for the next Monday. Would the Englishman reach the Bavarian capital in time to keep the agreed rendezvous? Every seven-day delay increased the danger. But patiently, Paco waited.

In Moscow the son of a Georgian cobbler also waited – waited as he tried to decide whether he could trust the reports from Woodpecker, whether he could take military action on the basis of the stream of signals which kept coming in via Lucerne.

'The arrival of the Englishman with Hitler at the Berghof is my greatest anxiety,' Stalin confided to Beria as the two men sat alone in his office inside the Kremlin. 'It is a pity the first attempt to kill him came to nothing. . .'

'I understood from earlier Woodpecker reports this Lindsay does not officially represent Churchill,' Beria responded cautiously.

Stalin stared at the secret police chief contemptuously, puffed at his pipe and then rested it inside an ash-tray. He sat back in his chair and clasped both hands before speaking.

'If Hitler can find a way to bring the forty German divisions now guarding Western Europe to our front we are finished! You understand, Beria? Finished,' he repeated bitterly. 'And now I learn that Englishman is alive and well and has journeyed with Hitler to the Berghof. Quite obviously he has gained the Führer's confidence. At this very moment he may be negotiating terms for a separate peace. Whatever happens he must be killed before he can return to England. *Killed*! I am handing over the responsibility for his fate to you. . .'

Stalin also was – *waiting* . . .

Chapter Eighteen

Five days had passed since the arrival of the Führer at the Berghof. It was Saturday, which, Lindsay thought grimly, would be succeeded by Sunday and *Monday*. And still he had no plan for escaping to keep the Munich rendezvous with Paco. Escape was vital. Reaching London was urgent. What a weapon for Churchill – if he could broadcast to the world that a pseudo-Hitler had been installed. . .

'These will be your quarters,' Bormann had told him brusquely when they reached the Berghof. 'The Führer has agreed you are to undergo intensive interrogation. . .'

On this encouraging note the Reichsleiter had left the Englishman alone. The first surprise was the quarters allocated to him. They included the large room at the foot of a flight of stairs where Lindsay had witnessed a nightmare scene on his earlier visit.

Inside this room he had seen through a half-open door the mirror image of the Führer practising a speech – a Führer surrounded by a circle of mirrors as he thundered at the top of his voice, studying the effect of his body language while he gestured violently. All the mirrors had vanished.

As soon as he was on his own, Lindsay had examined the highly polished floor carefully. The mirrors had been heavy cheval glasses. The supporting legs should have left traces on the woodblock floor. He found nothing. Someone had gone to considerable trouble to remove all traces.

There was the faint aroma of fresh polish. The surface of the woodblocks gleamed. He suspected the floor had first been stripped. He opened a drawer at the base of a heavy wardrobe. It contained books by Clausewitz, von Moltke and Schlieffen – all the classic military authorities. Many had the corners of pages turned down, passages underlined. He found an unused 1943 diary. On impulse he pocketed it.

Christa Lundt had come to see him soon after he had unpacked his few things. She had entered without knocking, closed the door and placed a finger over her lips to stop him greeting her. She had then spent a quarter of an hour checking the apartment.

'No microphones,' she pronounced eventually. 'So we can talk.'

'You've been to the Berghof before, of course? I imagined so. Have you ever been down here?'

'Never! It was closely guarded – sealed off from the rest of the Berghof. Access was under the personal control of the previous Commandant, the one who committed suicide. . . .'

'*Committed suicide*? How long ago was this, Christa?'

'About two weeks ago. It must have been just after you

flew to the Wolf's Lair. I'm talking about Commandant Müller. . .'

'Müller!' Lindsay was pacing the room, frowning. 'I met Müller when I was here before – that man never committed suicide. What the hell is going on here?' He stopped pacing and faced Christa. 'How did he commit suicide?'

'Well . . .' Christa hesitated and the Englishman waited silently. 'The first report was he had an accident. He fell four hundred feet from the outer platform of the Kehlstein. That's the Eagle's Nest, the eyrie the Führer had built at the peak of the mountain. You get up there by a lift which ascends inside the rock face. . .'

'Go on,' Lindsay urged as she paused.

'Commandant Müller was supposed to have slipped on the ice and plunged over the wall when he went up there by himself. . .'

'Why would he do that – at this time of the year?'

'I never heard of him going there before. Afterwards we heard rumours that the accident story was to cover up the fact that he had killed himself. . .'

'And who was appointed in his place? Who did appoint his successor, by the way?'

'Colonel Jaeger, whose responsibility was the SS detachment here, was appointed in Müller's place.' Her expression softened. 'The Colonel is a tough, professional soldier. But underneath he's a decent man. As to who appointed Jaeger, Martin Bormann himself handled the whole affair. . .'

'How do you know that?'

'Am I in the witness box? Are you cross-examining me?' Christa lashed out sarcastically.

She sat down on a hard-backed chair, crossed her legs and looked at her fingernails. Lindsay pulled up a similar chair, swung it round, straddled the chair and leaned his arms along the top so he faced her directly. She made a great show of looking anywhere except at him, her chin set.

'There's a complicated jigsaw of intrigue – maybe murder – which I'm trying to put together,' he said quietly. 'So, I'm asking you again. *How do you know*?'

'Because I transmitted Bormann's message to the Berghof confirming Jaeger's temporary bloody appointment as Commandant,' she flared.

'And that instruction was purely Bormann's? Not by order of the Führer. . .'

'It was!' she said through clenched teeth. 'He added the words "by order of the Führer" himself. At that time Hitler was still on his way back from the Russian front. It was the time when he was delayed and landed at another airfield. Anything else you'd care to know, Wing Commander?'

'I doubt if you have any other worthwhile information,' Lindsay replied in an off-hand tone calculated to get under her skin.

'Except that there's something very odd about the Führer ever since he did get back from Russia! If I told you that was pure feminine instinct you'd laugh at me. . .'

Lindsay extracted a pack of cigarettes and lit one, watching her while he did so. He delayed his reply until he had taken several long puffs. Her face was flushed with fury.

'No,' he commented eventually, 'I wouldn't laugh. You're his chief secretary, you're intelligent – I'm simply stating a fact. So I'd consider your instinctive reactions very seriously – and they happen to coincide with things I've experienced which don't add up. . .'

He chose his next words very carefully.

'I'm wondering if we're witnessing one of the greatest confidence tricks in history. . .'

Her eyes warned him. She was in a position to see the door into the room which he couldn't because it was behind him. Lindsay continued to puff at his cigarette. He had not heard the door opening but he did hear it close.

'I always seem to find you two together – which is pleasant when the world is at war. To find a German girl striking up a friendship with an Englishman. . .'

The familiar voice was that of Major Gustav Hartmann of the Abwehr.

'One of the greatest confidence tricks in history, I believe you said,' commented Hartmann. 'Care to enlighten me on your extremely intriguing assertion?'

Christa had left the room and Lindsay was alone with Hartmann who had sat down and was lighting his pipe, watching the Englishman as he puffed out clouds of blue smoke which formed a veil between the two men.

'This is an official interrogation?' Lindsay asked.

'Just call it a chat between two individuals whom the chances of war have brought together for a brief time.'

'The Soviet spy you're searching for,' the Englishman replied and said no more, forcing the German to give him a few more seconds to think.

'I don't quite understand – the link between the two factors. . .'

'*If* a Soviet spy has penetrated the Führer's entourage surely he is bringing off the greatest confidence trick in history,' Lindsay replied.

Hartmann tamped his pipe and stared hard at the Englishman. For a moment Lindsay glimpsed a second man behind the interrogator's normal air of casual amiability, a ruthless pursuer who never gave up. It was an observation he was to recall later.

'You know something,' the German said thoughtfully, 'you are much cleverer than anyone has realized. With the possible exception of the Führer. He has an almost feminine instinct where people are concerned. *Why* did you come to Germany, Wing Commander?'

'You know – to try and arrange some sort of accommodation between Great Britain and the Third Reich. The real menace is Russia. . .'

'So,' Hartmann interjected, 'we come full circle again. I see no point in taking up more of your time – or mine. . .'

He stood up, his expression grim and resigned. He left the room without another word, closing the door noiselessly.

The Abwehr man moved like a cat. Lindsay recalled his unexpected appearance on the station platform at Salzburg – how he seemed to have guided Christa and himself away from the danger of the doorway guarded by SS. Or had he? You could never tell with Hartmann.

Lindsay, disturbed by something he couldn't put his finger on, also left the room. Outside the SS guard positioned there by Jaeger watched him stroll along the corridor to the window at the end. So long as he remained in sight the guard would leave him alone.

From the window he looked straight down to the entrance to the Berghof. He could feel the guard's eyes on his back. He lit a cigarette. Someone had cleaned off the condensation from the big sheet of glass. The whole place was kept spotless. Staring down at the snow-clad scene he suddenly froze, the cigarette half way to his mouth. He knew now how they could escape from the Berghof.

'I have a plan to test the Englishman – to lead him into a trap,' Colonel Jaeger informed Gruber.

'You have the authority to carry out this plan?' the Gestapo man enquired.

The two men were the only occupants of the viewing platform from the Kehlstein. Despite his leather great-coat and the collar pulled up behind his thick neck the fat Gestapo officer was chilled with the icy wind blowing across the valley from the nearby mountains.

Jaeger, clad in his full uniform with his peaked cap jammed down over his high forehead, seemed immune to the temperature. Beneath the peak his aquiline nose and firm mouth expressed determination. A commanding figure, he exuded confidence and his voice was clipped and decisive.

'Martin Bormann himself has agreed unofficially that I put the plan into action. . .'

'*Unofficially?*'

There was a probing query behind the word. Jaeger made an impatient gesture. The only reason he was confiding in this creep was to keep him out of the way, to prevent him botching up everything at the critical moment.

'He has given me his verbal agreement. Coming from the

Reichsleiter that is enough for me. You think I am accustomed to getting all my orders in writing?'

From Bormann, yes I would, Gruber thought, but withheld comment on the point. The Gestapo officer had worked his way up to his present position by ensuring that every action he took had the unquestioned backing of his superior, preferably in the presence of witnesses.

Gruber now decided his policy should be to encourage Jaeger to proceed on two counts. If his plan succeeded it must be seen as a combined exercise on the part of Gruber and Jaeger. Should it fail, he must be in a position to disengage – to disclaim all responsibility for what he would term 'this foolhardy act'. . .

'How soon do you propose to operate this plan?' he asked.

'Tomorrow – Sunday!' Jaeger replied promptly.

'And the details?'

Gruber would have given anything to continue their conversation inside the shelter of the luxuriously-appointed rooms of the Kehlstein behind them. But out here perched on this elevated refrigerator there was no danger of anyone overhearing them. Pressing his gloved hands inside his coat pockets, Gruber forced himself to stand still without shivering. Jaeger was a man who despised any sort of weakness. He began speaking enthusiastically.

'The guard outside this Wing Commander's quarters will be removed. It will not seem so strange, considering it is Sunday. Lindsay will think our security is lax. I hear he frequently comes out to walk along the corridor. . .'

'Yes, yes! Colonel, can I ask you to be concise? I have duties which will not wait much longer. . .'

Gruber was frozen stiff. He began to suspect Jaeger was subjecting him to this ordeal by cold deliberately. And he was right. Jaeger continued his explanation in a leisurely manner.

'The staircase continues to the main hall and entrance. A car will be left empty where he can see it from the window at the end of the corridor on his floor. All guards will be withdrawn from that part of the Berghof. . .'

'Go on. . .'

'God in Heaven! Don't you see? If he is waiting his chance to escape he will seize it, take the car and drive away. I suspect he may be accompanied by Fräulein Lundt. Have you not observed they spend time together? My guards have clear orders. . .'

'So, they leave in the car, according to your theory. How far do they get?'

'The detail guarding the first checkpoint on the road to Salzburg will be withdrawn. . .'

'Supposing they do actually escape? No, they have to drive on past two more checkpoints. . .'

'All guards withdrawn from the second checkpoint, and from the third. The road to Salzburg wide open!'

'Good God, man – you are crazy!' Gruber gasped.

Jaeger grinned, looking down at his small companion. Gruber's face was turning blue with exposure to the freezing temperature. The colonel was enjoying himself. He went on speaking.

'Except that both those checkpoints will be heavily re-inforced with concealed troops.' He gestured towards the low parapet separating them from the four hundred foot drop to the abyss below. 'This is where Commandant Müller is alleged to have committed suicide, is it not?' he remarked.

'It was an accident,' Gruber said, bewildered at this unexpected turn in the conversation.

'The Romans used to throw men from the Tarpeian Rock. . .'

'What does that mean?' Gruber demanded harshly.

'I wonder. Shall we go back to the lift. . .'

Without waiting for a reply Jaeger led the way. He had ended the conversation leaving the Gestapo man in a state of anxiety. In some ways his technique was not unlike that of Hartmann: he kept the opposition off balance.

Sunday dawned with the threat of heavy snow. The sky was leaden, obliterating the peaks, and the view from the corridor window on the floor occupied by Lindsay was dramatic and menacing.

The first thing the Englishman noticed after rising early and shaving quickly was the absence of the usual SS guard outside his door. An eight-hour roster was normally operated. Was it possible that because this was Sunday fewer guards were available for duty? He walked quietly down the staircase into the main entrance hall.

The same unnatural quiet met him. No guards. He walked over to the giant double entrance doors and examined them for alarm systems. Another memory of the crash programme at Ryder Street. A Cockney electrician had put him through his paces.

'Look for concealed wires, mate. No wires, no alarm system. If it's the SS you're up against they rely on brute force – they think no further than a man with a gun. The Abwehr? A tricky bunch, that lot. They've got tradition, which means they rely on patience. Finally, our old friends the Gestapo. They'll use anything, including alarm systems. . .'

But the Gestapo had no permanent control of security at the Berghof. Lindsay grasped the large handle of the right-hand door and eased it downwards. Slowly he eased open the massive door on its well-oiled hinges. At any moment the muzzle of a machine-pistol would be shoved in his face.

Nothing. . .

Lindsay peered out and the cold came in and met him, chilling his face. There was no one anywhere in sight. They must be relying on the checkpoints lower down the road on the way to Salzburg. He closed the door and heard a slight sound behind him. What a fool he had been to assume the main entrance would be deserted.

He turned round, thankful he was at least on the inside of the doors, his mind juggling with reasons for his presence. Christa Lundt stood staring at him, framed in an open door. She wore ski pants and a weatherproof suede jacket. One finger raised to her lips warned him to remain silent. She gestured for him to join her.

Closing the door behind her, she leaned against it and let out her breath as Lindsay walked round a large anteroom, checking the room he had not been inside before. There were

168

no other doors, no open fireplace which might conceal a hidden microphone. When he turned round Christa was in the same position, with a certain look which disturbed him.

'I think we could make the attempt today,' she said. 'There is a car outside. I suppose you saw it from the corridor window upstairs?'

'No, I didn't. And I came downstairs only a few minutes ago. . .'

Puzzled, Lindsay went over to the window and stared. A large green Mercedes with snow on the running-boards was parked to one side of the window. The vehicle was empty, the windscreen frosted over.

As he studied the car Christa joined him, linked arms and nestled close to him. He remembered the affectionate way she had watched him from the door and felt even more disturbed. Was she growing too fond of him?

He cursed himself for indulging in the passionate act they had performed at the Wolf's Lair. Because that was all it had been for him – a reaction to the extreme tension he had laboured under. For her, had it been something more?

'Lucky we both got up so early,' she murmured. 'There is no need to start up that car and risk someone hearing the engine as we leave. Don't you see!' She tugged at him impatiently. 'The front wheels are perched at the edge of the road where the slope begins. We put it in gear, release the brake, give it a push and jump aboard. The momentum will carry us a kilometre down the hill before you have to switch on the motor. . .'

'I didn't see that car from the corridor window upstairs because it is parked just out of sight. If it was further to the right – so I could have seen it – then it would not be at the top of the slope. . .'

'What are you on about, for God's sake? I know there is a most appalling risk but. . .'

'I'm wondering when it was parked there,' he speculated.

'Oh, I can tell you that. Not ten minutes ago. Two SS guards pushed it round from the garage at the back, then went away – to their barracks, I suppose.'

169

He stared down at her. 'I'd like to get this clear – exactly what happened. You say the guards *pushed* the Mercedes? Why the needless expenditure of energy? Why not drive it from the garage to park it here?'

'Because then they might have woken up the Führer, silly! You know he goes to bed at the ridiculous hour of three in the middle of the night and doesn't rise until about eleven in the morning. And his bedroom suite is round the side, right above where they would have had to drive the car. . .'

'There's no one about. No sign of a guard. Is that usual at this hour in this part of the Berghof?'

'How should I know? I'm not usually up myself this early. And I'm in another part of the Berghof except when I arrive and leave.'

Lindsay was in a quandary. He could feel the warmth of her body pressed into his side. He liked her – but that was all, and her behaviour unsettled him. Her explanation about why the car had been pushed made sense. Everyone on the Führer's staff was house-trained to avoid causing him the slightest inconvenience or discomfort.

'It's all pretty convenient,' he commented. 'That car just waiting for us to take off. . .'

'I've brought a small case down. You'd better pack your things quickly so we can leave before someone does arrive.'

There was a sense of her rising impatience – due, he guessed, to her taut nerves. She wanted to get on with it. At least she was not one of those women who hesitated at a crucial moment.

'I wonder how much petrol is in the tank,' he mused while he decided whether she was, after all, right.

'Christ! Go out and find out!'

'Stay here,' he warned. 'Under no circumstances leave this room until I get back. Where is your case? Behind that cupboard? You leave it there for the moment. If I'm caught and they find you, say you couldn't sleep and were going out for a walk. . .'

The marble-floored entrance hall was still deserted and eerily silent as Lindsay padded across to the entrance. Standing by the great door he listened, his head cocked on one side. He waited three minutes by the second hand on his watch. If there was anyone about they couldn't remain still for that period if they were watching.

An intake of breath, the squeak of a shoe brought on by a cramped leg, there had to be some tiny, betraying sound. Finally, Lindsay was convinced he was alone. He opened the door and stepped out into the snow.

The surface was solid, crisp and he moved with long strides to the side of the Mercedes. Who was it waiting for? With his hand on the front passenger door handle he paused. Suddenly he looked at the upper floors overlooking the car, searching for any sign of sudden movement – a shadow stepping back from a window, the twitch of a curtain.

Nothing.

It was uncanny. Had they struck lucky? It did happen – especially in wartime. Then you didn't waste a moment. You *moved* – so maybe Christa was right. He turned the handle and the unlocked door opened. *Unlocked*? A lousy kind of security they operated in this neck of the woods.

Leaning inside he checked the gauge. The petrol tank was full. There was even a pile of road maps on the passenger seat. And on the back seat lay a Schmeisser machine-pistol with a loaded magazine. He closed the door without touching anything.

Before returning to the Berghof he smeared his isolated footprints, carefully leaving intact the faint imprint of the two SS men who had pushed the car to this point. And Christa was right. The merest shove, with the brake released and the gear in 'neutral', would propel the Mercedes down the sloping road to where it curved round the mountain and disappeared in the distance.

He returned to the entrance hall, his hands frozen. He heard the sound as he perched against the closed door to slap snow off his boots with a handkerchief. A faint grinding sound like the creak of a slowly-approaching tank track.

He grabbed for the door handle and glanced over his shoulder. In the far distance across the valley a puff of white showed where massive snow had slipped. Spring was on the way. He went inside. Christa would be waiting, keyed up for their great gamble.

Colonel Jaeger stood behind the open barracks window, a pair of binoculars pressed to his eyes. The lenses were focused on the point where the road descending from the Berghof curved in a wild hairpin before disappearing behind a mountain wall.

Beside him stood his deputy, Alfred Schmidt, a tall, thin man with an intellectual appearance who wore rimless glasses. Schmidt moved his feet restlessly, grinding a heel into the floor. With an irritable gesture Jaeger lowered the glasses and let them dangle from the loop round his neck.

'Well, Schmidt, what is it?' he demanded.

'I'm worried the Englishman may never even see the car. If we had moved it a few metres further he would have looked straight down on to it from that window in the corridor. . .'

'Which would have been bloody obvious,' Jaeger snapped.

'If he is anxious to escape he will grab the first chance which comes to hand. . .'

'You have not spoken with him. I have!' Jaeger rapped harshly. 'Make it too obvious and he will smell a trap. It is always a mistake to underestimate your opponent.'

'Well, *if* he does take the bait, he won't get far,' Schmidt observed.

He looked outside the window where a file of two motor-cyclists and a further back-up of two motor-cycles and side-cars waited with armed SS in position. The passengers in the sidecars held their machine-pistols at the ready.

'*If*!' Jaeger exploded. 'You worry like an old woman. . .'

'I still think we should be in a position to observe what is going on at the front of the Berghof,' Schmidt persisted. 'We could have placed a man in one of the upper rooms overlooking the exit doors. . .'

'Everything depends on our target feeling sure he is not observed. When the car reaches that bend we take off. Now shut up and let me concentrate, for Christ's sake!'

Chapter Nineteen

'We take that car! We leave within ten minutes. . .'

Inside the large anteroom Lindsay and Christa were in the middle of a ferocious argument. The Englishman made no reply to what she had just said as she fought to drive him into a decision. She had been alternately pleading and berating. Now she grasped both his lapels, stood up on her toes so their faces were level and tugged hard as she went on speaking.

'Listen to me! Did you see anyone while you were outside?'

'No. . .'

'Did you *look* to see if anyone was watching the car?'

'Yes, but. . .'

'No "buts", for God's sake! That file on me Gruber has sent to Berlin for will reach here any day now. Do you want me to end up in a concentration camp?'

Gently he took hold of both her wrists and released himself from her grasp. Still holding on, he pushed her into a chair, motioned to her to stay put.

'It's all too easy and convenient,' he said. 'No one about inside the place, no one outside. . .'

'It's Sunday. . . !'

It was so bloody tempting, Lindsay thought. The timing was right. If they got away today, tomorrow was Monday – the day for contacting Paco. And with luck Christa – with her local knowledge – could get them through to Munich from Salzburg. He began thinking aloud.

'Having met Jaeger I have some idea of what makes him tick. If he were setting a trap he'd do it something like this. . .'

'He'd at least have parked the car where you could see it from the corridor window upstairs. You said you couldn't see it. . .'

'I couldn't. . .'

'Well then!'

'If I were Jaeger,' Lindsay persisted, 'I wouldn't make it that obvious. And I wouldn't post watchers where they could be seen. I'd stay back and wait. . .'

'Wait! Wait! Wait! That's all you can think of!'

'I remember when I met Hitler before the war. We had a very long conversation. He told me that in any crisis he always waited until events developed, until something gave him a sign as to which was the direction he should move in. I'm a bit like Hitler. . .'

'You lack his resolution,' she retorted bitterly.

'I've noticed there's a big laundry truck which arrives daily – to collect dirty linen and deliver fresh. The guards have become used to that truck. I've watched them from my corridor window. What I don't know is does it call on Sunday?'

'How should I know?' she asked sulkily. 'I'm kept occupied the other side of the Berghof. Why are you wasting time on this truck?'

'It arrives each day with commendable Teutonic promptness at the same time – exactly eleven o'clock in the morning.' Lindsay was walking slowly backwards and forwards while Christa fidgeted on the chair. 'There is only one man with that truck, no guards, just the driver, a short, fat man in overalls who heaves inside great bales of fresh laundry. Then he takes out the dirty stuff in white sacks, dumps them in the back, hauls down the door and drives off. There's the name of some firm in Salzburg on the side. Salzburg is where we want to go. . .'

'Where do we go from there?' she asked.

'Later. . .' He was determined not to reveal their destination until the last minute. 'That laundry truck could be our transport to freedom,' he continued. 'When the door is up I can see inside from that window. There's a whole load of stuff that isn't unloaded here we could hide under. And my guess is the checkpoints are so used to the truck by now they won't search it, just so long as the alarm hasn't been raised here. Where are you supposed to be at eleven this morning? And

174

while I remember it, have you any idea how long the truck should take to get back to Salzburg, assuming it has no more calls?'

'I have seen the truck leaving,' Christa said thoughtfully. 'He drives like a maniac – in a hurry to get off duty, I suppose. My guess is he has to be in Salzburg one hour after leaving here. As to my whereabouts, I'm off duty today. Traudl is taking down the minutes at the midday conference. . .'

'So where would you normally be?'

'Reading, resting, doing washing and ironing in my room. No one comes near me.' She looked up, her expression more relaxed. 'You could be missed quickly.'

'It's the luck of the draw. Gruber grilled me yesterday – and went away disgusted. I could be left alone today. Sunday. They bring me breakfast at eight, collect the tray half an hour later – and lunch isn't until one-thirty. . .'

'So. . .' Christa was becoming absorbed in the details. 'The truck takes one hour, which means we reach Salzburg at midday. I looked up trains to both Vienna and Munich – since you're so cagey about our destination. I suppose you'll trust me one day. . .' A wistful – not resentful – note crept into her voice. Again Lindsay began to worry about her feelings towards him.

'I have people to protect,' he said shortly.

'I do understand. We reach Salzburg about midday. It's going to be a tight schedule, whichever way we go. There's an express to Vienna at 12.15, one to Munich at 12.30. If it is Munich we might just make it before they realize you are gone. The express arrives at 1.30 p.m., the very moment they bring your lunch. Vienna is well over three hours. . .'

'We'll have to take our chances,' he said quietly. 'There are a lot of imponderables. Whether the truck goes anywhere near the station is just one of them. . .'

'And whether the laundry truck calls Sunday is another,' she reminded him. 'We meet here later?'

'Yes, as near to 10.45 as we can make it.'

'I still think we ought to grab that car.' She stood up and went to the window. 'We know that is available.'

He came up behind her and squeezed her arms reassuringly. 'The laundry truck it is. I've made up my mind.'

'All right.' She turned, looked up at him and produced a Luger 9-mm. pistol from her jacket pocket. 'I took this from a place where it won't be missed for days. I have a spare magazine. I'll give them to you just before we leave. . .' She hesitated.

'Christa, what is it?'

'Ian, I want you to promise me something. If we're on the verge of being captured, shoot me, please. Then maybe you'd better use the next bullet on yourself. . .' She turned away, her voice trembling. 'If we have to go . . . I'd like us to go together. . .'

He felt like hell. He couldn't think what to do, what to say. Just helpless. He reached out to touch her as she remained with her back to him and then dropped his hands to his sides. Her feeling for him was worse than he'd thought. And he couldn't reciprocate the emotion.

'Let's see first whether that truck does call Sundays,' he said roughly and left the room.

'Move the bloody car back into the garage,' Colonel Jaeger rasped.

It was ten o'clock in the morning, heavy snow was falling and the far side of the valley and the mountains beyond were blotted out by the white pall. Jaeger, stiff with standing in one position for so long, so fixed had been his concentration watching the hairpin bend, was frustrated and in a rage.

'We could wait a little longer. . .' Schmidt began.

It was the wrong remark. Jaeger turned on his subordinate and exploded. 'Are you mentally unstable? A few hours ago you were criticizing me for not parking the bloody Mercedes on the front doorstep! Now you propose we hang about here for ever! The men outside from the motor battalion are freezing to death. Do as I damned well tell you. . .'

Schmidt hurried outside the barracks to issue orders to the troops who sat with their legs astride the motor-cycles, banging their gloves together to bring the circulation back into frozen hands. When he had despatched a team he returned nervously to where the SS colonel was striding up and down, pausing to warm his hands at an old-fashioned log-stove.

'They are collecting the car,' he said breathlessly.

'Bormann will be delighted with the great success of the whole idea,' Jaeger commented savagely.

'It was *his* idea?' Schmidt queried as he used a silk handkerchief to clean his glasses. The lenses had steamed up with condensation during his brief excursion outside. The temperature was dropping rapidly.

'Now it hasn't worked, it will become *my* idea – I know Bormann. He always phrases his orders obliquely. And this one was not by order of the Führer. . .'

He broke off as he heard the sound of the Mercedes being driven back towards the garage. It was a tribute to the car that the bloody motor had started up after standing outside for hours in these conditions.

'Those men were supposed to *push* the machine back,' he blazed.

'I'll reprimand the sergeant. . .'

'Oh, don't bother! What does it matter. The whole operation is a farce. I'm going to get something to eat.'

'Colonel,' Schmidt began tactfully, 'the three checkpoints are still on full alert. Shall I phone them orders to stand down?'

At the doorway to the barracks canteen Jaeger paused while he considered the suggestion. Snow flakes were beginning to adhere to the outside of the windows, masking the view. It was going to be a raw outlook.

'Good idea,' he said. 'Men kept on alert pointlessly lose their edge. Tell them to relax. And then come and join me for breakfast. I need someone to talk to – so I can contradict them!' He sighed. 'Sunday! I always hated Sunday – ever since I was a little boy. . .'

Lindsay heard the faint sound of a car engine being started up. He heard the sound because he had left the door of his room slightly ajar after the orderly collected his breakfast tray.

By leaving the door open he would be warned if a guard was posted outside. So far none had appeared. He had no way of knowing that, apart from withdrawing the normal guards to entice him into the trap, Jaeger had sent a large contingent away from the Berghof to reinforce the checkpoints and provide a reserve group of shock troops at a camp close to Salzburg.

Lindsay checked his watch yet again. Exactly 10 a.m. Another three-quarters of an hour before he joined Christa in the anteroom. He opened the door wider and peered out into a deserted corridor. Walking swiftly and silently he reached the window and looked down. The Mercedes had driven forward into view.

The vehicle was now halted with the engine warming up. Two SS men were scraping ice from the windscreen, pausing to melt a fresh area by pressing their gloves over the glass. The unseen driver turned on the wipers which operated jerkily and then settled down into a regular rhythm.

Lindsay stayed well back behind a curtain as he watched the two SS soldiers climb into the back. The car was driven in a sweeping semi-circle and headed out of sight in the direction of the barracks. Lindsay continued to wait but there was no sign of further activity.

At 10.30 he checked the corridor, staircase and entrance hall. When he found they were deserted he slipped down with his case and went inside the anteroom. Christa was pacing restlessly, trying to stifle a sensation of growing panic.

Lindsay watched her while he hid his case behind a huge chest of drawers standing clear of the wall. He would have been much better on his own he thought – but he couldn't leave her now. Advice he had been given by Colonel Browne in Ryder Street kept coming back.

'If you're on the run don't be tempted to link up with anyone – it multiplies the risk of capture ten-fold. Statistics show. . .'

Bugger statistics. He had to get Christa across the border into Switzerland. There he could leave her with a clear conscience – to sit out the rest of the war. She was German-speaking, so she could merge with the population.

'The car is gone. They've taken it away,' Christa remarked and her tone was edgy. 'I suppose you'll say that proves it was a trap they set for us. . .'

'I really don't know. Maybe someone was going to use it and the weather changed their mind. . .'

'You're just saying that to pander to me. . .'

He took three long strides across the room and grasped her with both hands. His voice was low and brutal, his eyes hard.

'Now listen! In less than thirty minutes we're walking out of that door – if the laundry truck ever turns up. We have to dodge the driver, hide ourselves in the back of the truck and from that moment there's no turning back. . .'

He let go with his right hand, reached down and pulled up the leg of his trouser, exposing the knife he had stolen from the galley on board the Führer train.

'I may have to kill the driver,' he went on. 'At some stage the killing will start. So, my girl, unless you get a grip on yourself damned quick you'll be a liability.'

'I was all right at Salzburg when we got off the train,' she said quietly. 'It was just bad luck that Hartmann intervened and stopped us. I'll be all right again – once we're on the move. Ian, I won't let you down. It's the waiting which twists me into knots. . .'

'Join the club.'

He released her and regretted his outburst. She was, of course, right. On previous form she could be relied on. You should always go on previous form, not what people say.

'Are you staying here with me?' she asked.

'Yes.'

'You don't have to. I can wait it out on my own. If someone checks your room it would be safer for you if you were up there – if they search me I'm carrying the Luger. . .'

'Either way it's a risk,' he told her in a businesslike tone as though she were the last consideration. 'I've managed to get down here unseen. My door is closed. If they post a guard they'll just assume I'm inside. They always have done. But if I'm inside, then I have to get past him to get down here again.

179

There's no ideal formula for this kind of situation.' He smiled. 'So just keep on pacing. . .'

At 10.45 he asked her to give him the Luger and spare magazine. He shoved the pistol under his jacket and inside his belt. They went on waiting and neither of them seemed to be able to think of anything to say.

It was debatable which of them checked their watches more regularly. The minutes crawled. 10.50. Outside it was still snowing but less heavily. Lindsay prayed it would keep on falling. Bad weather – plus the fact it was Sunday – were the two factors which might keep everyone indoors long enough. They both checked their watches at the same moment. Their eyes met. *10.59.*

Time is relative the man said, whatever that might mean – whoever the man was – but one thing is certain. Sixty seconds never took longer to tick past. Neither moved. Both stood well clear of the window overlooking the entrance. *11.00 a.m.* . . .

Lindsay had his head cocked to one side, listening for the first sound of the laundry truck's motor. A leaden silence. Outside the snow was falling more thickly, heavy flakes drifting down, spinning slowly in tiny somersaults. *11.01.* . . .

'It isn't coming. . .' Christa began.

Lindsay shushed her with a shake of his head, listening intently. Christa couldn't keep still. She clenched and un-clenched her small hands. The Englishman remained quite motionless, his mouth tight as he concentrated. Waiting it out. Pure hell. A nerve-drainer.

He raised one hand to keep her quiet, held it in mid-air. The distant sound of an engine approaching fast. 'He drives like a maniac,' Christa had said the previous day. Something like that. He motioned her to keep still and moved to the window, sidling close to a curtain edge.

A shape loomed through the snow, burst through the pallid veil, swung in a wild skid through a hundred and eighty degrees so the bonnet faced the way back to Salzburg. He was staring straight at the back of the closed vehicle with a roll-top shutter door. The laundry did call Sundays.

Through an inch-gap in the slightly-opened anteroom door Lindsay looked into the entrance hall. The driver wore a white coat and trousers – overalls – and a peaked cap. He had opened one of the double doors and staggered inside carrying a huge white sack over his shoulder. He disappeared through a doorway on the far side of the hall.

'The truck door's wide open,' called out Christa who was watching from the window.

'Then we move!'

They were both holding their cases. Lindsay opened the door wide and shoved Christa through first. He was careful to close the anteroom door behind him. Christa had already vanished outside. There was no way of knowing how quickly the driver would reappear. Lindsay ran light-footed across the marble floor disfigured with snow patches from the driver's boots and followed Christa.

It was less cold than he had expected, the snow was thinning, the flakes smaller, fewer. She had followed his instructions – he could just see the indentations where, walking on her toes, she had dug into the snow. Moving on his heels, he took great strides. There must be no traces of footprints prominent enough for the driver to see.

He hauled himself up inside the truck and her voice called softly. 'Back here. . .' She had scrambled over piles of linen sacks to the very back of the truck, just behind the driver's cab. He couldn't see her in the semi-dark and that encouraged him. With luck they would remain undiscovered by the driver, unless he searched for a sack close to the cab.

Lindsay buried himself under the pile and she snuggled close to him. He was lying on his case but movement now would be dangerous. Reaching under his jacket, he pulled out the Luger. Her lips spoke direct into his right ear.

'Why the gun? You're not going to shoot him. . .'

'Only if he finds us. Then I grab the driving wheel and we take off. . .'

181

'Let's hope not. . .'

She subsided. *Let's hope not*. Christ! Shooting the driver at this stage would be the last resort. Later, Lindsay would have no compunction, but parked outside the Berghof there were so many hazards.

Someone might hear the shot. The body would have to be concealed. How would they get through the checkpoints with Lindsay at the wheel? He felt Christa stiffen. The driver was returning for a fresh load. They heard him bang his boots against the outside to kick off snow. Submerged under the linen piles they heard him rummaging about and it seemed he was very close. Lindsay hoped to God that – if it came to it – he could eliminate the man with a blow from the barrel rather than firing the weapon.

Clump! He had dropped to the ground with further supplies. They heard the crunch of his heavy-footed tread on the snow. With luck any traces their own feet had left in the snow would be gone. But Lindsay's nerves were tingling. The delivery seemed to be taking forever. And every second they lingered at this point increased the danger of someone noticing he was missing.

Three more times the driver made trips inside the Berghof. Now each time he returned he brought back sacks of dirty linen which he tossed carelessly towards the back. On the third occasion Lindsay saw something which made him freeze.

The driver was approaching the truck. Through a gap between the sacks Lindsay saw exposed – in full view – the forefoot of Christa's left boot. A sack which had previously covered her foot had slithered away. To miss seeing that boot the driver would have to be blind. The crisis had arrived. He took a firm grip on the butt of the Luger.

'God in heaven! This bleedin' weather. . .'

The driver was talking to himself as he scrambled aboard. A man of method, he climbed aboard to ensure the dirty linen was stored at the very back of the truck. Standing upright he

182

peered towards the back, holding the new sack of dirty linen while he recovered his breath.

'Finished, Hans? This weather suit your driving? You bastard, you should be restricted to the autobahn. . .'

Belatedly, an SS guard had appeared and was joshing the driver who stood still holding the sack. He glanced back over his shoulder and shouted at the guard.

'Gunther, you can piss down your trouser leg. I'll be back in Salzburg before noon. Care to join me in the cab?'

'In this weather! You're a bloody lunatic! The checkpoints should slow you down – if you haven't turned the truck over. . .'

Lindsay held his breath. Christa's boot was still sticking out. He dared not mention it to her. And when the driver spotted it he'd call to the guard. . .

The sack of dirty linen sailed through the air and landed on her foot, completely concealing it. *Clump!* The driver had jumped to the ground. There was a grinding rattle. Darkness. He had shut the door.

Crouched over his wheel inside the cab Hans switched on – the fog-lamps, the motor. Gear in, brake released. He was away. He rammed his foot on the accelerator. The truck took off down the winding slope.

Under the sack pile Christa grabbed hold of Lindsay and held on as the vehicle began to sway from side to side. The vehicle picked up more speed. The sacks cushioned them from the buffeting but under them they could feel the wheels sliding. Lindsay guessed they were approaching the hairpin bend. He waited for Hans to reduce speed.

Hans accelerated. He had wiped a peephole in the windscreen but it was still partially misted over. The eery yellow beams of the fog lamps showed the hairpin coming up. He kept his foot well down.

Lindsay held Christa tightly. He felt the rear wheels swinging out of control. Hans let the truck go with the skid. No braking. He held the wheel steady, went with the skid until the vehicle was moving slowly, then gently applied the accelerator. He had navigated the hairpin. He pressed his foot down and headed for the first checkpoint.

In the back of the truck Christa clung to Lindsay. There was sweat on the Englishman's forehead. She let out her breath in a deep sigh.

'He's going to kill us,' she said.

'Rear wheel skid,' Lindsay said in a clipped tone. 'He coped with it perfectly. I'll tell you now where we're heading for – Munich.'

'That's the second express then – the one that departs at 12.30 from Salzburg. If we make it we reach Munich at 1.30 – which is when they'll be bringing your lunch to your room at the Berghof. The alarm will be raised almost at the precise moment we get to Munich. Bormann will react fast – he'll put out an alert for us all over Bavaria.'

'Let's get to Salzburg first,' Lindsay suggested. 'And we'll have about a twenty-four hour wait in Munich before I can meet our contact. Where the hell we'll hole up I don't know. . .'

'I do! Kurt had a small attic hideaway which should still be available. . .'

'Whereabouts in Munich?' he asked casually. 'Near the Feldherrnhalle or the Frauenkirche?'

'Very close to the Frauenkirche. It's in a small alley. It's not much of a place but his aunt hates the Nazis. They put her husband in a labour battalion. It's one reason why Kurt chose the place. . .' She broke off. 'We're stopping. Christ! This is the first checkpoint.'

Inside his cab Hans swore when he saw the barrier like a frontier pole was barring his way at the checkpoint. Bloody fools! Had they nothing better to do in this weather. And there seemed to be more guards about than usual.

He braked but kept the motor running as a strong hint. With a sense of relief he recognized the SS officer approaching as he lowered his window. Hans never alighted from his cab – not for any time-serving bloody soldier!

184

'You are trying to break a record, Hans?' the thin-faced SS man enquired. 'We saw you coming down the mountain – you're going to end up breaking your neck.'

'I'm late for my meal. What's all the fuss? Why the circus?'

'We are searching all vehicles. An exercise. Orders from the Berghof last night. . .'

'Well get on with it – and then lift that ruddy pole!'

'Always so polite, Hans!'

Every word of the conversation could be clearly heard inside the truck. Lindsay gripped the butt of the Luger again. They had to be discovered if the truck was searched. Could he cold-bloodedly press the muzzle of the Luger against Christa's temple and pull the trigger? He had never killed a woman before. . .

A grinding rattle as someone raised the rear door. The temperature dropped even lower as air flooded inside. Christa grasped his gun-hand carefully, lifted it slowly and placed the tip of the muzzle against the side of her head. He didn't take the first pressure on the trigger. Would they use bayonets to prod the sack pile?

A scraping noise – followed by an intake of breath. Someone had clambered up inside the truck. Lindsay felt moisture on the palm of the hand holding the pistol. Christa lay quite inert. What the hell must her thoughts be at this moment? Lindsay had never felt so helpless, a sensation he detested.

A clump of jackboots moving closer. Outside the sound of several voices. He could feel the tension inside Christa's body. The poor kid was petrified with terror. Sounds followed each other in rapid succession. The groaning rumbling of a half-track vehicle nearby. The now familiar rattle of the door at the back being closed. 'Piss off, Hans, and get your lunch. . .' Gear change. Brake release. The truck was moving. . .

'Hans!' A bellowing shout. 'Drive straight through the next two checkpoints.'

They were on their way.

185

Chapter Twenty

At the Berghof the Führer rose at his normal late hour – 11 a.m. – within minutes of Lindsay's and Christa's escape to Salzburg. Following his normal routine, he had gone to bed at 3 a.m.

His bedroom, which had a connecting link via a dressing room with Eva Braun's, was furnished in a spartan fashion. The only decoration on the walls was an oil painting of his mother copied from an old photograph.

One of the most powerful men in the world, he shaved and dressed himself without any help from his valet, Krause. His garb was as ordinary as his late breakfast. He wore his brown tunic with the red swastika armband and trousers.

His breakfast – never varied – consisted of two cups of milk and up to ten pieces of zwieback, the German black rusk. He also consumed several pieces of semi-sweet chocolate which, he was convinced, gave him energy.

He ate alone and standing up, leafing through the latest reports of DNB, the German News Agency. Breakfast was finished in five minutes and then he was ready for the day. He opened the midday military conference attended by Bormann, Keitel, Jodl and other high officers with an unusual remark.

'I have the odd feeling that something disturbing has happened.'

'What might that be, *mein Führer*?' purred Bormann.

'If I knew, I would have told you! Now let's get on. . .'

He adopted a characteristic pose while he listened to Jodl outlining the present position on the Eastern Front, standing with both hands clasped over his lower abdomen. He said nothing, nodding his head occasionally as though in agreement. His silence had the effect of creating an atmosphere of tension.

At one moment he left the conference table over which was spread a large-scale map of Soviet Russia. He stood peering out of a window and then returned to the table. He had been gazing towards Salzburg.

Bormann went berserk when he heard the news. The military conference ended abruptly when Hitler glowered at his generals and left without a word. It was 1.30 p.m. Since it was Sunday, the cook had prepared Lindsay's meal a few minutes early because he was anxious to finish and get away for a few hours. The tray was delivered to the Englishman's empty room at 1.25.

'God in Heaven, Jaeger!' Bormann fumed. 'What kind of security are you running. You plan a trap for Lindsay earlier, it flops – later in the morning he escapes. . .'

'I was handicapped. . .' the Colonel stood his ground '. . . by the fact that my detachment of guards was dispersed over a wide area to spring the trap. A trap you originally suggested. . .'

Bormann, the top of his head level with Jaeger's chest, paused in his tirade. He recognized a quagmire when his foot felt the surface subsiding. If the Führer launched an investigation, this SS hyena would share the blame for the disaster – with himself.

'How could he have got away?' he demanded.

'May I say something?' requested Schmidt, who was standing two paces behind his chief.

Bormann stared at the thin-faced officer who wore rimless glasses. He disliked rimless glasses: they always reminded him of his bitter enemy, Himmler. But Schmidt had an analytical mind. They made a dangerous combination, this pair. Schmidt provided the intellect; Jaeger was the man of action. He nodded: permission to speak.

'There may, I regret, be further bad news,' Schmidt informed him. 'Fräulein Christa Lundt is known to have frequented the company of the Englishman. She, also, appears to be missing. . .'

'Two of them gone!'

'I believe,' Schmidt continued, 'there is only one method of escape they could have used. The laundry truck which calls daily at eleven in the morning. The timing is right. . .'

'The checkpoints!' Bormann raved.

'The alert was cancelled after our plan for the Mercedes trap clearly had not worked,' Jaeger intervened.

Bormann noted the word *our* and suddenly calmed down. Schmidt took the opportunity to make a suggestion. Jaeger would be most grateful if he could divert Bormann's fury.

'The driver of the laundry truck may have information. Shall I call him on the phone?'

It took Schmidt only a few minutes to track down the driver at his home. He passed the phone over to the Reichsleiter who was careful not to panic Hans.

'What was that? An SS officer's uniform missing . . . your depot is close to the railway . . . a couple was seen walking towards the station . . . an SS officer and a girl . . . the Munich express . . . hold on. . .' He looked at Schmidt. 'A railway timetable. Quickly. A train to Munich about 12.30 . . .' He spoke a few more words to the driver before ending the call.

The meticulous Schmidt had already located a timetable and was leafing through the pages. He found the right place as Bormann gave the instruction to Jaeger.

'Get me the chief of Munich SS on the line. I will talk to him. An SS officer's uniform sent for cleaning in that truck has gone missing. Well, Schmidt?'

'If they were able to board the express – and the Lundt girl would probably manage that for them both – they departed Salzburg at 12.30 and arrive Munich at 1.30. . .'

Bormann glanced at a wall-clock. 1.39. 'Let's hope to God it arrives late – they usually do these days.'

Jaeger was holding the receiver, one hand clamped over it while he spoke. 'I have the Munich SS chief on the line. His name is Mayr. . .'

'Bormann speaking. Mayr? Two fugitives from the Berghof . . . an Englishman and a German girl . . . descriptions . . . suspected they are aboard the 12.30 express from Salzburg arriving at Munich about this moment. The man may be wearing SS uniform . . . seal off the station. . .'

'The train is going to arrive late,' Christa commented. 'It was that hold-up at Rosenheim. . .'

Lindsay borrowed her hand-mirror to check his appearance. He was wearing the SS officer's uniform Christa had seen projecting from one of the linen sacks in the laundry truck. There was a blemish on the left sleeve. Otherwise it was in impeccable condition. It fitted him better than he had feared. A bit tight round the collar. He adjusted the peaked cap so it hid the top part of his face and glanced round the mailvan they had travelled inside from Salzburg. He checked his watch. 1.40 p.m. Ten minutes late.

Moving slowly, the train began to rumble over points. He looked at Christa who stood close to the door with her suitcase. They'd agreed they must leave the coach as soon as it stopped. Earlier he had used his knife to try and manipulate the outside bolt open. On the verge of giving up, he felt the bolt elevate and clang as it dropped free.

'We're coming in now,' Christa said calmly. 'There's a system of points where the tracks converge. . .'

'Get to the far end of the coach,' Lindsay ordered.

'I know this station – it's huge,' she protested.

'Do as you're bloody well told.'

She glowered and then obeyed his instruction. Lindsay took up a position to one side of the sliding door, the knife held in his right hand, the suitcase in his left. Slipping inside the mailvan at Salzburg had been easy. Munich could be more dangerous.

Major Hugo Bruckner of the SS stood on the platform as the Salzburg express came in. A burly man of medium height, he took his duties very seriously. He had a particular detestation for army deserters – probably because he had served a long stint on the Russian front. They travelled about on trains. A favourite hiding-place was the mailvan which he could see approaching.

189

The passenger coaches slid past him, doors already opening as troops and civilians prepared to alight and join the jostling mob in the concourse. He stiffened as his keen eyes spotted the loose bolt on the mail-van. It looked as though he might gather up more cannon fodder for the Eastern Front – the inevitable destination of deserters caught in the act.

The train stopped. Bruckner stood on an isolated portion of the platform and noted the door was ajar a couple of centimetres, enough for anyone hidden inside to peer out. The darkness inside the mail-van was making it difficult for Bruckner to see into the coach but he had no fear of slimy deserters. He threw the door to one side and climbed aboard.

The coach was empty. He looked to his right and Lindsay was now within three feet of him. It was the SS uniform which momentarily froze Bruckner's reflexes – the last person he had expected to encounter was an SS officer. . .

Lindsay's right hand flashed up and drove down with all his strength behind the vicious lunge. The blade slid off the edge of the German's breastbone and plunged up to the hilt. Lindsay let go of the handle and Bruckner staggered back inside the coach with a grunt of surprise.

Christa watched, one hand to her mouth, watched Bruckner toppling back with the knife protruding from his chest like a decoration. A red lake had appeared and was welling over his uniform. Lindsay put an arm round his neck, well clear of the blood, hauled him deep inside the van and dropped him in the place where they had hidden.

He piled mail-bags on top of the dead German with furious haste. Christa had peered out and had dropped to the platform. He grabbed his case and followed her. Catching up with the girl, he saw her face was white.

'I think I'm going to be sick. . .'

'Reactions come later. Get a hold on yourself! You said you knew this station. So do your stuff – get us out of it. . .'

His violent verbal assault did the trick. She glared at him and recovered, then quickened her pace. 'Look at those post trolleys coming towards us – they're heading for the mail-van. . .'

Killing the German had been a reflex action, something he knew he would have to do sooner or later. The crocodile of mail trolleys, proceeding down the platform towards them, was something unforeseen. They'd never get clear of the station before the body was found. . .

Christa was moving at almost a running pace, taking long strides, and now they were approaching the end of the platform. No inspectors at the barrier – in Germany tickets were checked on the train while in motion. He glanced back. The trolley cavalcade, pulled by one man, pushed by another, had almost reached the mail-van. They walked through the barrier.

They were caught up in the milling mob, submerged by it as people criss-crossed the concourse. Christa linked her arm inside his and guided him towards an exit. At the sight of the SS uniform other passengers made way for them. It speeded their passage but drew attention to them.

'How far is it to this flat your fiancé had?'

'Not far. Five minutes by tram. . .'

'If there is an alarm out they'll be looking for two people – a man and a girl. We must separate. . .'

'All right. . .'

No more arguments as she continued walking, opened her purse and instructed him.

'We board the same tram. I get on first – so you can see what I do. Here is the coin you'll need for the fare. You get *on* at the front – *off* at the back. So find a seat *behind* me.'

Again it amazed him. She was so incredibly cool when the pressure was on, thinking ahead, every little detail. That brief lapse after the killing of the SS officer. Who wouldn't get the urge to vomit – the macabre sight of the German stepping backwards with the knife sticking out of the middle of his chest. . . ?

'I'm going ahead now,' she warned. 'Oh, my God! Look – the SS are arriving! *Don't* lose me. . .'

The SS were indeed arriving in force. Responding swiftly and efficiently to Bormann's personal call, SS chief, Mayr, was deploying his troops round the main station.

191

'Swamp the place!' he had ordered. 'Throw a cordon round the whole district! Check all papers – pay particular attention to personnel in SS uniform already there. You are looking for an officer – with a girl. The Reichsleiter himself says they must be captured. . .'

Proceeding systematically, the first truckload was spilling out troops at the main entrance at the very moment Christa, followed by Lindsay, walked out of a side entrance.

She headed straight for a tram where the last passengers were filing aboard. Climbing inside she bought her ticket and walked along the crowded central corridor. There were no seats left so she stood.

Lindsay was the last passenger to board the tram. Collecting his ticket, he made his way towards a position behind where Christa stood. A lame man with his leg thrust out into the corridor looked at the new arrival apprehensively and slowly stood up, offering his seat.

The Englishman very nearly told him to sit down and then remembered the uniform he was wearing. He sank down in the seat and gazed ahead. Staring over her shoulder, Christa gave a sigh of relief. The doors closed, a warning bell rang and the tram moved off.

It was turning in front of the station to proceed down a main street when – through the rear window – she saw an SS man standing in front of the next tram to stop it moving off. New truckloads of SS were passing the tram in the opposite direction, horns blaring as the drivers forced other traffic to the kerb.

Three motor-cycles with sidecars filled with more SS reinforcements roared past towards the station. Should they get off at the next stop before whoever was in command thought of sending those motor-cycles in pursuit of their tram, Christa wondered?

She had never known a tram seem to move more ponderously. She forced herself to keep an expression of indifference on her face as she noticed a man in army uniform watching her. He stood up.

'Take my seat, Fräulein. You look tired. You have had a long journey?'

'Thank you.' She gave him a brief smile. 'But I'm getting off at the next stop. . .'

The short encounter was unfortunate, could even be dangerous. The German sergeant who had taken a fancy to her – she had seen it in his eyes – would remember her if questioned later. Worse, he would remember the stop where she alighted.

The tram was stopping. She picked up her case and walked past the sergeant without a glance in his direction. Lindsay waited until she was descending the steps, got up quickly and followed her. He was behind her on the crowded pavement when he glanced back. The tram they had travelled aboard was surrounded by army motor-cycle patrols. An SS officer was entering the vehicle with the obvious intention of questioning everyone aboard.

The Führer's moods were always unpredictable. He took the news that the two fugitives had escaped from the train at Munich with surprising calm, even caution. Removing his spectacles – he was never photographed wearing them – he laid aside the papers he had been studying and listened as Bormann ranted on.

'Mayr did not move fast enough. That phone call from him at the Munich station proves it. They travelled in the mail-van. They killed the SS officer Bruckner whose body was found in the mail-van and fled. . .'

'Army deserters often travel in mail-vans,' Hitler observed.

'Mayr also reported a tram which had just left the station was stopped by motor-cycle patrols. Witnesses aboard provided very clear descriptions of two passengers who had just left it, one man in the uniform of an SS officer and a girl who sounds exactly like Christa Lundt. . .'

'Now he tells me. . .'

Hitler, seated on a couch, looked at Jaeger and Schmidt while he played with the spectacles in his lap. Keitel and Jodl, who had returned to clear up a point arising from the midday conference, were also present. So far they had preserved a discreet silence.

'What do you think, Keitel?' the Führer asked suddenly.

'They won't get far. . .'

'Mayr is instituting a search of the whole city. . .' Bormann burst out. 'I agree with the Field Marshal. . .'

'That's because neither of you knows what you are talking about,' Jaeger intervened bluntly. 'Mayr has a monumental task. . .'

'So,' the Führer commented, using a phrase which expressed his general attitude and summed up the secret of his rise to power, 'a way can be found for everything. . .'

An hour later Mayr had returned to his Munich barracks when the strange phone call came through. He picked up the receiver and identified himself. It was the Berghof again.

'Bormann speaking! Information has reached me that Lindsay has a rendezvous with an Allied agent at the Frauenkirche. . .'

The voice was oddly muffled. Mayr thought it hardly sounded like the Reichsleiter. Still, he was not a man whose identity it would be wise to question. The voice went on talking.

' . . . the agent waits at the rendezvous at 1100 hours every Monday. Make your dispositions accordingly and on no account mention this call to anyone. By order of the Führer. . . !'

Still mystified, Mayr replaced the receiver. Tomorrow was Monday. He would be waiting for this Allied agent at the Frauenkirche.

Chapter Twenty-One

'Just in time,' said Christa. 'Here we are, and we're clear of the street.'

'They'll search the whole area,' Lindsay warned. 'Checking on that tram was only the start. . .'

They were standing in a narrow alley between ancient walls and the only sign it was daytime was the thin avenue of sky way above their heads. There was a smell of tomcat. The cobbles beneath their feet were slimy. The buildings had a condemned look. She extracted a key from her purse, inserted it into the lock of a new solid wooden door decorated with iron studs and paused before she opened it.

'Kurt came here on leave and when he was on the run. His Aunt Helga lives here. As I told you, they took her husband for the labour battalions. She hates the Nazis. Your uniform will frighten her. Wait on the third landing while I talk to her. . .'

It was so dark inside, Lindsay could see nothing when she had shut the outer door. He felt his way up the narrow staircase on his own, clutching the greasy banister rail. Counting the landings, he waited on the third while Christa went on up the fourth flight. He wrinkled his nose at the musty smell; the place had an uninhabited feel. Was the aunt the only occupant, he wondered? Above him he saw light filter out as he heard a door open.

There was a whispered conversation which went with the atmosphere of the place. A pungent odour of urine drifted out from an open door on his landing. He peered inside and saw by the half-light a window smeared with dirt, a lavatory that had not been flushed for some time.

'Ian! Come up.'

Christa's voice. His hand slipped easily up over a section of recently polished banister. At the top, a middle-aged woman with strong features stood beside Christa. Ignoring the uniform, she frowned as she examined his face. 'He has some identification?' she demanded.

'Have you?' Christa queried. 'This is Aunt Helga. She is very cautious. . .'

'You need to be these days,' the woman interjected grimly. 'It is rumoured there is an underground network which smuggles Allied fliers to Switzerland. The Gestapo use their own agents in the guise of British or Americans to try and infiltrate the network. . .'

'I have my RAF identity card,' Lindsay began.

'And why did they not take this document from you?' demanded the gaunt-faced woman as she took the folder from Lindsay and checked it carefully, comparing the photograph with its owner. 'Christa has told me you were a prisoner. . .'

'They did. . .' Lindsay caught Christa's warning glance. He was to reveal only the minimum information. 'A Gestapo man called Gruber kept it for two days – doubtless to have it photographed for his files. . .'

'They let him have it back on orders from higher up,' Christa said quickly. 'He is a Wing Commander and I think they hoped to obtain valuable information from him. . .'

'Take it!' Helga had used her flowered apron to wipe it clean of her fingerprints and thrust it at him, holding it between the cloth of the apron. 'Come inside. I must insist you give me that uniform so I can burn it.'

'The smell will be foul,' Lindsay observed with an attempt at humour but Helga remained stern and aloof.

'We burn anything these days to keep warm. We live with foul smells.' She closed and locked the door of the apartment and went over to the stove where she picked up an iron poker, raised the lid and stirred the smouldering contents. He had the impression she had just armed herself with a weapon. Her next question confirmed his suspicion.

'Where did you obtain that SS uniform from?'

'Aunt Helga!' Christa protested. 'I got it for him – it doesn't matter how. You've got to trust him. I have been to England

and I tested him when first we met. Show him the hiding-place.'

'The one Kurt made for himself and was never able to use?' she said bitterly. 'Very well, but I will need that uniform to burn piece by piece. . .'

The uniform seemed to be an obsession with her. Lindsay guessed she was younger than her weathered appearance. God knew what she had suffered.

'We will get warning this time,' Helga remarked, 'if there is an emergency. A good friend of mine in the country built a fresh door in the alley strong enough to resist cannon-shot. They have to ring the bell now and wait. When they came for Kurt they simply smashed the door in. . .'

The hiding-place was reached by an ingeniously camouflaged trap-door hinged in the roof alongside a cross-beam. Helga fetched a pair of steps from the kitchen, stood them in a certain place and climbed up, holding a thin-bladed knife.

'You insert the knife tip next to this hook on the beam,' she explained. 'Shove it up like you would your tool into a woman. . .' Lindsay glanced at Christa, who stared across the room, blushing. 'The knife tip,' Helga continued, 'impinges on a steel bar which Kurt attached to the trap-door. Push it up. So. . . !'

A square section of the seemingly continuous ceiling elevated to expose a dark hole. Helga dropped the trap in position and came back down the steps. She was carrying them back into the kitchen when she growled the invitation.

'If you are hungry I can provide some discoloured and tasteless liquid which we call soup. At least it will be hot. . .'

'You've been accepted!' Christa whispered.

At 3 p.m., precisely, one hour after their arrival at the spotless apartment of Helga, a police detachment called to search the whole building.

The clapper of the large bowl-shaped bell above the apartment door was hammering away like a machine-gun non-stop. Christa swallowed the remnants of her watery coffee and jumped up from the table.

197

'What the hell's that?'

'Front door bell in the alley,' Helga said laconically.

She opened a window and leaned far out beyond the dormer overhang to look down a sheer wall into the alley beneath. Waving a hand, she shouted something Lindsay, who had also stood up, did not catch. Withdrawing her head she walked into the kitchen and came back with the pair of steps.

'Looks like the whole Munich police force is down there. Stay in the attic until I tap three times on the trap with my broom-handle. Don't forget your cigarette pack, Mr Lindsay. . .'

He took the knife she handed him and shinned up the steps. He managed to operate the primitive opening device first time and reached down for his suitcase which Christa was holding. Helga was clearing the table of cups and plates, leaving only crockery she had used herself.

The bell started hammering again. Lindsay carted Christa's case up to the attic while the girl collected stubs of cigarettes, wrapped them in a piece of newspaper and shoved it inside her coat pocket.

'My cap. . .' Lindsay called down.

She rammed it on her head and climbed the steps, grabbing the hand the Englishman extended to haul her up inside the attic. Helga came back, took the steps away and reappeared holding a stick with a knobbly handle. She developed a limp as she went towards the door, looking up at the two faces peering down.

'Rheumatism,' she said drily. 'Takes me ages to get down those stairs. . .'

It was the nearest Helga had come to displaying a sense of humour since their arrival. Lindsay closed the flap and felt for the bolt. He rammed it home and waited. The trap-door was made of knotted wood like the rest of the ceiling. Poor Kurt had made a skilful job of concealing the trap-door. Christa switched on a small torch she had brought from the kitchen.

The attic had a Disney-like character – roofs slanting at steep angles instead of walls. The floor was boarded over the rafters. Two tiny dormer windows had been masked with heavy curtains which let in no daylight. There were even two sleeping bags and Christa had settled herself on one.

'Get on the other sleeping-bag,' she warned. 'The floor-boards creak. . .'

'You know this place well?'

'Yes.' She nodded, her expression wistful. Lindsay reflected she had spent time with Kurt in this tiny, hidden world. He had eased himself on to the sleeping-bag next to the trap-door when they heard voices below, voices they could hear with surprising clarity. The police had arrived.

In the room below, Helga was chiding police sergeant Berg, a man of fifty-eight with an ample stomach and a flowing moustache. He had two men with him and instructed them to start the search.

'A body can't even finish her meagre meal without you invading her privacy,' Helga growled, leaning on her stick. 'There ought to be a law against it. . .'

'We are the law,' Berg reminded her amiably.

'Then there ought to be a law against the law!'

'We're looking for a man and a woman,' Berg explained in a conciliatory tone. 'The man is wearing an SS uniform. . .'

'I would let the SS into my place! Give him a meal – make him feel at home! Like bloody hell I would. . .'

'Now, Helga, I'm only doing my duty.'

'Then tell them to be careful in my kitchen. I can hear them messing about with crockery.'

It was at that moment when the knot of wood fell from the trap-door into the room below. Lindsay had pressed his ear to the trap to hear more clearly and was appalled. He distinctly heared it *ping* on the floor of the room below during a brief pause in the conversation. He heard Berg's reaction.

'What was that?'

The Englishman saw Christa's hand clench before she switched-ed off the torch. Without touching the woodwork, he peered down with one eye through the hole the fallen knot had left. He had a clear view of the room.

Berg had been standing looking out of the window with his back to Helga when the knot fell. Helga sighed and moved her stick four inches, covering the knot with the tip of her stick. Berg had turned round and was looking suspiciously at her. There was no smile on his face now. He had become the official policeman.

'The stove, of course!' rasped Helga. 'Sometimes,' she went on with withering sarcasm, 'I get hold of a piece of wood I can actually burn in it! Is there a law against that too?'

Through the spy-hole Lindsay watched and held his breath. The knot of wood was larger than the tip of her stick. Berg had only to look down. . . His next move would be to look *up*. And since the policeman was not wearing glasses his eyesight was probably excellent.

Helga, her mouth tight and surly, held Berg's gaze, then she went on talking, her manner aggressive. 'You haven't looked inside that big cupboard yet. Maybe I have your SS man hidden away behind my few clothes. There's plenty of room, dumbhead!'

Berg was so annoyed he went to the cupboard and opened both doors. Helga stooped quickly, picked up the knot of wood and hobbled over to the stove. She used one hand to lift up the lid with the poker and with the other flipped the knot inside. Berg closed the doors of the cupboard and swung round.

'Helga, I don't like this any more than you do. The man wearing SS uniform is British. . .'

'I know! He has a hooked nose and a scar on his right cheek.'

'You've seen him!'

'Berg, you fell for that one, you old fool!' She cackled, waving her stick at him in a mock threatening gesture. 'Time they put you out to grass!'

She glared as the other two policemen reappeared respectively from the bedroom and the kitchen. They both shook their heads. Pointing her stick at the door to the outer landing, Helga growled at them.

'You know the way out, or have you forgotten the layout of this luxurious apartment?'

Berg made a gesture for them to leave, closed the door and came back into the room. He stood exactly beneath the hole in the trap-door. He only had to glance up. . . Lindsay tensed. Did he know of the existence of the attic?

Berg reached inside his coat pocket and brought out a round tin which he presented to Helga. 'My brother came on leave from Tunisia a week ago. They captured an English truck which had lost its way in the mountains. Stacked with the stuff – English coffee. Lyons. Something for the trouble you've been caused. . .'

'Bribery! Black market, too!' Helga's claw-like hand reached out and grasped the tin. 'You're a villain, Berg. You know that? I may drink your health with the first cup.'

'I'll be going – but to save you more trouble I'll leave this document which confirms this building has been searched.' Producing a piece of paper he spread it on the table, dated and signed it and gave it to her. 'If the SS arrive wave this in their faces. It's signed by the Munich chief of police as well as myself.'

'I'll see you downstairs. No, don't argue! I want to make sure that outer door to the alley is locked and bolted myself. You wouldn't believe the people who find their way down that alley in the dark.'

'Believe me, I would,' Berg said vehemently.

The door closed and the flat was suddenly unnaturally hushed. In the attic Christa let out a sigh of relief and stretched her aching limbs. She had remained cramped in one position during the whole tense ordeal.

'When that knot of wood came loose I could have screamed,' she said.

'How did you know?'

She grasped his hand and pointed it upwards. Lindsay saw above him a distorted blip of light on the slanting roof, light from the room below. He told her what had happened.

'She's a gutsy old girl,' he remarked. 'Now she's making sure they leave the premises. While she's away there are things you should know in case something happens to me before we make the rendezvous tomorrow. At exactly eleven in the morning in front of the Frauenkirche. . .'

He explained every detail of how to link up with the agent, Paco. She nestled up close to him in the dark, listening carefully. He then went on to tell her something else.

'If you alone get through to Switzerland with Paco. . .'

'We *both* get through or not at all,' she said fiercely.

'It's wartime. For God's sake, listen. The Allied Command want to know the location of the Führer's secret headquarters. You can tell them that better than I can. The second thing they want to know is who is controlling the German war machine. Well, it's the Führer himself. . .' He paused, wondering whether to go on.

'There's something else, isn't there?' she said quietly. 'About the Führer. . .'

'Go on. . .'

'Ever since he returned from that trip to the Eastern Front at Smolensk he's seemed different. I don't think other people have noticed because they're so frightened of him – including Keitel and Jodl. And ever since he arrived back he's either listened and said nothing – or else screamed at them. The way he walks isn't quite right. There are other things, little things only a woman would notice. It's uncanny – I've felt I was in the presence of his twin brother – except that he hadn't one. . .'

'You said *hadn't* – past tense. Your feeling must be strong. I notice you didn't mention Bormann when you referred to Keitel and Jodl. . .'

'Bormann also has been acting strangely since the Führer's return. Every time during a military conference when I looked at the Führer, trying to work out what seemed different, I found Bormann watching me like a cat – as though trying to make up his mind about something.'

'Something about the Führer?'

'No! Something about *me* – whether I had noticed the change. . .'

'*The change*. Christa, you've put your finger on it. They've found a dummy Führer – Bormann has, I'm certain. While at the Berghof the first time I witnessed a nightmare scene. . .'

He told her about the man gesturing and screaming at the top of his voice inside the circle of mirrors. Her fingers gripped his arm tightly as he went on. At one moment she had been stroking the edge of his jaw but now she was motionless.

'When was this?' she said eventually. 'I told you – that part of the Berghof was always sealed off by Commandant Müller. . .'

'When I saw the spit image of Adolf Hitler pirouetting inside the circle of mirrors at the Berghof, the Führer was a thousand miles away at Smolensk. . .'

'There are *two* of them? How is that possible, Ian?'

'I don't know. All I know is that it is a fact. Now what you say confirms that the Hitler who boarded the plane for Smolensk was not the same man who stepped off it when the plane returned. . .'

'Is it a plot?' she wondered aloud.

'People always think of plots, conspiracies – when so often the truth is quite simple. What holds up the entire edifice of the Nazi regime, stops the generals launching a military coup?'

'The Führer. . .'

'So whatever happens there has to be a Führer. Bormann, Goebbels, Goering, Ribbentrop and all the others – to say nothing of Keitel and Jodl, the whole SS and Gestapo apparatus – all of them depend for *their* continuing existence on the continuing existence of the *Führer*!'

'You mean. . .'

'Let me finish. If any one of those top people *did* suspect a switch had been made would they dare even mention it? They'd go along with the deception. . .'

'What about the generals who disagree with Hitler. Guderian, for example. . .'

'How often do men like that visit the Führer these days now he's locked himself away at the Wolf's Lair with occasional trips to the Berghof?'

'Very seldom. They *expect* to see the Führer. . .' Christa said slowly.

'So the fact that a substitute may have taken his place would never even cross their minds – especially if the double is convincing enough. And from what I saw during my first stay at the Berghof this unknown man has had plenty of time to perfect his act.'

'There's Eva Braun,' Christa reminded him. 'She's bound to detect the impersonation. . .'

'And how strong is her position without the Führer? What's she like, incidentally?'

'Attractive and empty-headed. Spends most of her time at the Berghof making herself up and thinks of nothing except clothes. She's vain, often grumbles about the lack of attention paid to her by the Führer. . .'

'So the dummy has been on the spot to entertain her during the Führer's long absences. They could even have been carrying on an affair,' Lindsay suggested. What would *her* position be without the Führer?' he repeated.

'She'd find herself in the gutter.' Christa's tone was unequivocal. 'She's hated by the wives of the other Nazis – Ribbentrop, Goebbels and so on. My God, I'm beginning to think you could be right. It would also explain why Commandant Müller sealed off that area of the Berghof. . .'

'And why Commandant Müller had to have an "accident" just about the time the switch would be made by Bormann. I'm sure Müller was murdered – he wasn't the type to commit suicide – or fall over the edge of the Kehlstein parapet. Didn't you say there was a very loud explosion about the time the Führer's plane was due back from Smolensk?'

'It was like a bomb going off. . .'

'His plane must have crashed,' Lindsay conjectured. 'Who went to the airfield to meet the plane?'

'Martin Bormann.'

'The Brown Shadow. Always at his master's side – and wielding immense power "by order of the Führer". Only someone with that power could work the trick.'

'You think the plane crashed by accident?' Christa asked.

'What was the weather like?'

'Diabolical. The fog was at tree height. They said the plane had diverted to another airfield.'

'I'm a flier. I've seen that fog at the Wolf's Lair. Landing a plane under those conditions would be near-suicide. . .'

'The Führer was always impatient. He probably over-ruled the pilot.'

'You realize what this means if we're right? Bormann will send out a horde of men to catch us with orders to shoot on sight. We know too much to live.'

Chapter Twenty-Two

It was crisis Monday – the day of the rendezvous with Paco. The previous night Christa and Lindsay had slept inside the sleeping-bags in the attic, to protect Helga in case the SS arrived.

'It's a grey day – come and look,' said Christa.

She had pulled aside the curtain masking the tiny dormer window perched high on the top of the building. Lindsay joined her and peered out. Above nearby rooftops loomed two giant domes – once copper-coloured and now green with verdigris. Christa pointed to them.

'That's the Frauenkirche.'

'Close enough. According to the map I studied in London there's a large open space in front. At eleven o'clock will there be many people about?'

'Housewives going from shop to shop trying to find some place which has just had a delivery. Everything is whipped the moment it arrives. Do we walk together this time? You'll be in civilian clothes. . .'

'Yes.'

It wasn't the perfect arrangement – there would probably be patrols out looking for a man and a girl but he sensed her

205

need for reassurance of his presence. Also he had no idea how Paco planned to get them away. If a vehicle was involved they wouldn't want to waste a second getting inside it.

By 10.30 a.m. they had eaten the meagre breakfast Helga supplied, but she had generously reinforced it with two large cups of the Lyons coffee Sergeant Berg had given her.

'You're not wasting any time,' Lindsay observed.

Up early, Helga had spread the SS uniform out on another table and, using a pair of pinking shears, had cut it into small pieces ready for burning. She had removed the metal buttons and stored them in a small bag.

'They go down a drain three kilometres from here,' she remarked.

An old wooden chair stood near the stove with a large axe on the seat. Helga gestured towards it. 'I break that up – the wood will help to burn the cloth. The tray of cold ashes go into another bag and will be dumped in a litter bin – again a good distance from my apartment.'

She provided Lindsay with a selection of shabby trousers, coats and jackets and he tried them on quickly. The trousers fitted him well but the jackets were tight and a little short in the sleeves.

'It doesn't matter,' Helga commented. 'In Germany today we wear anything we can lay our hands on. Your problem will be your face.'

'My face?'

'Too young – the face of a possible deserter.' She fetched the stick she had used to fool Berg. 'Take this and limp – you've been badly wounded, unfit for further service, discharged from the Army. I suppose it's the same in England – the streets crawling with cripples. . .'

Lindsay was careful not to disillusion her. Unlike the Wehrmacht, the British had not been minced up in the barbaric Soviet grinding machine, had not fought Cossacks who, when German troops raised their hands in surrender, rode down the line slicing off the hands at the wrists with their swords.

He checked himself in a mirror and was amazed at the

transformation. His blond hair helped – it gave him a Teutonic look. He shoved his Luger down inside his belt, left the jacket loose for ease of access and fastened only one button of the overcoat.

'These were Kurt's things?' he asked quietly.

'Yes. Berg knew he was here but said what the hell – the war was crazy anyway. Would the average Englishman hate the average German if he met him? Or the other way round?' She drew herself up erect. 'You're English – do you hate me?'

'For God's sake, after what you've done. . .'

'You'd better go or you'll be late for your appointment,' she said severely, cutting off the Englishman in mid-sentence.

Christa hugged Helga and, picking up her suitcase, ran out of the apartment, her eyes brimming. Lindsay picked up his own case, looked at Helga who had picked up the axe and waved it to get him moving. He heard her lock the apartment door as he fumbled his way down the beastly staircase.

'. . . you'll be late for your appointment.'

The old woman was clever. She'd dismissed them as though they were on their way to attend some business meeting, knowing the tension they must be experiencing as they made their way to their uncertain rendezvous.

High up in the attic overlooking the Frauenkirche, Paco focused the lenses of the field-glasses and slowly scanned the Neuhauser-Kaufigerstrasse, lingering on the open space in front of the great church. A road-sweeper stood near the entrance, wielding his bristle-broom which was almost worn down to the handle. Nearby stood his innocent-looking wheeled trash-bin. As he cleaned the pavement he dragged his left leg.

Paco checked the time. *10.55.* If the English agent was coming he had to appear within the next five minutes. So far there was no suspicious activity in the area – only a handful of housewives wearily trudging past on their way to the next stop. Some of them would have been up at six o'clock to make an early start.

Paco climbed down the winding staircase from the observation point and hurried to the ground floor. Dressed in an astrakhan coat with a matching Russian-style hat pulled well down over the ears, Paco was a sturdily built figure who gave an impression of some wealth.

From a secret cupboard on the ground floor the agent collected a violin case. Inside it was a Schmeisser machine-pistol, fully loaded.

Christa led the way through a maze of cobbled alleys. Looking up, Lindsay caught the occasional glimpse of the twin green domes. It told him how close they were to their destination. How the hell was Paco going to get them away safely? The problem had irked him for some time.

'Stop! Get into a doorway!'

Inside yet another slit-like alley Christa called out the warning and pressed herself into the alcove of a doorway. Lindsay obeyed, the case in his left hand. His right hand slipped under his jacket and gripped the butt of the Luger. He peered along the alley to the street at the end.

A camouflaged military truck, moving very slowly, slid across the gap at the alley's end. He even saw rifles projecting from the open rear, presumably held by troops sitting inside the vehicle. He checked his watch. *10.58!* God, they were going to be late. Would Paco wait – or even turn up at all?

'All right now,' Christa called out.

'How did you know?' he asked as he caught up with her.

'You learn to recognize the sound of an Army truck – I just hope they're not deploying in front of the Frauenkirche.'

'There must be a lot of military stuff moving through here all the time,' he said confidently. 'How close are we?'

'Across that street, down the alley opposite – and then we've arrived.'

'So now I take the lead. If there's trouble – if only one of us can get away with Paco – you're elected. . .'

'No, I couldn't leave you. . .'

'Don't give me trouble now, you bloody fool!'

He left her behind, but not before he saw the stricken look on her face at the way he had reacted. He had never spoken to her like that before. He emerged from the alley, glancing both ways. A queue of people formed a long crocodile outside a shop. Others hurried to join it. No police. No troops. He crossed the street and entered the alley. Behind him the click-clack of Christa's shoes hurried to catch up. He paused inside the alley and turned. He hugged her briefly, still holding his case.

'I'm sorry,' he said quickly, 'but someone has to get to London with the information. It's vital.'

'I do understand, Ian.'

Her face flooded with relief. She smiled bravely. He kissed her briefly. She bit her lips to hold back the tears.

'I won't be a burden, I promise. . .'

'A burden! Good God, I'd never have got this far without you. Now, come on, we have to get moving. What's that bell striking?'

'Eleven o'clock. The Frauenkirche is at the end of this alley.'

A turmoil of emotion. Nerves tautened with stark fear. It was inevitable, Lindsay thought as he walked rapidly down the shadowed alley with Christa at his heels. If only the girl hadn't fallen in love with him.

They were out in the open. It was a visual shock. After scuttling like rabbits through a series of warrens, the wide open spaces were frightening. You felt so exposed. Lindsay paused, Christa beside him, to survey the view.

The vast edifice of the Frauenkirche towered above them to the right. A Volkswagen with an ugly contraption mounted on its body – a device for storing synthetic fuel – drove slowly past, its motor sputtering. In the distance a uniformed chauffeur opened the rear door of a green Mercedes while a booted figure wearing an astrakhan coat and hat climbed inside.

Nearer to the Frauenkirche a large delivery van stood parked by the kerb while the driver buried his head under the bonnet. It was getting so that nothing worked for long. Most skilled mechanics were at the front. A road-sweeper nearby brushed the flagstones with a bristle broom, dragging one leg. Lindsay walked in front of the Frauenkirche, placed a half-smoked cigarette in his mouth with his left hand, lit it, smoked a few puffs and stubbed it beneath his left foot.

The sky was heavily overcast. A sea of grey clouds pressed down on Munich. The atmosphere was turgid, plucked at the nerves. A gentle, chilling drizzle began to fall, casting a misty veil over the city. Lindsay wondered how long he should stay there, conspicuous by his lack of movement.

The green Mercedes was moving now, heading towards them at speed. Lindsay watched it approach – it seemed unlikely. . .

'Papers! Your papers!'

'Look out, Ian. . . !' There was desperation in Christa's urgent cry. '*Behind you!*'

The bastards had hidden inside the church. Two SS men. One, a tall individual confidently extending his hand for the demanded papers. The second, shorter and plump, cradled a machine-pistol under his arm.

Lindsay spun round, had a snapshot vision of the two men, then his attention was caught by movement beyond the Frauenkirche. The driver had lifted his head from underneath the bonnet of the delivery van and men in grey uniform carrying rifles were jumping out of the back.

Which way to go?

There was a skidding scream of tyres, a grinding jamming of car brakes. The green Mercedes slid to the edge of the kerb close to them. The figure in the back had thrown open the rear door.

The road-sweeper had lost his limp, had dropped his broom, was rummaging inside the wheeled trash-bin. He jerked erect holding something in either hand. Lindsay recognised the stick-grenades he was gripping. They sailed through the air, landed in front of the grey-clad soldiers from the delivery van. They detonated with dull thumps.

The soldiers performed weird acrobatic motions, jumping upwards like marionettes on strings, hurling their rifles away, toppling backwards. The road-sweeper had hurled his third missile. It landed close to the same spot and a balloon of dark

210

vapour spread and blotted out van and stricken soldiers. Smoke bomb. . .

A hand reached out from the rear of the Mercedes and gripped his wrist. A voice called out the order. In English.

'Get inside, you fool! You want to get us all killed. . .'

'The girl first. . .'

Lindsay turned to grab Christa, to throw her if necessary head first inside the back of the car. She wasn't within grabbing distance. A horrific sight met his eyes. He yelled like a crazed animal.

He had dropped the suitcase. The astrakhan-clad figure who had given him the abrupt order still clung to his left hand with an iron grasp. With his right hand he hauled out the Luger and aimed it. He was beside himself with terror.

The SS man – the short, fat-bellied swine – with the machine-pistol was pointing the muzzle at Lindsay to cut him down. But Christa was standing in the way – deliberately masking his line of fire. Oh God, Oh God, Oh dear God. . . !'

The SS man pressed the trigger, emptied half the magazine into her. She slumped forward, both hands holding her stomach. The blood was drenching the pavement. Above her drooping body the fat SS man appeared. He raised the muzzle of his weapon. Lindsay shot him twice in the face, his aim true, his hand steady as a rock.

He fired a third time but the hand gripping his other wrist had jerked him at the same moment and the shot went wide. It made no difference. The SS man had fallen alongside his victim.

'If you don't get into this car I'll shoot you myself,' the voice in English snapped. 'She's dead – can't you see that. . .'

He climbed inside the car, slamming the door shut, aware now that other things had been happening. The road-sweeper had grabbed his case, dived into the front passenger seat and shut the door. The car took off.

Lindsay twisted round and stared through the rear window. He had only one last glimpse. Christa's shattered body lying crumpled on the pavement. He hoped she had died immediately. Her slim legs were sprawled at a strange angle.

211

'She saved my life,' he said.

No one seemed interested. The powerful engine of the Mercedes carried them through the streets of Munich at manic speed. The astrakhan-clad figure by his side had a machine-pistol in its lap, an open violin case on the floor which presumably had concealed the weapon.

Lindsay felt he no longer cared whether they got away or not. He couldn't stop thinking of Christa acting as a human shield to save him. Minutes earlier he had called her a bloody fool. The car slowed down as it entered a deserted street and then swung left into a cul-de-sac.

A hand closed over his own. He looked down and realized he was still clutching the Luger. He'd forgotten all about the blasted thing – the gun Christa had provided. His companion's tone of voice was critical.

'The safety catch is still off. . .'

'All right! All right!'

He put the safety on and stared ahead. They were nearly at the end of the cul-de-sac. Now he saw a garage was open. The car slid inside, stopped. The chauffeur jumped out, closed the doors. Nobody said anything as he climbed out on to a concrete floor and an overhead light came on. A stench of petrol.

The figure in the astrakhan coat and hat walked round the car and stared at Lindsay. The same height as the Englishman, the wearer's voice was abrupt when it asked the question.

'The mission was to collect you. Who was the girl?'

'A German secretary of Hitler's. Without her help I would not have been there for you to collect.'

'*C'est la guerre*. . .'

The figure removed the astrakhan hat, revealing thick blonde hair, a well-shaped nose and chin – strong bone structure – and greenish tinted eyes. Lindsay was staring at a girl. She would be about twenty-seven, held herself very erect and was extremely attractive.

'I'm Paco,' she said. 'Now all we have to do is get you back to the Allied lines. Simple? Yes? No?'

Chapter Twenty-Three

'We establish a battle headquarters! Its sole objective – to track down the two fugitives! I shall take personal command. . .'

Bormann, clad in his normal uniform, his trousers thrust inside jackboots, his squarish face flushed, stopped in mid-sentence as the Führer made a gesture of disagreement.

'Really, Bormann,' Hitler commented mildly and with some amusement, 'we are not fighting Zhukov and his Soviet divisions. Not here, anyway. We are talking about two people.'

It was a muddle and the Reichsleiter had caused it. What should have been a military conference had been side-tracked by Bormann bringing up the problem of Lindsay and inviting the wrong people to attend the meeting. Eight men were seated in the huge living room with the famous picture window at the Berghof.

Keitel and Jodl sat side by side on a sofa, scarcely bothering to conceal their annoyance. The other four were Colonel Jaeger with his deputy, Schmidt; the Gestapo representative, Gruber; and Gustav Hartmann of the Abwehr.

'I understand, *mein Führer*,' Bormann agreed hastily.

He leaned back in his chair and crossed his short, stocky legs as the phone began ringing shrilly. Bormann practically leaped on the phone and pressed the receiver to his ear.

'Yes, Mayr, this is Bormann. You have caught them?'

There was a pause while he listened and Hartmann, watching his expression, felt certain he knew what had happened. He was also dying to light his pipe but there could be no smoking in Hitler's presence. Still, Bormann's face was a picture. . .

'Mayr, this is impossible,' Bormann protested. 'I made no

call to you about any Lindsay rendezvous with an Allied agent. What's going on here? Why didn't you check back? Wait a minute. . .'

He cupped a pudgy hand over the speaker and stared at the seated men. 'Someone here at the Berghof impersonated me when they called Mayr.' His gaze rested on Keitel and Jodl.

Keitel, his chin perched on the point of his baton, looked into the distance as though Bormann did not exist. Jodl folded his arms and regarded the Reichsleiter with a saturnine expression. The atmosphere was tense. Bormann continued the call.

'Listen, Mayr!' he exploded. 'You say someone pretending to be me told you about this rendezvous, that you acted on the information, that Lindsay did turn up – so presumably you have now got him . . . All right, go on. . .'

The other men in the room remained silent. The Führer studied his fingernails with a bored expression. Hartmann kept his face blank, enjoying the whole incident.

'This morning, you say. . .' Bormann sounded incredulous. 'Wait a minute,' he repeated. He stared at the others. 'There has been a massacre outside the Frauenkirche, soldiers killed.'

'Give me the phone!' Hitler snapped.

His passive manner changed in one of his unpredictable switches of mood. He stood very erect, the phone pressed to his ear.

'The Führer speaking. This is taking too long. Tell me in a few words what happened. . .'

Hitler listened intently, occasionally acknowledging what was being said to him with a simple 'Yes' or 'No'. This was another myth about the Führer, Hartmann reflected as he reached for his pipe and put it in his mouth without lighting it. The myth that Hitler could never listen. When he was intrigued by a subject, the Führer was one of the world's most attentive listeners.

'Do what you can, Mayr,' the Führer said eventually. 'Spread a massive dragnet as you suggest. The Englishman must not leave Germany. I prefer he should be taken alive.

Report regularly to Bormann about your progress. Do your best, Mayr.'

He put down the phone and began pacing the wide spaces of the room in an agitated manner, hands clasped behind his back. It was several minutes before he spoke.

'There has been a terrible accident. Christa Lundt, my favourite secretary, has been shot dead.'

'By the Englishman, Lindsay. . .' Bormann jumped in.

'No!' Hitler glanced at him with a look of contempt. 'I would greatly appreciate it if you could keep quiet until I have finished speaking. And you may be interested to hear Christa was shot by a member of the SS. . .'

Hartmann looked at Colonel Jaeger and actually saw the blood drain from his face at the news. One by one, the Führer was using the event to unnerve almost everyone present. He stopped in front of Gruber who started to rise to his feet.

'Sit down!' Hitler snapped. 'Apparently on the basis of information received a trap was laid this morning. The Gestapo were conspicuous by their absence. They don't seem to know what is going on even in Munich. . .'

He turned on his heels and stared down at Hartmann. The Abwehr officer stared back, his unlit pipe clenched between his teeth. Hitler's mood changed again with the same startling abruptness and he addressed Hartmann in a calm manner.

'Did the Abwehr have any knowledge of this – something to do with a rendezvous in the centre of Munich?'

'Not a word, *mein Führer*. Otherwise you would have been the first to hear. . .'

Which was not strictly speaking, necessarily true – but the opportunity to score over Gestapo and SS was too good to overlook. He watched as the Führer nodded – as though to say that is exactly what I would have expected. Hitler made a dismissive gesture.

'Deal with it in any way you like, Bormann. I leave the whole sorry business in your hands. Make sure flowers and condolences are sent from me on my behalf to Christa's relatives. I am going to my room to rest.'

215

It became a battle royal after Keitel and Jodl followed Hitler out of the room – with two organizations fighting for supremacy in the struggle to hunt down the Englishman. Gestapo and SS – Gruber and Jaeger – confronted each other while Hartmann sat listening.

It was a typical ploy of Bormann's – learned from the Führer – to set different power groups competing against each other. Bormann laid down the ground rules by phoning Mayr again to issue fresh instructions.

'Mayr, the Englishman, Wing Commander Lindsay, is a spy and is to be shot at the first sighting. Understood? By order of the Führer!'

He slammed down the phone and Hartmann almost expected him to give the Nazi salute. He made one of his rare interventions.

'Reichsleiter, that order is wrong. Hitler himself told Mayr "I prefer he should be taken alive."'

'That was earlier,' Bormann snapped. 'Later, when he became aware of what had happened he specifically told me to deal with it in any way I liked. You, also, are involved. You interrogated Lindsay, you know the man. From now on you will devote all your waking hours to locating this English spy. You will pursue him – to the ends of the earth if need be. . . .'

'Then I'll need a lot of money,' Hartmann said quickly.

'Unlimited funds will be placed at your disposal. Gruber, what measures do you propose we take?'

'Seal off the entire city of Munich. All exits must be closed.'

'That is not enough,' Jaeger interrupted. He unfolded a map of Bavaria on the table and stabbed at it with his finger. 'Where is Lindsay likely to head for? That is the key to the whole operation and I believe I know the answer.'

'Well?' Bormann demanded.

'Switzerland! We must flood the area between Munich and the Swiss frontier with troops. All trains to that area must carry special plain-clothes inspection teams. It requires concentration of our forces. Road-blocks must be set up on every route leading to the Swiss border. All airfields must be discreetly guarded – *discreetly* – since we are setting up a whole series of traps.'

'Why bother about airfields?' Gruber enquired.

Jaeger looked at him with a hint of contempt. 'Have you forgotten Lindsay is a *Wing Commander*? That he was originally flown to the Wolf's Lair from the Berghof in a Junkers 52? He may have spent his time observing how the plane is operated. . .'

'I see what you mean,' Gruber mumbled and subsided.

Sitting quietly, puffing his pipe, Hartmann had to admire the SS colonel's energy and organizing ability. A successful criminal lawyer in peacetime, Hartmann placed great value on *evidence*. He asked a question.

'You are banking everything on the logic that Lindsay has to be heading for Switzerland?'

'Well, is it not logical?' Jaeger turned on him aggressively. 'I have put myself – as I always did at the front – inside the mind of the enemy. You have a comment?'

'I prefer to listen to your meticulous planning,' Hartmann replied ambiguously.

'In any case,' Bormann broke in, 'you are a strictly one-man show, Hartmann. We rely on you to contact via Berlin the Abwehr agents inside Switzerland. Any information you obtain should be passed to Colonel Jaeger.'

'Tell me, Bormann, precisely what happened in Munich this morning? You used the word "massacre".'

'Mayr botched the operation. As to what happened. . .'

Hartmann listened intently as Bormann recalled in detail his phone conversation. Colonel Jaeger was already on the line to Mayr in Munich firing off a series of orders. Hartmann frowned as Bormann came to the end of his story, an expression which irked the Reichsleiter.

'What is the matter now, Hartmann?'

'I find it disturbing. This rescue of the Englishman was planned brilliantly – like a military operation. The road-sweeper who hurled grenades and smoke bombs at our troops – a masterly touch.'

'You call it that!' snapped Bormann. 'A number of our men were killed.'

'Furthermore,' Hartmann continued, 'we have no descriptions of this three-man group who snatched Lindsay from under the noses of our elaborate trap. The leader sounds to be the man who wore the astrakhan hat and coat. No description. Then there was the roadsweeper and the uniformed chauffeur who drove the Mercedes – again, no descriptions. How the hell did they get hold of a Mercedes?'

'Obviously they stole it!' interjected Gruber who was feeling he was being ignored.

'Possibly, Gruber,' Hartmann agreed amiably. 'Now, the Gestapo spends vast sums and has I don't know how many men on its staff. So tell me, what information have you about an underground group operating in the Munich area?'

Gruber, now he was the centre of attraction, looked uncomfortable. Bormann stared at him. Jaeger had just finished his phone call to Mayr and also stood watching.

'There are so many rumours we have to check. It is wartime. . .' he rambled.

'Gruber!' Bormann's voice dripped sarcasm. 'I could have told you myself it is wartime. We all labour under that same handicap but we still do our duty.'

'A specific group, I mean, Gruber,' Hartmann persisted gently. 'They could be saboteurs – in which case you may have discovered explosives. They could be spies – in which case your signals section may have detected unauthorized radio transmissions. They could be subversives – in which case you may have found anti-Nazi propaganda. Well?'

Even Bormann felt a grudging admiration for the way the Abwehr officer was spearing Gruber to the wall. Gruber sucked in a deep breath, his palms moist with sweat as he replied.

'We know of no such group,' he snapped. 'Obviously these assassins came into the city from a long distance, rescued the Englishman and departed. . .'

'*Obviously*!' roared Jaeger. 'How could they be sure when Lindsay would escape? He has been inside Germany for some time – and most of that time he was at the Wolf's Lair! Clearly these men have been waiting inside Munich for him to make his break – and the Gestapo hadn't an idea they existed! Criminal incompetence!'

'I shall report that slander to Reichsführer Himmler,' blazed Gruber. 'Your remark verges on treason. . .'

'So!' Jaeger made a contemptuous gesture. 'While you enjoy a cosy chat with Himmler I will devote my energies to tracking down not only the Englishman – but also we will scoop up in our net this trio of subversives and spies who have been operating under your nose!'

Only Hartmann observed the smug satisfaction on Bormann's face. Divide and neutralize the power of all potential rivals. He sat motionless as Gruber and Jaeger glared at each other and Bormann intervened, his tone of voice now reasonable and soothing.

'I do agree that Colonel Jaeger's plan for sealing off the Swiss border sounds reasonable. On the other hand, I am sure with all the resources at its disposal the Gestapo has a major contribution to make. This meeting is adjourned.'

The three men walked out of the room, leaving Hartmann alone. Standing up, he crouched over the large-scale map Jaeger had spread on the table. A solitary man, Hartmann had developed the habit of murmuring to himself to clear his mind.

'The last thing anyone would expect would be for Lindsay and his rescuers to move from Munich to Salzburg. . . After all, Lindsay has just left Salzburg. . . It depends on how good their intelligence is. . .'

He used his pipe stem to trace the route from Munich to Salzburg and let it continue on. The next destination was Vienna.

'Now, Wing Commander Lindsay, you are safe – you fit the description we have been given,' Paco told him. They had also exchanged the quaint password Browne had provided in London.

219

'And if I hadn't?' Lindsay enquired.

'I would have strangled you. It is quieter and saves bullets.'

The man who had acted as chauffeur gave this morale-raising reply. Paco, who seemed to command the group, turned on him.

'You will not talk like that again to our guest. He is a very important man. The nephew of a British duke. . .'

Half an hour had passed since Lindsay was bundled into the Mercedes and taken on the mad drive through Munich which ended inside a garage. A concealed door inside a cupboard at the back of the garage led to a staircase which they had descended to a basement – a large room with two double-tiered bunks against separate walls.

Once the concealed door had been closed – it was made of sheet steel faced with heavy wood so no amount of tapping inside the garage would have produced a hollow sound – Paco introduced her companions.

'This,' she said, indicating the hard-faced 'chauffeur', is Bora. He speaks good English. Shake hands, Bora. . .'

He was as tall as Lindsay, about thirty years old, his eyes were hostile and the Englishman instantly disliked him. Fortunately he had the foresight to stiffen his hand because Bora had a grip like a wrestler's and exerted full pressure.

'Do behave, Bora,' Paco said softly. 'I saw that. . .'

'Bora is the name of a strong dry wind which blows up the Adriatic,' Lindsay observed.

'Now you know why we gave him that code-name.' She turned to the second man – maybe forty years old with a weatherbeaten face and a humorous glint in his shrewd eyes. 'This is Milic. He also speaks English, but do not expect perfection.'

'Milic is most pleased to meet the Englishman . . . the girl bulleted by the Nazi was very close friend?'

'He means,' Paco interjected in her direct manner, 'were you in love with her. Were you?'

'No,' Lindsay said tersely.

'But I think she was in love with you,' Paco continued. She had a soft, appealing voice which contrasted strangely with

220

her poise, the erect way she held herself. Her slow-moving, wary eyes watched him closely.

'It was a tragedy,' Lindsay replied.

'There is so often one who loves, one who is loved – I think your writer, Somerset Maugham, said something like that.' She changed the subject abruptly. 'I will tell you a little about myself.'

Paco – it was a code-name – was twenty-seven years old. She had been born of an English mother and a Serbian father, a professor of languages at Belgrade University. Educated at the Godolphin, an English boarding-school, she had gone on to a Swiss finishing-school and then returned to Jugoslavia. She was fluent in English, German and Serbo-Croat.

'When Hitler bombed Belgrade both my parents were killed. In one night I became an orphan. No need for sympathy, Wing Commander – it has happened to so many in England also. I joined the Partisans. In Jugoslavia it is almost as common for a woman to carry a gun as a man. And my German is useful – it allows me to operate inside the Third Reich.'

'You must have contact with London,' Lindsay suggested.

'There is a limit to what you need to know,' Paco said brusquely. 'But a little information about the people your life now depends on – and equally whose lives may depend on you at a critical time – will help us to work as a team. You know, Wing Commander, I have to point out you are a novice at this dangerous game. . .'

'I did escape from the Berghof,' Lindsay snapped.

'True.' Her greenish eyes surveyed him. 'I do find that a most promising omen for the future.' She became stern again. 'Bora. He has killed many Germans and trusts no one. His wife was killed in the bombing the same night my parents died. But I think he found his natural vocation as a fighter. You would not believe it – he was a furniture-maker, carving fine chairs. . .'

'You find that amusing, Paco?' Bora, who had been cleaning the machine-pistol, leaned forward, his manner aggressive.

221

'I find it strange – you use your skilled hands to build complex explosive devices. Once you created, now you destroy. . .'

'It is the war.'

The girl was not in the least disturbed by Bora's attitude. As she lit a cigarette, Lindsay was struck by the serenity which never seemed to desert her. She stroked her blonde hair, gazing at the third member of her group.

'Now Milic here. . .' Her tone of voice became more affectionate. '. . . he was a stone-mason who once worked in the quarries. He has no idea what has happened to his wife and two children. They were on holiday in Zagreb when the war came. He is very strong – and very controlled. You follow me?'

'I think so,' Lindsay replied, not looking at Bora.

'So now,' Paco went on, 'we have to move very quickly – to take you out of Germany before the highly-efficient Nazi apparatus has time to get organized. No later than tonight.'

'That's quick,' Lindsay commented.

'I just hope it is quick enough. You may stay here. Milic and I have to go out to see what is happening before we escort you to safety. . .'

'May I ask where is safety?'

'Switzerland.'

Colonel Jaeger stood with his hands on his hips surveying the scene inside the main station at Munich. A cold wind was blowing, sending pieces of paper scuttering along the rail tracks, chilling everyone. Jaeger was glad of his fur-lined military great-coat and his deputy, Schmidt, who had just joined him, clapped his gloved hands together.

'All the barricades to Switzerland are manned,' Schmidt informed his chief. 'There is the usual desperate shortage of personnel but they will not slip through by road.'

'Nor by train,' Jaeger affirmed. 'Every train to Switzerland is carrying a special team. They have the Englishman's de-

222

scription, orders to check the papers of all passengers irrespective of that description. We may scoop up other interesting fish in our net. . .'

He paused and Schmidt followed his gaze. A tall, blonde-haired girl in her late twenties had just been stopped by one of Jaeger's patrols. She wore an expensive leather coat and a fetching black fur cap perched on the top of her head. She glanced across, her eyes met Jaeger's, then she resumed her conversation with the two soldiers.

'She's a beauty,' Jaeger said appreciatively. 'Maybe the lady could do with a little help.'

He left Schmidt who smiled cynically. The Colonel was noted for his keen eye for attractive women. As Jaeger approached, the two soldiers stiffened to attention and saluted.

'What seems to be the trouble?' Jaeger enquired affably.

'These men are harassing me. . .' Paco turned her eyes and held Jaeger's in a long look. 'I am the Baroness Werther, the niece of General Speidel. . .'

'I think you can leave this to me. . .' Jaeger dismissed his men with a curt gesture, his eyes still on Paco as he returned their salute. 'They are looking for an English spy,' he explained, 'so they sometimes show excessive zeal.'

'I look to you like a spy, Colonel?' asked Paco.

'Of course not, Baroness.' Jaeger bowed. The girl really had an instantaneous effect on him and Jaeger regarded himself as something of a connoisseur of the fair sex. Of course, all this Aryan propaganda was claptrap, but the sceptical Colonel began to wonder whether there was a point to it as he continued to stare at this vision.

'Since you have military connections,' he suggested, 'could you possibly join me for lunch so I may express my regrets in a practical way at the inconvenience you have just suffered? I do have a table permanently reserved at the Four Seasons. . .'

He waited, somewhat surprised at his impulsive action and even more surprised when he realized he was almost holding his breath for her reply. She looked at him steadily, taking her time while she considered his proposal. It would be a rejection, Jaeger felt sure.

'Is that the real reason why you extend this invitation, Colonel? Simply to express regrets?'

She was holding him on a tightrope of anticipation. It was quite ridiculous but he desperately wanted to get to know her better – and she had thrown him completely off balance.

'It would be an honour,' he said frankly, 'to walk into the Four Seasons graced by your company. Simply lunch – I promise you as an officer. . .'

'And a gentleman?' She smiled to take the sting out of her playfulness. 'I would be very glad to join you – for lunch. . .' said Paco calmly.

'Alfred,' Jaeger informed Schmidt, 'this is the Baroness Werther, niece of General Speidel. You will assume command of the operation while we take lunch at the Four Seasons. Good hunting!'

Paco dipped her head a fraction in acknowledgement of Schmidt's bow, her eyes catching briefly those behind the rimless glasses of Jaeger's thin-faced deputy. Something about the man disturbed her.

The Colonel was a buoyant, full-blooded personality who enjoyed life and radiated a warmth of feeling, a man a woman could understand – even if at times he might prove a handful. 'Alfred', she sensed, was a very different proposition.

'Who was that man you introduced me to?' she asked as Jaeger escorted her from the station to his waiting car.

'Schmidt, my deputy,' Jaeger replied impatiently. 'A good man – but hardly your type. Before the war he was a policeman! Now, in a matter of minutes we can get to know each other better in the comfort of the Four Seasons. . .'

The little alarm bell at the back of Paco's mind kept on ringing.

It was quite true that in peacetime Alfred Schmidt had been in the police force. Blessed with a sixth sense that the Führer would have appreciated – and a first-rate mind – Captain

224

Alfred Schmidt had been Chief of Police in Düsseldorf.

When war came on 1 September 1939 his obvious destination was the Gestapo. Schmidt, a man with a wide knowledge of international police forces and security organizations, appreciated some specialist outfit was needed to guard the state. He knew that England had its Special Branch, America the FBI, and so on.

But the Gestapo had already built up a certain reputation – to put it bluntly Schmidt didn't like the smell of it. To avoid being co-opted into the Gestapo he volunteered for the SS. Even after several years of war his policeman's instincts had not deserted him.

For one thing no one had checked 'the Baroness's' papers. He had observed the two soldiers had been shown nothing by the time Jaeger arrived. He had noted the girl's long glance in the direction of his chief. The colonel he highly respected and liked was lunching with a girl whose credentials were quite unknown.

Schmidt was in a dilemma. To check on Jaeger's lunch companion he must use a 'safe' telephone – which meant driving to the SS barracks, and the Colonel had left him in charge at the station.

It was probably all a wild goose chase anyway, but – like Paco – the ex-police chief had a sixth sense which warned him that something was wrong. With such a beautiful escort he estimated Jaeger would be away at least two hours. He made up his mind.

'Klaus!' he called out. 'Take command of operations here – I'll be back later. . .'

He drove himself to the barracks, leaped from behind the wheel and ran upstairs to his office. The lines were busy – so it took twenty minutes to get through to Gestapo headquarters in Berlin. He asked to be put through to Gestapo chief Heinrich Müller.

'It is lunchtime,' a bored voice informed him. 'He is out. Who did you say was calling?'

'SS Colonel Jaeger's deputy from Munich. Who am I speaking to? It is an urgent matter. . .'

'Brandt. I have been seconded here temporarily. No, everyone else is out – I told you, it is lunchtime. . .'

'Then you must deal with this personally. Can you check the General Records? Good. I need information as to whether there exists a Baroness Werther, niece of General Speidel. How long will that take? You can't say? God Almighty. . . !'

He arranged for Brandt to phone back the information to his secretary, replaced the receiver and instructed his secretary.

'Type out the reply from this half-wit, Brandt. Have a despatch rider standing by. Give him the reply in a sealed envelope and tell him to race like hell to the main station and hand it to me.'

He drove back to the station and was relieved on arrival when Klaus reported nothing had happened in his absence. Now it was a matter of waiting for the reply. If something *was* wrong he could phone Jaeger direct at the Four Seasons.

Chapter Twenty-Four

It was 4 p.m. when the despatch rider from the SS barracks pulled up his machine in front of Munich station bringing a sealed envelope for Captain Alfred Schmidt. Since Jaeger had still not returned, his deputy assumed he must really be enjoying himself with the Baroness.

'Dumbhead!'

Schmidt swore to himself as he watched the motor-cyclist brake at speed, causing his machine to skid alongside the kerb and very nearly hurl its rider over the handlebars to kingdom come. And all because a group of SS troops stood watching. Sheer, stupid bravado!

'If I ever see you behave like that again I'll have your stripes, Sergeant!'

'Sorry, sir. . .'

The despatch rider held out the envelope. He was going to make the excuse the brake had slipped but something in Schmidt's eye warned him to keep quiet. Taking the envelope, Schmidt glanced behind the sergeant, stiffened and spoke quickly.

'That is all, Sergeant! Back to barracks immediately!'

A Mercedes had just arrived and Jaeger was climbing out of the vehicle. He seemed to be in high good humour, pausing while talking to the SS troops and saying something which caused them to laugh. A popular officer, Jaeger. Schmidt, anxious to conceal the message he had just received unless it was alarming, tore open the envelope and pulled out a folded message sheet.

He had taken a chance. No senior officer, even one as comradely as Jaeger, likes a junior snooping on his private excursions. He heard another burst of laughter, this time from Jaeger himself, as he swiftly scanned the wording his secretary had typed after hearing from Brandt.

The news was alarming – from two sources. Milic arrived back first in the basement hideaway. He wore cleaner's overalls and an old peaked cap. He looked serious as he removed his cap, nodded to the Englishman and scratched his thatch of grey hair.

'Well?' Bora demanded.

'Switzerland is the trap,' Milic said, speaking in his careful English for Lindsay's sake. 'We go that way and we see Gestapo prison. . .'

'Why?' asked Bora impatiently. 'Give details. . .'

'I cycle three roads south . . . every road has the barrier. Many troops. They look at papers, use their telephones. . .'

'The station then,' snapped Bora. 'We take him out by train. . .'

'No train.' Milic shook his head. 'At the station I watch the trains to Switzerland. Men – not in uniform – are on these trains. They look at the papers. . .'

He broke off as Paco arrived and closed the secret door.

She took off her fur cap and dropped it on a crate. Gazing at Lindsay she used her hands to tidy her blonde hair. He could read nothing in her expression.

'We have a problem,' she said quietly. 'The Swiss route is shut down. They have sealed the border. Any attempt to smuggle you there will end in disaster.' She paused. 'I have just had an excellent lunch with Colonel Jaeger of the SS. . .'

'You've done what!'

Bora jumped up from his crate, staring at her as though she were mad. His eyes swivelled briefly to the door and back again to the girl.

'You could have been followed. We had better leave at once – if it is not too late already. . .'

'Bora. . .' She placed her hands on his shoulders and stared at the Serb. 'You think I am an amateur? Of course I was not followed. I took all the usual precautions, although they were unnecessary. Now, sit down and *listen*!'

She turned to Lindsay and produced a large envelope which she held under his nose. He took the envelope, extracted the documents and read them. Each carried at the head the German eagle clutching the swastika between its claws. All of them carried the signature of *Egon Jaeger, Colonel, SS*.

'My God, these are transit papers to Vienna. Why Vienna?'

'Now, *you* listen! I obtained these for myself, and my servants travelling with me, from this Colonel Jaeger. . .'

'How did you manage that?' asked Lindsay.

'Not by going to bed with him – which I can see is what you're thinking. Would it have worried you had I done so?'

Lindsay did not reply at once: he was uncertain how to react and he was aware the greenish eyes were watching him with a hint of amusement. He bit his lip and avoided the subject.

'They are for travel by train. . .'

'Don't you see!' She punched him as though irked by his slow-wittedness. 'You very recently travelled by train from Salzburg to Munich. The route to Vienna is from Munich via Salzburg. At the station I noticed they are not watching the Vienna expresses. The Nazis will never dream you would dare to go back the same way you came in. . .'

'One of these documents is for a Franz Weber, chauffeur. . .'

'You will be Weber. I want you to try on the uniform Bora wore when we snatched you from in front of the Frauenkirche. I'm sure it will fit – you are about his height and build. You speak excellent German.' Paco went on, her tone confident. 'You can drive? You drive the car to the station.'

'Yes. What will I be driving?' Lindsay asked.

'The Mercedes, of course. There is nothing else and a baroness is expected to travel in style. Munich is full of green Mercedes staff cars – and I'm certain no one recorded the registration in the panic we created. . .'

'What about Bora and Milic?'

'They come with us in the back of the car. Bora is my steward. Milic we must drop off in a quiet street near the station. He will make his own way. . .'

'And you are?'

'The Baroness Werther, of course! Sitting alongside you in the car so I can guide you to the station. . .'

'Supposing they decide to check up on this fictitious baroness?'

'But she *exists*! I met her at my finishing-school in Switzerland before the war. Any more questions?'

'Supposing someone thinks of checking your description?'

'That would be just too bad. Look, Lindsay, we use these transit documents to clear out fast. No one knows where we've gone. . .'

'Where are we going after Vienna?'

'Let's take it one stage at a time. . .'

For the second time Paco showed caution in the amount of information she was prepared to give Lindsay. For the first time he rebelled.

'I don't like it. I'm supposed to pass vital information I have to my people urgently. . .'

'*You* don't like it!' Bora reared up, his face ugly. 'To us you are a dangerous burden. You have no experience of operating underground – and we're supposed to risk our lives babying you along. . .'

'Shut up!' Paco told him. She grasped Lindsay by the arm, guiding him to a corner of the basement where she sat on a crate and pulled him down beside her. She lowered her voice.

'The people I represent have a bargain with the British – so many guns, so much ammunition in return for smuggling English agents out of Germany. Please cooperate – Bora is right, but he's unpredictable. The Swiss route is suicide. It has to be Vienna – and on from there. . .'

'O.K. But when do we move – or is that classified too. . . ?'

'Lindsay. . .' She placed a hand on his arm. 'Don't go bitter on me. We catch the 8 p.m. train from Munich which arrives in Vienna at 11 p.m. It's an express. . .'

'Thank God. Let's get on with it. I've only been inside this cellar for a few hours but the walls are closing in on me. . .'

'Now you are thinking like Bora – and that is good.' She paused. 'If we run into an emergency and have to separate, go with Milic. He will never abandon you. He likes you. . .'

'But Bora might abandon me?'

'Let's not think about negative things. . .'

Which meant, Lindsay realized, that without admitting it, Paco did agree with him on the greatest danger – that someone would check her description before they were clear of the Third Reich.

It was 4 p.m. when Paco arrived back at the basement and began her conversation with Lindsay.

It was 4 p.m. when the despatch rider delivered the message to Schmidt at Munich station. He read the typed words and folded the sheet, hiding it in his pocket as Jaeger left the troops he had been joking with and approached him.

Baroness Werther, niece of General Speidel, is heiress to a large steel fortune. Her father is close friend of Reichs-marschall Goering. Brandt.

Schmidt felt relieved at the contents of the message but at the back of his mind he felt he had overlooked something. He concentrated on greeting Jaeger who looked like a man who had enjoyed a most satisfying lunch. He clapped a hand on Schmidt's shoulder.

230

'Everything in order, Schmidt? Good. You really must work hard for your next promotion. The perks available to a high-ranking officer are unbelievable. . .'

He winked and exuded satisfaction and good humour as he glanced round the concourse. Schmidt probed delicately.

'Your companion was . . . interesting, I trust?'

'*Interesting*!' Jaeger lowered his voice. 'I will tell you, my friend, there is something about that woman which gets into your bloodstream. I am over the moon. . .'

'You will be meeting again?'

'But of course! Within a week at the outside. They all play hard to get at first – those really worth getting!'

'She lives in Munich?'

'I really don't know. . .' Jaeger watched two of his men bullying an old woman officiously. 'You! Over there! She is old enough to be your mother – your grandmother. Have a little patience while she finds her papers. The labour battalions require more recruits. . .' He turned to Schmidt. 'Now, you were saying?'

'I was just asking where the Baroness lives. . .'

'We didn't get round to that.' A roguish gleam came into the Colonel's blue eyes. 'We had other topics which absorbed all our attention. She has promised to ring me at the barracks within a week – I gave her my private number. . .'

Jaeger stood with his hands on his hips and began humming *Lili Marlene* to himself. He's got it badly, Schmidt thought. Seldom had he seen his chief in such a mood of euphoria. The girl must have hypnotized him.

'Schmidt,' the Colonel said suddenly, 'have you had any lunch? I thought not. Push off. I'll keep an eye on things here. . .'

His deputy walked away and got behind the wheel of his car. He drove slowly back to the barracks, half his mind elsewhere. The Colonel was also dreaming. Lisa, the Baroness, had told him she was visiting her uncle in Vienna but only expected to be there two or three days.

'Really it is a duty visit,' she had remarked. 'I shall be back here as soon as I become bored – which will be very quickly.'

231

He remembered the expression in her eyes over the rim of her wine-glass. The transit papers he had been glad to provide to avoid her being subjected to any annoying interrogation. And the scene he had just witnessed of two oafs pestering some poor old woman made him even happier he had supplied the documents.

Schmidt, driving on automatic pilot, recalled the wording of the message from Gestapo headquarters in the Prinz Albrechtstrasse in Berlin. It confirmed the existence of a Baroness Werther. It confirmed that she was an heiress. It confirmed that she was a niece of General Speidel. He remembered what it did *not* confirm – because he had forgotten to request the information.

Schmidt ran to his office at the barracks, told his secretary to get Brandt on the phone again. As he waited at his desk, he realized he was fiddling nervously with his pencil, that his secretary was watching him. He pretended to read a report. To his surprise the call came through quickly.

'Schmidt from Munich here again. I got your message, Brandt – for which many thanks. You must excuse me, but I omitted to ask for one further minor detail. A precise description of the Baroness Werther. This also is an urgent enquiry. I need a reply by 7 p.m. at the latest. . .'

Chapter Twenty-Five

At the Munich station SS chief Mayr looked over the trio who were travelling to Vienna. He had chanced to be standing by the barrier when they arrived. He noted the girl's expensive outfit, the equally top quality luggage carried by the uniformed chauffeur, and the steward who limped – doubtless a war wound. He was opening his mouth to speak when Paco smiled at him and produced a sheaf of papers from her handbag.

'You are SS, I see,' she remarked. 'So undoubtedly you know my friend, Colonel Jaeger. . .'

She gave the word *friend* a certain inflection. At her mention of the name, Mayr's attitude changed. An amiable man of forty, he bowed and removed his cap which he tucked under his arm.

'Of course! My duty is to random check passengers' papers – so you must excuse any inconvenience. . .'

'Look at the clock!' Paco said sharply. 'It would be more than an inconvenience if you cause me to miss the Vienna Express. I have transit documents signed personally for myself and my servants by Colonel Jaeger. Do be quick. . .'

Mayr glanced at the clock, saw Jaeger's signature on the papers and hastily gestured for her to pass on to the platform.

'A safe journey.' Mayr wished her.

Lindsay was careful not to look at the German as he shuffled past with the cases, and followed Bora and Paco who was walking briskly past the coaches until she came to an empty compartment. Opening the door, she climbed aboard, leaving her companions to follow as she glanced along the corridor. It was deserted.

'You handled that brilliantly,' Lindsay remarked after he had put the cases on the rack. The express was moving out of the station. His admiration was genuine: she had employed just the right mixture of arrogant confidence and feminine wiles.

'One obstacle overcome,' responded Paco and removed her fur hat, then used her hands to settle her blonde hair.

'This superb luggage – Bora's *loden* garb – where did you get all this from?' Lindsay asked.

'None of your business,' snapped Bora.

'Don't be liverish,' Paco chided him amiably. 'It is a reasonable question.' She looked at Lindsay. 'We broke into a villa outside Munich and stole everything. Nothing impresses the officer class more than an impression of great wealth – which means power.'

'What about tickets?' Lindsay asked suddenly. 'In Germany they inspect them on the train.'

Paco opened her handbag and produced three first-class tickets which she gave to Lindsay. 'The chauffeur carries things like that – and you speak German. You know, Lindsay, you're learning quickly – to think of details. I bought those this morning when I saw at the station the Swiss trains were being watched. . .'

'They're return tickets – to Vienna and back. . .'

'So,' Paco replied, 'if Jaeger should check before we leave the train he'll think I'm coming back, as I said I would. That is the one unfortunate episode I wish we could have avoided – my having to use Jaeger's name with that SS officer. They may find out the train we are travelling on.'

'Does that matter?' asked Bora in a casual tone. 'In only three hours we shall be in Vienna.'

Lindsay stared into the corridor. A cleaner wearing overalls and a railman's peaked cap was collecting rubbish with a dust-pan and hand-brush. It was Milic. He winked at Lindsay and proceeded towards the front of the train.

'Yes, using Jaeger's name might matter,' Paco told Bora. 'Don't you see,' she went on, 'back in the basement Lindsay raised the spectre of what could happen if someone checks on my description. . .'

The express was now picking up speed, the wheels clicking in a hypnotic rhythm. Lindsay said nothing. Three hours to Vienna. . .

In his office Schmidt had fallen asleep at his desk, his head resting on his forearms. The remains of a meal were on a tray. It was very silent inside the large building. The shrill sound of the 'phone ringing brought him awake with a start. He looked at the clock. Christ! *10.45 p.m.*

'Schmidt. . .'

He got no further. Brandt started speaking, his voice surprisingly alert. There was a sense of achievement, too.

'I have the Baroness Werther's description. It took delicate handling. I gave as the reason for the enquiry some problem of mistaken identity. You were not mentioned. . .'

Schmidt changed his mind about Brandt. The Gestapo man

had shown a discretion he would not have expected. He was relieved: it kept Jaeger out of the picture. He held a pencil poised over his notepad.

'Thanks, I appreciate it. Let's keep it that way. Now. . .'

'Height 1.5 metres, a brunette, on the plump side. Twenty-nine years old. Wears glasses – short-sighted as a bat. Any help?'

Schmidt kept the alarm out of his voice. 'Yes, that's extremely helpful. I am most obliged – and sorry to keep you working so late.'

'Gives me a good excuse to arrive home in the early hours – I have a little detour on the way,' Brandt concluded sardonically.

Schmidt replaced the receiver and felt sick. Another subordinate would have used the information to harpoon his chief – clear the way for his own promotion. The thought never entered his head. He twisted round in his chair as the door opened. Jaeger peered in – behind him stood Mayr.

'It's about the Baroness Werther,' Schmidt said cryptically. 'I would appreciate a word in private. . .'

Jaeger said something to Mayr, entered the room and shut the door. He was in an ebullient mood as he stripped off his gloves and tossed them on to a desk with his cap. Swivelling round a hard wooden chair, he straddled the seat and leaned his elbows along the back.

'You look worried, Schmidt. Never worry. Problems have a habit of solving themselves. Never stir things up unnecessarily. It is one of the Führer's favourite maxims.'

'This is a description of the Baroness Werther. . .'

Jaeger read the wording on the sheet Schmidt had torn from his notepad. Most men would have wasted time questioning the source of the information, the reason why Schmidt had involved himself in the matter. Jaeger simply handed the sheet back.

'I have been taken for a ride, Schmidt. And what a ride! She – whoever she may be – is superb. I gave her transit documents for herself and her so-called servants!'

'Are there copies in the files?' Schmidt asked quickly. 'Transit to where?'

'No copies, comrade. Transit by rail, Munich to Vienna.'

He broke off as the door opened. Mayr walked into the room and closed the door. A tall, thin man, he looked puzzled.

'Excuse me, but I've been thinking it over. Did I hear you make a reference to the Baroness Werther?'

'Yes,' Jaeger said immediately, and waited.

'I saw her aboard the Vienna Express this evening with her entourage. She showed me the transit you had signed. She's a real looker, that blonde. . .'

'Who comprised her entourage?' Jaeger enquired casually.

'A uniformed chauffeur. I can't describe him – he had a peaked cap pulled down over his forehead and was lumbered with luggage. Then there was another man – he looked like one of those stewards you find in the country looking after an estate. He was limping, a relic of his war, I imagine. Is it important?'

'Sheer curiosity,' Jaeger replied promptly. 'There was a third man?'

'No, quite definitely. . .'

'Which train? What time?' asked Schmidt.

'Departed on time at eight o'clock. There is no problem?'

'Not on the basis of what you have told us,' Jaeger replied.

'Then I'm off to bed. See you both in the morning.'

Schmidt had crossed the room and was grasping a railway timetable off a shelf as Mayr closed the door. He leafed through it quickly, checked with his finger down a series of times. His finger stopped. He looked at the clock. 10.51.

'It's still on the way. . .' Schmidt had trouble suppressing his relief. 'Arrives in nine minutes. 2300 hours. Who do we know. . . ?'

'In Vienna? Anton Kahr – in charge of SS. An old buddy of mine – we served together on the Russian front. . .'

Schmidt checked a list of classified numbers, picked up the phone and asked for a top priority call. He held on to the earpiece as the operator contacted Vienna. Jaeger, as controlled as though on the eve of a battle, thought out aloud.

'Mayr will be compelled to keep quiet when I have to tell him – he saw them aboard the train. The odd thing is, there should have been another man – there were three of them when they lifted Lindsay out of the Frauenkirche. . .'

'Kahr on the line. . .' Schmidt handed the phone to his chief and watched the clock as Jaeger talked rapidly and concisely. It was still only 10.54 when he completed the call.

'Six minutes before the express arrives,' Schmidt said.

'And when it does, Kahr and his men will be waiting concealed on the platform. The Baroness is due for a little surprise. . .'

Chapter Twenty-Six

They disembarked on to the platform at the Westbahnhof, mingling with the other passengers. Paco showed Lindsay the luggage store and stood where she could watch him. Bora had again proved difficult as the express was approaching the terminus.

'Lindsay,' Paco had said, 'you will leave the cases at the luggage store. Wait for the numbered receipt and here is the money you will need. We will not be coming back for the cases. . .'

'Then why not leave them here?' Bora demanded irritably.

'Because a porter or cleaner will find them quickly. Left at the baggage store they may not be found for days.' She looked at Lindsay. 'We are going next to Graz, capital of the Austrian province of Styria. From there we go south and cross the border at Spielfeld-Strass into Jugoslavia. There are a few Allied agents with the guerrillas. . .'

Lindsay had to repress an almost irresistible urge to leave when the Austrian official took the cases from him, but he forced himself to wait. The official seemed to take forever laboriously producing the receipt which he eventually exchanged for the fee.

The platform with its gloomy lighting projected by cone-shaped shades was deserted by the time he left the baggage store. Lindsay felt naked. Paco was smoking a cigarette as he joined her.

'Where are the others?' he asked.

'They will take a separate taxi. This way, if anyone checks we are two separate couples – two men and a man and a girl. Not what they will be looking for. . .'

'You're nervous about something,' he suggested.

They were walking out of the station into a huge open space and there was very little traffic about – mostly military vehicles. Paco strode away from the station and they walked a long distance before she summoned a taxi.

'The train was fifteen minutes early,' she said. 'It arrived at 10.45. . .'

The council of war, as Bormann termed it, was held at the Berghof at 12.15 a.m. the next morning. It had been one hell of a rush – Jaeger, Schmidt and Mayr had flown from Munich to Salzburg airstrip. Hartmann also attended the conference.

Cars had been waiting to drive them out of the city and up into the mountains along treacherous, icy roads. The meeting was held in the large living-room with the giant picture window. The Führer had personally presided over it. To Jaeger's relief – and surprise – Hitler had taken the news calmly, speaking quietly.

'So, you let the Englishman slip through your fingers. Always I have said the English are tough and dangerous. It is a great pity they will not yet see reason and ally themselves with us . . .'

'I am entirely and solely responsible for this débâcle,' Jaeger had begun and his admission was pounced on by Bormann.

'In that case you will have to pay the penalty . . .'

'Bormann! Please . . .!' The Führer lifted a conciliatory hand. At that hour Hitler was the freshest man present, but it

238

was his habit never to retire to bed before 3 a.m. 'Apportioning the blame will get us nowhere. We must move on – decide on how we're to track down Lindsay and have him brought back here.'

Débâcle was the word. Due purely to the chance fifteen-minute early arrival of the express, SS chief Kahr in Vienna had found the station deserted. No trace of the fugitives. His men checked everywhere – including the baggage store.

'There is one interesting fact,' ventured Hartmann and Bormann again charged in like a bull.

'This no longer concerns the Abwehr . . .'

'Bormann, please!' repeated the Führer, showing exemplary patience. 'I would like to hear what Major Hartmann has to say.'

'Apparently – according to Mayr – when this group left Munich they had two expensive cases,' Hartmann began. 'These cases have since been found in the baggage store at Vienna station. The description of the uniformed chauffeur who handed them in coincides with the chauffeur Mayr saw at Munich station. The cases contain an expensive wardrobe for a woman . . .'

'You do not think they will come back for the cases?' asked the Führer.

'Exactly,' agreed Hartmann. 'They have dumped them. That tells us something – and I am convinced the group is directed by the girl who so confidently impersonated the Baroness Werther . . .'

'A girl! For God's sake . . .!'

Bormann was contemptuous. He was also irritated that Hartmann was holding the centre of the stage – that Hitler was listening so attentively. Again he was scolded.

'Bormann, do keep quiet! There have been some truly remarkable cases in the West of the English sending women agents to liaise with the French underground. These women have shown courage and the most audacious initiative. Proceed, please, Hartmann . . .'

'The puzzle is what they will do next, where they will go . . .'

239

'Vienna is a labyrinth,' Hitler remarked. 'I should know – the days of my poverty-stricken youth were spent there. They could hide – if they know the city – and we would not find them in years.'

'*If* that is their intention,' Hartmann continued, 'which I suspect it is not.' He warmed to his subject, so absorbed he produced his pipe and used it to emphasize points. 'Let us assume this girl is their leader – she certainly has the nerve. At each stage I sense she has worked to a plan – this is no wild rush into nowhere. On past form – always judge people on that – she will have a definite plan for reaching their next destination. All we have to do is to work out where that is – and get there first.'

He sat back and almost lit the pipe. He hastily put it inside his pocket.

'You make it sound so very straightforward,' Bormann said.

'A decision must be taken!' Hitler jumped up, displaying one of his sudden bursts of energy as he began pacing back and forth, his hands clasped behind his back. 'Gruber is already on his way to Vienna with a fellow officer flown from Berlin You will go, too – Jaeger and Schmidt forming a second unit. Major Hartmann will also proceed to Vienna . . .'

'All these personnel to catch one Englishman?'

Bormann was aghast. Always sure of how to proceed, the Reichsleiter was completely nonplussed by this development. The Führer didn't even hear his mild intervention as he spoke briskly, his voice growing in power.

'This way we have three independent forces on their tails – the Gestapo, the SS and the Abwehr. If one of them cannot track down this subversive group we might as well pull down the shutters and close the shop! Bormann, you will furnish them with all the funds, facilities and weapons they need. Stay up all night, if necessary!'

He stopped pacing, folded his arms and stared hard at the group of men listening in silence. This was no moment to interrupt the Führer.

'I expect you all to be in Vienna before dawn – then you

240

have all day to scour the city. And remember, gentlemen, the Gestapo is already there – one jump ahead of you . . .'

His arm still folded, Hitler waited with a stern expression as the men hurried from the room. Once alone with Bormann, his mood changed dramatically. Throwing himself into a chair he spread his arms wide and shook with laughter.

'Bormann, did you see their expressions! It's like a race – who will catch the Englishman first? Nothing gingers up men like competition. And you know who I predict will track down our target?'

'Gruber.'

'Of course not!' The idea sent Hitler into another paroxysm of mirth. 'Hartmann,' he gasped out when he had recovered. 'That wily Abwehr type knows a thing or two – he even gave the others a clue and they were too thick to grasp it . . .' His manner changed yet again. His face stiffened, he sat up erect, his voice harsh. 'What are you still doing here? They will be waiting for you downstairs, Bormann! You are holding up their urgent departure . . .'

Bormann, short and stocky, a ridiculous figure in his jackboots when he skipped hurriedly across the polished floor, paused at the door.

'*Mein Führer*, you said Hartmann gave them a clue?'

'The cases they left behind! The cases full of expensive clothes for a woman. Now, hurry!'

He listened to the fading scurry of Bormann's boots tiptapping up the curved staircase and then relaxed in his chair with a broad smile. He spoke quietly to test her hearing.

'Eva, you can come in now, you little minx. They've all gone. You've been eavesdropping again, haven't you?'

It was 2 a.m. when the Condor transport plane carrying Jaeger, Schmidt and Hartmann landed at the aerodrome outside Vienna. A car was waiting to take them into the Austrian capital. Bormann was a strange man, but his enemies – which included almost everyone except the Führer – all admitted he was a superb organizer.

241

Schmidt sat in the front beside the driver while Jaeger and the Abwehr officer occupied the rear seats. During the longish drive into the city Hartmann remained deep in thought. His silence irked the more extrovert SS colonel.

'How are you going to set about this impossible task?' he asked.

'Where are you going first?' countered Hartmann.

'To SS headquarters, for a consultation with Kahr. You are welcome to attend our meeting.'

'Would you think it discourteous if I asked you to drop me off at the Westbahnhof?' Hartmann suggested. 'I imagine the luggage they left behind is still there?'

'I presume so. What can that tell you?'

'I won't know till I see it, will I?' Hartmann replied.

'You're a close-mouthed bastard,' Jaeger commented amiably.

'But, if I may say so,' Schmidt added, turning round in his seat, 'a shrewd one, too . . .'

Schmidt sensed a certain fellow-feeling with the ex-lawyer. His methods were not unlike those Schmidt had employed as a police chief in those far-off days in Düsseldorf. It all seemed a century ago.

Hartmann alighted from the car outside the station. It was exactly 2.30 a.m. He made his way to the luggage store, extracting from his wallet a document he had obtained from Bormann. It gave him powers to question anyone, regardless of rank. *By order of the Führer.*

'I'm just going off night duty,' the baggage store supervisor remarked and his manner was surly.

'This is my authority,' Hartmann told him crisply. 'Are you the man who received the luggage impounded by the SS?'

Yes, he was the man. Yes, he could provide a description of the passenger who had deposited the luggage. Hartmann smoked his pipe and listened in silence as the supervisor described the chauffeur. It was not a positive identification but he felt convinced Lindsay had been inside that uniform. He asked to see the bags.

Hartmann spent some time carefully sifting through their

contents, being careful to replace things as he found them. He was naturally tidy and both cases contained a woman's complete travelling wardrobe. The clothes were smart, very expensive. He paused when his agile fingers touched a folded astrakhan coat and matching hat.

An astrakhan coat and hat . . . The detailed report of the rescue group in front of the Frauenkirche had mentioned a *man* clad in just such an outfit, the 'man' in the rear of the green Mercedes who had hauled Lindsay inside. Except that it had not been a man – it had been a woman . . .

'Found any clues, Major?'

Hartmann glanced over his shoulder and saw Schmidt standing behind him. The SS officer smiled and made a friendly gesture as he spoke.

'Jaeger sent me to find out what you are up to. I was nothing loath to come – I'm equally curious . . .'

'The Baroness Werther – her impersonator – was at the Frauenkirche massacre. This is the coat and hat she wore – the hat doubtless well pulled down over her head. Hence no one realized she was a woman. She has now abandoned all her finery. What does that suggest to you, Schmidt?'

'That she has no further use for it . . .'

'Carry that thought to its logical conclusion,' Hartmann pressed.

'I'm road-blocked . . .'

'We shall find the Englishman not by concentrating on Lindsay – we must out-guess the Baroness, as I shall continue to call her. A worthy opponent, I suspect. Schmidt! She is changing her level, moving on a different plane. So far she has travelled as an aristocrat. She may be going to the other extreme – to the peasant level.'

'To confuse us? So we have the wrong description . . .'

'Partly that,' Hartmann agreed. His dark eyes gleamed and he reminded Schmidt of a bloodhound who has picked up the scent. 'But this fact may point to her general destination – she may *have* to assume a new appearance because of her surroundings. You would not resent a suggestion?'

'My God! No.'

243

'Warn the watchers at all bus depots and the captains of all ships plying the Danube to look for a peasant group – three men and a girl. And there is another station here, I believe . . .'

'The Südbahnhof. Trains to Graz – and Jugoslavia beyond . . .'

'Watch that station.'

Schmidt glanced at the huge clock suspended from a girder. It was 2.45 a.m.

Everything in the Südbahnhof district was worn-out, derelict – or at best shabby if a building was occupied – when you could see anything through the sour fog which clung to the area like a plague. Gaunt wrecks of buildings like huge rotting teeth loomed in the dirt-laden mist. It reminded Lindsay of a no-man's-land abandoned long ago by battle-weary armies.

Paco and Lindsay had travelled in a taxi which sagged to one side, the monstrous synthetic fuel attachment making the vehicle look distorted. She paid off the taxi in the middle of what appeared to be a desert of rubble and waited until it vanished in the grey pall.

'We walk the rest of the way,' she said briskly, 'then if the cab driver is picked up and questioned he can't lead them to us . . .'

'Lead them to where?' Lindsay wondered how she knew the direction to take. 'This isn't my idea of Strauss's Vienna at all . . .'

'It's one of the poor districts,' she said, striding out. 'Quite possibly Hitler knew it well in his younger days. You can see how it could drive a man on to get somewhere in the world . . .'

They were treading across an open area of rubble when two youths loomed out of the fog. Shabbily dressed, capless, they had an ugly look. One carried a length of iron pipe. The youth with the pipe hoisted it to strike Lindsay's skull a shattering blow.

The Englishman stopped Paco with his left hand. He jerked up his right foot and kicked his assailant between the legs with all his strength. The youth screamed, dropped the weapon, crouched over, moaning horribly. The other youth vanished. Raising his foot again, Lindsay placed it on the shoulder of the crouched youth and shoved hard. The youth spun over backwards and sprawled among a debris of stones and broken glass. Blood oozed from his head.

'Move!' Lindsay snapped. 'And put that thing away . . .'

That thing was a short-bladed knife Paco had produced – Lindsay wasn't sure where from. They hurried through the night as he went on talking.

'If you'd knifed one of them the police would have started swarming. That we can do without . . .'

'I know. This way . . .'

'And get rid of that knife . . .'

'I didn't expect . . .'

Paco stopped in mid-sentence. She must be ruddy well played out, Lindsay thought. He knew what she had stopped herself saying: 'I didn't expect you'd cope with those two thugs . . .'

'You're learning fast, Lindsay.' She linked her arm through his, and a trace of the normal Paco returned as she smiled mischievously. 'You may even survive. Now, you mustn't be able to identify this place we're staying for the night.'

A fat chance of that, Lindsay almost retorted. The three-storey building they were approaching had plaster peeling off the drab walls. In the swirling fog he made out the word Gasthof but the name which had once followed it had peeled away.

It was a slum. Torn curtains with ragged edges hung across the windows at crazy angles. Nearby he heard the muffled thump of engines shunting freight wagons. Were they that close to the Südbahnhof? Then they were inside a gloomy hall and he shut the warped front door. An interesting contradiction – the hinges were well-oiled, making no sound.

Paco went up to a plain wooden counter behind which a gnarled old man in a threadbare green waistcoat waited. The place had a musty, dank smell mingled with stale urine. Were they going to spend many hours in this hell-hole?

'You know me – Paco,' she said in a firm, confident voice. 'I am expecting two men . . .'

'What kept you?'

Bora appeared out of nowhere half-way down a rickety staircase. Behind him, smiling warmly, stood Milic. Bora ran lightly down the rest of the steps, making no sound. He paused at the bottom to stare hard at Lindsay. The English-man had had enough of the arrogant Serb and stared back. Bora turned to Paco.

'There has been some trouble in the area recently . . .'

'Stop rattling your guts in public!' It was the old boy behind the makeshift reception counter who growled out the words. From his manner he had as little liking for Bora as had Lindsay. He turned to Paco, ignoring the Serb.

'The police have already been. They looked at the register. They went away. They won't be back. They're looking for a killer.'

'A killer?' Paco queried softly.

'Two youths in civvies – they're probably army deserters. They attacked two soldiers and robbed them blind. Attacked them with lengths of iron piping. One soldier killed, the other in hospital. They got good descriptions from the one who survived. It's stirred things up round here, I can tell you.'

'Where are the suitcases I left?' Paco interrupted brus-quely.

'Room 17. Your friends have already collected one. I've put them in Room 20. You two will be sharing . . .?'

The question drifted off into space as the receptionist looked over Paco's shoulder at Lindsay who remained silent. Nothing lecherous in the old man's expression – just a straightforward enquiry.

'We'll be sharing,' said Paco.

'Money in advance . . .'

'I know! This payment includes warning in time for us to escape if the police return. And that front door is still open . . .'

'It won't be!' Lifting a flap in the counter, the receptionist trudged to the entrance, inserted a large key in the lock, turned it and began shutting bolts. Lindsay counted four. The old man peered up at him and winked. 'Take a cannon to blow this door in. That's solid yew . . .'

Paco counted out a large pile of banknotes. Picking up the key, she gestured for Lindsay to follow her. Bora and Milic preceded her up the stairs. She waited until they were alone at the end of a long corridor before speaking.

'Bora, we're catching the 4.30 a.m. train from the Süd-bahnhof to Graz – so get what sleep you can. No problems on the way here?'

'Our cab broke down – his scrap metal engine exploded. We walked two miles. This murdered soldier worries me. By morning the area could be swarming with Gestapo . . .'

'So we're catching the earliest train we can. Go to bed, Bora.'

Lindsay followed Paco along the narrow, bare-boarded corridor to Room 17. It was larger inside than he'd expected – dim light filtered through the uncurtained window. He went across and looked out. The view was restricted – a blank wall opposite, a thread of an alley below. He closed the curtains carefully and Paco switched on the light, a naked bulb the equivalent of forty watts.

Paco sank on to the edge of the large bed. 'Thanks for keeping quiet about those two thugs we met – they must be the men who killed that soldier. The receptionist would have been alarmed. And Bora would have had a fit . . .'

'You gave that receptionist enough money. I was amazed. We can trust him?'

'The price of secrecy. We can trust our money. Funny, isn't it, for that amount we could have stayed at the Sacher . . .'

'Why didn't we? This place is quite a dump.'

'Lindsay, you've stopped learning again. If by any quirk of fate they've traced us to Vienna they'll check the top hotels first – the places where the Baroness Werther would stay at. To say nothing of the problem of registration. And here we're a stone's throw from the Südbahnhof. I'm dog-tired – get me the suitcase out of that big wardrobe . . .'

The furnishings were simple – primitive might have been a

better word. A large wardrobe with a door which didn't close properly, a cracked mirror. The large bed with varnish peeling off the headboard. A cracked wash-basin which exuded a peculiar aroma if you stood too close. He placed the case on the bed and sat at the top with the case between them.

'We're peasants from now on,' she said. 'We change into our new clothes before we sleep – then if we have to leave quickly by the fire-escape we're dressed. It's at the end of the corridor . . .'

Dropping from fatigue, Lindsay changed into the outfit Paco had chosen for him – a thick shirt with a worn collar, a pair of green corduroy trousers which had been repaired many times and a heavy, shabby jacket.

Paco was quicker and by the time he had changed she was in bed under the down quilt and fast asleep. Wearily he climbed in the other side, careful not to disturb her and lay down. Closing his eyes, he slipped into blessed oblivion.

It was 3 a.m. At SS headquarters in Vienna all the men seated round the table could hardly keep their eyes open except for one. Gustav Hartmann seemed tireless and capable of going on for ever without sleep.

Gruber was holding forth. By his side sat his new colleague, Willy Maisel, a thin-faced man of thirty with a thatch of dark hair who had a considerable reputation for shrewdness.

'This Englishman and the subversives have now killed a German soldier near the Südbahnhof!' He was working himself up into an excited state. 'This is the second time they have murdered . . .'

'Oh, for God's sake,' interrupted Colonel Jaeger, 'don't get so bloody theatrical. Certainly not at this hour.'

By his side Schmidt lifted his eyes to heaven and flung a pencil down on the table. In the brief silence the noise was like a pistol shot.

'The evidence points in another direction,' ventured Willy Maisel. 'We have precise descriptions of the two assailants, both youths who sound to me like deserters. Nothing at all to do with Wing Commander Lindsay and his friends.'

'Thank you for your support,' Gruber said nastily. 'At least I have taken some positive action, which is more than anyone else could claim, I suspect . . .'

'Oh, what action is that?' Hartmann enquired jovially.

'Gestapo agents and their network of paid informants are at this moment checking all the top hotels in the city. This pseudo-Baroness likes to live well, the murdering bitch . . .'

'Good for you,' Hartmann replied with a straight face. 'I'm sure tying up your forces on that mission will prove highly profitable.'

'I'm declaring this meeting closed.' Jaeger stood up and shoved his chair back against the wall with a hard kick of his boot. 'I want some sleep. We'll start again in the morning . . .'

Schmidt strolled over to Hartmann, glancing back at the table to where Gruber and Maisel still sat with their heads together. The SS officer waited until they were in the corridor before he asked his question.

'Do you think Gruber knows what he is talking about – this obsession with the Südbahnhof?'

'Maisel is the clever one,' Hartmann replied cryptically. 'He supplies the brains, Gruber the brute force. A perfectly balanced Gestapo team. They should go far!'

'Which means you're evading my question,' Schmidt remarked without malice as they continued along the corridor.

'The Südbahnhof is a working-class area – one of the really poor districts. Good night . . .'

Schmidt watched the Abwehr man disappearing down a flight of ill-lit steps. He suspected Hartmann had been giving him a clue – but he was too exhausted to work it out.

'Wake up, Lindsay, you lazy slug. You've had hours of sleep!'

Lindsay's head was full of cottonwool. He opened his eyes as Paco shook his shoulder again. He felt he had just gone to sleep. Would it never stop – this pushing on and on and on? Christ, he wished they'd been able to make Switzerland.

'What time is it?' he asked as he sat up and forced his legs out of bed.

'Four o'clock. Train leaves in thirty minutes. Get something inside you. I brought breakfast up.'

Breakfast was one slice of dark bread which tasted like sawdust sprinkled with charcoal. There was a chipped mug containing some liquid he couldn't identify. Sitting at a small table he looked at Paco.

She was wearing a faded head-scarf tied under her chin which hid her blonde hair. A heavy bolero-style jacket and a cheap skirt which billowed out completed her new ensemble. It made her look plumper.

He finished the bread and swallowed the rest of the liquid. The battered old suitcase stood on the floor. He gestured towards it.

'We take that?'

'Yes, you carry it. We change clothes again when we arrive at the refuge in Graz. Any talking needed at the station you leave to me. I've already got our tickets. Ready?'

'No! So let's go . . .'

He picked up the working man's cloth cap and pulled it down over his forehead. The clothes felt strange – and not only from sleeping in them. The material was stiff and unyielding. He had picked up the case when he caught sight of himself in the cracked wardrobe mirror.

'I haven't had a shave . . .'

'I want you whiskered, you clot! You're a peasant. Some people can't think of the simplest things . . .'

'Oh, stop your nagging, for Christ's sake!'

'That's better,' she told him. 'I want you alert. We go out by the fire-escape – the receptionist says a policeman is watching the front entrance . . .'

The fire-escape was a rusted contraption clinging precariously to the side of the rear of the building. It led down into the narrow alley Lindsay had seen from the bedroom window when they had arrived.

'I don't like the look of this . . .'

'Go on!' she hissed.

One of the metal treads gave way under his weight, then stabilized at a slant. Bora and Milic were waiting for them in the alley. Lindsay noticed Bora also carried an ancient suitcase. Both men were clad in peasant garb. Paco pushed past them and Lindsay followed her out of the alley into the open.

Smoke. In the pre-dawn atmosphere the whole district appeared to be shrouded in smoke. It was the relics of the overnight fog. They passed the silhouettes of slum tenements and then he had his first glimpse of the grim building which was the Südbahnhof. More like a prison than a railway station.

Stooped figures like ghosts drifted towards the building. He followed Paco inside the booking-hall where more figures, huddled in the cold, formed queues behind the ticket windows. They went through the door on to the platform. A train stood waiting with destination plates attached to the coaches: *Graz*. At this moment he saw Gruber, the Gestapo chief from the Berghof.

'Do as I tell you and don't bloody argue . . .'

Lindsay grabbed Paco by the arm and held on tightly. She was compelled to stop and he knew she was furious. He didn't care. *Gruber!* Suddenly he was alert. The taste of his filthy breakfast was forgotten. He glanced both ways along the crowded platform.

'What the hell do you think you're doing?' she whispered.

'Keep still a minute!'

He kept hold of her arm, forcing her to do his bidding. Two youths who had been strolling towards him stopped in their tracks. They were the youths who had attacked him with an iron pipe. Lindsay, sensing Gruber's closeness to his left, stared hard at them.

The one who had run away saw him first, said something to his companion, who then also stared back at Lindsay. They turned away. They began to run, knocking down an old woman in their haste. It became a commotion.

'*Halt!*' Gruber's voice, a harsh shout. 'Halt, I say – or we fire!'

Gruber rushed straight in front of Lindsay, a Luger in his right hand, followed by two more men also holding pistols.

The three men stopped, aimed their weapons. Lindsay counted six shots. One of the youths flung up both hands like an athlete at the winning tape and crashed forward on to the platform. The second youth screamed, stopped, grabbed his left leg and sank down on one knee.

'Come on! Now!'

Lindsay hustled Paco aboard the train, glanced back, saw Milic and Bora close behind, and pushed Paco along the corridor. She found an empty compartment and sank into the corner seat next to the corridor. He closed the door as Bora and Milic moved on to another compartment.

'That was Gruber of the Gestapo,' Lindsay said quietly, heaving the case on to the rack. 'He questioned me before we escaped from the Berghof . . .' No point in telling Paco about the existence and location of the Wolf's Lair. 'Those two thugs thought I was going to point the finger at them. They saw me, they saw Gruber – Gestapo written all over him. They panicked – as I hoped. The perfect diversion for us. Any comment?'

He sat down and she leaned her head back and studied him. Her breasts were heaving as she struggled to get her breath back. She smiled.

'You really have learned fast, haven't you, Lindsay?'

It was all over Vienna in no time – the news that the Gestapo had shot one of the two murderers of a German soldier and had the other in custody. Gruber saw to it that the triumph was broadcast. This put the Gestapo one up against the SS and the Abwehr. What he did not foresee was that within twenty-four hours this would bring Hartmann to Gestapo headquarters where the surviving deserter was to be interrogated.

Hartmann had no difficulty in persuading the officer on duty to give him access to the prisoner. He simply waved Bormann's document under his nose. At that moment Gruber was preoccupied in his office trying to get through to the Berghof.

'I am Major Hartmann,' the Abwehr officer informed the

252

deserter who was lying on a bed in a cell with his leg bandaged. 'You realize your position? You will be tried and sentenced on the evidence of the soldier who survived your brutal assault . . .'

'It was Gerd who killed him . . .' the youth protested.

'If I am to help you,' Hartmann interrupted, 'you must tell me what happened at the Südbahnhof. I cannot understand why you panicked. No one had seen you . . .'

'The man and the girl had spotted us . . .'

The youth stopped as though he had said too much. Hartmann leaned forward as he raised a warning finger.

'I am short of time. I am the Abwehr. Once I leave here you are alone – with the Gestapo. What man, what girl?'

'The previous night we stopped them near the Südbahnhof. The funny thing is they were dressed so differently I might never have recognized them at the station – but the man kept staring at me . . .'

Hartmann had the whole story out of him in ten minutes. The youth had seen the man and the girl boarding the Graz train. Hartmann stood up, called the guard, left the cell and left Gestapo headquarters. Reluctantly he decided he had better report his findings to Bormann before he headed for Graz.

Chapter Twenty-Seven

The Bureau Ha, the section of Swiss Intelligence which dealt with Lucy, was based in the Villa Stutz, eight and a half kilometres from the suburb where the Roesslers had their apartment.

This three-story, stucco-faced building was tucked well out of the way in a discreet location on a lonely cape projecting into Lake Lucerne. From the outside it had the appearance of being the residence of a wealthy Swiss. No uniformed soldiers were ever seen in the vicinity; its wrought-iron double gates were guarded by men in civilian clothes.

It was to the Villa Stutz that Roger Masson summoned Roessler to an interview in his office at midnight. The late hour was chosen deliberately. It enabled Roessler to make the trip to the Bureau's headquarters without being seen. At that time – as Masson knew – Switzerland was swarming with German agents who had slipped across the frontiers.

Masson sat stiffly behind his desk as the stooped figure of Roessler was shown into the room. This alone made Roessler nervous – it was unlike Masson who normally greeted him in the most friendly manner. The Swiss launched his verbal onslaught as soon as Roessler was seated opposite him.

'You are a German. Our arrangement was that you would operate your transmitter on the clear understanding that copies of every signal from Woodpecker would be sent to me . . .'

'There have been no signals to send . . .'

'You expect me to believe that for several weeks Woodpecker has been off the air every night? Has the system broken down then? Do you think Woodpecker has been caught by the Gestapo? All this is highly unsatisfactory. Has a man called Allen Dulles, an American, been near you?'

'I have never heard of such a person,' Roessler protested.

Masson leaned back in his chair. Roessler's statement carried conviction. But the American agent who had slipped into Switzerland via Vichy France earlier was proving a bloody nuisance. He travelled about openly, making no attempt to conceal himself. He practically advertised his existence. Already the Germans knew he was in Switzerland. As these thoughts drifted through his mind, Masson watched his visitor who stirred restlessly as he glanced round the room. Floor-length curtains shrouded the windows and the silence was increased by the mist rolling in from the lake.

'It really puzzles me – this sudden gap in Woodpecker's flow of information,' Masson said suddenly.

'You think it doesn't puzzle me? And the season for the

summer campaign on the Russian front is approaching – so Moscow should be avid for details of the Wehrmacht's order of battle. Hitler could destroy them with the huge forces under his control . . .'

'I know. Well, we'll have to see. You may go now . . .'

Masson sat alone at his desk for a whole hour after Roessler had left. If Hitler won on the Eastern Front his next objective might be the invasion of Switzerland. There had been that unnerving reference to Switzerland his code-breakers had still not managed to unravel. Lucy's activities – if ever discovered – were a tremendous provocation to the Nazis. Masson simply couldn't make up his mind whether to let Roessler go on.

At the end of April 1943 Woodpecker's transmissions were resumed. Masson had no way of knowing that this event coincided with the movement of the Führer and his entourage back to the Wolf's Lair aboard the *Amerika*. Among the people who travelled back with him on the train were Reichsleiter Martin Bormann; the stiff-necked Field Marshal Wilhelm Keitel; and the amiable but wily General Jodl.

The *Amerika* was steaming steadily closer to the Wolf's Lair when Bormann entered the dining-car. Hitler sat at a table with Keitel and Jodl and had commenced his meagre lunch consisting of a bowl of celery soup.

'*Mein Führer*,' Bormann announced as he sat in the empty chair, 'there is news of the English fugitive, Lindsay . . .'

'They have captured him? Alive, I hope . . .'

'Well, no – not yet. But Hartmann has reported they are making for Jugoslavia. He is following them . . .'

'Ah, Hartmann!' Hitler was amused at Bormann's expense. 'I recall at the Berghof you wished to entrust this mission solely to the Gestapo and the SS. Was it not I who insisted Hartmann should join the search?'

'It was your decision alone, *mein Führer*, once again confirming your infallible judgement,' Bormann agreed obsequiously.

Jodl nearly choked on the particularly succulent morsel of pork he was enjoying. The Reichsleiter's self-abasement

255

almost made him throw up. Jodl was one of the few men capable of standing up to Hitler. There had been a famous pre-war incident when he had engaged in a shouting match with the Führer, contradicting him to his face.

'I don't know how you can stomach that meat,' Hitler remarked. 'A vegetarian diet . . .' He stopped himself launching into a long lecture and continued questioning Bormann. 'So, Lindsay and his associates did not head for Switzerland – as you were certain they would. The expensive luggage abandoned at the Westbahnhof should have warned you, Bormann. They were adopting a different role. Where does Hartmann think they are heading for now?'

'One of the British agents parachuted in to liaise with the Jugoslav guerrilla forces . . .'

'Which one specifically?' Jodl enquired.

'He gave no further information except that he was continuing on their trail,' Bormann replied.

Keitel remained silent, apparently absorbed in his meal and the view out of the window. It was going to be one of the first warm spring days.

'Jugoslavia?' Hitler repeated thoughtfully. 'I wonder if they all realize what awaits them down there? They are entering the gates of hell . . .'

By 2.30 on the following morning, the *Amerika* had long ago pulled up in the small railway siding at the Wolf's Lair. Hitler and his entourage were settled in at their familiar quarters inside Security Ring A. There was one exception.

A shadowy figure made its way alone through the darkness of the engulfing pine forest until it reached the log pile. Agile hands removed the few logs concealing the transceiver. The coded signal the hands tapped out was in two parts. The first gave the new German order of battle decided on by the Führer at his midnight conference.

The second part, in special code, reported Hartmann's news as to the present whereabouts of Wing Commander Lindsay and his likely destination. The transmission completed, the hands replaced the concealing logs and switched off the small, masked torch. Woodpecker had resumed communication with Lucy.

As you drive into the Kremlin you enter a city within a city – like one of those Russian, hand-painted wooden dolls which opens to reveal inside a smaller replica of the original doll. You drive acrosss a vast courtyard surrounded with medieval houses and ancient churches and the great entrance doors close behind you, sealing you off from the outside world. It is like travelling back through several centuries in time.

At five o'clock on the morning of 1 May Laventri Beria was in a foul humour as he sat in the rear of the black limousine – the only colour known to Soviet manufacturers of luxury cars. Seeing nothing of the inner city, he tried to guess what emergency could have caused Stalin to summon him at this ungodly hour. Beria was getting very short of sleep.

The Generalissimo, fully-dressed in his simple uniform, freshly shaved, waited for the NKVD chief in his office in the modern block. He remained standing and made a gesture for Beria to sit down. This compensated for the Georgian's lack of height and put his visitor at a psychological disadvantage.

'That Englishman, Wing Commander Lindsay!' Stalin's voice was harsh, his manner venomous. He paced around the gloomy room for a few moments and Beria froze. Seldom had he seen the Georgian so disturbed. 'He is escaping to Jugoslavia . . .'

He used the word *escaping* in a tone of withering sarcasm. 'Do you really think, Beria, it would be possible for a man to escape from Berchtesgaden without the Führer's connivance?'

'You have clearly detected some conspiracy?' Beria suggested cautiously and then waited. He was accustomed to Stalin using him as a sounding-board for his own thoughts – especially if he was under great stress. The atmosphere reeked with tension and that mixture of odours old Western hands associate with Russia – human sweat, repellent Soviet soap and disinfectant.

'I have received another signal telling me not only that this

Englishman is making for Jugoslavia but also – listen to this, comrade – that he will attempt to get in touch with spies dropped by parachute into that country by our so-called Allies. You see the next development, of course?'

'Perhaps you would enlighten me?' Beria requested.

'It is all a capitalist trick!' Stalin's face suddenly flushed red as the blood coloured his complexion. 'Lindsay *is* a peace emissary from Churchill! He has agreed terms with Hitler which he is carrying back to London. Hitler goes to great lengths to conceal this from me – by returning Lindsay by a devious route. He hides his real aims even from his closest associates. Can you imagine the atmosphere of intrigue and mistrust which must prevail at the Hitlerite headquarters – one man pitted against the other?'

Beria could imagine it only too well, but was careful not to say so. It described perfectly the regime in the Kremlin.

'Perhaps the problem is not insoluble?' he ventured.

'I have already taken steps to deal permanently with our Wing Commander,' Stalin informed him.

On 2 May in London it was raining, which was no great surprise, a steady drizzle which could soak you in five minutes if you were outside. Tim Whelby was outside.

He wore an ordinary, drab raincoat and pretended to be reading a newspaper in the dreary surroundings of Charing Cross station. It was also chilly and he shivered as he checked his watch. 10 p.m. Exactly. Another three minutes and he would go back to his flat.

'An urgent signal has arrived from Cossack . . .'

The words were spoken in a whisper. Savitsky had appeared out of nowhere. He stood a foot away from Whelby and shook water off his umbrella over the Englishman. He turned and apologized in a normal voice.

'That's all right. I was wet through anyway,' Whelby replied in a sarcastic tone. He lowered his voice. 'Do get on with it, the police patrol round here . . .'

'Our Wing Commander is heading for Jugoslavia. We

understand he hopes to contact one of the Allied agents there . . .'

'He's on his own?' Whelby could not keep the surprise out of his question. By now he had pieced together a fairly complete picture of Lindsay. He knew for certain the RAF type spoke fluent German but no one had mentioned Serbo-Croat. The whole thing seemed highly unlikely. 'Are you sure about this information?' he asked.

'All my information is correct,' the Russian said with some irritation. 'And no, he is not alone. He linked up with a group of Allied agents. They got him out of Germany.'

'What do you expect me to do about it?' Whelby demanded sharply. 'My area is the Iberian peninsula. He was coming out via Switzerland and on to Spain. I might have done something then.'

'He must not reach Colonel Browne alive. Even if you have to intercept him personally. That comes from the top. I'm going . . .'

'I would if I were you,' Whelby replied with a trace of bitterness. For God's sake, did they imagine he was a trained assassin?

Marooned in southern Austria, Wing Commander Lindsay had no inkling how many different enemy groups were closing in on him. On the German side there were Colonel Jaeger and his deputy, Schmidt; the Gestapo, led by Gruber and his more intelligent colleague, Willy Maisel; and Major Hartmann of the Abwehr.

Stalin was being kept constantly in touch with the Englishman's progress. He was further doing everything in his power to bring about the Wing Commander's early liquidation.

Finally, there was the most trusted quarter – London – a haven Lindsay was desperately trying to reach. And here Tim Whelby was waiting with orders to ensure that the Wing Commander never survived to deliver his report on his visit to the Führer.

At this stage all the leading characters in the Great Game were living in a state of chronic anxiety. Stalin was sweating it out in case the Allies made a separate deal with the Germans. Roger Masson was having nightmares because he could not rid himself of the dread that Hitler would invade Switzerland if he found out the activities of Lucy. Roessler was worrying because he seemed to have lost the confidence of his Swiss protectors.

The key to all this desperate insecurity was that in May 1943 the Germans still stood a good chance of winning the war. They had the resources, the men – and the generals – to destroy Soviet Russia.

In London Tim Whelby was only too aware of the military situation. His most recent encounter with Josef Savitsky had shaken him badly. Although he had earlier had the briefest of meetings with Lindsay he had hardly noticed the man. Others had been present – men whom it had seemed more important to observe and cultivate.

'During a recent trip to Madrid,' he remarked casually to Colonel Browne shortly after the Charing Cross meeting, 'I was told of a rumour we might be exploring the possibilities of a separate peace with Hitler if the terms were right . . .'

'Really?' Browne hardly appeared to be listening as he stooped over the papers on his desk. 'Who told you that?'

'Just an informant I'd sooner not name. I told him the whole thing was a load of rubbish. How do these rumours start?'

'The way all rumours start, I suppose . . .'

'The same informant told me . . .' Whelby invented the story while he went on talking '. . . that Lindsay was sent on a peace mission to Hitler and is now negotiating a treaty with him . . .'

'Really?' Colonel Browne's tone expressed sheer disbelief in what he was being told and he reached for another document.

Whelby dropped the subject. It would be dangerous to pursue the topic any further. The devil of it was he had still not obtained Browne's confidence so he would open up on Lindsay's real role.

When Paco and Lindsay – with Bora and Milic – reached the ancient town of Graz from the Südbahnhof they did not linger. They arrived well after dark. Mingling with the hurrying crowd of other passengers, they walked out of the station without interference.

'No sign of security or police checks,' Lindsay commented.

'This is a backwoods place, remote from the war,' Paco replied as they continued on foot. 'No taxis here – and the last bus left an hour ago. You can walk three kilometres. You've been sitting down for a whole day!'

'There's a different atmosphere.' He glanced behind and Bora was following with Milic in the distance. The moon shone brightly on cobbles worn by centuries of footfalls. 'It might be a country at peace, like Switzerland.'

'Don't get too rhapsodic,' she warned. 'We hide up here for about three weeks in case they're watching the frontier for us. Then we cross into Jugoslavia at the Spielfeld-Strass border post – and that may be no picnic. . .'

'We're all going over together?'

'You and I together. We change clothes into Serbian costume. Bora and Milic provide the diversion to help us through . . .'

'I should help them . . .' he began.

'You should do as you're bloody well told! This is my territory. You're a package we have to deliver to one of the Allied military missions . . .'

'Maybe I should apologize for existing . . .'

'Now, don't go all sulky. That I can do without . . .'

During the verbal flare-up Paco had kept her soft voice calm as though they were carrying on a normal conversation. She glanced sideways at him as he stared straight ahead.

'You saved our bacon at the Südbahnhof when you rushed me aboard the train. We make a good team, Lindsay.' She grasped his free arm. 'We're all exhausted – that's the moment to watch it. We've just passed a couple of Austrian policemen in uniform . . .'

'I never even saw them.'

'Because we were too busy arguing like a normal couple. I

saw one of them grin and make a remark to his companion . . .'

'You devious little bitch!'

'It's nice to be appreciated . . .' She squeezed his arm and began walking faster. He stared at her – she had deliberately provoked the row to get them past the policemen. Her quickmindedness and ingenuity never ceased to amaze him. This, he thought, was how Paco's group had survived so long.

'What did you do before the war?' he asked. 'I don't know much about you . . .'

'I worked for an advertising agency in Belgrade. I was what they call in London an account executive. To survive in *that* job you have to be very persuasive with all types.'

'You joined the Partisans after Belgrade?'

'I joined the bloody Četniks – they support the monarchy, which I was quite happy about. That is, until I found they were collaborating with the Germans. I went over to the Partisans because they *were* fighting Germans. As simple as that. . .'

They spent the harrowing waiting time in an old house overlooking the river Mur in the centré of Graz. An old couple occupied the staging post. On Paco's instructions Lindsay exchanged not a word with either of them. He slept in a tiny bedroom with a window facing across the river to a weird clock tower perched halfway up a steep hill rising from the opposite bank.

He slept badly, tossing and turning on the unfamiliar bed and through the open window chill air flowed into the room – he opened it so he could hear if the police called in the night. On the day they left the place he wondered whether the lack of sleep had been due to premonition. The crossing at Spielfeld-Strass was a bloody affair.

PART THREE

THE CAULDRON:
Der Kessel

Chapter Twenty-Eight

In forty years Spielfeld-Strass has not changed. It is the same today as it was in 1943 – when Paco and her companions arrived in a six-coach train drawn by an ancient steam engine. It is more like a wayside halt than a frontier station.

As Lindsay alighted, following Paco, he saw another train waiting in a siding. The destination plates hanging from the coaches carried the legend *WIEN SUDBHF*. They crossed the tracks coated with early morning frost and went inside the small station building through the door marked Ausgang. No one was about to collect the tickets they had purchased at Graz.

Paco walked without appearing to hurry, descended some concrete steps and they were out in the open. The station stood perched on the side of a small hill. Down a short slope they walked into Spielfeld, a handful of houses and a police station, a two-storeyed building with a tiled gable and a tiny dormer window like a dovecote. Over the entrance were the words Gendarmerie and Postenkommando.

It was all so entirely unexpected. Lindsay transferred his suitcase to his left hand and caught up with Paco.

'There's no sign of troops or defences.'

'Wait till we get to the border crossing. It's not far.'

'What's happened to Bora and Milic?'

'Questions, questions, questions! You're at it again. They've gone a different way to create the diversion if we run into trouble at the crossing point . . .'

Lindsay said nothing. He was recalling how he had wandered into the kitchen of the house at Graz. Milic had been packing equipment inside a bag – the 'equipment' had included stick grenades and what looked like smoke bombs. Presumably he had collected his travelling gear from some

265

secret weapons store inside the house. He had not enquired.

'Don't stop!' Paco warned. 'Keep walking – ignore the police van.'

The police station stood at the edge of a deserted square. On the far side reared a huge chestnut tree, gaunt with naked branches along which were perched rows of sparrows. Behind the tree huddled an ancient inn with faded, colour-washed walls. *Gasthof Schenk.*

It was so incredibly peaceful. The other passengers seemed to have made off in the opposite direction – which made Lindsay feel conspicuous and nervous of the police station. Coffee-coloured hens trod the paving stones, jerking their red wattles. The birds chattered testily. The only other sound was the click of billiard balls from an open window in the Gasthof. It was 11 a.m., the sky was a sea of surging grey clouds and there was the smell of rain to come.

Two uniformed policemen sat in the cab of the police van parked under the chestnut. As they walked past the vehicle which bore the word Polizei in white across the front, Lindsay was aware of two pairs of eyes studying him. The two men remained motionless but he knew they were watching. He waited for the metallic grind of the handle being turned as the door opened.

Paco waited until they were descending a country lane before she spoke. Behind there was a faint flapping and Lindsay almost jumped. It was the birds taking off.

'They wouldn't stoop to speak to the likes of us,' she remarked in a perfect Cockney accent. 'The way we're dressed!'

They had changed into different clothes at the house in Graz. Now Paco wore a peasant jacket and skirt of Serbian style with a brightly-coloured handkerchief wrapped tightly round her head – again concealing her blonde hair.

Lindsay was similarly attired in the male equivalent and, at Paco's suggestion, had again not shaved so he was well-whiskered. They passed a high green knoll as they proceeded down the empty country lane and now the only sound was the distant whistle of an engine followed by the clang of shunted coaches.

'Milic and Bora may have to wipe out the frontier post if we are stopped,' she remarked casually. 'In case of trouble, put as much distance as possible between yourself and the guards. We have arrived . . .'

Acts of violence are shocking not so much by the casualties they create as in the suddenness with which they occur. Rounding a corner in the country lane they were confronted with the frontier post, with war.

German troops mounted guard over the crossing point, men clad in field-grey uniform who moved restlessly about to combat the morning chill. They paused to stamp their booted feet on the iron-hard ground crusted heavily with frost in a hollow. They slapped their gloved hands round their shoulders to get the circulation going. In the descent from the station the temperature had dropped ten degrees.

The rail track had reappeared, the line leading south into the Balkans, into the battlefield. A goods wagon stood in a siding and men loaded it with wooden boxes from an Army truck. Lindsay stiffened and Paco's arm linked inside his kept him moving.

The boxes were rectangular in shape, made of wood and stencilled with broken lettering. Ammunition boxes. The rail wagon was almost fully-laden. Sentries with machine-pistols at the ready patrolled on both sides of the track.

'A bad moment to arrive,' Lindsay murmured.

'A good moment,' Paco murmured back. 'Their attention is taken up with that wagon.'

Lindsay glanced up at the grassy knolls topped with copses of trees surrounding the hollow. He was trying to imagine where he would position himself if he were Milic and Bora. There was no sign of the two men. Paco produced some grubby papers and they joined a queue of no more than half-a-dozen peasants waiting to cross into Jugoslavia.

The two old women immediately in front of them chattered in a strange language, a sing-song, zizzing sound. Lindsay had never heard people speaking in that way before. Paco, who was watching him, whispered.

'That's Serbo-Croat. You'd better get used to it, you're going to hear a lot of that . . .'

Strange, Lindsay reflected, her calm confidence that they would reach the Promised Land, Jugoslavia. The border post was a small wooden hut very much like those he remembered night watchmen had sheltered inside in England before the war. All papers were being examined minutely by a young Army captain.

'Be careful,' he warned Paco, 'the young ones are the worst.'

'Not for me!'

She really was quite incredible. Lindsay's nerves were twanging. Then he noticed why such a youngster occupied this passive occupation. His left sleeve hung loose like a draped curtain: he had only one arm. He observed the tight mouth, the bitter expression. Paco could have misjudged this man.

The queue shuffled forward. Beyond the hut, maybe a hundred metres beyond, stood a huge tidy log pile stacked in a cube. Some of the logs from this pile formed a fire which crackled close to the hut. The captain waved a man across the border. Safety was simply permission to continue walking down a country road – on to Jugoslav soil.

Now only the two old women in front of them had to be checked before it was their turn. Lindsay had never felt so helpless in his life – no experience at the Wolf's Lair, at the Berghof, while they were spending the night at the tumble-down Gasthof near the Südbahnhof, had been as bad as this. He felt so horribly *exposed* . . .

'I thought my aunt looked surprisingly well – considering how ill she has been. Don't you agree?' asked Paco, speaking German in a calm voice.

She caught Lindsay off guard. He had been studying the topography close to the border point. He realized she was making conversation for the benefit of the officer checking papers.

'It was a waste of time our coming in my opinion,' Lindsay responded.

The two old women ahead were handed their documents and the German studied Paco before taking her papers. She smiled at him but he showed no interest, which was exactly what Lindsay had expected. 'These papers are not in order,' he said after only a glance.

The top of the green knoll closest to the frontier post below was occupied by three men. Two were alive. One was dead. The German machine-gunner who had guarded this key position sprawled behind his weapon had never heard Milic creeping through the trees. His first inkling that he was not alone was when Milic rammed home the knife.

British field craft, as taught in the training camps in England was an amateurish affair compared with the Serb's expertise. Now it was Bora who lay sprawled behind the gun mounted on a tripod.

Next to him Milic lay on the cold grass with a pair of field glasses focused on Lindsay and Paco as they waited for their papers to be examined. Alongside Milic in neat rows lay the stick grenades he had extracted from the canvas satchel he had carried on his back. A parallel row of smoke bombs lay behind the grenades.

'I think there is trouble down there,' Milic observed.

'What is wrong?' snapped Bora. 'They may get through without trouble. Trust Paco . . .'

'She has just given the signal,' Milic replied equably.

Through the lenses of the glasses he clearly saw Paco raise a hand to the handkerchief covering her head. It was the agreed warning. *We are in danger . . .*

'The special stamp recently introduced is absent from both of these documents,' the captain at the frontier post informed Paco.

'But, Captain, these papers were stamped in Graz yesterday . . .'

'You mean they were forged in Graz yesterday!'

269

Paco raised her hand to her head as though straightening her handkerchief. She went on talking, holding the captain's attention as she produced another set of papers. Her manner became even more self-assured and with a hint of arrogance.

'We are on a mission. Have you not been informed? We should have been passed through without question. These papers, as you will see, are signed by SS Colonel Jaeger of the Berghof . . .'

Lindsay glanced round the hollow again, surveying the enclosing knolls as the captain, his eye caught by the embossed eagle holding the swastika in its claws at the head of the documents, began to study the transit orders.

A short, wide-shouldered figure appeared at the crest of the knoll closest to the frontier post. His right hand held something which he hurled in an arc. The object landed close to a group of soldiers and detonated.

The dull thump of the explosion knocked down the soldiers like a row of skittles. A second grenade landed. Lindsay made a fist and hit the captain in the centre of his chest. He toppled back inside the hut. Grabbing Paco by the arm he hustled her forward until they were running.

'That log pile!' he shouted. The peaceful frontier post had erupted into activity and soldiers milled around like confused ants. 'We must get down behind it – the ammunition wagon . . .!'

He threw her down bodily as bullets from a machine-pistol streamed at them, spinning chips of wood off the top of the pile. Peering round a corner he saw the next grenade describing an arc and dropping inside its objective – the ammunition wagon . . .

The world came apart in a shattering roar. The ground under their feet – the frost-coated, iron hard ground – trembled as though shaken by an earthquake. Lindsay lay on top of Paco, shielding her as debris rained down. The log-pile remained firm.

He risked another glance round the corner. The wagon had disappeared. A section of the track had disappeared. The Germans who had patrolled alongside the wagon had disappeared. Men with rifles – well spaced out – began advancing up towards the crest of the knoll from which Milic had hurled his grenades. Now, crouched out of sight, he tossed smoke bombs down the slope.

They burst just in front of the advancing file of troops and a wall of fog billowed between them and the top of the knoll. Sprawled full-length behind the German machine-gun, Bora stared along the gunsight. The first German broke through the smoke. He waited. More troops appeared.

Lindsay checked carefully the position inside the hollow. Confusion still. Distant shouted orders. The frontier post hut had also vanished when the ammunition wagon exploded.

'We go now,' he told Paco. 'No one is watching the road to Jugoslavia. What about Milic and Bora . . .'

'They look after themselves. That was the arrangement. They join us later . . .'

'Follow me. I'm going to run. Zigzag – it makes a hard target to hit. Keep well away from me . . .'

He took one final look and started running. Paco followed and kept to the side of the road. Lindsay was running down the centre, dodging from side to side. At the extreme right flank of the file of troops moving up the knoll a soldier saw them.

He stopped, turning as he lifted his rifle to shoulder level. He took careful aim at the Englishman, trying to anticipate his next position. He was aiming slightly ahead of Lindsay. He took the first pressure. He was a marksman – which was why he was a flanker.

Bora swivelled the barrel of his gun. He sighted it on the man aiming at Lindsay and pressed the trigger. He kept his finger on the trigger, sweeping the weapon's stream of bullets along the line of climbing Germans. The flanker was dead. The steady rattle of the machine-gun continued, then ceased.

They were spread along the lower slope – every man who a moment earlier had been advancing towards the crest. In the hollow there was carnage but no sign of life. Black smoke drifted slowly from a large crater where the ammunition wagon had stood. The truck which had brought the ammunition boxes had vanished. Peace – a peace of horror – settled over Spielfeld-Strass.

'The incident bears the clear signature of the group we are pursuing,' Hartmann remarked as he extinguished his pipe.

The Junkers 52 which had flown the two men from Vienna to Graz was beginning its descent. Beside the Abwehr officer sat Willy Maisel. For weeks Hartmann had combed the Graz district for the fugitives without success, eventually returning to the Austrian capital. Now events had confirmed his judgement. Before boarding the Junkers he had phoned Bormann. He had heard Bormann repeating what he said and in the background the voices of Jodl and Keitel. The Reichsleiter's security was a farce.

'Signature?' queried the mystified Maisel.

'Their *modus operandi* – a repeat performance of the affair in front of the Frauenkirche in Munich. The report from Graz about the attack at Spielfeld-Strass spoke of grenades and smoke bombs. The same technique as in Munich . . .'

'I see,' Maisel replied. 'You think then . . .'

'I don't think, my dear Maisel, I *know*! Lindsay and his escort crossed into Jugoslavia at Spielfeld-Strass this morning. I tried to warn Bormann – Switzerland might not be the answer . . .'

'So now we enter Jugoslavia ourselves – into the cauldron as the Wehrmacht calls it,' Maisel commented without enthusiasm.

'An excellent description – you can get scalded before you know what has happened,' Hartmann replied cheerfully. 'And *I* have to go into Jugoslavia. You are a free agent, Maisel . . .'

'I have my duty to do,' the Gestapo officer said stolidly.

The wheels of the plane bumped as they touched down and taxied along the runway. A building carried the legend *Graz Flughafen*. Hartmann was secretly amused at Maisel's trepidation. At Vienna the Gestapo man had joined the plane at the last moment – sent, as Hartmann was perfectly aware, by Gruber to keep an eye on his investigation.

Hartmann had always preferred to operate on his own. Already he had laid plans to lose Maisel at the first opportunity. When they disembarked from the machine and Maisel began walking in the direction of the airfield building Hartmann dropped his case and stretched his arms.

'I'm going to exercise my legs . . .'

'I need coffee – I'm parched,' Maisel replied and walked on.

Hartmann waited until he had disappeared, then picked up his bag and walked rapidly across to the small Fiesler-Storch parked near the runway where a pilot stood smoking. He stubbed his cigarette quickly as Hartmann approached.

'Gustav Hartmann,' the German introduced himself breezily. 'I phoned from Vienna for a feeder aircraft to take me on to Spielfeld-Strass . . .'

'At your service, Major. Erhard Noske. May I take your case?'

'Fuelled? Ready for immediate take-off?'

'Of course, sir! Your orders were explicit . . .'

Five minutes later Willy Maisel, a cup of coffee in his hand, stared out of a window as the tiny plane took off, gained height and turned on a south-easterly course. Swallowing the rest of the coffee, which tasted like real coffee – these rustics out in the wilds knew how to take care of themselves – he ran to the control tower.

'That plane which just took off. Who was aboard? What is its destination?'

'All flights are subject to the most stringent security. Who might you be?' enquired the late middle-aged Austrian.

'I *might* be Gestapo . . .' Maisel produced his identity folder. 'I *am* Gestapo. You want me to ask you again in words of one syllable?'

'Major Gustav Hartmann of the Abwehr is the passenger. He is flying to the airstrip nearest Spielfeld-Strass . . .'

'Bastard!'

'I beg your pardon – I have answered your questions.'

'Not you. At least I don't think so,' Maisel replied drily.

The airstrip materialized like a conjuring trick. They had flown the whole way from Graz in a heavy overcast, grey damp clouds like the thickest of ground fogs. Hartmann – who disliked flying – had spent most of the time trying to recall that there were *no* mountains in the way between Graz and the border. They dropped like a stone.

The airstrip – no more than a preserved grass runway – lay beneath their landing wheels. They were down before Hartmann had time to adjust to the fact that they were landing. A Mercedes stood waiting, two men in the front seat.

'Very efficient of you, Noske,' Hartmann commented as he shoe-horned himself out of the plane and accepted his bag from the pilot. 'To have the car I ordered waiting. And a chauffeur as well, I see. The other man is a guard?'

'I have no idea who those people are,' Noske replied.

'You haven't? I see,' Hartmann responded grimly and took his time lighting his pipe.

He walked slowly to the open Mercedes, pausing to get the pipe going properly. There was an icy breeze blowing across the hard, rutted field. Let them ruddy well wait his convenience. It was Colonel Jaeger – with Schmidt beside him – who greeted Hartmann affably.

'Jump in the back seat! I'll drive you to Spielfeld-Strass. That is your destination, of course?'

'Of course . . .' Hartmann settled himself comfortably as though he had expected the two SS men to be waiting. He continued the conversation while Jaeger steered the car across the bumpy ground on to a nearby highway.

'Since when has the SS taken to tapping my phone calls? I used a phone at your headquarters to avoid Gruber .. .'

'It's by way of a compliment,' Jaeger replied. 'Your reputation for solving the insoluble is nation-wide.'

'You know something?' the Abwehr man commented. 'If we spend so much energy spying on each other, the Allies and Russia will have won this war before we realize what has happened.'

'You suspect Lindsay went over at Spielfeld-Strass?'

'Someone did,' Hartmann replied non-committally.

'We've just come from there . . .' Jaeger's tone changed, a bleak note entered his voice. 'It's a bloody terrible business that took place down there . . .'

'What do you expect? Someone tosses a match into an ammunition wagon.'

'It wasn't a match – it was a grenade,' Jaeger growled and his eyes met Hartmann's in the rear-view mirror. 'Waffen SS troops died in that holocaust . . .'

'A lot of people died when Goering carpet-bombed Belgrade . . .'

Jaeger was so furious he jammed on the brake and swivelled in his seat. 'Whose side are you on, anyway? Tito's?'

'I was a lawyer before this bloodbath we call a war started,' Hartmann said mildly. 'My job was sometimes for the prosecution, sometimes for the defence. That way you get to look at other people's point of view. Are we going to get to Spielfeld-Strass today?'

Jaeger released the brake and resumed driving at speed along the winding country road. His expression was grim. He was blazing with rage. He carefully avoided meeting Hartmann's eyes in the rear-view mirror a second time. The Abwehr officer placidly smoked his pipe.

Once Schmidt turned round and stared at their passenger briefly, the ghost of a smile on his face. Hartmann knew what he was thinking. *You devious bastard* . . .

It was Schmidt he would have to watch, Hartmann reflected. A police chief before the war, his mind was attuned to analyzing motives. Hartmann had deliberately provoked the bluff Jaeger to distance himself from the SS colonel – and Schmidt had understood his tactic.

Jaeger remained silent until he drove the car down the country lane past the railway station and pulled up in the hollow where the Spielfeld-Strass frontier post had stood.

The scene was dramatic. The catastrophe had occurred at eleven-thirty in the morning. It was now three in the afternoon. A gigantic crane mounted on a flat-car was slowly backing away towards Graz, drawn by a steam-engine. Army engineers, their work completed, stood drinking beer.

Fresh track had been laid, renewing the link between Austria and the line continuing south to Zagreb in Jugoslavia. Hartmann stepped out of the car and again threw Jaeger off balance with his opening remark.

'With organization like this we should still win this war.'

'It is essential communications be maintained,' Jaeger responded gruffly. 'Along this route travel all the supplies for twenty divisions engaging the guerrilla forces. Twenty divisions! Can you imagine what we could do with those transferred to the Russian front?'

'Perhaps the Führer should have gone round Jugoslavia rather than through it,' Hartmann suggested.

'And let the Allies launch an attack on our flank?'

'They have yet to do that in Spain. Neutrals – they're worth their weight in gold. They don't tie up priceless troops. Tell me, did anyone survive?'

A large canvas structure had been erected on the edge of the hollow and Hartmann had observed a medical orderly entering the marquee. Jaeger gestured towards it.

'A Captain Brunner was the only survivor. The extraordinary thing is he was apparently inside a flimsy wooden hut when hell broke loose. The hut just vanished but he escaped with little more than shock. So they told me over the phone.'

'I think I'll have a word with him . . .'

Hartmann started to walk towards the marquee. Jaeger fell in beside him, followed by Schmidt. The Abwehr man stopped and removed his pipe. His manner was quite sharp.

'Alone, I meant. Now would it be sensible to confront a shock case with an SS colonel, an SS captain and myself? He will feel overwhelmed – may even suspect we're interrogating him prior to arrest. Bormann will certainly try and make someone responsible for this débâcle. Who is made to order for the role? The sole survivor.'

'All right.' Jaeger's agreement was grudging. 'We'll see him later.' His sense of humour asserted itself. 'Unless, of course, you bring us a detailed report of every word Brunner says. *Every* word!'

'Of course!'

Hartmann's tone expressed amazement that Jaeger should imagine any other outcome was possible. On his way to the makeshift field hospital he checked to make sure he was carrying a pack of cigarettes. In the past they had worked wonders in interrogations. The medical orderly came out of the entrance.

'Can your patient smoke if he wants to? Can I ask him just a few questions?'

The orderly, a stoop-shouldered man in his fifties, stared. He looked as though he was adjusting to a unique experience.

'They don't usually ask, they just barge in regardless. Yes, he can smoke, in fact, he's panting for a cigarette. The shock is wearing off rapidly. I'd say you'll be good for him . . .'

Brunner was lying on a stretcher perched between two crates with a pile of stacked pillows to keep him upright. He watched the new arrival warily as Hartmann manhandled a spare crate to provide himself with a seat. The act of adopting a sitting position reassures the subject you are interrogating.

The injured captain's hand was bandaged, so Hartmann lit a cigarette and placed it between Brunner's lips. The eyes still had a wary look. He nodded his thanks for the cigarette.

'I'm Abwehr . . .'

The transformation in the atmosphere was almost ludicrous. The man on the stretcher physically sagged back on the pillows with relief.

'I was expecting the Gestapo.'

'Well, this is your lucky day – if you ignore this . . .' Hartmann gestured towards the bandaged hand. 'You survived.' He glanced at the loose left sleeve which contained no arm. 'The Eastern Front? I thought so. And here you must have felt confident you had rendered your service to the Reich – that you could enjoy the quiet life until this accursed war ended.'

Perhaps it was his lawyer's training – more likely it was simply his natural flair for psychology – but Hartmann had a

277

gift for saying the right thing. He saw Brunner's eyes light up, the reserves come down.

'You're so right,' Brunner agreed passionately. 'Then out of the blue this morning the world blows up. You know I'm the only survivor? I had friends in this unit. If it had been Russia . . . But at this dot on the map no one's ever heard of – and it was all the work of that bitch, I'm certain.'

'Tell me about . . . the bitch,' Hartmann coaxed.

It came flooding out, the events prior to the moment when the world had blown up. Hartmann listened without interruption and offered a fresh cigarette which Brunner lit himself. The descriptions of the couple whose papers Brunner had questioned seconds before the disaster made Hartmann uncertain.

'What colour was the girl's hair?' he asked eventually.

'No idea. She had it covered in one of those handkerchiefs these peasant women wear.'

'And she spoke German – fluently?'

'As well as you and I are talking . . .'

His description of the man who had accompanied her was vaguer. Hartmann felt fairly sure this could have been Lindsay – but again there was no certainty. And no, Brunner had not seen any sign of the guerrillas who had attacked the post.

'First time they've ever come this far north,' he went on, thinking aloud. 'Can't understand the reason – probably the ammunition wagon was their objective.'

'It was common knowledge the wagon was to be loaded today?'

'God no! You wouldn't believe the security on things like that. First indication we get is when the wagon appears and the feeder truck rolls up . . .'

'So there would be no way the guerrillas could have known in advance the wagon would be here today?'

'Come to think of it, no.'

'Where are they sending you?' Hartmann asked as he stood up and prepared to leave.

'I've got compassionate leave. I'm months overdue. The

Colonel in Graz is a decent type. It's a long way. Flensburg. Know it?'

'On the Danish border . . .' Hartmann smiled wryly. 'What used to be the Danish border before 1940. When you get home apply to the local military commander for a permanent discharge. You have done your bit for the Fatherland. Good luck, Brunner . . .'

It was pure chance that Hartmann met the medical orderly outside the field dressing station. The orderly was hurrying and his brow was furrowed. In his hand he held a piece of paper.

'Something troubling you?' Hartmann enquired.

'The patient, Captain Brunner, has to be kept here. I was just arranging for him to be moved to Graz . . .'

'Why the delay?'

'A Gestapo officer, Gruber, is on his way from Vienna to question Brunner. He is expected in three hours' time . . .'

Hartmann reacted instantly. 'You will move Brunner by plane to Graz immediately! Have another machine standing by to fly him on direct to Flensburg in Schleswig-Holstein via Frankfurt . . .'

'But what about Gruber?'

'What I have instructed you to do is by order of the Führer . . .' Hartmann produced the authority signed by Martin Bormann giving him full powers. 'Read that. Does anyone know your name?'

'No. It was all such a rush. I came straight down from Graz.'

'Travel back there with Brunner and see him safely aboard the transport to Flensburg. He is your patient. This, you never received . . .' Hartmann took from the orderly's hands the signal sent by Gruber, screwed it up into a ball and pocketed it. 'I cannot tell you the reason why the swift evacuation of Brunner is imperative. It goes right up to the Führer himself. Understood?'

'Yes, I will do as you say at once.'

The orderly carefully handed back the Bormann document he had read, Hartmann replaced it inside his wallet and walked back to the station to enquire when the next train left for Zagreb. He had left the frontier post unnoticed by Jaeger and Schmidt who sat on the ground leaning their backs against the Mercedes while they ate army rations obtained from the engineers.

'That train departs for Zagreb in five minutes,' the station master at Spielfeld-Strass told Hartmann. 'Normal service will be resumed now the track is repaired.'

There was an atmosphere of the front line now about the sleepy little halt. Waffen SS troops armed with machine-pistols stood inside the cab with the engine-driver and fire-man. One man with a heavy machine-gun was perched on top of the coal-tender. In the rear coach, a mail-van, a platoon of troops was hidden – a helmeted figure peered out briefly before slamming the door shut.

Hartmann chose an empty third-class compartment with uncomfortable wooden seats to make his presence less notice-able. Within five minutes the train started moving south. He kept his head out of sight as they chugged slowly through the hollow across freshly-laid track.

The Mercedes had gone. Presumably Jaeger, beside him-self with fury at the trick played on him, was searching for Hartmann. The temporarily-erected field hospital was also gone. The orderly had spirited Brunner out of Spielfeld-Strass.

Alone at last! He lit his pipe and eased his back against the hard seat. He must get something to eat later – but Hartmann could go long periods without food. At the station he had drunk two bottles of mineral water from the tiny army canteen. He said the words out aloud.

'Well, I've done the best I can.'

'And that, I am sure, is a very good best, Major . . .'

Hartmann turned his head very slowly and looked up at the man staring down at him with a satisfied smile. Willy Maisel, the Gestapo official he had left behind at Graz Flughafen, looked as contented as Hartmann had felt a minute earlier.

Chapter Twenty-Nine

'There will be a train for Zagreb at Maribor,' Paco whispered to Lindsay.

'Where the hell is Maribor?' he enquired.

'It is the next stop down the line from Spielfeld-Strass. Of course there will be no trains coming down from Graz today with the track shattered . . .'

They were perched at the back of a farm wagon drawn by a pair of horses. In front of them was a pile of freshly-cut logs, and behind the farmer holding the reins sat Bora and Milic. They had caught up with Paco and Lindsay by hurrying down the country road after their break through the frontier post.

The farm wagon had emerged from a rutted side track while they trudged along the road in the early afternoon. Paco, speaking Serbo-Croat, had persuaded the farmer to give them a ride. Her story had been ingenious.

'We are taking the train to Zagreb when the engine broke down at Spielfeld-Strass. It was going to be hours before they mended it and we have a rendezvous we must keep at all costs.'

A rendezvous. She had spoken the words in a certain way and the moustachioed old farmer with grizzled hair had studied her for a moment. Then, without speaking a word, he had gestured them to climb aboard.

'What was all that about?' Lindsay had murmured when they were settled inside the wagon.

'He thinks we are linking up with a Partisan group. He is a patriot, like most farmers who have been robbed of their crops by the Germans. He just doesn't want to know any details . . .'

The wagon moved at a surprising pace as the two powerful horses hauled the wagon steadily forward along a deserted

281

road. There was no sign of the Germans, no checkpoints. Lindsay still felt uneasy but could not put his finger on what was bothering him.

'There's no danger of a train getting through from Spiel-feld-Strass?' Lindsay persisted.

'Do you always worry like this, question everything?' Paco wondered. 'You yourself saw the state of the track when we fled from the place.'

'You have to be right, I suppose.' Lindsay sounded unconvinced. 'As to worrying, yes – except when I'm in a fighter plane.'

'I'd have thought that was when you did worry . . .'

'You're too preoccupied – watching in all directions, especially your tail.' He glanced at her. 'And then you have no one to think about except yourself . . .'

'And what does that mean?' she asked, staring straight ahead.

'Just a remark off the top of my head . . .'

'You're a funny man, Lindsay. Still, I'll soon have you off my hands when we pass you over to one of the Allied military missions.'

There was relief in her tone at the prospect, Lindsay reflected bitterly. As the wagon creaked and wobbled along the road they kept bumping into each other. He could feel the warmth of her body, the firmness of her flesh beneath the thick jacket she wore.

Occasionally she stole quick glances at him, studying his face as he now stared rigidly ahead. Bora, who had a machine-pistol concealed in a multi-coloured carpet bag, perched on the logs as he watched the road constantly. The farmer never spoke to his passengers, sitting drooped forward with the reins in his hands. Time passed like a dream with the gently swaying motion of the wagon.

'We're coming into Maribor,' murmured Paco. 'Here you *do* let me carry on any conversations. It has to be Serbo-Croat from now on. You are a deaf mute.' There was a trace of humour in her voice. 'Make the effort, try and act dumb . . .'

The farmer dropped them outside the small station and

again they split up into pairs, Lindsay accompanying Paco while Bora and Milic kept to themselves. The first shock came when Paco enquired about the next train to Zagreb.

She conversed with a gnarled old railway official who could not have been a day under seventy. Lindsay listened to the same sing-song, zizzing sound he had first heard when they had queued up behind the two old women at the Spielfeld-Strass frontier post.

Thanking him, she linked her arm inside Lindsay's and led him on to the platform where peasants with large bundles waited. She was careful not to speak until they were by themselves, close to the end of the potholed platform.

'Why are there so many old people about?' he asked. 'I noticed it as soon as we came into Maribor – not a youngster anywhere. In Germany it's understandable . . .'

'For the same reason,' she said tersely. 'The young ones are in the mountains – with the Partisans or the Četniks. Damnit, Lindsay, you were right. We'll have to decide what to do . . .'

'The problem is . . .'

'It's quite incredible – but I double-checked with the old boy. The next train for Zagreb is due – and it's coming through from Spielfeld-Strass!'

'Never underestimate the enemy. We'd better miss this train and catch the next one . . .'

'Which is some time tomorrow. Maybe! And there's a German headquarters in this town. It's small, I don't know anyone – and it's Croat territory. Wait here and we could get caught by a routine check. What's the matter with catching this train?'

'Paco, we don't know who may be on board. Who will they have sent after us? Because you can guarantee they've sent someone to track me down. Colonel Jaeger? Gruber? Hartmann? Take your pick . . .'

'I hope it's not Jaeger. I'm sure he'd recognize me – even in these clothes. We spent hours at the Four Seasons in Munich together when I wheedled those transit documents out of him . . .'

'You never did tell me how you managed that . . .'

'Here we go again. I've told you once already. I didn't have to sleep with him – that's what you're thinking, isn't it? And Jaeger is a professional soldier, an honourable man whose concern is to do his duty – at least that was my impression. His hobby just happens to be women. What difference does it make to you?'

'So you're prepared to risk this train from Spielfeld-Strass?'

'When the alternative is hanging about in Maribor, yes! And there won't be anyone dangerous on that train. We've moved too fast for them.'

In London during the evening Tim Whelby met Savitsky in a crowded pub in Tottenham Court Road. When he walked into the place at exactly nine o'clock he was surprised to see the Russian sitting in a secluded corner with half a pint of mild and bitter in front of him. It was the first time his contact had arrived early at a rendezvous.

Whelby ordered a double Scotch at the bar and threaded his way among the tables. He paused before taking the vacant seat on which Savitsky had perched his hat to keep the chair occupied.

'Do you mind if I sit here? It's packed tonight.'

'Please join me.'

Whelby swallowed half his Scotch and observed that the Russian watched his action with disapproval. To hell with this pedant of a messenger boy. He swallowed some more and placed the glass on the table.

'Lindsay has crossed the border into Jugoslavia.'

'The Germans aren't doing very well, are they?' Whelby commented. 'When did this happen?'

'Earlier yesterday. In the morning.'

Whelby was badly shaken. He grasped his glass casually and deliberately held on to it without drinking. It was important never to display any signs of agitation in Savitsky's presence. Whelby had no doubt regular reports assessing his ability and potential as a Soviet agent were despatched to Moscow.

But how the hell had this information reached the embassy

in Kensington Palace Gardens so swiftly? There had to exist a truly extraordinary system of communication. It began to look as though the system originated inside Germany itself.

'So where do you think he's heading for now?' Whelby asked.

'It's obvious – one of the Allied military missions working with the guerrillas. He could be air-lifted out any time now. Much more speedily than we ever anticipated. You have to stop him ever reporting back to London . . .'

'Thanks a bundle,' Whelby said laconically.

'I beg your pardon? What does that mean?'

'You've told me all this before – about the need for stopping him. A reason would help . . .'

'You have your instruction. The reason behind an instruction is not your concern. Surely your people must have received a communication from Lindsay about this latest news . . .'

'If they have, they're not telling me.'

'You must make enquiries – discreetly, understand?'

'That's reassuring,' Whelby said quietly. 'You remember, I hope, that my area is Spain and Portugal. If you check with an atlas when you get back you'll find they're some distance from Jugoslavia.'

'You make it sound difficult, so when you solve the problem it will make you seem so much more clever.'

'That's right,' said Whelby. 'You've got it in one.'

It was well after dark when the masked lamps of the engine hauling the train from Spielfeld-Strass approached the platform of Maribor station. Hartmann, pleading a need for fresh air, had left Maisel in the compartment while he went into the corridor, lowered a window and peered out.

His pipe – his trademark – was in his pocket. On his head he wore an old, peaked cloth cap not unlike those worn by so many middle-aged workers in Jugoslavia. Unless viewed very close up, not even his friends would have recognized Major Gustav Hartmann of the Abwehr.

He had excellent night vision which was rapidly adjusting to the darkness as the train chugged slowly towards the station. There were a lot of people waiting to board the train. Hartmann was recalling in photographic detail the descriptions he had coaxed out of the wounded Captain Brunner, descriptions of the girl and the man whose papers he had found out of order just before 'the world blew up'.

On the platform at the far end near the point where the engine would pull up Paco and Lindsay wearily watched the oncoming train. Earlier they had risked leaving the station to get something to eat and drink at a small café in a back street – the bill was outrageous because the proprietor produced meat which he had obtained on the black market.

'I'll sleep all the way to Zagreb,' Paco said. 'You'll lend me your shoulder for a pillow, won't you?'

'We'll take it in turns,' Lindsay snapped. 'One of us has to stay awake all the time in case of an emergency.'

'I know! I know! There's a whole Panzer division aboard and their sole job is to find us.' She paused after the outburst which was so unusual. 'Sorry, I'm dog-tired. It's the responsibility. You're right, of course. We'll agree some kind of roster. Oh, Jesus, Lindsay – you are right!'

They could see the engine-cab as it glided past – the armed troops inside. And then the coal-tender with the machine-gun mounted on top. What they did not see was the head of a man poked out of a window in a rear coach, a man wearing a cloth cap with a peak who was staring at them.

Colonel Browne was working late in his office at Ryder Street when Whelby arrived back on the pretence of collecting papers he had forgotten. It was becoming a habit for Browne to catch up on his own paperwork when everyone had left the building.

Daytime hours were occupied more and more with futile conferences as the momentum of the war built up. Browne blamed the Americans – it seemed they could only communicate verbally. He laid down his pen and stretched his aching limbs.

'Take a seat, Whelby. Care for a drink?'

'I've just had a couple – at a pub in Tottenham Court Road. I was chatting to a Flying Officer Lindsay – no relation to the Wing Commander who trotted off to Berchtesgaden, I suppose?'

'Doubt it. Our Lindsay is an only child.'

'Any word from him yet since he took off?'

Tired out, Browne hesitated, and Whelby noted the brief pause. 'Not a dicky bird,' the Colonel replied curtly. 'We'll hear in due course . . .'

'Must be worrying – the waiting,' Whelby probed.

'No more than a dozen other problems.'

Whelby was in a cleft stick. He knew that the command structure in the Mediterranean had recently been changed. Allied Forces HQ under Eisenhower and Alexander in Algiers controlled operations in North Africa, including Monty's Eighth Army which was now involved in the final stages of the Tunisian campaign.

But subversive operations in the Balkans, including Greece and Jugoslavia, were directed by the Middle East Command with GHQ in Cairo. Whelby could see no way of introducing Cairo into the conversation because he was not supposed to know where Lindsay was. He'd just have to wait: events had a way of playing into his hands.

'Something on your mind?' Browne asked.

'Yes, getting to bed. Good night, sir.'

Bormann had talked at the Wolf's Lair about Lindsay's suspected escape into Jugoslavia. The information reached him via two sources. When Hartmann had temporarily ditched Willy Maisel at Graz Airport the Gestapo official immediately phoned Gruber in Vienna.

'Hartmann, the wily bastard, gave me the slip. He's flying on his own, in a Fiesler-Storch he had standing by, to Spielfeld-Strass to investigate an incident. He thinks Lindsay crossed the border today . . .'

'What incident?' Gruber demanded sharply. 'What evidence has he to support this crazy theory?'

Gruber knew Martin Bormann, knew how cautiously the

Reichsleiter proceeded. He would need convincing *evidence* of what could so easily be a rumour. God knew there had been enough false sightings of the Englishman.

And Bormann always demanded evidence because that was how the Führer's mind worked. How many times had he heard Hitler rave at generals who presented him with bad news and then backed down on cross-examination.

'There was a guerrilla attack,' Maisel explained and told him the whole story. 'Hartmann linked it with the Frauen-kirche . . . stick grenades and smoke bombs . . . the same technique . . .'

Gruber was sufficiently convinced to decide it would be dangerous *not* to forward this report to Bormann. After all, he was now able to emphasize he was merely passing on information which had originated from Willy Maisel. If there was any backlash it would be Maisel at whom the finger could be pointed.

He at once phoned Bormann, who listened in silence. Gruber knew the Reichsleiter was working out all the angles as to how this new development might affect *his* position.

'I will pass on your message to the Führer,' Bormann decided, careful not to reveal he had already heard direct from Hartmann. 'The incident at Spielfeld-Strass is not, of course, conclusive.'

'It comes from Maisel,' Gruber stressed. 'And he bases what he told me on a conversation with another source – Major Gustav Hartmann.'

'Ah, the Abwehr! Who trusts that nest of traitors any more!'

Apparently the Führer did. When Bormann reported the news to Hitler he called for a large-scale map of Southern Europe which he personally spread out over the large table in the conference room. His finger traced a route from Munich to Vienna via Salzburg.

'It makes sense,' he pronounced. 'Bormann, you sealed off all routes from Munich to Switzerland? Yes?'

'It was the obvious escape route.'

'And the group which is endeavouring to smuggle Lindsay home again is professional . . .'

'We have no evidence of that . . .' Bormann objected.

Hitler exploded. 'You have forgotten what happened at the Frauenkirche? Only professionals could have pulled that off! They made fools of the troops who were actually waiting for them! What happens next? Hartmann searches the luggage they abandoned at Vienna Westbahnhof – which tallies with the description of the luggage the so-called Baroness Werther and her so-called chauffeur were carrying when Mayr saw them boarding the Vienna Express at Munich. You agree, Jodl?'

The two other men in the room, Colonel-General Alfred Jodl and Field Marshal Wilhelm Keitel had so far listened in silence. Jodl nodded his head.

'It would seem so, my Führer,' he replied cautiously.

'Next,' Hitler continued excitedly, 'we have the incident the following morning at the Südbahnhof. Later, under interrogation one of the two murderers of a German soldier describes how he saw a girl and a man boarding the train for Graz. And where does the line south from Graz lead to? Spielfeld-Strass, where there is a far more serious incident. Agreed, Keitel?'

'It is logical, my Führer.'

'Hartmann now reports his conclusion that he discerns the same signature – an apt word, that – in the grenade and smoke bomb attack at the frontier post as was used at the Frauen-kirche.'

Hitler spread both hands on the map, his arms rigid, and stared round at the three men listening to him in total silence. His expression was cynical.

'I have five million Bolsheviks facing me on the Eastern Front. I have to give daily orders as to how to destroy this barbaric horde. On top of that I have to play detective to point out how Lindsay is trying to escape with the aid of the only man after him who has any brains at all! Hartmann! Gentle-men, this conference is adjourned.'

His voice dripped with contempt as he marched out of the

room and along the corridor which led to the outside world.

It was by an equally complex communication route that the news of Lindsay's likely escape route reached London. Within hours of Hitler ending the conference, Rudolf Roessler at his apartment in Lucerne received a signal in the special code from Woodpecker.

He immediately re-transmitted this to Cossack in Moscow, where Stalin once again summoned Beria into the Presence. Silently, he handed the signal concerning Lindsay to his secret police chief. It was his policy always to show the white-faced man with pince-nez signals from Lucy. Should anything go wrong, Stalin was then in a position to off-load the full blame on to Beria. Lucy would become a Beria operation.

'You think this Lindsay is trying to contact one of those Allied espionage missions?' Beria suggested.

'Surely that is the only possible conclusion,' Stalin remarked acidly. 'When the time is ripe they will send a special aircraft to pick him up and transport him to Algeria, then on to London. We cannot trust Tito to liquidate him, so what is the solution?'

'Your agent in London will have to see he never reaches his chief.'

'Good.' Stalin retrieved the signal from Beria's limp hand. 'On your way out, send in my personal coding officer.'

In the darkened room lit only by a cone-shaped light on his desk Stalin sat down and composed the message, phrasing it with great care. When the coding officer arrived he remained crouched over his desk as though no one had entered, finishing the job. The officer, standing rigidly to attention, saw only a hand holding the slip of paper extend itself past the light.

'Send this immediately to Savitsky at the London Embassy.'

This intricate sequence of events explains why in London the Soviet agent, Savitsky, surprised Tim Whelby by arriving first at the pub in Tottenham Court Road.

For the first time in Savitsky's experience a signal from Cossack had carried the word *Urgent*. The Russian was also thankful that – by pure coincidence – a routine rendezvous had previously been arranged for this particular evening. Emergency, hastily arranged, meetings were highly dangerous.

And now, so far as Savitsky was concerned, the ball had, thank God, been passed to Tim Whelby. In Washington, London, the Wolf's Lair, Vienna and Moscow, life was not so very different. If you were handed a grenade with the pin out, you passed the deadly gift into other hands as swiftly as possible.

As the train from Spielfeld-Strass pulled into Maribor station Hartmann returned to his compartment to find Willy Maisel hauling down his case from the rack. The Gestapo man fastened the top button of his coat to muffle himself against the night cold.

'Not leaving, I trust?' Hartmann enquired with just the right tone of apparent interest.

'I have to keep Gruber in touch with developments which, as far as I can see, amount to zero. I can phone him from military headquarters here. By now he'll be like a cat on hot bricks to report again to Bormann . . .'

'I think I'll stay on board this train to Zagreb,' Hartmann remarked casually as he settled into his seat and lit his pipe.

'Please yourself. I think it's a waste of time.'

Hartmann waited until Maisel had gone and then went back into the corridor and lowered the window again. He peered out along the platform and was just in time to see Paco and Lindsay board a coach near the engine.

The train had left Maribor some time earlier and was proceeding south through the night when Willy Maisel reached army headquarters, flourished his identity folder and tried to call Gruber in Vienna.

He was informed by the operator that for security reasons all calls had to pass through the headquarters in Graz. He gave his name and waited, suddenly aware that he was ravenous. An aroma of food cooking drifted up into the room where he sat. He was quite unprepared for what happened next.

'Is that Willy Maisel speaking?' a gruff voice demanded.

'Yes, I have already asked to be put through . . .'

'Colonel Jaeger speaking, Maisel. What are you doing in Maribor?'

'I left the train which came through from Spielfeld-Strass. I was with Major Hartmann of the Abwehr . . .'

'Put him on the line, please.'

'I said I *was* with him. That was about an hour ago. He stayed on the train.'

'Did he give any reason for that decision? Where is he headed for now? Is there any sign of the Englishman, Lindsay?'

The questions were fired at him as though Jaeger were issuing commands to troops prior to an attack. Maisel cursed the infernal luck which had put him in touch with the SS colonel. He had no information, so what harm was there in relaying this negative factor?

'Hartmann decided to go on to Zagreb. I have no idea why – it seemed a pointless decision. There is no sign of Lindsay . . .'

'Hold the line!'

Jaeger covered the mouthpiece and turned to Schmidt who stood next to him. He explained briefly the gist of the conversation. 'See what you can get out of him,' he suggested.

'Schmidt here, Maisel. Can I ask you to be very precise about the sequence of events, please? Now, what exactly did Hartmann do?'

'Nothing!' Maisel was mystified and not a little irritated. 'As the train was coming into Maribor he went into the corridor and looked out of the window. He said something about needing a breath of fresh air . . .'

292

'Which side of the train was he looking out of? The platform side?'

'Yes, that's right . . .'

Maisel was beginning to wonder whether he had missed something but could not fathom what the devil it might be. Why the hell didn't they get off the line and let him speak to Vienna?

'Now, please think carefully,' Schmidt continued. 'Before he went into the corridor and peered out of the window had he given any indication he was staying on the train?'

'None at all. Only after he came back. I was surprised . . .'

'Thank you, Maisel. I'm handing you back to the operator who will transfer you to Vienna now you are identified. All calls are monitored since the massacre at Spielfeld-Strass . . .'

'How many were killed . . .?'

'Here is the operator – goodbye, Maisel . . .'

Schmidt put down the receiver and looked at the Colonel. He had just taken a nip of cognac from his hip flask and offered it to his deputy who shook his head. Jaeger replaced the screw cap before he spoke.

'You put him off the track, I hope? Get anything out of him?'

'He'll be smarting over the curt way I ended the conversation – which will stop him wondering what I was getting at. He sounded exhausted, I'm glad to say.'

'That's the way I like the opposition,' Jaeger commented with some satisfaction. 'Exhausted! Now . . .'

'It is interesting. Hartmann looked out of the corridor window as the train was approaching the platform at Maribor. Only after that did he announce he was continuing on to Zagreb. I think he spotted someone on that platform, someone waiting to board the train . . .'

'And I think you could be right. That clever bastard always was a loner. The train takes a good six hours to reach Zagreb from Maribor. Why don't we steal a march on our secretive friend, Gustav Hartmann?'

'Fly direct to Zagreb from here and be waiting for him at

Zagreb station when the train arrives?' Schmidt suggested.

'You're a mind-reader, my dear fellow,' Jaeger said jovially. 'So, what's keeping you? Arrange the flight and we'll leave for Zagreb at once.'

Chapter Thirty

Heljec, commander of the Partisan group operating north of Zagreb, chose a deep gorge near a place called Zidani Most to ambush the train. Six foot two tall, Heljec had thick black hair, dark and wary eyes, prominent Slavic cheekbones and a strong nose and jaw.

Thirty years old, Heljec had been an engineer building dams in peacetime. Now his life was dedicated to destruction. He stood at the brink of the gorge looking down with his deputy, Vlatko Jovanovic, by his side. In his right hand Heljec held a German Schmeisser machine-pistol.

'What time is it, Vlatko?' he asked.

'Almost 3 a.m. The train should arrive shortly. The men are in position. They know what they must do . . .'

'They must knock out the guards in the engine-cab. They must eliminate the machine-gunner on top of the coal-tender. They must wipe out the troops secreted in the mail-van coach at the rear. No prisoners. We cannot afford them.'

'It is all arranged,' Vlatko reassured him. 'Don't worry.'

'The day I stop worrying, this unit ceases to exist . . .'

Heljec spoke in a throaty voice – he consumed eighty cigarettes a day. There could hardly have been a greater contrast between the appearances and temperaments of the two men. Heljec had taken to the war like a duck to water. His men were in awe of his presence and stamina. He could make his way across country impassable to German commanders at a pace of thirty miles a day.

Vlatko Jovanovic, a shoemaker by profession, was small and tubby. Fifty years old, he was appalled by war and destruction, a genial and pacific man who had decided there was no alternative but to fight. A calm and careful man – for twenty-five years he had been the finest shoemaker in Belgrade – he complemented Heljec's savage vigour perfectly.

'You did a good job at Maribor,' Heljec remarked.

He made the comment automatically, his eyes studying the curve of the rail track at the bottom of the gorge at a point where the train would be moving up a steep ascent and, therefore, going slowly.

'It was routine, just a question of constant alertness.'

'The journey back was difficult.'

It was a statement Heljec was making. He expected miracles of endurance from his men but he never forgot to express his thanks afterwards. Jovanovic nodded his round head and pulled at the tip of his magnificent moustache, his most distinctive feature.

'Again, it was a question of alertness,' he replied.

This whole operation of ambushing the train was an experiment which had been personally sanctioned by Tito. They were, in fact, deep inside the hated Četniks' country. The plan was to provoke the Germans into heavily reinforcing this area of Jugoslavia which, at the moment, was lightly held, and largely by Četniks.

A major success north of Zagreb would send shock waves through the German command which could well extend to Berlin. Heljec was well aware of what was at stake and looking forward all the more to dealing the enemy a blow under the belt. It was *worthwhile*.

'I am sure we have enough troops for the job,' Heljec remarked.

'Forty men,' Vlatko again reassured him. 'All strategically placed. And we outnumber them heavily. That is the secret of war, Napoleon once said. Mass your forces – even if inferior – at the point where you will be superior to the enemy. Then you strike with everything you've got.'

'You're right, of course,' Heljec agreed. 'It is the unexpected I am always watching for.'

'So, at Maribor I found the data needed to plan this operation.'

It had, Vlatko reflected without saying so aloud, been tricky on Maribor platform. The crowds had helped as he mingled with them observing the train which had just arrived from Spielfeld-Strass. A meticulous man, Vlatko had counted the number of cars. Eight, including the mail-van at the rear.

The Germans, knowing the area was swarming with spies, had acted with great secrecy. Not one of the Waffen SS hidden inside the mail-van had been allowed onto the platform to stretch his aching legs. Vlatko, who had once produced hand-made shoes for royalty, was unusually observant. He noticed *omissions*.

Intrigued by the fact that *no mail was unloaded*, he loitered against a wall and watched. His patience was rewarded when the officer in charge opened the sliding doors a few inches and peered out. Vlatko, by the light of a lamp outside the coach, had a glimpse of German Army uniforms before the door closed again.

'How long before the train leaves for Zagreb?' he had asked a railway official.

'Half an hour at least. Maybe longer. Water has to be siphoned aboard.'

'Then I have time for a drink if I can find a bar open?'

'Have one for me.'

Slipping out of the station, Vlatko had mounted the cycle he had left hidden in an alley and made his way out of the town to a remote farmhouse. Here he had paused to use a concealed transmitter to radio a brief message to Heljec.

His work at the farmhouse completed, he had changed from using the cycle to an ancient motor-bike, speeding through the night along a devious route following little-used side roads. He had reached Heljec's group waiting above the gorge before the train arrived.

Even at this stage of the war, the Partisans' system of communications was remarkably well-organized. The Germans had attacked Jugoslavia in April 1941. Two years later the guerrillas had a whole network of couriers who travelled by pedal- and motor-cycle. They further employed numerous radio transmitters used only for the most urgent signals – hence the German radio-detector vans had so far not tracked down a single Partisan transmitter. As Vlatko had remarked, it was routine . . .

'I have kept back one piece of unfortunate news,' Vlatko said in a hesitant voice.

'What is it?' rasped Heljec. 'You know I like to hear about any problems immediately.'

'This we can do very little about.'

'Spit it out man, for God's sake!'

'While on the platform at Maribor I saw Paco boarding the train. I think she had a man with her . . .'

'On the train we are waiting for? You think it was the Englishman we are supposed to receive weapons for?'

'Possibly. I could not risk trying to warn her . . .'

'Of course not! She must take her chances . . .' Now it was Heljec's turn to hesitate, a rare reaction. 'Which coach did she get inside?' he asked eventually.

'A dangerous one – the coach immediately behind the engine and the tender with the German machine-gunner.'

Heljec remained silent and brooding. Paco was the best courier he had ever met. She could, and would, go into areas any man might cringe at the thought of penetrating. For Christ's sake, she had just taken a group into and out of the Third Reich itself.

'She is born lucky,' he said eventually.

'You salve your conscience with illusions . . .'

'Damn you, the whole operation is set up!' Heljec blazed in an outburst of intense frustration. Why had Vlatko to tell him something like this at the last moment? Better that he should not have known until after the ambush had taken place. Better for myself, he thought. Heljec always made a great effort to be honest with himself.

'Go down and tell the section attacking the engine and tender to use grenades as a last resource, to rely on machine-pistols.'

'Too late. Here comes the train . . .'

Paco had the corner seat away from the corridor and facing the engine. Her eyes were closed and her head was flopped on Lindsay's shoulder as the train crawled up a steep gradient. He found it a comforting sensation.

It was his sole consolation. The compartment was crammed with peasants shoulder to shoulder, most of them fast asleep. Leg-room was non-existent: a tangled sprawl of legs filled the space. It crossed Lindsay's mind that in case of emergency they were in a good position – next to the door.

He checked the time, carefully easing up the cuff of his sleeve to avoid disturbing her. 3.10 a.m. He should have woken her at three. They had worked out a roster so one of them would always be awake. He decided to let her sleep on.

'You're cheating, you nice bastard,' she murmured. 'I saw the time . . .'

'Get back to sleep – I'm quite fresh.'

'Liar, nice liar . . .' She suppressed a yawn. 'Where are we? Why are we travelling so slowly?'

'As far as I can see we're moving through some kind of gorge . . .'

'Zidani Most will be the next stop, then Zagreb . . .'

'If you say so . . .'

'Lindsay, you're comfortable to sleep against . . .'

'Now she tells me – just when we have all this privacy.'

She snuggled up closer and watched him through half-closed eyes. 'Lindsay, I might accept your suggestion to get some more sleep. You know what? You're a corrupting influence. I think I like it – being corrupted . . .' She kept her voice so low no one could have heard her using his name. She closed her eyes and immediately opened them as she felt him stiffen. The soft murmur was replaced by an urgent whisper. 'What's wrong?'

'It's crazy. I thought I saw someone on the track outside.'

The first phase of the attack opened when one of Heljec's men jumped on to the train step of the slow-moving coach next to

298

the mail-van. Easing his way round the end, he took a grenade from his belt, extracted the pin, laid the grenade on the coupling and jumped off.

In the confined space between the two coaches the grenade detonated with a muffled thump. The coupling snapped and the mail-van started running backwards down the steep gradient. Near the end of the train a second man flashed a light on and off twice, signalling to the group opposite the engine and tender.

The commander of the Waffen SS unit inside the mail-van reacted in the only way he could, sliding back the door to see what was happening. The muzzles of several machine-pistols poked through the opening at the very moment five grenades landed inside the coach. A series of explosions shook the coach which was now moving at speed.

The rear wheels smashed into the huge tree trunk dragged on to the line, half-mounted the obstacle, then the mail-van left the line, smashing over on its side. Flames appeared and the van began to burn. No survivors appeared.

At the front of the train the flashing of the lamp triggered the second phase of the attack. The German soldier crouched behind the machine-gun saw vague shapes moving in the dark. He pressed the trigger, unaware that a grenade had landed on top of the tender a few inches from his side.

The gun began to stutter. The grenade exploded with a loud crack. The German and his weapon were lifted off the tender and hurled on to the track. On either side of the engine dark silhouettes had mounted the footplate. Knives were wielded with savage efficiency and neither of the two Germans in the cab loosed off a shot. The attack had occupied the space of less than a hundred seconds.

'We're getting out . . .'

Lindsay had grabbed both cases from the rack as Paco threw open the door. She snatched her case off him and beyond the open doorway felt with her foot for the train step. No point in breaking an ankle. She was by the side of the track as Lindsay jumped down and joined her.

Confusion. Chaos. Men tumbling in panic to leave the

train, shouting. The slap of doors opening, slamming against the side of coaches. Women screaming. The horror had only begun.

'We must get clear of the train . . .' Lindsay.

'It's a Partisan ambush . . .' Paco.

'Up the side of the bloody gorge!' Lindsay.

He grabbed her arm, hauled her up what seemed like the face of a mountain cluttered with boulders. A searchlight stabbed out from a coach half-way along the train. It helped them to scramble round the huge boulders, climbing higher and higher. A group of Partisans were caught in the glare of the light. The stutter of machine-pistols rattled out a fusillade – *from the train*.

'The Germans are among the passengers,' Paco gasped.

The hail of fire cut down the Partisans illuminated by the powerful light. Out of the corner of his eye Lindsay saw men falling in grotesque attitudes, somersaulting down the slope, falling where they had stood.

'Keep climbing!' Lindsay ordered, dragging her up when she hesitated at the sight.

Retaliation came, ruthless and terrible. Grenades exploded near the searchlight, many falling among passengers trapped on the lower slopes. Intermingled with the thud of grenades, the rattle of machine-pistol fire, came the agonized screams of terrified and wounded passengers.

Regardless of the Jugoslav civilians, the Partisan attack continued to concentrate on killing Germans. It was a bloodbath. A tangle of petrified passengers followed the wrong route, still using the illuminated path of the German searchlight to get away. Lindsay saw more grenades fly through the beam, land and detonate among them.

'Shoot out that bloody searchlight, you crazy fools,' he snarled at the unseen attackers above.

'They have to kill the Germans,' Paco gasped.

There was a sudden silence – as though some unseen commander had ordered a cease fire. Then three rapid rifle cracks. Lindsay heard – in the eery hush – the trickling shatter of glass. The light dimmed, faded, vanished.

'Thank God!' Lindsay was appalled. 'Call this war? Could it be the Četniks?'

They paused, two-thirds of the way up the gorge, their aching legs hardly able to carry them another step. Oddly enough, both still hung on to their cases. Lindsay had stopped because they were partly sheltered by a semi-circle of boulders.

'No,' Paco said, 'they're Partisans. The Četniks have allied themselves with the Germans . . .'

'It's bloody slaughter. Did you see those peasants? A woman had her whole arm shot clean away.'

'This is the way we have to fight.'

'And long after the war is over we shall hear about the brave Partisans who took to the mountains – but massacres like this will go unreported. If this is the filthy Balkans you can keep it.'

'You fool . . .!'

With her free hand she slapped him hard across the side of his face. Quite deliberately he slapped her back, stinging her skin.

'If that's the language you Balkan women understand. Now, let's get to the top . . .'

Her reaction was unexpected. He had anticipated a vehement verbal onslaught; instead she quietly followed him up the mountain-like slope. From the bottomless pit of the gorge, the occasional pistol shot reverberated up to them. The Partisans finishing off wounded Germans, Lindsay imagined. There was a sudden crackle of rifle fire close by. Answered at once by a grenade which landed a few yards ahead of Lindsay. It detonated like a bomb. He fell into oblivion.

'He is suffering from the concussion.'

The strange voice spoke English with a careful precision like a man who uses the language occasionally but knows it well. The shape of the man was blurred but becoming more distinct, a man stooped over Lindsay. Everything suddenly became quite clear.

Lindsay was lying on the ground propped up against a boulder softened by something like a folded blanket. Then he saw Paco crouched beside him, studying him closely.

'Lindsay,' she said quietly, 'you can understand me? Good. This is Dr Macek – a proper doctor . . .'

'She means,' Macek intervened with an amused tone, 'that I am assumed to know the profession I practised in the peacetime. You will need much rest . . .'

He was a man of possibly forty with dark hair, a trim, military-style moustache and dark, almost hypnotic eyes. Like the other men Lindsay could see by the light of a watchman's lamp perched on the ground and which hissed, Macek wore a mixture of peasant clothes and army uniform. Despite the sartorial muddle Macek still seemed to preserve a neat appearance lacking in his compatriots . . .

'Another German? So, we will execute him . . .'

The voice, speaking Serbo-Croat, so Lindsay didn't understand a word, was vigorous and dominant. Beyond Macek stood a giant silhouette against the lamp's glow, a giant with thick black hair and holding a pistol in his right hand.

To Lindsay's horror he saw two Partisans dragging forward a familiar figure, the prisoner maintaining an erect stance despite the fact his hands were bound behind him and he looked exhausted. Major Gustav Hartmann. Blood on his forehead. The giant's gesture with his pistol was eloquent.

'For God's sake, stop him! That's Major Hartmann of the Abwehr,' he told Paco. He had an inspiration despite the feeling that at any moment he would lose consciousness again. 'I can persuade him to provide valuable information . . .'

'Heljec! Leave him alone!' Paco instantly jumped to her feet and stared at the Partisan leader who swung round to face her. 'I mean what I say!' she continued. 'He is Abwehr . . .'

'He is German . . .'

'Heljec . . .' A small, round-faced man appeared in the glow cast by the lamp. It was Vlatko Jovanovic. 'Paco has earned the right to speak for this prisoner . . .'

'I lead this group!' Heljec raised his pistol again. 'You have no rights. Paco has no rights. *I* have the rights . . .'

'Then we settle this dispute in the customary manner . . .'

Vlatko drew a knife, a curved weapon with a long blade. Lindsay fought to retain consciousness, amazed at the courage of the rotund figure. It was Paco who flew into a fury, stepping forward until she was almost standing on the giant's feet as she glared up at him.

'A head count! I killed so many Germans today – you're only interested in increasing your prestige with Tito. How dare you say I have no rights! Who led a group deep inside the Third Reich to rescue the Englishman? Who spent hours dining with an SS colonel in the centre of Munich to obtain transit papers?'

She laughed in his face. Then she looked round the group of fascinated Partisans who had formed a circle to see the outcome.

'This is a very brave man who leads you – while he is on home ground,' she flailed on. 'You think he would dare set one of his outsized feet in Germany.'

'I speak no German . . .' Heljec began.

'Neither do I, but I, too, was there in Germany.'

Milic, who had travelled on the train with Bora, still spoke calmly but his moustaches quivered. He carried a machine-pistol and the muzzle was aimed point-blank at Heljec.

'You will speak with more respect to Paco,' Milic continued. 'The Abwehr is not like the Gestapo – as the Partisans are not like the Četniks. You wish to behave like a Četnik, Heljec? I will not permit it.'

'You wish to take over leadership of this group, Milic?'

'Only if you persist in murdering prisoners who may help Tito plan his future strategy . . .'

During this tense exchange Hartmann had stood, his wrists still bound, with a blank expression. He stared at Lindsay as though attempting to convey some message.

There was a long silence after Milic made his final pronouncement. From the gorge below there drifted up from the rail track the sound of people in pain moaning, the

303

stench of cordite. Heljec thrust his pistol back inside his belt.

'We must move fast,' he decided, 'before German motor-ized troops arrive. The German can walk so he comes with us. Tito will tell us his fate. Make a stretcher to carry the Englishman.' His voice rose sharply. 'What is the matter with you all? I said we must move . . .'

Paco turned her back on him without a word and came back to kneel beside Lindsay. She placed a reassuring hand on his shoulder.

'The doctor says you have concussion. You will be carried. No! No argument! You are valuable merchandise – one Englishman for many guns. That was the arrangement . . .'

Lindsay opened his mouth to speak and dropped into a dark pit of unconsciousness.

'He is suffering from glandular fever. You observe both the sides of the neck – the swellings? And the temperature . . .'

Lindsay was bemused as he heard the voice speak precise English, the voice which strung out the words with careful deliberation. This was a repeat performance, a theatrical play in which he had appeared before.

He opened his eyes and his vision was blurred. Two figures stooped over him. A man and a woman. The figures became more distinct. Everything suddenly became quite clear. He blinked. Damnit! He was occupying the same posture, propped up against something as he sat on the ground in the open.

'How are you feeling?' asked Paco.

'Awful – bloody awful. Don't worry – I shall feel worse . . .'

'Ah! The sense of humour,' commented Dr Macek. 'I trained at St Thomas's in London. I enjoyed the British – masterly understatement. Do I have that right?'

'Yes,' said Lindsay. 'Where the hell are we? How far from that frightful gorge?'

'Many miles away,' Paco replied. 'That was four weeks ago. You have had . . .'

'*Four weeks!*' Lindsay was suddenly disorientated and very alarmed. Was he going mad? Where had the time gone?

He could remember nothing since the train ambush, the subsequent confrontation between Paco and Heljec. *Heljec!* He could remember the bastard's name. That brought back a little self-confidence. Paco took his right hand in both of hers and began speaking in her slow, soft voice.

'You had concussion. A piece of a grenade struck you on the forehead. Men have taken it in turns to carry you on an improvised stretcher. You have insisted on walking at times . . .'

'And now,' Dr Macek intervened cheerfully, 'my patient, who is almost cured of the concussion, has contracted glandular fever. So you have the swellings at the sides of the neck and must rest . . .'

'Bloody hell, no more!' Lindsay struggled to his feet, swaying as he stared round. Paco placed a walking-stick in his hand. He grasped it automatically and to his surprise the stick felt familiar.

'Milic made you that stick,' she said. 'You have covered a great distance with your three legs. Now you must listen to Dr Macek . . .' A teasing note entered her voice '. . . who was trained at St Thomas's so you will trust him . . .'

A grim, dramatic panorama met his eyes as he hobbled across the rough, rock-ribbed summit. They were perched on top of a small plateau surmounted by the relics of an ancient fortress, so derelict it could scarcely be distinguished from the scramble of huge boulders it had once been erected above.

It was mid-morning, he suspected, a clear, crisp day when the saw-toothed edges of distant mountains looked as though they had been cut from metal silhouetted against a cloudless sky. Perfect flying weather.

Something was disturbing Lindsay, a sense of unease nagging at the back of his mind. Paco and Macek had propped him against a boulder under a copse of stunted trees. Other trees clustered the plateau below the fortress – which had long ago lost all form of roofing. He found himself keeping to the shelter of the trees as he left the other two behind and hobbled with the aid of the stick at a fast jig-jog towards the fortress which, he instinctively felt sure, was Heljec's headquarters.

'Wait for us!' Paco called out. 'God, he's moving like a racehorse.'

Then Lindsay heard it again and stopped abruptly under a well-foliaged tree. The muttering engine of a light aircraft. He'd heard that sound at the moment of regaining consciousness but he had been distracted by Macek's remark, by his general sense of not knowing where he was. They caught up with him and he cautioned them.

'Keep under cover, out of sight of that plane . . .'

'It's a German Storch,' Paco said with irritating patience. 'I have learned to live with the sound . . .'

'But have you learned to die with it?'

The violence of his question, his sudden burst of energy, the incredible pace he had kept up moving towards the fortress, stunned both Paco and Macek into temporary silence. To Lindsay's great relief. He could listen – with a pilot's ear.

He stood with his head cocked on one side. Flying very slowly. Almost lowest possible speed. Much lower and the engine would stall. As he thought, it was describing a circle – round the perimeter of the plateau.

Perching both hands on the stick to steady himself, he stared up through the foliage, craning his neck as he sought a loophole through which he might glimpse the plane. Then he saw it. The machine, tilting. The pilot's head, craned like his own – but staring down through the goggles.

'What are you getting so agitated about?' Paco asked. 'The Germans are always flying over Jugoslavia.'

'Was a machine like that flying overhead just as I woke up?'

'Yes, there was an aircraft . . .'

'And how many times today has a German light aircraft flown over this area? Think, for God's sake.'

'All right . . .!' Paco began to protest.

'Six times, I think,' Macek broke in. 'This is the sixth . . .'

'And it's only eleven in the morning . . .' Lindsay checked his watch.

'I kept it wound up for you,' Paco snapped.

'Six times. I see! That plane was so low it knew what it was

306

looking for, where to find its objective. Hear it flying away?'

'I told you . . .' Paco began again.

'Heljec must be warned a major bombing attack – maybe even a parachute landing – is imminent. We must evacuate this area at once.' Lindsay's tone was terse, decisive. 'How many men have you billeted up here?'

'Thirty men – the whole unit,' Paco replied. 'Now look, Lindsay. There's no point in starting a panic . . .'

'No! You listen! Heljec may be the expert at ambushing trains, shooting Germans – including prisoners when he can – at sacrificing civilians wholesale for the greater glory of Communism. A fat lot of joy some of those poor bastards left in the gorge are going to get out of any fanciful Communist paradise. Heljec may be expert at all these things – but when it Goddamn well comes to planes he'd better go back to school. I know the warning signs. I saw enough of them when I was footslogging it to Dunkirk after my machine went down. Where's Heljec?'

'In the fort.'

It was Macek who told him. The sound of the spotter plane had faded to the distant hum of a bee on a summer's day. Lindsay grabbed Paco's arm, took a firm grip on his stick and hustled her up the slope to the fort's entrance. Despite his physical weakness his certainty of the appalling danger was producing adrenalin at a tremendous rate.

He paused at the sight inside the fort. Heljec was crouched with Jovanovic over a map spread out over a large rock. On the ground against a crumbling wall slumped Hartmann. The side of his jaw was discoloured with a recent bruise. He grinned wryly at the Englishman.

Lindsay addressed the Abwehr man in German, taking no notice of Heljec who had spun round and was glaring at him.

'How did you get that bruise, Hartmann?'

'I tried to warn this stupid brute – a spotter plane has been over and the next thing will be . . .'

'I know. Leave it to me.' He turned to Paco, still ignoring Heljec who was showing signs of growing annoyance. He pointed his stick at the Serb. 'Paco, you once said it was often

307

difficult to get people to do the simplest things – a remark I was not too appreciative of at the time. Now, tell this stupid brute what is coming to him if he doesn't instantly sound a general alarm and evacuate. Tell him I'm a pilot and know about aerial warfare. He's about to be *annihilated!*'

Paco began speaking rapidly. At one moment she stamped her foot. In his frustration at this waste of precious time Lindsay walked backwards and forwards with his stick. Jovanovic joined in the heated conversation. Paco turned to Lindsay.

'Tell me again quickly your reasons. Forcefully. Heljec will be watching you.'

He repeated what he had said. One. Two. Three. Finally he turned on the giant and raised his stick like a weapon.

'Tell him if he doesn't act quickly I'll beat some sense into him with this stick,' he shouted at the top of his voice.

She spoke only a few words when Jovanovic interrupted her and made a gesture beyond the fort, rolling up the map as he finished. Heljec ran through the exit and out of sight.

'Your threat to attack him convinced him,' Paco said. 'We are evacuating at once . . .'

As they emerged from the fort Lindsay was astounded to witness the sudden appearance of Partisans everywhere. They seemed to rise out of the ground from invisible trenches. He followed Paco to the edge of the plateau where the terrain dropped steeply in a series of gullies. She stopped to help him but he waved her on.

'Just show me the way. I'll keep up. Good God, there's Bora. The devil looks after its own.'

The descent was precipitous and Lindsay half-walked, half-stumbled down a flight of natural steps formed by rock ledges jutting from the mountain-side. Somehow he kept his balance as Paco kept glancing back and he kept waving her on, certain there was little time left to get clear of the plateau.

He remembered his case. Below them he saw Bora carrying it and below him Milic carrying another. Paco's, he presumed. As he continued the diabolical descent he thought of Hartmann and looked back. The German was a few yards behind, followed by Milic who carried his machine-pistol. That was when his experienced ears caught the first distant sound of a fleet of planes coming.

The guerrilla force slipped down from the plateau inside a series of deep gulches and defiles, some of which in winter would be raging torrents. The slither of small pebbles told Lindsay that.

He was now close enough to the winding gorge they were heading for to see the dark shadows on the opposite slope which were mouths of caves. Those would be their refuge and their shelter when the bombardment started. If they got there in time.

Paco stopped briefly as Milic called down to her. Hartmann was close behind Lindsay who still kept up a furious pace as he went on stumbling down the fiendish descent, saving his balance again and again with the aid of the stick.

'Tell the German if he attempts to signal to the planes I will shoot him instantly,' Milic had warned.

'For Christ's sake, he was the one who tried to warn Heljec they were on their way.' Her tone was scathing. 'Go back to your shoemaking if that's the best you can do! And shut up. We haven't much time . . .'

She repeated the gist of the exchange to Lindsay and then, agile as a goat, continued on her way. *We haven't much time.* She was right, Lindsay thought. They were almost at the bottom but now the sound of the incoming planes was an ominous roar.

The gorge was a river bed. Green water frothed and tumbled over boulders but the winter level had dropped. Paco waited, grabbed Lindsay's arm and helped him use the boulders as stepping stones. He was vaguely aware that to left and right Partisans were scurrying across and disappearing inside the caves. He concentrated on looking down, watching where he placed his feet. Then they were on the other side.

Still clutching his arm, Paco hustled him up a short slope strewn with stones which slithered and rattled under his feet. The mouth of a cave, about eight feet high, loomed up and she hurried him inside. There was a sudden drop of temperature as they paused in the gloom.

Paco was taking in deep breaths, her bosom heaving with their efforts. She saw him watching her and looked away as Hartmann arrived with Milic practically treading on his heels.

'Get this enthusiast off my back,' Hartmann said drily and sat on one of the huge boulders which littered the interior of the cave.

Commonsense told them to retreat deep inside the cave. Curiosity – the same curiosity which brought Londoners into the streets in 1940, staring up at the German bombers overhead – took them to the mouth of the cave to see what was happening. Lindsay immediately witnessed a grim incident.

A Partisan in the gorge crouched behind a massive boulder was aiming his rifle skywards. Heljec appeared behind the man, raised his pistol and shot him dead. The Serb skipped across the river and vanished inside another cave.

'The murdering swine!' protested Lindsay.

'Heljec had given strict orders,' Paco said quietly. 'There must be no firing at the planes to give away our positions.'

She had just spoken when Lindsay heard a sound which took him back to France, 1940. The high-pitched scream of an aircraft engine. He peered out cautiously. A second plane was following the first over the summit plateau where the crumbling fortress which had been Heljec's headquarters reared up like the mountain's summit.

The plane, a small black dart at a great height, turned on its side and plunged in a vertical dive at tremendous speed. A stick of bombs from the first machine straddled the plateau. The roar of bursting bombs reverberated down in the gorge. A hailstorm of splintered rock flew into the air. A wall of the fortress toppled, spilled down the gulches, dissolving into a thousand fragments. A cloud of dust rose from where the wall had stood.

'Jesus Christ!' said Lindsay. 'Stukas – dive-bombers. If we were up there now . . .'

The air armada – the sky seemed full of machines – systematically pattern-bombed the plateau from end to end.

Then the air commander changed his tactics.

'They've spotted the caves!' Lindsay shouted. 'Get well to the back . . .'

A crouched, running figure dashed inside their cave. It was Dr Macek. He saw Lindsay and looked amazed. At Paco's urging he joined them at the rear of the cave behind a rampart of rocks. A stick of bombs trod its lethal way along the floor of the gorge, one exploding close to their own entrance. Sharp-edged bits of stone like shrapnel flew about inside their cave, clattering against the rampart.

Crouched down with Paco on his right and Macek on his left, Lindsay felt the reaction to his exertions starting. His legs and hands trembled uncontrollably. Macek placed a gentle hand across his forehead and frowned at Paco.

'All right,' snapped Lindsay, who had seen his expression and mistrusted doctors, 'what is it?'

'You've drained yourself coming down that mountain. I did say you have glandular fever. I did say you needed rest, a lot of rest . . .'

'So they carried me down instead,' Lindsay commented sarcastically. 'You think we'd ever have made it . . .?'

His last recollection was glancing beyond Macek and noticing Hartmann watching him – punctuated by a whole fusillade of bombs filling the gorge with their hellish sound and dust drifting inside the cave. Then, oh God, he was falling into oblivion again.

Chapter Thirty-One

Kursk! July 1943 . . .

A town in Russia south of Moscow few people have heard of. It was at Kursk in the summer of '43 that the outcome of the Second World War would be decided.

Here a gigantic Russian salient like a thumb protruded into the German front. The Red Army had crammed the salient with their élite divisions ready for the attack.

311

This vast area was dangerously over-crowded. There were the huge T-34 tanks, the latest Soviet self-propelled guns, the most battle-experienced infantry and armoured divisions. No fewer than one million Russian troops assembled in this confined pocket waited the order to advance. And Stalin hesitated.

There was no hesitation at the Wolf's Lair. The Führer had made up his mind and his most able commander, Field Marshal von Kluge, fully supported the plan: to attack first, to slice off the base of the thumb and close the immense trap which within days would encircle one million Russians.

'The road to Moscow will then be open,' von Kluge continued at the Führer's midday conference on 1 July. 'There will be nothing left for Stalin to throw in our path. We take Moscow, the hub of the Bolshevik railway system, and Russia is wiped out.'

'We launch the offensive on 5 July,' Hitler agreed. 'Then, once Russia is destroyed we transfer one hundred and twenty divisions to France and Belgium. Any attempted landing by the Anglo-Americans will end in catastrophe. Gentlemen, *Operation Citadel* is on. I have decided.'

He looked round the table at Martin Bormann, Keitel and Jodl, who duly nodded their agreement. The Citadel was Kursk. Once it fell, the gates to Moscow were thrown wide open.

Hitler dismissed the meeting and told Bormann to accompany him to his quarters. He strode out of the *Lagebaracke*, across the compound and entered his own simple hut. Once inside the Führer threw the cap he had donned onto a table and told his deputy to shut the door as he settled himself in an arm chair.

'Bormann, you must by now agree that everyone accepts me for who I am. Citadel is the biggest operation Germany has so far launched in the whole war.'

'*Mein Führer*,' began Bormann, 'I have only one anxiety. There is still no news of the killing or capture of Wing Commander Lindsay.'

'Who cares about him any longer? How could he affect me?'

Bormann noted he used *me*, not *us*. Since the impersonation which had begun the previous March, Bormann – who had expected to manipulate Heinz Kuby like a ventriloquist's dummy – had found himself relegated to his earlier role under the original Führer. And, he reflected, there was not one thing in the world he could do about it without destroying himself.

'I have studied Lindsay's file carefully,' Bormann persisted. 'He was once an actor used to studying mannerisms and he was very close to that promiscuous Christa Lundt. Before they escaped together I caught her watching you closely. I think she detected something wrong.'

'So, what do you propose?' Hitler interjected impatiently.

'That SS Colonel Jaeger be sent back to the Balkans in the hope that he can pick up Lindsay's trail.'

'Jaeger is taking command of his unit again for Citadel,' the Führer said brusquely. 'We need every experienced man we can lay our hands on to pull this off. Just so long as that Soviet spy Hartmann insisted was here does not pass on details of Citadel to the Russians. Everything depends on the element of surprise . . .'

That evening at the pine-shrouded Wolf's Lair on 1 July the atmosphere was tense. It was going to be another sultry, humid night and so much hinged on Citadel.

Three of the leading personalities passed through the various checkpoints separately. None of the trio was likely to want the company of one of his colleagues. Keitel was regarded by Jodl as a stuffed shirt who had been promoted above his level of ability. Martin Bormann was possessed of one universal attribute. He was detested by everyone except the Führer. And Hitler's dog, Blondi.

Keitel considered Jodl a tricky individual, not a man you would ever strike up an intimacy with. Certainly an officer it would be wise to hold at a distance. And so it came about that the three men went their own ways, seeking brief relief from the claustrophobia of the Wolf's Lair before the midnight conference.

In these northern climes it was dark at 11.15 p.m. when once again experienced hands opened up the log pile concealing the powerful transmitter in the forest. The signal tapped out with the aid of a pocket torch was unusually long. The operator replaced the logs and returned just in time to attend the Führer's conference.

'Anna, I am exhausted,' Rudolf Roessler exclaimed as he closed the flap inside the cupboard which hid his own transceiver. 'I feel something very important is imminent.'

'And how do you know that?' Anna enquired as she handed her husband a cup of coffee which he drank greedily.

'I have received, in normal code, the longest signal yet from Woodpecker. I have immediately re-transmitted it to Moscow. I suspect it gives the order of battle for a very major operation . . .'

'Well, you have done all you can,' Anna said briskly, 'so we shall just have to see.'

Roessler swivelled round in his chair and stared at her, his face lined with fatigue. 'From what has happened so far we know Stalin is not making full use of the information I send. Will he ever come to trust me?'

'Kursk! It could be a huge trap to destroy us . . .'

Inside the small office in the Kremlin it was the early hours and the atmosphere was strained as Stalin spoke. Two other men stood alongside each other, listening. The aggressive General Zhukov and the quieter, more intellectual Marshal Vassilevsky, Chief of Staff.

Stalin was holding the long signal just received from Lucy which had originated from Woodpecker. Never before had Stalin received from this source such a detailed order of battle for the German Army. It was quite terrifying, the vast amount of war material the Wehrmacht had assembled. If it were true. The Generalissimo read the signal again slowly, repeating aloud a few of the details.

'Tiger and Panther tanks . . . Ferdinand mobile guns . . . General Model to attack from the north . . . General Hoth from the south . . . The pick of the German generals . . . a huge mass of their élite divisions. This is a colossal force. If it is true we could make our own dispositions and destroy them.'

'Could I ask,' Vassilevsky began casually, 'what is the record of this Woodpecker-Lucy espionage ring so far?'

'The information has always proved correct.'

'So it could be correct again. At some moment we have to take our courage in both hands, and gamble everything on the belief that Lucy is right . . .'

'Zhukov?'

Stalin, who was also standing in the gloom of his office lit only by the shaded desk lamp, glanced sideways at the General. Vassilevsky sighed inwardly. Stalin was up to his old tricks – enticing others to express opinions which could be employed against them if there was a disaster.

The trouble was Stalin had never lost his crafty Georgian origins. Treacherous and devious by nature, he saw trickery everywhere – and Lucy could be Hitler's pawn, luring the Red Army into a gigantic trap from which it would never extricate itself.

Zhukov did not hesitate. The only general capable of contradicting Stalin to his face, he spoke out vehemently.

'Woodpecker tells us D-Day is 5 July – three days from now. He further tells us H-Hour for the attack is 1500 hours, a most unusual time for the launching of a German offensive, so it has the ring of truth. I wish to return immediately to GHQ to make our dispositions on the basis that Woodpecker *is* telling the truth.'

'You would take full responsibility for such a decision?'

'Yes, Generalissimo!'

'We must consider the problem further, gentlemen. Prepare yourselves for a long night,' Stalin replied.

At 2.30 p.m. on 5 July Colonel Jaeger's old leg wound began to play him up. Perched in the turret of his enormous Panther tank, he was commanding a section of an armoured division of General Model's 4th Army which was to drive a hammer-blow south at the base of the Russian 'thumb' to link up with General Hoth's 9th Army advancing from the south. Between them the two armies would amputate the thumb – encircling one million enemy troops.

It was a hot sultry afternoon as Jaeger checked his watch and surveyed the endless rows of tanks drawn up for battle. His leg wound always troubled him just before the start of a great offensive. Looking across to the next Panther he saw Schmidt wiping sweat off his forehead.

'In half an hour it will be really hot!' he shouted jovially. 'Save your sweat for then!'

There was the sound of laughter from the turrets of tanks nearby. Jaeger was a commander who had the gift of breaking almost unbearable tension with a joke.

'Colonel!' Schmidt shouted back. 'Your sweat pores differ from ours. When the time comes you will sweat beer!'

There was another burst of laughter. Jaeger, anything but a stiff-necked, Prussian-type officer, was always ready to bandy words with his men regardless of rank. At precisely 1500 hours he gave his driver the order through his throat-mike.

'Forward! And don't stop till you see the whites of General Hoth's eyes!'

The immense leviathans began to rumble southward on their massive tracks. There was the thump of heavy artillery opening up a non-stop barrage. The endless, mind-wearying steppes of Russia spread before them as Jaeger's Panther pushed ahead of the vast tracked armada. Ignoring the shell-bursts which began to crater the sun-bleached earth, Jaeger directed his Panther straight ahead. South – ever south – until the link-up with Hoth and the pincers closed behind the Red Army cooped up inside its huge salient.

Altogether, on that humid July day, Field Marshal von Kluge had over half a million German troops under his command. They included seventeen Panzer divisions equipped with the monster new Tiger and Panther tanks, countless mobile guns

– all backed up by motorized infantry. It was the largest force ever thrown against a single objective. *Citadel*.

H-Hour, the starting time – three in the afternoon – should certainly have taken by surprise the enemy who was accustomed to dawn attacks. It was anticipated that before Zhukov grasped what was happening he would find himself surrounded.

And in addition, the 2nd Army – comprising six Panzer and two infantry divisions – was attacking the tip of the 'thumb', as a diversion to draw Soviet troops away from the main battle area.

Earlier than he had expected, Colonel Jaeger found himself staring at two Soviet T-34 tanks advancing towards him about one hundred metres apart from each other. An average commander's reaction would have been to slow down, to wait for reinforcements to catch up with him. Jaeger was not an average commander.

'Increase speed!' he ordered.

As he had foreseen, he could see the huge gun like a telegraph pole on each tank traversing to aim at him. Their traverse was too slow because the last reaction they had expected was for the Panther to continue on course at higher speed: on a course which would naturally take the German tank between the two Soviet T-34s with fifty metres to spare on either side.

The Russian guns began to move more rapidly to bring their muzzles to bear on Jaeger at point-blank range. The Colonel timed it carefully. Just before the traverses were completed he spoke again into the mike.

'Maintain course. And give me everything you've got. Go like hell!'

The Panther rumbled forward, suddenly at top speed. The guns of the T-34s were traversing a little too slowly. Jaeger was midway between them when the Soviet commanders realized this maniac was continuing to advance past them.

They ordered their gunners to traverse to an angle of ninety degrees. The guns went on turning. Jaeger went on advancing. The Soviet commanders gave the order simultaneously.

'Fire . . .!'

A second earlier Jaeger passed beyond them. The guns of the two T-34s faced each other. The shells passed each other in mid-flight and detonated. Looking back, Jaeger saw the tanks burning, flames leaping from the turrets. So far he had not fired a shot.

'Continue to advance on the same course . . .'

Earlier he had seen the two tanks approaching, one behind the other before they separated to avoid bunching into a solid target. Jaeger could clearly see the marks of their tracks and he guided his Panther along the same avenue.

Minefields! The everlasting gut terror of all tank commanders. By keeping to the track course of the burning T-34s Jaeger knew he was safe from mines. The wisdom of his judgement was vindicated a moment later when he heard a series of explosions.

To his left and right three Panthers were disabled or destroyed. One had a track sheared off the chassis and stood motionless in the battlefield. Two more were burning where they had encountered mines. Jaeger wirelessed back to the remainder of his squadron.

'Follow in my tracks. Precisely. Pathway through major minefield.'

As he completed his instruction to his operator Jaeger began to worry. Instinctively the incident he had survived told him something strange was happening. *Minefields . . .*

The Russians had sown no fewer than 40,000 mines *in a single night*, each mine capable of disabling a Panther or Tiger tank.

They had sown these lethal weapons in each sector where they knew the Panzer divisions were coming. In the early hours of the morning of 2 July inside the Kremlin, Stalin had finally decided to trust the Woodpecker signals. Given the go-ahead, the Soviet generals had reorganized their entire defences inside the Kursk salient, converting it into the greatest military deathtrap in history.

The Germans still fought hard. Low-flying Stukas equipped

with cannons swept over the battlefield, wiping out a large number of T-34 tanks. Across a vast area savage tank duels were fought but Hitler had lost the vital element of surprise.

It does not take all that much skill to win a battle if you know in advance exactly what the enemy plan is. The two men who really won the turning-point battle of Kursk were absent from the field of carnage. Woodpecker was at the Wolf's Lair in East Prussia. The middle-aged, shabbily-dressed Rudolf Roessler was in Lucerne.

Even so, the Russians did not find it a walkover. Fighting continued to rage from 5 July to 22 July as the salient became a charnel house. The casualties on both sides were enormous. Medical personnel on the German side described their field hospitals as slaughterhouses.

Throughout the long days and nights the sound was deafening as the artillery continued to pound, the tanks to fire and the bombs to fall. The earth was desecrated, turned into a desert – a desert littered with shattered planes, tanks, and men.

Colonel Jaeger survived the holocaust – and saved Schmidt. Two Panthers had been blown up under the Colonel and he was in the turret of the third in the midst of chaos and milling confusion when he saw Schmidt, hit by a sniper's bullet, topple over the side of his turret.

'Halt!' he ordered.

Clambering down onto the churned-up earth he ran across as Schmidt's tank detonated a mine. A huge length of track splayed out and slapped onto the ground. Schmidt, sprawled on his side, looked up.

'Get out of it, Chief! The medics will come for me . . .'

'Shut up and keep still!'

Jaeger gathered up Schmidt in both his arms and carried him to his own tank. He had reached the Panther when he felt a thump against his leg. He ignored it, hoisting up Schmidt as his wireless operator reached down to grasp the injured man.

'Colonel! Your leg!' the wireless operator shouted to make himself heard above the mind-numbing thunder which never ceased.

'Get Schmidt inside! I can get up myself. That's an order. . .'

Blood had soaked through the trousers covering the upper part of his leg and the pain was starting. There was a ping against the side of the Panther. That damned sniper again! Gritting his teeth, Jaeger hauled himself rapidly up to the turret, inside and closed the lid.

'There is a bloody spy at the Wolf's Lair – and I'm going to track the bastard down when I get out of here.'

Jaeger was talking to Schmidt in the next hospital bed a week later. By using the Führer's name the SS colonel had managed to get them both transported to a hospital in Munich. He had a definite purpose in choosing this location for their recuperation.

'Why are you so sure now?' Schmidt enquired.

'Kursk!'

'So, we lost the battle – it doesn't mean we lost the war . . .'

'I fear, my old friend,' Jaeger said sombrely, 'it means just that. At Kursk, history – it is not an original phrase – trembled in the balance. We *should* have won, but the Bolsheviks knew our order of battle in advance. I forced my way into the presence of Field Marshal von Kluge afterwards. He agreed with me. The Führer was right, there is a top-level Soviet spy at the Wolf's Lair.'

'Well, there's nothing you can do about it,' Schmidt observed.

They occupied a small two-man ward and both were recovering from their injuries. Jaeger had been shot in the upper right leg, the bullet embedding itself only a few centimetres from the place where he had been shot during the final stages of the 1940 campaign in France.

The doctor had suggested he be invalided out of the Army when final recovery took place. He was exhausted by his exertions in so many campaigns. Jaeger's reaction had almost put the doctor into one of his own beds. Grabbing the walking-stick by his bedside the Colonel had thrown back the bedclothes and rested his good leg on the floor.

'You may be a good doctor but you're a bloody lousy psychologist!' he had roared. 'I have a specific job to do – and by God I'm going to do it!'

He waved the stick in a threatening manner. Hauling the bandaged right leg out of bed he stood up, supporting himself by the stick as he hobbled forward menacingly. The doctor backed away from him until the wall stopped his retreat.

'Colonel, you should be in bed . . .'

'I should be in the Cauldron – searching for a lead to the man who put me here, who left so many thousands of my comrades dead amid the flies and dust of Kursk. I have only one instruction for you, Doctor, get me mobile at the earliest possible moment.'

'I can only do that if you rest, stay in bed . . .'

The doctor's face had lost its normal colour, confronted by Jaeger who was the picture of ferocity. Holding on with one hand to the bottom of Schmidt's bed, Jaeger raised his stick with the other to emphasize his command.

'Agreed – on one condition. Each day a little more exercise so I can be discharged at the earliest possible moment. There is a war on, or hadn't you heard . . .'

'The same request applies to me,' Schmidt interjected. 'You're to discharge me on the same day as the Colonel leaves . . .'

'That may be possible,' the doctor agreed cautiously. 'Your chest wound is healing nicely. It was fortunate the bullet passed right through, missing all the vital parts . . .'

He broke off in mid-sentence as a nursing sister entered, stopped and stared in bewilderment. She was not a particularly attractive woman, arrogant by nature, and on the first day of his admission Jaeger had had to speak severely to her.

'We are holding an important conference,' he informed her with a straight face. 'No bedpan interruptions at the moment.'

'You have a visitor, Colonel. A Mr Maisel. He says you are expecting him . . .'

'And he speaks the truth, so usher him in at once, please . . .'

'Is everything all right, Doctor?' she asked.

'He's not feeling too good this morning,' Jaeger replied in his most jovial manner. 'You can see he's lost his usual colour. I prescribe rest, possibly a short period in bed.'

'Is it correct that you wished to see me, Colonel?' enquired Willy Maisel.

The thin-faced Gestapo official with a thatch of dark hair was dressed in a well-fitting navy blue suit and his shrewd gaze switched backwards and forwards between Jaeger and Schmidt. He made no reference to their state of health.

'Where the hell is that Englishman, Wing Commander Lindsay, at this moment?' Jaeger rasped.

Willy Maisel was sitting down on a chair drawn up close to the Colonel's bedside drinking a liquid the hospital hopefully termed 'coffee'. Jaeger had winkled out of him the reason for his initial distant manner. *Gruber*.

The Gestapo chief, still based in Vienna, was being driven mad by a constant stream of phone calls from Martin Bormann at the Wolf's Lair. Regardless of the normal person's routine he was plagued with these calls from the Reichsleiter at all hours. Three o'clock in the morning was one favourite time and Gruber by now felt he was one of his own suspects in the cells where sleep was deliberately denied.

'He is worn out,' Maisel explained. 'When he heard that you wanted to see me he swore foully. He was terrified that I might pass on any information to you . . .'

'Why?'

Jaeger was intrigued. There was something very odd going on. Maisel, a shrewd man, seemed relieved to be away from Gestapo headquarters – thankful to talk to someone in the outside world.

'Because Bormann is venting his spite on him, preparing him as a potential scapegoat would be my guess . . .'

'A scapegoat for what?'

'The inability of anyone to track down the Englishman, Lindsay. At times Bormann seems petrified at the idea Lindsay may reach London. Jodl and Keitel, too. They have

322

both phoned Gruber at different times about the same subject, which I find odd.'

'Any idea why?' Jaeger asked.

'The Führer wants to see Lindsay again, I gather. After Kursk, I suppose. There are constant rumours Hitler is desperate to do a deal with Churchill . . .'

'So the more people who are after Lindsay the better the chances of locating him?' Schmidt intervened.

Jaeger smiled to himself. In all apparent innocence Schmidt had laid a trap – and Maisel walked into it. The way was now being paved for Jaeger and Schmidt to join the search for the fugitive.

'Yes, I suppose it comes to that,' Maisel agreed.

'When exactly, and where, was Lindsay last sighted?' Jaeger asked.

'Nowhere really – not since that night I talked to you from Maribor. But our Intelligence people in the Balkans keep reporting these rumours. A blonde girl and Lindsay are travelling with a Partisan group – probably the same lot that attacked the train before it reached Zagreb. And strangely enough we keep hearing Major Hartmann of the Abwehr is alive and with them. After all, we know he was on the same train . . .'

'Hartmann!' Jaeger sat up very erect. 'The clever bastard is a survivor. Any fuller description of this blonde girl?'

'Only that she is in her late twenties, is very attractive and it is rumoured she is called Paco. Obviously a code-name. Also she seems to carry great authority with the leader of the group. Now we hear a full-blown Allied Military Mission has landed from a plane in Jugoslavia, flown in from Tunisia, we assume. In the Balkans nothing is cut and dried . . .'

Jaeger sat in silence for some time after Willy Maisel left the ward. Used to his chief's moods, Schmidt was careful to say nothing. Then Jaeger seemed to make up his mind. Throwing back the bed-clothes, he reached for the stick, eased himself out of bed and began his daily pacing back and forth.

'The English fought well at Dunkirk. You remember that

323

wall we could not break through, Schmidt? The Führer is right – we should be allied with them. He should never have allowed that fat mental deficient, Goering, to bomb London. If the Russians win they will menace the whole western world for generations . . .'

'It is a tragedy,' Schmidt agreed, 'but what can we do?'

'Lindsay is the key,' Jaeger replied. 'You and I must find him. It's going to be a race against time. If we're not quick that Allied Military Mission will airlift him out. We may be able to checkmate them if the Mission's whereabouts is known. That's our first job . . .'

He was talking to himself, thinking aloud as he forced his body upright, marching slowly round the ward, managing without the stick as much as he could.

'How do we checkmate the Mission?' Schmidt enquired.

'I'm going to phone Bormann and get the Führer's backing – we send instructions to the local Luftwaffe commander in the area to concentrate every plane he's got on the area where the Allied Mission is operating. We bomb the hell out of them – keep them on the run so Lindsay can't link up with them until we get down there.'

'I still don't understand why Lindsay is the key . . .'

'I was very struck by his intelligence. Look how he escaped from the Berghof with Christa Lundt in that laundry truck, how he did *not* take the bait of the Mercedes we left waiting for him earlier that morning. He really fooled us, the devil! I think that during the two weeks he spent at the Wolf's Lair he found out a lot. He may even have detected the identity of the Soviet spy at the Wolf's Lair – with the help of Lundt. And, by God, I want to put a bullet through that one myself.'

'It's a long shot,' Schmidt reflected.

'I've played them all my life – long shots . . .'

Chapter Thirty-Two

Brigadier Fitzroy Maclean was probably one of the most daring and colourful characters of World War Two, a man whom Colonel Jaeger would most certainly have appreciated. He arrived in the Balkans while the German was recuperating in the Munich hospital.

Maclean literally jumped into the Cauldron – with a parachute – at night, landing in Bosnia with the rest of his team and guided by fires lit by the Partisans. His aim was to contact Tito – which he did – but soon after arriving he found himself unmercifully harassed by the Germans.

He was machine-gunned from the air. He was bombed. The group he joined had to move fast and constantly, often escaping by the skin of their teeth from heavy German motorized forces. For this encouraging welcome he had Colonel Jaeger to thank.

Within one hour of Willy Maisel leaving the hospital ward the Colonel was speaking over the phone to Martin Bormann at the Wolf's Lair. He did not mince his words.

'I expect to be out of this place in a few weeks. I'm going after Wing Commander Lindsay.'

'An excellent notion, Colonel,' Bormann agreed unctuously. 'I can promise you my full and unreserved support to hunt down this Englishman alive or dead,' purred the Reichsleiter. 'I will send you a signed authority . . .'

'What I want now is the phone number of the Luftwaffe air chief in Jugoslavia, plus your backing for me to give him orders to take certain measures . . .'

'It will be done at once.'

There was an interruption at the other end of the line, voices speaking rapidly, and then the Führer himself came on the line.

'Colonel Jaeger! At your convenience I wish you to fly here so I can confer a decoration on you for outstanding performance at the battle of Kursk. Had the generals shown half your determination and courage we should have won an earth-shattering victory. As for Lindsay, he must be brought back alive, unharmed. The outcome of the whole war may depend on your success in this task I personally place on your shoulders.'

'I will do my best, *mein Führer*,' Jaeger replied drily.

The phone was handed back to Bormann who had already found the 'phone number Jaeger needed, and promised to call the Luftwaffe commander. The swine was at least efficient, Jaeger admitted to himself.

Ending the conversation, Jaeger replaced the receiver on its cradle. Schmidt, sitting on the edge of his bed, waited for the news as the Colonel turned with a cynical smile.

'We have nothing to worry about – Bormann has given us his full and unreserved support . . .'

'How can we surrender to the Allies immediately?'

'The same thought crossed my mind. Incidentally, there is something very odd going on at the Wolf's Lair. Before the Führer came on the line I could hear voices arguing and I'm sure I recognized Keitel and Jodl as well as Bormann. Why should they be so interested in Lindsay?'

'You're thinking of the Soviet spy?'

'Yes.' Jaeger's manner became mock-jovial as he hobbled round the ward with the stick. 'Oh, there's one other small matter you may be interested to hear, Schmidt. Hitler wants us to retrieve Lindsay, I quote, *alive, unharmed*, close quote . . .'

'Out of the Balkans? Jesus Christ . . .!'

'No – he might be easier. Wing Commander Lindsay, at this moment possibly a guest of the Partisans, or even maybe dead. I'm counting on those rumours Maisel spoke of being true. I suppose I need my head examining. One other things buoys me up . . .'

'Which is?'

'Another rumour – about a certain blonde lady who carries

326

such authority with one Partisan group, and who sounds remarkably like the ex-Baroness Werther I once had high hopes of getting into bed with.' He smiled wryly. 'The only bed that blonde has put me into is a hospital bed.'

'I keep wondering where Gustav Hartmann is,' Schmidt speculated.

'Ah! Now you're talking. Find Hartmann and we've found Wing Commander Lindsay. Hartmann is a hard man to kill . . .'

For over three months they had been bombed from one refuge to another. The Englishman and the German sat side by side on a rock ledge which formed a natural seat at the summit of a cone-shaped hill. The sun glared down on them at midday out of a burning blue sky. A few metres away a shallow fissure in the rock formed a slit trench in case – once again – the planes with the iron crosses on their fuselages appeared out of nowhere. The German had grown almost as sick of his compatriots' warlike efforts as the Englishman.

'What do you think they're doing now, I wonder?' mused Hartmann.

Below, the Partisans, under Heljec's whiplash commands, shifted great boulders with iron crowbars, levering them to the brink of a sheer drop above a road like a thread.

'Another ambush – for another German column – for yet another good day's work of slaughter, I suppose.'

'You expect to get out of this alive?' Hartmann enquired as he produced a worn, leather pouch, fingered tobacco from pouch into pipe bowl and tamped the result with a brown-stained index finger.

'Do you? And how the blazes do you keep yourself supplied with tobacco?'

'I buy it, from the Partisans who, in their turn, have taken it from German soldiers they have killed.'

He saw Lindsay's expression. He lit the pipe and puffed at it for a few minutes. Then he spoke again in a carefully off-hand tone of voice.

'My friend, this is the Balkans. I do not think you have yet

327

come to terms with where we are. For centuries Croats have been killing Serbs. And vice versa. The Bulgars hate the Greeks – and again, vice versa. Hitler should never have introduced us to this part of the world. It is a place where you kill or be killed. As to your first question, I hope to survive. Smoking my pipe helps me to think clearly. What was it about the Führer you found strange when you were at the Wolf's Lair?'

'I visited him in Berlin before the war. Because of my links with the British aristocracy he took an interest in me. I was also an actor at one time. So I notice people's mannerisms – tiny things which pass unnoticed by others.'

'I understand that. Please continue.'

'At the Wolf's Lair when I first met Hitler he looked like the same man but I sensed he wasn't. Christa also thought something strange had taken place while he was away on that trip to Russia. And Bormann kept watching her closely after Hitler's return . . .'

'What is it you are really trying to say?' Hartmann persisted gently.

'Simply that some change had taken place . . .'

'What you are really saying is that the Hitler who returned late from Smolensk was not the same man who went away?'

It was out in the open. Lindsay made a helpless gesture with his hands. 'I'm saying they have put in a substitute . . .'

Hartmann grilled the Englishman, searching for a loophole in this theory. Lindsay welcomed the experience, it tested the validity of an event he himself had questioned over and over again. He told the Abwehr man of the nightmarish scene he had witnessed when he first arrived at the Berghof.

'And at that time the real Führer was visiting the Eastern Front,' Hartmann commented.

'I've told you the dates . . .'

'What about Eva Braun? He'd never have fooled her . . .'

'I don't think he had to,' Lindsay explained. 'Later on I caught a glimpse of this same man with his arm round her

328

waist as they went into the bedroom she occupies at the Berghof . . .'

'She was having an affair with the double? Now that would be in character,' Hartmann said. 'She's attractive but she's also shallow and flighty.'

'And surely her whole position rested on the existence of the Führer? If he vanished from the scene . . .'

'Goodbye, Eva Braun. She isn't popular – especially with the wives of the leading Nazis.' Hartmann was becoming convinced. 'It would explain something else,' he suggested.

'What's that?'

Hartmann settled himself back against the rock. Puffing at his pipe, he glanced round to make sure no Partisan was near.

'The débâcle at Kursk. Hitler is still controlling the military strategy. He showed himself to be a genius in the early years of the war. The attack on Poland – the generals were nervous. Hitler was the driving force. The astonishing campaign when we seized Denmark and Norway. Again, it was Hitler's decision to launch the attack under the command of Falkenhorst – and again the generals shivered in their boots, predicting a disaster! France in 1940 – Hitler backed the audacious plan produced by Manstein – and put into operation by Guderian. The General Staff almost had a nervous breakdown. It would be a catastrophe! Instead it was a total victory . . .'

'He went wrong at Stalingrad,' Lindsay reminded him.

'A myth! Jodl told me Hitler was certain Stalin was massing armies behind the Don – but our Intelligence, the Gehlen lot – insisted any attack would be at Smolensk, hundreds of miles to the north. The general agreed. For once Hitler gave in and let them go ahead. But how do you account for the fact that the double now at the Wolf's Lair is able to cope with directing the war?' Hartmann asked.

'When I was brought back by train to the Berghof for the second time I was given the same room where I had earlier watched the man with the mirrors. They had cleared the place out but missed a drawer at the base of a wardrobe. Inside I found a whole collection of military works – Clausewitz, von Moltke and others . . .'

'The very books I know the Führer himself studied,' Hartmann confirmed. 'This new Hitler must have studied for his role in every aspect, maybe over a period of years. Obviously that included the same military manuals the real Hitler read. But he will lack his predecessor's flair – the war is being handed to Stalin on a plate . . .'

'You think I'm right, then?'

'Yes – and for another reason. Hitler no longer makes use of his old powers of oratory in public – the talent that lifted him to the heights. A strange omission – until you realize that is one activity a pseudo-Führer would never dare indulge in because he couldn't pull it off. That is the clincher. And here comes Paco . . .'

'You wish to see how determined we are to fight the Germans?' asked Paco. 'Come with me, both of you . . .'

She led the way from the rock pile across the slope of the hilltop towards where the Partisans had completed constructing their rampart of boulders at the brink of the drop.

'This is not my idea,' she told them. 'It is Heljec who insisted on this . . . demonstration.'

'Demonstration?' queried Lindsay.

'Of the Partisans' will to fight. I argued with him but still he insists. So, you will see . . .'

Heljec stood with a group of his men behind the boulders, his waist decorated with grenades slung from a belt, a normal Partisan technique Lindsay found most alarming. They were all there. The amiable, round-faced Milic who smiled at Lindsay. Bleak Bora who looked away at the trio's approach. Dr Macek whose expression was anything but happy (Lindsay wondered why). Heljec's deputy, Vlatko Jovanovic who, behind Heljec's back, made a gesture of resignation to Paco. What on earth was going on?

Heljec himself seemed delighted. He beckoned them forward and placed them between two massive boulders where they could stare down the vertical drop into the abyss. He

330

even laid an arm across the Englishman's shoulder and said something to Paco.

'He wants you to watch the road,' Paco translated. 'They are coming now,' she added.

In the depths a file of tiny figures was marching steadily along the winding thread of a road. As the column came closer, began to pass underneath them, Heljec handed a pair of field-glasses to Lindsay and spoke again. Hartmann was provided with his own pair of binoculars.

'He wants you to study the column,' Paco said tersely.

Mystified, Lindsay focused his glasses. In the twin lenses he was astounded to see the entire column was composed of women, women between approximately the ages of twenty and forty, women armed with every conceivable weapon.

At their waists swung the inevitable hand grenades, festooned round them like some hideous decorations. Pistols were shoved inside their belts. Sheathed knives adorned their sides. Many carried rifles, a few machine-pistols.

They wore the Partisan cap with a red blotch which, Lindsay assumed, was the five-pointed Communist star. There was an eery atmosphere about the endless column which plodded past remorselessly. Not a single woman glanced up to the sheer rock wall rising above them, although Lindsay felt sure they knew a group of their compatriots was watching.

'Who are they?' he asked, lowering his glasses.

'The Amazon Brigade,' replied Paco tonelessly.

Heljec began talking excitedly and Paco, her eyes blazing, turned to confront him, arguing back, her voice and manner as cold as ice. Heljec's expression became ugly as Paco shook her head. He raised his pistol and pointed it at Lindsay. For Hartmann's benefit Paco spoke in German, turning her back on the Partisan leader.

'Heljec wishes me to tell you both this. The Amazon Brigade are the survivors of a small town which was attacked by a German company. All their men were killed in the battle. They formed themselves into this so-called Amazon Brigade, trained with the Partisans – and then went to hunt down the

331

company which had attacked their town. You both understand that I am telling you this story only at Heljec's urging?'

'Get it over with,' Lindsay suggested.

'They thought they had found the Germans they sought
trapped in a defile. The Germans were surrounded, had not
eaten for days and were exhausted. They surrendered . . .'

'Go on,' Lindsay said quietly.

'After the Germans surrendered, those women down there
castrated every man with their knives. The next bit Heljec
does not know I am telling you. They had found the wrong
Germans. The men were innocent. Now Heljec parades those
women to show you how all his people – women as well as men
– fight the enemy. Sometimes I wish I had never joined these
people.'

Hartmann's expression was grim. Heljec lifted his pistol
and placed the muzzle against his forehead. He said something to Paco.

'He wants you to look at those women through your
binoculars again,' Paco told him. 'He says if you don't he will
pull the trigger . . .'

'Tell the murdering swine to go ahead . . .'

Hartmann threw the field-glasses at the Partisan leader's
feet and braced himself. Lindsay saw Heljec take the first
pressure. Paco burst out with a stream of Serbo-Croat. The
Englishman had never seen her look so contemptuous. Heljec
pulled the trigger.

There was a click.

There had been no bullet up the spout. Hartmann remained very still. His face was now bloodless. Heljec removed the weapon and spoke again.

'He says you are a very brave man,' Paco translated.

'Tell him I can't repay the compliment,' Hartmann retorted.

The German shoved both hands inside his jacket pockets
and walked away. Paco and Lindsay followed him up the hill
to the rocks where they had sat earlier. Hartmann sat down
and looked at Lindsay.

'You know why I concealed my hands? They are trembling

uncontrollably. I nearly messed myself back there . . .'

'We have to get away from these bastards as soon as we can,' Lindsay said savagely.

The Heljec incident seemed to have forged a bond between the German and the Englishman. And Paco made no attempt to object to what had just been said. *Escape . . .*

Chapter Thirty-Three

They brought Sergeant Len Reader into the Partisan camp after darkness had fallen like a black cloak. It might be more accurate to say Sergeant Reader brought in the three Partisans – led by Milic – who had found him.

Dressed in British Army serge uniform, Reader marched in front of the group as though in charge. Twenty-seven years old, about five feet eight inches tall, he had a beaky nose, alert eyes, was clean-shaven and exuded an air of confidence.

'Who's in charge of *this* bloody mob?' he enquired.

'You're English . . .!'

Lindsay stood up, holding the bowl of food he had been consuming with no great enthusiasm, stupefied by the appearance of the new arrival. Reader displayed no such surprise. He addressed his compatriot as though meeting him was the most natural thing in the world.

'London, born and bred. Sergeant Len Reader, Royal Corps of Signals. Plumber by trade – so naturally they say we're going to make a wireless operator of you, Reader. Oh, I'm insubordinate, too. Would you by any chance be Wing Commander Lindsay?'

'I would.'

'Sir!' Reader threw up the most impressive salute he had encountered. 'Any of these buggers crowding us understand English?'

'Only a blonde girl called Paco – she's elsewhere just now . . .'

333

'So I can talk and only you'll get my drift?'

Reader was holding in one hand a sten gun and Lindsay was beginning to understand how he had managed to retain possession of the weapon. From his belt hung ammunition pouches which appeared to be bulging to capacity. A backpack completed his equipment.

'Yes, Sergeant. And this would be a good moment to talk . . .'

'I was supposed to join up with the Brigadier – Fitzroy Maclean, that is – who jumped with his lot from the first aircraft. I was with the team in the second plane. I jumped all right then my bleedin' parachute has to drift away from the rest of 'em. So I find myself all on my ownsome. Funny thing, the container with my transmitter lands plonk! Nearly bashed my brains out.'

'This Brigadier Maclean – can you tell me what he's doing in this part of the world?'

'Suppose I can tell *you* – seeing as part of the job was to airlift you out and fly you back to where we came from . . .' Reader lowered his voice. 'Tunisia. Maclean's main job is to contact the Partisan boss over here, better not mention *his* name, seeing as we're surrounded with all these Peeping Toms. So I find myself wandering round for days dodging Jerries and some of the locals who seem to be hobnobbing with the enemy. A right balls-up, if you ask me . . .'

'Četniks,' murmured Lindsay, 'the locals collaborating with the wrong people . . .'

'We was warned about them. Had a lecture – situation appraisal as the toffee-nosed Intelligence lot call it. Slovenes, Croats, Serbs and God knows what they've got over here. A regular goulash of a place this is. This lot who found me didn't get the old transmitter,' Reader added with some relish.

'What happened to it? That could be vital . . .'

'Buried it, didn't I? Just before they arrived. I could take you to it now, it's not half-a-mile away. Better keep mum about that, hadn't we?'

'Yes, Sergeant, I should keep very mum indeed. I may want you to send a signal back when we can. How did you manage to hang on to that sten gun? I'd have expected Milic to confiscate it on the spot.'

'If that's Fatty you're talking about, he did try it on. I couldn't tell a ruddy word he was blathering but I made sure he understood me.'

'And how did you manage that, Sergeant?'

'Pointed the muzzle at his belly, cocked the gun and told him if he didn't keep his bleedin' hands off it he'd get half a magazine for breakfast . . .'

'And not understanding one word of English, I imagine Milic got the message?'

'Too right, he did!' Sergeant Reader looked round at the staring faces. 'Scruffy bunch, aren't they? No discipline. I'd get them licked into shape in no time . . .'

'I expect you would, Sergeant.' Lindsay lowered his voice. 'I want you to remember something in case anything happens to me. In my right-hand jacket pocket there is a small, black, leatherbound notebook I pinched from the Berghof. I've used it as a diary – noted down everything I've observed since I landed in Germany. Including the identity of a man I think is a Soviet spy at Hitler's operational headquarters. That book must reach a Colonel Browne of SIS in Ryder Street, London . . .'

'Nothing's going to happen to you while I'm around,' Reader said chirpily, 'so hand it to him yourself.'

'But if it does,' Lindsay persisted, 'you get my diary and see it reaches London.'

'Wing Commander,' Reader suggested, 'let's you and me stroll off quiet like on our own and have a little chat.'

Chapter Thirty-Four

Lindsay and Reader perched themselves on an isolated boulder and the sergeant glanced round the hilltop before he asked the question and gave his companion the shock of his life.

'Got any form of identification to prove who you are, mate? And this sten isn't aimed at your guts for the fun of the thing.'

'What the hell . . .'

'We can do without the indignation bit, Wing Commander,' Reader interrupted in a voice of quiet menace. 'I've been on this underground lark long enough not to trust my own grandmother – unless she has her papers. Have you?'

'Here you are,' Lindsay said wearily, extracting his RAF paybook. 'I don't normally pull rank, but . . .'

'So don't pull it now. The man with the gun outranks everyone. Something else I learned down there in Greece. Same bleedin' set-up. Only there they call themselves EDES and ELAS. One lot Commies, the others Royalists and both more keen on cutting each others' throats than fighting Jerry. The whole Balkans is one big shithouse . . .'

While he was rambling on, Reader was examining Lindsay's identity papers with great care, even testing the thickness and feel of the material with thumb and forefinger.

'Checking for forgery?' Lindsay queried sarcastically.

Reader's reply stunned him and he studied the outwardly phlegmatic sergeant all over again as though he had never seen him before.

'Checking for just that. The Gestapo boys have a whole printing outfit at No. 9 Prinz Albrechtstrasse, Berlin. Work like beavers day and night producing false papers. Some of them to infiltrate their own people into the underground escape route for RAF fliers from Brussels to the Spanish border. You know what, old boy? You pass scrutiny. Lucky for you. If you hadn't passed muster I'd have been obliged to put a bullet into you after nightfall . . .'

Lindsay returned the identity papers to his pocket. He was trying to absorb the complete change of accent in Reader's voice in his last four sentences. In contrast to the earlier Cockney they had been spoken by a highly-educated man.

'And, incidentally,' Reader continued with a wintry smile, 'I'm not all that heavily out-ranked by you. I'm a major. Army Intelligence . . .'

'I knew there was something phoney about you,' Lindsay replied quietly. 'You'll excuse me – your performance was a bit hammy. I used to be a professional actor a millenium ago.'

'I thought I was pretty good . . .' Reader sounded a trifle put out. 'Where did I go wrong?'

'The usual faults they knock out of you at RADA. Exaggeration, of gesture, accent and so forth. Economy is the secret, gaining the maximum of effect with the minimum effort. The art of doing nothing can take you a long way . . .'

'The object of the exercise was to fool this rabble. That I did pull off. What a ghastly crowd they are. Positively wallowing in butchery. Some of them, anyway. They'd have been lost without a war . . .'

'We have to remember this is the cradle of war throughout most of history. Why the cover role? *Major!*'

They had left the boulder and wandered slowly round the crown of the hill. In the distance Milic and his men watched them uncertainly. Smoke like a poison gas cloud drifted from a nearby slope and brought with it a stench like burning flesh. Reader wrinkled his long, enquiring nose.

'The whole Balkans stinks. Literally. My cover role? Enough about the set-up out here filtered through to London to give us something of a picture. Nobody trusts anyone. Strangers – new arrivals – are automatically suspect. It's like one of our English villages. Twenty years in the place and maybe they'll give you the time of day. Just maybe! Can you imagine the reaction of Tito if he heard Army Intelligence had arrived? From what we've gleaned he's the biggest neurotic of them all . . .'

Lindsay rather liked *gleaned*. As they walked, Reader couldn't keep his hands still. His fingers walked up and down the barrel of the sten as though he were itching to use it. Probably he was missing his tightly-rolled Dunhill umbrella. Unless . . . Lindsay went on probing in his off-hand manner.

'Care to tell me why you are out here? Why you downgraded yourself to sergeant?'

'Cover again. We thought the sergeant touch rather good. Gives me some air of authority with the locals, but an officer, no! A Communist gang is going to take a very questioning look once an officer lands in their lap. God knows, you must have found that out by yourself now . . .'

'Not really. You were going to tell me what brought you into this earthly paradise.'

'Was I?' A hint of mockery crept into Reader's tone. 'Surely you asked me. Well, here goes. What I told you earlier – doing my Cockney bit – was gospel. I'm the bloody chaperone – escort Wing Commander Lindsay out of the Balkans, Reader, they said . . .'

'And who may they be?'

'Nice bit of syntax there. The Lord's anointed. Colonel Browne. None other . . .'

'He still smokes those foul cigars?'

'When he can get them, yes. He sends you his regards. Thought you'd appreciate that out here.'

'So you're not a radio operator at all?' Lindsay went on grimly. 'We have no communication with the outside world?'

'Begging your pardon.' The mockery had turned to mild indignation. 'Before I transferred to Intelligence I was in Signals. Came out top of the form for transmitting at high speed.'

'So there is a hidden transmitter buried somewhere?'

'Bet your life on it.' Reader paused, his tone sardonic now. 'Come to think of it, chum, that's what you are doing – betting your life on that box of wires and circuits. We have to get you out of here. All we need is a radio signal sent in secret. An airstrip for the Dakota from Africa to land on. The Dakota itself. Piece of cake, wouldn't you say?'

'Major, I've just realized something,' Lindsay ruminated aloud. 'You made a big thing about my identification. I haven't seen yours yet.'

'Thought you'd never ask . . .'

Earlier Paco had reappeared in the distance, talking briefly to Milic before she resumed strolling by herself a hundred yards or so away from the two Englishmen. Lindsay examined the Army paybook Reader handed him. He opened the stiff

338

brown cover and checked the pages, glancing up several times.

'That blonde girl, Paco,' he murmured, 'speaks better English than you do. In fact, she is half-English – on her mother's side. Thought you ought to know before you meet her. Security. She's a Partisan . . .'

Reader took back the paybook Lindsay held out to him and with a sleight of hand made it disappear somewhere inside his uniform. As he handed back the brown folder Lindsay found himself recalling something Reader himself had said earlier.

The Gestapo boys have a whole printing outfit at No. 9 Prinz Albrechtstrasse . . . Work like beavers . . . producing false papers . . .

'Wing Commander,' Reader commented out of the blue, 'I would say you're head over heels in love with that girl. Are you?'

'What the hell are you talking about?' Lindsay snapped.

'Fact One: the way you said her name. Fact Two: while we've been talking you've hardly taken your eyes off her since she appeared. You watch her every movement as though you're watching a goddess. Fact Three: your expression since I started talking about her – *mind your own bloody business* is written all over your face . . .'

'Why don't you do just that, *Sergeant*?' Lindsay rapped back.

'This might just be the moment to get clear of this bunch of peasants,' Reader suggested, not in the least disconcerted by his companion's reaction. 'They're all grouped together quite a way from where we are now. Take it one step at a time. Head for the spot where I buried the transmitter . . .'

'Could I take a look at that sten of yours?'

The question was so unexpected that Reader handed over the weapon almost as a reflex action. Lindsay stepped back a few paces, grasping the weapon firmly as he performed a simple action.

'Watch out!' There was genuine alarm in Reader's voice. 'You just released the safety catch – and that's a full mag.'

'I know. And I'm aiming it at you point-blank. Colonel

Browne is a chain-smoker – of cigarettes. He's never touched a cigar in his life . . .'

'I've been hoping to hell you'd pick me up on that . . .'

'Really, Sergeant? May I ask why?'

'Like I tells you before, mate.' Reader was lapsing back into his awful Cockney. Out of the corner of his eye Lindsay saw that Paco was approaching. Reader was quick as a knife, he'd grant the bastard that. He went on, gabbling out the explanation. 'We was told to be especially bleedin' careful in this dung-heap. No one is what they say they is until they've been triple-checked, then don't make any cosy assumptions. Those cigars was thought up by the Colonel himself as a trick question. You could have been anyone . . .' Reader rattled on, 'seeing as the Allied Mission is a prime Jerry target. Had to be sure. No offence . . .'

He broke off as Paco arrived, swept off his cap in an elaborate gesture of politeness and stared at her with blatant interest as she stood and stared back.

'And who have we here, Wing Commander? When they told me you're for the Balkans, my lad, I never expected to meet the Queen of Sheba? I am right? I 'ave to be . . .'

'This,' Lindsay introduced him to Paco, 'is Sergeant Len Reader who, you may already have gathered, has a habit of speaking his mind – and hardly ever stops doing just that. Reader, meet Paco.'

'Pleasure's all mine.'

They shook hands. Paco's sleepy eyes studied Reader and under her scrutiny he became oddly restless.

'Could I have my hand back now?' Paco suggested. 'I only have two of them . . .'

'A thousand apologies, lady. No offence meant – but out here a man gets bowled over when someone like you turns up. And when you speak the King's English . . . This sing-song chatter I've been hearing ever since I arrived . . .'

'*When* did you arrive, Sergeant Reader?' Paco enquired.

'It's all right,' Lindsay assured her. 'I've checked his identity.'

'I'd still like to know *when* he arrived, *where* and *how*?'

It was the first time Lindsay realized one of Paco's duties was to act as Intelligence Officer for the Partisan group. The irony of the situation intrigued him – she had little idea that she was interrogating a man who himself was undoubtedly highly-trained in the sophisticated craft of interrogation.

'The when was days ago. The where Mickey can tell you – me I've no flaming idea. The how was by parachute, dangling by my braces over the Black Hole of Calcutta. Anything else you'd like to know, Lady Bountiful? Blood group? I can show you me birthmark if you're not shy.'

'Mickey?'

'I think he means Milic who brought him in,' Lindsay explained.

Paco ignored him as she continued studying Reader who stared back with what Lindsay felt sure he would have described as 'dumb insolence'. Lindsay sensed a growing hostility between the pair.

'Milic,' Paco said with quiet deliberation, 'tells me he found you wandering round in the middle of the night. No sign of any parachute.'

'So I buried it under some rocks, didn't I? You think I'm going to leave it lying around for Jerry to find? Next thing we know is a whole bleedin' Panzer division is on me heels. First thing you do when your arse hits enemy territory is hide the 'chute.'

'I know . . .'

'Why ask then, for Christ's sake?' Reader flared up. 'We come here to help you people out and you try and stand me in the witness box. Why did you do this? Why didn't you do that? My boss is going to love you . . .'

'And just who is your boss?' Paco asked sharply.

'Brigadier Fitzroy Maclean . . .' Reader leaned his face close to Paco's. 'And let me tell you something. He's been in more scraps than you've had hot dinners. We started fighting 'itler in 1939. You joined the party a bit late, didn't you?'

'I think that's enough, Sergeant,' Lindsay intervened.

'Well keep your girl friend off my back or I'm liable to get a bit shirty. She wouldn't like that is my guess.'

341

Taking his sten from Lindsay, Reader marched away at a steady one-two, one-two. Paco waited until he was out of hearing before she spoke.

'Lindsay, I don't trust that man . . .'

'Just because you didn't hit it off with him? He's come a long way to . . .'

'It's the classic manoeuvre of the suspect under interrogation,' she insisted. 'Pick a quarrel, break the trend when the questions get dangerous . . .'

'He just hasn't attuned himself to the atmosphere out here. He only dropped out of the blue a few days ago.'

'You're sure of that? Milic found him roaming about. No one saw him coming down in a parachute. He's sensitive about that 'chute, as he calls it. And why did he call me your girl friend?'

The question, idly thrown into the conversation, caught Lindsay off guard. Paco was standing very close to him. He was excruciatingly aware of her physical proximity. The emotions he had clamped a lid down on flooded out. The lid was blown sky-high. Damn Reader and his careless remark to the flames of hell.

He stood very still, not looking at her. She waited in silence. He knew she was watching him as closely as she had so recently watched Reader. He took out one of his few remaining packs of cigarettes, cupped his hand against the breeze which was blowing up, and lit it.

'Could I have one?' Paco asked quietly.

'Here you are, take this one . . .'

He would have liked to place it between her lips but refrained from even this small gesture of intimacy. Instead, he handed it to her. He was pleased to see his hand was steady. This was unadulterated hell. Paco took short, quick puffs and then opened Pandora's box.

'Lindsay, I like you.' She paused. 'I like you a lot. But that's all. I'm sorry . . .'

'The feeling's mutual . . .'

He didn't know how he'd managed to get the words out. He

was worried his voice had sounded forced, unnatural. Paco, he knew, was a very perceptive girl. God knows he'd done his best to conceal his real feelings. If she went on like this he was going to give himself away.

'You're still very carefully not looking at me . . .'

'I'm watching Reader traipsing about. You said don't trust him.'

'Now you're changing the subject. What's your next move – to manufacture a row between us?'

He swung round violently and stared straight at her. 'What do you want me to say then?'

'Let's go for a stroll. I want to talk to you.'

She linked her arm inside his and he felt the gentle pressure of her right breast. They walked in step as she began talking.

'You don't know much about me. There is no one else, by the way. The war seems to have stultified my emotions. I've seen so much horror I've grown almost immune. That worries me, worries me more than you might imagine, Lindsay. I know how you feel – I wish I felt the same way. I don't. And a quick roll in the hay after dark isn't going to help either of us. I thought bringing it out into the open might help. I made a mistake. I can see that now. War is not the most amusing of human activities.'

She let go of his arm, bent down to stub out her cigarette on a rock and then dropped the dead stub in her pocket. Her voice changed, became matter-of-fact.

'The first rule of Partisan survival. Leave no traces for the enemy to find.'

She walked away, a slow, purposeful tread. The sun came out. It showed up the gleam of her neat, blonde hair. She had never looked more desirable.

Lindsay stopped at the edge of the abyss. The rock wall fell a thousand feet to a scatter of boulders far below. They looked no larger than pebbles.

He had to get his priorities sorted out. He was carrying – inside his head, in his diary – priceless information which London must know. It could even affect the outcome of the war. Getting back to Allied territory was his prime objective.

He found it poor consolation. He felt humiliated. Paco knew. It was, he now realized, her presumed ignorance of his feelings which had sustained him. He felt an emotional wreck. How often had he imagined making love to her in every erotic detail – her equally passionate response.

'We could make a break for it now, Wing Commander. I've found a hidden gulch which leads into the valley . . .'

It was Sergeant Len Reader. Of course.

Chapter Thirty-Five

'That bloody colonel commanding this column needs shooting,' Jaeger commented savagely to Schmidt. 'Jugoslavia isn't France, it isn't even Russia. To understand this theatre of war you go back to Wellington and the Peninsular War – the Spanish guerrillas. He's going to lead us straight into an ambush.'

'At least you persuaded him to position the mortar teams at the rear of the column,' Schmidt replied.

'Only by waving the Führer's signed order,' Jaeger growled. 'Look at the terrain – the way he's crammed everything together. We should be spread out in well-separated sections . . .'

They were well south of Zagreb and dusk was beginning to descend on all sides like a sinister cloud. The armoured column – comprising tanks, mobile guns and motorized infantry was entering a narrow, winding defile. On both sides rose precipitous heights. Jaeger frowned and raised the field-glasses looped from his neck to focus on a rampart of huge boulders which lay strewn along the brink of the right-hand ridge.

They were travelling as passengers in a half-track, the last vehicle in the straggled column. Immediately ahead of them crawled two canvas-sided trucks carrying the mortar teams. It was very silent apart from the purr of slow-moving engines and Jaeger sat as rigid as a statue, his twin lenses studying the boulder rampart poised far above them.

'There's something funny about those damned rocks,' he told Schmidt. 'Here, you take a look.'

'What am I looking for?' Schmidt asked as he peered through the glasses.

'The slightest sign of movement up there. That's a geological oddity – that line of boulders. There are too many of them. They're too evenly spaced. They're all perched just on the brink. That crazy fool, Schrenk, should have sent a patrol up there before he entered the defile. According to this map the defile is over four kilometres long. Don't like it . . .'

They had attached themselves to the column because it was the only way to get deep into Jugoslavia. Jaeger hoped for Partisan prisoners, men he could question as to the whereabouts of Lindsay and the girl he had come to refer to as the Baroness.

Schrenk's column was undertaking a punitive expedition. He was searching for the phantom Amazon Brigade. An informant had told him the Brigade had passed along this route only a few hours earlier. Jaeger had made himself unpopular by being sceptical, almost contemptuous.

'This informant,' he had demanded, '. . . he is a local?'

'A Serb,' Schrenk had replied. 'Greedy for gold. Always before he has proved reliable.'

'So he is trustworthy forever?'

Schrenk had stormed off and the two colonels had not met again since the column moved off seven hours earlier. At intervals a courier had driven back along the column on his motor-cycle with 'evidence' that they were on the right track. A discarded pair of woman's coarse pantaloons, a Partisan cap complete with the red star badge and a small tuft of feminine hair attached.

'Very convenient,' had been Jaeger's only comment.

'I still think this would be a good time to make a break for it,' Reader repeated to Lindsay. 'It will be dark in no

345

time. There's no one guarding that hidden gulch I found.'

Lindsay looked carefully round the hilltop. On surface appearances Reader was right. Dusk was falling suddenly, the way it did in this part of the world. There was growing activity among the Partisans who, under Heljec's prodding, were gathering behind the rampart of boulders.

They were now armed with thick wooden poles which they seemed to be preparing to use as levers. The ends of the poles were being rammed under the line of boulders perched on the brink of the drop above the gorge where earlier the Amazon Brigade had marched.

'Well?' snapped Reader impatiently, 'do we make a run for it or can't you tear yourself away from that Paco?'

'I'm just not too partial to committing suicide. You're not familiar with these peasants, as you call them, Sergeant. They can hide in a cleft in the ground, merge against the background of a rock cluster. They're everywhere but you don't see them – until too late.'

'I think it's Paco . . .'

'Think what you like,' replied Lindsay calmly, refusing to be provoked. 'Heljec will certainly know about that so-called hidden gulch of yours. The first warning you'll get that I'm right will be a knife between the shoulder-blades . . .'

'Have it your own way – we've lost our chance now, anyway. We have company.'

Through the purple gloaming which was becoming denser by the minute, Lindsay saw Paco approaching. She was accompanied by Milic who carried a German machine-pistol at the ready.

'Heljec insists you both come over and watch.' There was a note of disapproval in her voice. 'And could Sergeant Reader please hand over his sten to Milic for the moment? Heljec has ordered him to confiscate the weapon no matter what means he has to use. Humour him, for God's sake – for my sake . . .'

'Give him the sten,' said Lindsay, standing up.

'I'll give him a burst . . .'

'Don't be a bigger bloody fool than you have to. Look

behind us. We're surrounded. I warned you about men rising up out of the ground.'

'Christ Almighty . . .!'

A screen of a dozen or so Partisans stood silently, barely a few feet behind them. They carried a motley collection of guns, all aimed point-blank at Reader. The weapons were even more eloquent than their silence. With a curse, Reader handed the sten to Milic.

'Now you come with us very quietly. Heljec wishes you both to witness a demonstration of Partisan fighting . . .'

She led the way, and Lindsay walked beside her, towards where the main body of Partisans crouched behind their improvised wall of boulders. It was only as they came close that Lindsay saw Hartmann. He had been on the verge of asking Paco what had happened to the German.

Hartmann stood as erect as he could, turning his head to look at Lindsay. His wrists were bound behind his back. Again his eyes seemed to attempt to convey some message to the Englishman.

'Is that really necessary?' snapped Lindsay.

'Keep your voice down,' she hissed. 'It was done on the direct orders of Heljec. A German armoured column is approaching the gorge below. That is why the Amazon Brigade marched through it so openly earlier. It is a trap and the Germans are falling into it. Look down – not too close!' she warned.

The mutter of many slow-moving engines drifted up from the depths of the gorge. Peering over the edge, Lindsay saw the head of the toy-like column snaking its way along the twisting defile. There was just enough light to see that this was an expedition in force.

Armoured cars and motor-cyclists preceded the convoy. Behind came the tanks, nose to tail, their gun barrels swivelled to one side or the other at maximum elevation. Even to Lindsay's non-military eye this powerful cavalcade seemed useless, they would never be able to elevate the barrels to anything like the angle required to bombard the heights on which Heljec had placed his men.

And now he understood all the effort which had gone into shifting the boulders to the brink, the reason for the thick poles like pine trunks the Partisans had dug in beneath the rocks and which they manned like giant levers, two or three Partisans to a pole.

Doubtless the German commander had taken a gamble – because it was established military lore that in this part of the world the Wehrmacht never moved at night. He was hoping to slip through under the cover of dusk – to break out into the open plain beyond which Lindsay had seen earlier to the south.

It *was* military madness. It *would be* a massacre. Hartmann, compelled by Heljec to watch the destruction of his countrymen, stood close to Lindsay now with Paco between them. The Abwehr officer leaned forward to take a closer look into the abyss. He took a furtive step forward and Paco ground her booted heel hard on the German's foot.

'You want to die early, you maniac?' she whispered.

'What happened?' murmured Lindsay.

'Your German is a brave man. He was trying to kick a stone over the edge. He could have caused a gravel slide – warning the column down there. It is, of course, doomed . . .'

There was no hint of excitement, of triumph in her voice – only an infinite weariness at the thought of the imminent catastrophe and bloodshed.

Soundless as a cat, Heljec ran along the line of men holding the levers. Gentle as a cat, he touched each team leader's elbow as he passed. He was signalling them to launch the attack.

Only one truckload of infantry, the two trucks containing the mortar teams, and the half-track bringing up the rear remained outside the gorge. Within a minute they would have joined their companions inside the defile.

Jaeger had taken back his field-glasses from Schmidt and stared up like a man obsessed, the eyepieces screwed hard against his flesh. The caterpillar tracks ground forward under them. For a split second Jaeger thought fatigue was affecting his vision.

A giant boulder was wobbling. Rocking back and forth. Then the whole rampart began to tremble as though shaking under growing vibrations of an earthquake. A gap appeared on the skyline, still faintly visible. The giant had plunged down . . .

It struck an outcrop, ricocheted with all its massive weight across the gorge to hammer the opposite slope, bounced back in mid-air and then fell vertically. It landed smack on the top of the open turret of a tank. The commander was pounded to a jelly as the boulder collapsed the turret and concertinaed the chassis.

The squashed metal pile halted all the column behind it. More boulders hammered down, falling with tremendous velocity and landing on trucks full of men.

The screaming started. Agonizing, wailing screaming which went on and on and on. The night was filled with the cries of men mutilated, terrified, confused. The banshee-like wailing was the worst.

'Halt! Stop the bloody truck!'

Jaeger reacted instantly. Leaping from the half-track he ran to the lead truck carrying mortar teams, jumped on the running-board and yelled at the startled driver who jammed on his brakes and nearly threw Jaeger to the ground.

One other man had kept his head. Curiously it was the courier on the motor-cycle who earlier had brought to Jaeger 'evidence' from Schrenk of the earlier passage of the Amazon Brigade. In his anxiety to reach Jaeger he threw overboard a stringent order subject to immediate court-martial. He drove with his headlight full on. Standing up in the stationary half-track, his machine-pistol cocked, Schmidt watched the approaching headlamp weaving with great skill in and out among the rocks scattered over the lower slopes. What the hell message was he bringing?

'Colonel Jaeger . . .' The courier had skidded his machine to a halt and was gasping to regain his breath. 'You are now the senior officer . . . Colonel Schrenk is dead . . .'

'Get your breath back, man . . .'

'I'm all right, sir . . .'

349

'Take this instruction as a direct order to be obeyed without question by every officer in the column. Abandon all vehicles. The tanks – everything. Only portable weapons to be taken. You understand?'

'Perfectly, sir . . .'

'The surviving troops are to take up positions on the eastern slope – the *eastern*. Understood?'

'Yes, sir . . .'

'I will have any man who does not obey my next order shot. Under no circumstances are they to open fire on the enemy. Please repeat my instructions . . .'

In the distance they could hear the boulders falling, a clang of rock against metal. Desultory fire. Jaeger stood calmly and patiently as the courier repeated the orders almost word for word.

'Get going,' said Jaeger. 'And good luck . . .'

'I don't understand . . .' began Schmidt who had jumped down beside the Colonel as the motor-cyclist drove off, headlamp blazing.

'Neither will the enemy,' Jaeger replied grimly. 'Now, let's organize our own nasty little surprise for those swine on the heights.'

He ordered the mortar teams out of their trucks with all their equipment. They were to spread out. They were to take up position on the eastern slope opposite the heights where the Partisans were emplaced. Still limping slightly, he followed the mortar teams, moving with astonishing agility over the rough terrain.

'No firing until I give the order . . . aim for just behind the wall of boulders up there . . . take your time . . .'

This is the Jaeger I've always known, Schmidt thought as he followed his chief. Decisive, controlled, won't be rushed even when all hell is breaking loose.

All hell *had* broken loose. Because of Schrenk's stupidity the element of surprise was complete. The boulders continued tumbling down, rock clanged on metal as they hit the vehicles. And now grenades were tossed from the heights like exploding rain. There was the killing crackle of shrapnel.

350

But under Jaeger's command what had almost become a disorganized column fleeing in terrified chaos was taking up the designated positions. Jaeger waited until every mortar was emplaced to his satisfaction, then gave the order.

'Fire a ranging shot.'

On the hilltop Paco had borrowed a pair of night-glasses from Milic. She had focused them on the vague outline of the German column. Men sweated as they heaved at the poles to lever more boulders over the edge. Hartmann, still with wrists bound, stood next to her. His guards had abandoned him as they lobbed grenades into the black gulf.

On the other side she was flanked by Lindsay who glanced round and saw Reader close behind, his face oddly expressionless. As Paco continued staring through her glasses the darkness was illuminated by blue moonlight. A flare fired by the Germans hovered. Paco stared hard through the twin lenses.

'My God, it looks like Jaeger at the end of the defile . . .'

'You're imagining things,' Lindsay replied.

'I think we should get well back . . .'

It was Hartmann who had spoken to Lindsay. He made a gesture with his head towards the hilltop which was well clear of the edge of the precipice.

'Hartmann wants us to get out of this,' Lindsay told Paco. 'I think he may have a bloody good reason for . . .'

'I heard him.'

'Then for Christ's sake do something about it.'

'I've seen more than enough for one night,' she said.

Paco took Hartmann firmly by one arm and helped him to move at a gentle jog-trot up the hill slope. Lindsay followed and Reader brought up the rear. No attempt was made to detain them. The Partisans were totally preoccupied with what was going on below them. Heljec seemed to be in a state of euphoria, urging his men on.

The brilliant blue flare was still lighting up the night when the first ranging mortar bomb landed. It hit one of the large rocks.

351

'Now wait for what's coming,' said Hartmann as he continued his jog-trot while Paco supported his balance. 'Especially if that is Jaeger down there . . .'

One moment it seemed to be a massacre of the Germans trapped in the gorge, a leisurely process of annihilation. Then that first bomb landed. It took Jaeger's team seconds to adjust the angles of trajectory to a fractionally higher elevation.

A veteran fighter, Heljec had been perplexed despite his jubilation. He expressed his puzzlement to Milic.

'No opposition at all. It is strange . . .'

'We caught them with their pants down . . .'

'But no rifle fire even – not a single shot. What was that?'

That was Jaeger's ranging shot. By a miracle the men closest to the detonation escaped unscathed. The force of the explosion burst out back across the gorge. The flare sputtered, fizzled out. All activity along the precipice temporarily ceased while the Partisans adjusted to the sudden darkness which enveloped them. Then Jaeger's response began in earnest.

From below the SS Colonel heard, but could not see, the distant thump of the bombs exploding. He estimated they would be landing a hundred metres beyond the brink. His estimate was correct. The startled Partisans ran *into* the barrage they had hoped to flee from.

On the hilltop Paco looked back and saw Heljec's men falling, throwing up their arms as they plunged down onto the hard ground. It was ideal mortar territory: the hilltop was coated with half-buried rocks which increased the killing power of the bombs a hundredfold. Instant detonation created maximum blast. Shrapnel like knifeblades hurtling with tremendous velocity cut them to pieces.

It was Hartmann who called out the warning.

'We're not moving fast enough – he'll use a creeping barrage . . .'

'This is bloody stupid!' Paco snapped. 'Stop a second . . .'

Taking a knife from her belt she sliced through the rope

binding the German's wrists. Something fell heavily close to Lindsay. It was Milic's rotund, Falstaffian figure, the back of his head shattered. He was still clutching the sten gun. Reader bent down, tore the weapon from the lifeless hands and the spare magazines protruding from his jacket pocket.

'Hurry, for God's sake!' called out Hartmann over his shoulder.

They began running. Hartmann seemed to have taken over from Paco as leader of the group. The irony of the situation flashed through Lindsay's mind – an Abwehr officer guiding them into a less dangerous zone – from an attack unleashed by another German in the gorge below.

At that moment Jaeger was giving an order to his mortar teams which he had divided into two sections. He was leap-frogging them up the lower slope – so that one waiting section was always a hundred metres higher up than the other, its weapons elevated to fire the bombs a greater distance.

'Second team! Open fire . . .!'

The firing team fed bombs into the squat, sinister barrels – spread out over half a kilometre. It was all guesswork on Jaeger's part. It had to be, since he couldn't see what the hell was happening on the hilltop. He took encouragement from the fact that no more of the remaining rocks were being levered over the ridge which seemed deserted.

He would have been even more encouraged had he been able to view the hilltop. Five minutes earlier Heljec held the upper hand and the destruction of the entire column seemed inevitable. Now it was hell and chaos on the hilltop as the disorganized and bewildered Partisans ran on into the next barrage.

'If the shits had any sense they'd run back to the precipice,' Reader gasped out to Lindsay as he ran alongside him.

'We have to get to the edge of the hill and down the other side,' Hartmann shouted. 'Any bomb coming that far will fall into the other gorge . . .'

Paco ran alongside the German, careful not to trip. There might never be time to get to her feet again. She could hear the hateful hiss and rattle of the shrapnel close by . . . a big

353

enough piece could decapitate a man – or a woman. The barrage was horribly close, seemed to be scraping their heels. They were too late . . .

Hartmann grabbed Paco by the forearm, slowed her down. They had reached the far side of the hill where it plunged down into another gorge. He saw a narrow steep gulch descending like the start of a stream bed. He pulled her with him, feet slithering on a gravelly surface. The dried-up stream bed zigzagged between more boulders.

They came to an overhang of rock protruding far out, providing a natural roof. Panting for breath, Hartmann paused, let go of Paco and looked back and up. Lindsay was close behind. At his heels Reader followed, waving the sten as he staggered on the uneven surface.

'Get our breath back here . . .' Hartmann said. 'We're safe here from the mortar bombs. Sit down on that rock . . .'

Paco was trembling. He sat on another rock himself, took out a handkerchief and wiped sweat from his forehead. Lindsay, silent and withdrawn, had perched on another rock while Reader sagged against the rear wall.

'In a minute we'll have to get moving and fast,' Hartmann told them. 'Is there a way round into this gorge from the other one?' he asked Paco.

'Yes. This hill is like a lozenge,' she explained, 'cut off from the rest of the countryside by roads. Where the Germans came in there's a fork . . .'

'So, from the point where you saw Jaeger he could back-track, take the other fork – and he'd be coming along this gorge below which we have to cross to escape?'

'You're right,' Paco said, studying Hartmann. 'Except that I can't believe Jaeger has caught up with us, that the Germans will think of such a manoeuvre. They must be in a terrible mess.'

'If it's Jaeger he'll think of it, and he'll come,' Hartmann said firmly.

Lindsay was in a state of semi-shock. Locked into the cockpit of a Spitfire was one thing. But this was his first experience of real ground warfare. Illogically, he cursed his own slowness, the fact that it was Hartmann who had saved Paco was something he deeply resented.

Reaching automatically for a cigarette, his hand touched the hard outline of the diary in his pocket. That was all – was everything – which counted. He must get the information back to London. It was a hollow reflex thought. At that moment, watching Paco, he didn't really care what happened next.

The surviving Partisans had reached the edge of the hill and were fleeing into the gorge below down other gulches. Between the steady thump of the mortar bombs – like a martial drumbeat – Hartmann could hear on both sides the slither of fleeing feet, the slide of stones. He stood up.

'We must get moving – before they trap us . . .'

It was weird, thought Lindsay. Hartmann seemed to have taken command of their little group quite naturally. Even Paco was accepting his leadership. And poor Milic was dead, a man with only half a head. Milic who had – speaking not a word of German – travelled all the way to Munich as part of Paco's rescue team. A hand grabbed him by the shoulder and shook him roughly.

'Have you gone into a bloody trance? The others are half way down to the gorge . . .'

Reader, of course. Always Reader.

'I'm handing over command to you, Schmidt.' Jaeger gave the order as he stood in the back of the half-track studying a local map with the aid of a shaded torch. 'There's a fork barely a kilometre behind us. Remember? We took the right-hand turning. According to this map the left-hand one leads round the far side of this mountain. I'm going to trap the whole of this bloody Partisan group . . .'

'You'll get there in time?'

'That's why I've assembled this mobile force . . .'

Jaeger had achieved the apparently impossible twice over. He had – by cunning use of the mortar teams – converted potential destruction of the column into disaster for the Partisans. Now he had conjured up his mobile force – the half-track armed with a swivel-mounted machine-gun and a team of six motor-cycles with sidecars – the sidecars each carrying a man armed with a machine-pistol and grenades.

The half-track was crammed with infantry also armed with machine pistols and grenades. This, Jaeger was convinced, would be close-range – maybe hand-to-hand – fighting. As the first group of two motor-cycles and sidecars headed back for the fork he gave final instructions to Schmidt.

'Get the *men* out of the deathtrap they should never have been led into. Forget the transport, abandon the tanks. Save the *men*! They're to move – well-spread out – fast until they break out into the plain beyond. Regroup there and I'll rejoin you when I can.'

'Good luck, Chief.'

'Luck doesn't come into it,' Jaeger shouted as the half-track turned through a hundred and eighty degrees prior to moving back to the fork. 'It's firepower, mobility and getting there . . .'

Before he turned to face the way they were going, Schmidt was already kicking the starter of a borrowed motor-cycle ready for his swift journey along the column to issue the order. Evacuate!

Something very peculiar happened. At the time it made no sense to Lindsay, no sense at all. They had stumbled after Hartmann to the bottom of the serpentine gulch. The road along the gorge was little more than a rock-strewn track. Lindsay suspected it was a tumbling torrent in winter.

They had crossed the road as a rearguard: the more experienced Partisans were already on the far side, scrambling up another steep slope. They could hear the German motor-cycles and sidecars coming. They could *see* them coming as they roared forward with headlamps blazing.

Paco waited until they were several hundred metres above the road. They had reached a rock ledge at the mouth of a shadowed cave when, from underneath her jacket, she produced a Luger pistol and pointed it at Hartmann.

'If you make any attempt to signal our whereabouts to your compatriots I'll shoot you . . .'

'Shoot me!'

Hartmann began shaking with laughter. Lindsay thought the Abwehr officer's nerve had broken, that the strain had proved too much. The German extended a hand towards the pistol, suddenly stern.

'Who do you think got you off that hilltop? Who realized what was coming? Who just – but only just – saved you from the bombardment? Give me that gun immediately.'

He grasped the barrel, gently pulling it from Paco's grasp. He took hold of it by the butt and with a quick movement placed the end of the muzzle against Reader's skull.

'Hand over the sten to Lindsay. You've got three seconds and I've started counting . . . two . . .'

Reader surrendered the sten. The two men stared at each other. Hartmann gestured into the recesses of the cave. Reader shrugged, walked slowly into the shadows. Hartmann gestured again, this time to Lindsay.

'Go after him. Keep an eye on him. You have the sten . . .'

'Why?' asked Paco.

'Maybe because his enemy is down there. We shall survive only if we hide. There is more than the motor-cyclists . . .'

For the first time since they had started their brutal, aching climb Paco heard another, more sinister sound approaching above the erratic roar of the oncoming motor-cycles. The power and the grind of rumbling caterpillars. A tank? A half-track?

There was something macabre, almost comic, about the antics of the motor-cycles. They kept dashing backwards and forwards like frantic ants, never in one place for more than a second. Darting over a short distance, screeching round on their wheels, skidding, driving back the way they had just come. Then repeating the same process. And all the time the sound of the rumbling caterpillar tracks came closer.

'Get back from the edge,' Hartmann commanded.

He grabbed her forearm and hauled her closer to the mouth of the cave as he spoke. Just in time. The soldiers riding in the sidecars began scouring the lower slopes with a ferocious barrage of machine-pistol fire. They had spotted the fleeing Partisans on the higher slopes.

A man screamed, screamed as the Germans had screamed in the other gorge. The sombre thought crossed Lindsay's mind that the sounds had been the same. A body, arms and legs cartwheeling, fell through the air beyond the cave to land on the rocks a few hundred metres below.

The rattle of machine-pistol fire continued. Random shooting across the whole slope. The hail of fire became insistent. But this was only the hors d'oeuvres. Colonel Jaeger, remembering the other gorge, was about to serve up the main course.

On the same day it was very quiet and the street was deserted as the little, middle-aged man with glasses locked the outer door of the offices of Vita Nova Verlag in Lucerne. To clear up a backlog he had been working late and now he crossed the street to the tram stop and waited patiently.

The weather was chilly and damp and he wore his overcoat and soft hat as he checked his watch and peered along the street in the direction the tram would appear. The quiet, the lack of pedestrians was deceptive.

'There he is,' a man concealed in a shop doorway remarked to his companion, another ordinary-looking civilian. 'Every day he follows the same routine, the same route home. Even if he is late today. He must be crazy.'

'He never varies the route? You are sure of that?' the taller man asked sharply.

'We have watched him for a week now. He gives no sign of being a professional . . .'

'You are sure that is Rudolf Roessler? A man like that could have a double. We all have a double. Did I tell you once . . .'

'His tram is coming.' The first hint of excitement appeared in the voice of the smaller man. 'Be ready. The other teams are in position?'

'Of course.'

The tram rumbled wearily towards the stop. It had started to rain, a gentle, wetting drizzle like a sea-mist drifting in off the lake. Roessler absent-mindedly fastened the top button of his coat, a pointless action since in a moment he would be inside the tram. It stopped, its sides gleaming with globules of moisture, and Roessler climbed aboard. As was his habit he chose a seat at the back. A woman hurried aboard and sat beside him, much to the annoyance of Roessler who preferred to be alone. He glanced furtively sideways.

'Anna . . .!'

'Shush! Keep your voice down. You are being followed. You see those two men sitting in the seat near the exit door, the ones who came aboard at your stop . . .'

Roessler was bewildered. First the unprecedented appearance of his wife who had never before met him on his way home. Now this absurdly melodramatic story . . . To get his bearings he performed an everyday action, taking off his rain-smeared glasses to clean them. He was going to use the corner of his handkerchief when his wife took them from him.

'Give them to me. You'll smear them, make them worse . . .'

Without his glasses the world was a blur. He stared at the vague silhouettes of the backs of the two men. He had not even noticed them boarding the tram. His wife had taken a tissue from her handbag to clean the glasses.

'What is happening?' he asked. 'I don't understand – we are in Switzerland. We are safe . . .'

'We *thought* we were safe,' Anna corrected him.

She handed back the glasses. With a sense of relief he put them on and the world came back into focus. Droplets of rain ran down the windows of the tram. He followed one droplet as it zigzagged an irregular course. He was frightened.

'What are you talking about?' he asked. 'You said earlier I was being followed. By whom?'

His coat smelt of damp wool. He should have brought a raincoat instead. But earlier in the day . . .

'I don't know,' Anna replied, keeping her voice low. 'The first thing I noticed several days ago was the men following you to work in the morning. I was watching from behind the net curtains as you went off to catch your tram. Two men had been standing on the opposite pavement, apparently talking to each other. It was raining heavily. Neither had an umbrella and they were getting soaked. It seemed odd . . .'

'You're imagining all this,' he muttered.

'Wait till I've finished! Then tell me I'm imagining it. I went on watching. You crossed the street and you were no more than one hundred metres away when they began to follow you. As you disappeared round a corner they broke into a trot to catch up . . .'

'The same men as those sitting in that seat?'

He was beginning to believe her. Ever since they had fled from Germany before the war, he had felt secure once they crossed the Swiss border. He didn't want to believe her.

'Not the same men. A different pair . . .'

'There you are!' He relaxed, sagged against the back of the seat. 'It's all a coincidence. I told you it was your imagination . . .'

'Men are watching our apartment by day and by night . . .'

Oh, God! They sat there as the tram stopped, the doors opened, people got off, a man got on, the doors closed, they were off again. The two men Anna had pointed out remained in their seat, exchanging not a word. Roessler glanced up in the angled mirror to help passengers board and alight. One of the men in the seat was staring at him. Roessler looked away. It was becoming a nightmare.

'We're there,' said Anna. 'Get off as though nothing is wrong. Don't look at the men. Don't trip on the steps . . .'

They had reached the suburb of Wesemlin where they rented the small apartment they had taken in 1933. Anna is so strong, he thought. She walked to the exit with a firm tread, paused for him to catch her up, then stepped down into the street. On the pavement, in the reflection from his freshly-cleaned glasses, he saw the two men hurry down the steps seconds before the automatic doors closed. It was one of the worst moments of his life.

Chapter Thirty-Six

Jaeger timed the moment for the attack from the half-track with great perception. By now the motor-cyclists with their short-range barrage from the machine-pistols had the Partisans scrambling all over the slope, seeking altitude. Jaeger stood behind the powerful searchlight which had not yet been brought into play. An NCO called Olden manned the swivel-mounted machine gun with a range far greater than that of a machine-pistol.

'Olden,' Jaeger warned, 'I think we should have them scattering like ants. Brace yourself for when I turn on the light . . .'

'I am ready when you are, Colonel . . .'

There was a bitter note in Olden's voice. Back there in the other gorge he had lost comrades he had campaigned with in the wastes of Russia. Christ, one or two even went back to France, 1940!

The half-track went on rumbling forward, its caterpillars creaking and rattling. Jaeger aimed the powerful searchlight at an extreme angle, turned as far as it would go to the right.

'I'll sweep in a slow arc from right to left,' he called out to Olden. 'Maybe bob up and down a bit . . .'

'Understood, Colonel.'

Olden swivelled the barrel of his gun far right. They had to work in concert to gain maximum results. He was glad the Colonel was operating the light. Jaeger was alert, ice-cold at such a moment. His night vision was exceptional . . .

The light came on. A beam like an anti-aircraft searchlight lit up the slope. Tiny figures scattered across the slope made the fatal mistake of turning in surprise, and were blinded by the glare. Olden's gun began to chatter.

From the half-track they saw the figures dropping. The

noise of the engine, the tracks and Olden's gun drowned the screams of the Partisans caught in the open. The beam swept towards the left, paused, dropping and climbing while Olden's gun synchronized with the movement of the beam.

High up on the slope Heljec, leading a group of men up a defile, paused. Snatching a rifle from the man behind, he told them to continue without him and climbed out of the deep notch. Releasing the safety catch, he stood and watched.

Panic. Partisans were running like thoughtless rabbits to escape the probe of the deadly beam. The first priority was to shoot out that bloody searchlight. It would not be easy. The half-track's commander was a clever bastard. He was varying the speed of the vehicle. Not only a moving target – also an erratic one.

Heljec pressed the butt of his rifle firmly into his shoulder. He aimed a score of metres ahead of the half-track's progress, waited. Take out that light and the gunner was blind. Patiently he waited as the half-track crawled up to his line of fire.

The searchlight swivelled without warning. One moment it was a beam of light searching the slope over to his left. Then it moved, jerked, stopped. Heljec was caught in the full glare of the great eye of light.

Heljec dropped. Dropped his rifle. Dropped to the ground. He was rolling as he hit the earth. He spun like a child's top with incredible speed. Hands clasped on top of his head. Forearms protecting his face. Rolling. He reached the edge of the defile, rolled over the edge, dropped six feet and hit the base with a thud.

He had just reached the edge when Olden's gun began to hammer. As he dropped out of sight slivers of rock slashed off by Olden's bullets skimmed over his head. He lay where he had fallen on his bruised shoulder, listening to the drumfire. Waste your bloody bullets, you stupid mental deficient . . .

In the gorge below, both Olden and Jaeger were convinced they had scored another hit. There had been only a fraction in time between Olden's barrage following the searchlight beam and the figure with the rifle dropping.

'Cease fire!' he ordered Olden, *and doused the searchlight*.

From the viewpoint of military tactics he was correct. He had fully exploited the element of surprise. He had caused heavy casualties among the Partisans. The sight of a man standing aiming a rifle warned him the surprise was gone. The half-track – with the searchlight turned on – had become a potential target.

'We've tanned their hides!' Jaeger shouted. 'Now, get to hell out of it – join up with the others in the plain.'

'Perhaps we should walk past our apartment – to confuse the men who are following us,' Roessler suggested.

His glasses were already misted up again. He was confused and depressed. A superb wireless operator, a man of stubborn courage, he was hopeless in the present situation. Unlike his wife.

'Don't be silly,' she said. 'They know exactly where we live. The thing to do is not to let them know we've rumbled them. We carry on as usual . . .'

'It could be very dangerous . . . Anna,' he observed suddenly, 'look at that stationary car. You can't see inside it . . .'

'Don't try. Act normal. Just walk across the street to our apartment.'

She spoke confidently but the car – parked dead opposite to their apartment block entrance – had fine-mesh, dark-coloured curtains drawn. It was impossible to see whether there was anyone inside.

'Coffee!' Roessler said once they were inside their apartment.

'I'm already making it.'

Roessler had no vices except coffee – of which he consumed litres. He walked restlessly over to the window.

'Don't twitch those curtains!' warned Anna.

'What are we going to do? Those two men on the tram are standing in the rain with their hands in their pockets. This really is dreadful. And tonight I have to contact Wood-pecker . . .'

'You'll feel better after coffee. We must contact Masson.'

Roessler cheered up a little at her mention of the chief of Swiss counter-espionage. Then, standing by the window, careful not to touch the curtains, he froze. Blinking, he took off his glasses, put them on again and stared down into the street. He was excited as he called out.

'Anna! Brigadier Masson is here! He has just got out of that car. He's coming over to see us . . .'

'In broad daylight!' She appeared with the pot of coffee and cups on a tray. 'You must be wrong . . .'

Brigadier Roger Masson, dressed in civilian clothes, strolled over the deserted street and pressed the bell. Roessler operated the release button for the downstairs front door without even checking his identity on the speakphone. He had the apartment door open as the Swiss came up the stairs, his normally cheerful expression grave.

'You should have made sure who it was,' he said mildly. 'I must ask you from now on to take every precaution. Things have changed – and not for the better.'

Masson was choosing his words with care. It was a delicate business, this visit to Roessler at his apartment. He had to alert him – but not alarm him.

The Swiss counter-espionage chief was nervous and sensitive – attributes he normally concealed with a cheerful manner. The fact that he was dressed in his civilian clothes didn't help, he felt more at home in uniform.

'Coffee?' suggested Anna. 'Let me take your coat and hang it up – it's damp . . .'

'That's very kind of you . . .'

As he took off the coat Masson wandered over to the window and gazed into the street. Roessler joined him; his eyes behind the glasses had a feverish look.

'I am being followed. Since several days. It was Anna who first noticed . . .'

'For one week,' Masson said with typical precision. 'They are my men – working round the clock in relays. It is merely a precaution for your protection.'

'Why now? Something has happened?'

'I wouldn't say the timing has any particular significance. It

364

is simply that your work is so important – to us as well as to the Russians . . .'

Masson sat down in an arm chair by the small table where Anna had placed his cup of coffee. Roessler joined him in a nearby chair and drank greedily from his own cup, his eyes never leaving the Swiss.

'This is 1943,' he said after consuming half the cup. 'It is now over two years since Hitler invaded Russia. What has happened recently to make my work – so important is the phrase you used, I believe. You must be employing a lot of valuable men to have me guarded round the clock – again to use your own phrase, I believe . . .'

Masson forced himself to relax. He smiled and his bright blue eyes expressed confidence. The trouble was Roessler was shrewd – to say nothing of Anna. It was a godsend he had come to see them today. The moment he walked into the apartment he had sensed a new atmosphere – wariness on the part of Anna, something close to panic on the part of Roessler. He waved a reassuring hand.

'Before, there was this terrible shortage of staff. Suddenly I am allocated more men. Now I can look after you properly – as befits your importance . . .'

He sipped his coffee as Anna perched on the arm of her husband's chair. He was relieved to see Roessler trying to assume an expression of modesty which did not reflect his true reaction. It was certainly a truism, Masson thought to himself: flattery did get you somewhere. Cautiously he pressed a little further.

'When you visit us at the Villa Stutz it might be an idea if you varied the route and timing of your calls. It will give my men a little practice in keeping tabs on you. Regard it as a game . . .'

'I'll do that . . .'

Roessler had started on the cup Anna had just refilled, still revelling in the rosy glow of Masson's compliments. The feverish expression was disappearing. What a strange man this German is, the Swiss chief reflected. Outwardly so ordinary and middle-aged, you could pass him on the street and never recall you had passed anyone. Which was an advantage, of course.

Anyway, he had pulled it off. Best clear out before there was an unfortunate turn in the conversation. Leave well alone. He finished his cup, refused a refill from Anna and stood up, smiling amiably. Now, leave . . .

'Well, Hans, I think I managed that,' said Masson, settling himself in the front passenger seat of the limousine.

He sighed. He glanced at Roessler's apartment window as the driver performed an illegal U-turn and headed for the Villa Stutz. What a quaint man RR was.

The driver, the only other occupant of the large car, was Captain Hans Hausamann. In peacetime he had run a business which provided him with invaluable contacts all over Europe as far as Finland.

At the outbreak of war Hausamann had been recruited by the Swiss Commander-in-Chief, General Guisan. His business contacts provided a ready-made network which kept the Swiss High Command in touch with developments across the whole continent. He now controlled the highly secret counter-espionage system centred at the Villa Stuz known as the Bureau Ha.

'You sighed,' Hausamann commented. 'They gave you a rough ride?'

'Not really. After a little initial awkwardness I convinced RR our people watching him were a simple precautionary measure . . .'

'And he swallowed that one?'

'I think he did, yes.' Masson thought for a moment. 'Anna, of course, is a quite different proposition. She knows something is very wrong but I can rely on her to soothe RR . . .'

RR was how they referred to Rudolf Roessler. It was not a code reference – someone had started calling him that and it had become standard practice.

'You're sure about Anna?' Hausamann pressed. 'You know her . . .'

'We conspire over RR's head.' Masson smiled briefly. 'I

know her only concern is her husband's peace of mind. So she always goes along with me in an emergency. And, boy, have we got an emergency on our hands . . .'

They drove in silence the rest of the way. It is no more than eight kilometres to the district of Kastanienbaum where a lonely cape projects into the lake. Half a kilometre further, Hausamann pulled up outside the Villa Stutz. It is a very peaceful spot. But so is Bletchley, England, where Ultra operated from. And so was Prae Wood near St Albans, the headquarters of Section V where Whelby had his desk.

The wrought-iron gates in the outer wall were opened by a man dressed in a Tyrolean hat, a dark raincoat and leather boots. The gates were closed behind the limousine as it was driven up to the front entrance and stopped.

'I was just thinking,' Masson remarked, 'that when I first joined Intelligence I had ideals. I had no idea I would spend most of my life persuading others to tell the truth while I told nothing but lies. Even if by omission . . .'

'I don't follow you,' replied Hausamann who always spoke his mind.

'RR – I left him happy-happy. How would he react if he knew that Switzerland is now swarming with German agents dedicated to tracking him down? That this is the reason we blanket his life with our own men? At least we can console ourselves with the fact that the Germans – Schellenberg in particular, thank God – have no idea of what is going on . . .'

Masson did not realize it but this was probably the most naïve statement he made in his whole career.

NDA FRX . . . NDA FRX . . . NDA FRX . . .

It was exactly midnight when Roessler, hunched half-inside his cupboard over the transceiver, tapped out the call sign for Moscow Centre. Even then Soviet agents were in the habit of referring to Russian State Security headquarters as 'The Centre'.

Earlier Roessler had received a signal from Woodpecker which he was now trying to re-transmit to Moscow. He was crouched over the instrument when a hand appeared with a

367

cup of coffee. Still not sure that her husband had recovered from his fright earlier in the day, Anna had decided he would get extra coffee tonight.

She need not have worried. Once he was ensconced in his minute working quarters only one thing existed for Rudolf Roessler – the transceiver, the receipt and sending of signals. He had, in fact, forgotten all about the visit of Roger Masson.

He repeated the call sign two more times. As agreed, for this phase he was using the 43-metre band. And his 'fist' was firm and normal as he tapped out the dots and dashes.

His next move was to switch to the 39-metre band, again as per the arrangement. He waited. He drank half his cup of scalding coffee. He was busy. He was happy. He was ruling the world . . .

NDA OK QSR5 . . . NDA OK QSR5 . . .

Moscow was responding to his call. He waited again. Within seconds came a series of five letters and five figures – masking the code chosen for this transmission.

Roessler recorded the signal and only then did he begin to transmit Woodpecker's latest message about the present German order of battle. *All on the 39-metre band.* All was well with RR's world.

NDA FRX . . . NDA FRX . . . NDA . . . FRX . . .

At the Dresden Signals Monitoring Centre in Germany the call sign came through clearly. Walter Schellenberg, chief of SS Intelligence, listened on the spare set of headphones while Section Chief Meyer personally recorded the signal passing through the ether.

'It's stopped! You've lost him. This is the suspect call sign?'

'It is,' Meyer confirmed. 'It's taken me months to track it down. All I can say at the moment with the resources at my disposal is the transmitter is located somewhere along a line from Madrid through Geneva, Lucerne and Munich . . .'

'Can't you narrow that down?'

'If you're asking me to guess – and at present it is no more than a guess – I'd say it's located in the Geneva-Munich sector.'

'And it is a rogue transmitter?' Schellenberg persisted.

'I've checked the lists of all our call signs – hundreds of them – and it's not one of ours. It's the same man, too. I've come to recognize his fist . . .'

'Let me think a minute.'

Walter Schellenberg had been appointed chief of SS Intelligence as successor to Reinhard Heydrich when the latter had been assassinated by a team dropped into Czechoslovakia for that express purpose.

A tall, handsome and well-dressed man – he invariably wore civilian clothes – Schellenberg was one of the few Nazi leaders who could be described as a genuine intellectual, who preferred using brains to jackboots. Off his own bat – with Hitler's full approval – he had assigned to himself the task of hunting down the Soviet spy inside Germany he was convinced was passing to the Kremlin full details of the Führer's military planning.

Faced with such a task, an experienced gamekeeper – or spy-catcher – concentrates on the spy's weakest point, his system of communication. The method had often succeeded in the past. It required patience and determination – qualities Schellenberg possessed in full measure.

'You need use of our advanced mobile monitoring system,' he suggested.

'With that we could get a cross-bearing – pinpointing the precise source of the transmitter,' Meyer agreed. 'Could I suggest where it should be positioned?' he enquired.

'Tell me and it shall be done,' the SS chief assured him.

Meyer thought Schellenberg was a fine fellow. Despite his exalted rank he talked to you like an equal. Always smiling, charming, affable, not like some of the other thugs who came down from Berlin and threw their weight about.

True, Schellenberg had a downward curve to his lower lip which suggested ruthlessness. But a man like that shouldered enormous responsibilities. Drawing up a chair, Schellenberg sat down and waited patiently while the section chief considered his question.

For Schellenberg, Meyer was a valuable instrument. You

handled him with finesse and consideration, as you would a Stradivarius. Meyer could hold the outcome of the war in his hands if he tracked down this rogue transmitter. Schellenberg was convinced it was the route along which Germany's most cherished secrets were being passed to Moscow.

'Strasbourg,' Meyer said eventually after consulting a large-scale map of Europe on which he had traced the line, Madrid-Geneva-Munich. 'That's where I'd like the mobile monitor . . .'

'And another half-dozen men here allocated purely for your own use?'

'That would be a terrific help. It would save time . . .'

'Time is what we don't have. You are right. And always this call sign is on the 43-metre band? Then nothing more?'

'That's right. I think for the main transmission he switches to another waveband. We have to find that waveband. The extra men should do it.'

'Splendid! Splendid! I leave it to you, Meyer. Since you'll be directing a larger unit there will be promotion, extra pay, of course.'

This was another Schellenberg tactic. Dealing with anyone important to him, the SS chief always left them in a good mood, a mood of gratitude. It ensured their loyalty and support. And what Meyer had said was of great significance, confirming Schellenberg's growing conviction not only that clever Meyer had found the rogue transmitter, but also that the Soviets were involved.

It was known in the SD – SS Intelligence – that Russian agents used this little trick in wireless communication. Send out the call sign to make the initial contact on one pre-arranged waveband. Then switch to a second – also prear-ranged – waveband for transmitting the main signal.

Schellenberg cast one swift look round the vast floor di-vided up into glass, sound-proof cubicles. Inside each sat a radio monitor checking his own apportioned waveband. Dresden was the most efficient monitoring system which existed in the world at that time. He left the building and spoke to no one until he was seated beside his aide, Franz

Schaub, in the car which would take them to the airfield and the plane for Berlin.

'I'm pretty sure it's Switzerland, Franz. I've thought so all along. Why I don't know. Flood the place with more agents. I want them concentrated on Masson's lot. If Meyer can only give me proof, I have Masson by the balls. But *why* Switzerland?' he repeated with some exasperation.

As with most human activity, the outcome of great wars is often decided by eccentric characters.

The set-up in the summer-autumn of '43 was crazy. The Red Army should have achieved total victory all on its own by the end of the year, rolling all the way to the Channel. It had everything going for it.

On the Eastern Front two million German troops confronted *five* million Russians. By numbers alone a less tough and determined Wehrmacht would have been overwhelmed.

In addition, by this time, the German military machine was directed from the Wolf's Lair by a pseudo-Hitler with little of the military flair of his predecessor. Their main similarity was the new Führer's stubborn insistence on getting his own way.

On top of all these advantages, which should have handed the war to Stalin on a plate, the mysterious Woodpecker (via Lucy) was telling the Generalissimo in the Kremlin the movement of every German division. It should have been child's play to win, but the man with the withered arm, the ex-student from a seminary in Georgia, still couldn't pull it off. The Germans fought like tigers.

In Dresden Herbert Meyer, armed with his new resources, worked like the proverbial beaver to locate the rogue transmitter. Thirty years old, he should have been in the infantry or with the Panzers. But, like Goebbels, he had a clubfoot.

Tall as a beanpole, he had a head like a church mouse. A timid man, he had been the butt of his contemporaries at school. They had nicknamed him 'The Mouse', and the hated appellation dogged him in adult life. It may well have been this experience which led him to choose the solitary trade of watchmaker in peacetime.

Fate plays odd tricks on mere human beings. It was The Mouse's skill in working with precision instruments which eventually landed him in the great Monitoring complex at Dresden. He was the ideal man to hunt down Lucy. Chance and Walter Schellenberg had placed him in this unique position to decide the outcome of the Second World War.

The Mouse was now waiting to hear that the huge mobile monitoring system had been installed in the Alsatian city of Strasbourg. Then he could really get down to it and pinpoint the elusive transmitter he had nicknamed *The Ghost*.

In Lucerne, *The Ghost* – RR – continued to live practically off coffee and four hours' sleep a night. To catch the morning tram to the Vita Nova Verlag, studiously ignoring the loitering bodyguards who changed positions daily. To eat a sparing lunch, a meagre dinner.

All this was a chore prior to his real work which started late in the evening. The transmissions coming in from Woodpecker were longer now. Consequently, the signals to Moscow were also longer.

In his own quiet way, fussed over by the devoted Anna, RR was happy. The Swiss now thought him so important they provided this comforting protection. And after Kursk he knew that Stalin was listening to him. What more could a man want out of life?

'The Germans are smuggling in even more agents,' Masson warned Hausamann as soon as he arrived at the Villa Stutz and threw off his raincoat. 'Something very serious is taking place . . .'

Happiness was the last emotion Brigadier Roger Masson was experiencing. Hausamann, swivelling round in his chair away from a desk littered with papers, watched the counter-espionage chief.

'What are these agents doing?' Hausamann enquired – and received the last reply he would have expected.

'Nothing! Nothing at all! They are staying at hotels in Berne, in Geneva, in Basle. Not Lucerne as far as we know, thank God! They are so obviously *waiting*, Hans!'

Hausamann placed a pencil between his teeth, revolved it, and then asked:

'Waiting for what?'

'Hans, that is the hell of it. I don't know! It all smells of Schellenberg, of some devious master-plan . . .'

'You could kick them all out,' Hausamann observed. It was what he would have done.

'Then they send in a fresh detachment! Maybe next time we don't track them all. Maybe they slip through the net and we don't know they're here. Now that, Hans, would be very dangerous . . .'

'What could Schellenberg be up to at this stage of the game?'

'Another development has taken place which I don't like . . .'

Masson kept pacing round the room as though staying in one place for more than a few seconds was anathema. Hausamann could never recall seeing him so agitated.

'You know what this development is, Hans? Schellenberg sent me a personal message through Gisevius, the German Vice-Consul. He says he may wish to meet me very shortly – preferably on Swiss soil. It's nerve warfare. Or is it? Has he some ace concealed up his sleeve . . .'

'Wait for him to play it . . .'

Masson was still not listening. Hausamann would have bet a large sum his visitor had hardly registered a word said to him.

'I'm sure all this concerns Lucy in some way, Hans. I know my Schellenberg. If he ever finds out that we are protecting the man sending the German order of battle to the Kremlin we might as well take straight to the mountains. The Wehrmacht will kick in our front door the following day . . .'

'What I have never been able to work out,' Hausamann began briskly, deliberately changing the subject, 'is why

Woodpecker routes his signals via Lucy. Why not radio direct to Moscow?'

'That is something which has always puzzled me,' Masson replied. 'I'm probably worrying too much. Schellenberg himself may never make the connection.'

'You know, Schaub,' Schellenberg remarked to his aide in his Berlin office, 'I think I must be wrong about this Swiss thing. They would never dare to let anyone act as a post office to re-transmit our Soviet spy's signals to the Russians. The line Meyer drew on his map went through Munich . . .'

'You think Munich is his headquarters?' Schaub enquired.

'When Meyer comes up with the solution I think the answer may well be Munich, or somewhere outside the city. Now we must emulate the infinite patience of our excellent Meyer so let us turn our attention to other business, as the Führer would say . . .'

Neither Intelligence chief – Roger Masson or Walter Schellenberg – dreamed how long ago the communication system had been planned. Lucy – RR – was, in fact, acting as a post office for the onward transmission of signals between Woodpecker and Moscow in both directions.

In Soviet Intelligence jargon, Lucy was a *cul-de-sac*. A dead end. In case of emergency. Should the German monitors ever locate Lucy it would divert their attention from the original source of the signals – Woodpecker, operating from the highest level inside the Nazi apparatus.

This diversionary device had been planned so long ago – way back in the 1930's when Yagoda held Beria's post as head of the Ministry for State Security.

The Soviets had sown so many seeds in so many lands. Some, as they foresaw, fell on stony ground and came to nothing. It was the seeds which flourished that poisoned the wells of the West. Tim Whelby, burrowing his way upwards in London with his charm and habit of listening often and saying little. Woodpecker, Yagoda's crowning glory, scaling the summits in Hitler's Germany . . .

Chapter Thirty-Seven

'Oh, I don't know about that,' said Len Reader, 'he's just out of sorts. Not up to this kind of lark. He's one of the blue-eyed pilots from 1940. That was a million years ago – the Battle of Britain. Maybe he needs a woman,' he added with a wink.

'You *bastard* . . .!'

Paco's response was venomous. Crouched down beside Lindsay she had been dabbing the Englishman's feverish forehead with a cold damp cloth. Standing up suddenly, she drew back her right hand to slap Reader's face. He grasped her wrist in mid-swing and grinned.

'Don't tell me you've gone soppy over him, because I won't swallow that one. You're a real woman, you need a real man . . .'

'You are interfering with my patient . . .' The mild voice spoke from the entrance to the abandoned hovel. Reader swung round and faced Dr Macek who went on smiling as he regarded the Englishman through his rimless glasses. 'That I can't allow. You realize if I summon Heljec I can have you shot? Sorry to put it in such crude terms . . .'

'Bugger the lot of you creeps . . .'

Reader let go of Paco, his face flushed with annoyance. He walked out quickly, still holding the sten gun.

'We've just got rid of an expert in crude terms,' Paco said as she massaged her wrist where Reader had gripped her. 'I said at the beginning I didn't like that man . . .'

'And how is our patient?' Macek enquired, coming forward and frowning as he looked down at Lindsay who lay with his eyes closed on a makeshift straw palliasse. 'Sweating like a pig as they say. Unfortunate phrase . . .'

Paco waited while Macek examined the Englishman. They were many miles, *many weeks*, away from the gorge where

Colonel Jaeger had turned the tables on Heljec. Lindsay's glandular fever had grown steadily worse. He had become so weak and feverish a makeshift stretcher had been cobbled together at Macek's insistence and two Partisans carried him.

Their new temporary headquarters – one of a recent dozen – was a village of single-storey stone houses of the poorest kind. Perched halfway up the side of a mountain in Bosnia it rose in a series of steps, roof upon roof. Abandoned by the inhabitants who had fled before the advance of a German column, it was cautiously re-occupied by Heljec's Partisans.

By now they had made up the numbers lost in the firefight with Jaeger. In his more conscious moments Lindsay had seen the new men coming in. It was a weird phenomenon – they seemed to materialize out of nowhere. He had commented on it to Paco.

'Heljec has a reputation as an aggressive leader who never gives up,' she had replied wearily. 'So they come from scores of miles to find him, to join him as long as they have weapons. Weapons and ammunition are the Danegeld you need for him to accept you.'

Gustav Hartmann had been with them that night. He joined in the conversation. Unusually, he seemed depressed.

'They enjoy it, you see, Lindsay. Fighting. Killing. It has been going on for centuries in this accursed cesspit of Europe. They don't mind who they fight – just so long as the killing goes on. Read the history of the Balkans. Short of an enemy, they fight themselves. Croat against Serb, and so on. Tonight the news for you is good, for me it is bad, for all three of us it is terrible . . .'

'I don't understand,' said Paco.

By now they had come together almost as a small group of intimates. Lindsay, the Englishman; Hartmann, the German; and Paco, part-English, part-Serb. Dr Macek was not yet a fully paid-up member of the club, but he had visitor's rights.

'Reader,' Hartmann explained, 'brilliantly hides his transceiver by night and transports it by day on one of the mules. He has bribed the mule-train driver with gold. He keeps in touch with the outside world. Stalin has driven back the

Wehrmacht along the whole front. So, Lindsay, for you it is official good news. For me it is official bad news. You see?'

'No, I don't,' said Paco. 'You ended up by saying that for all three of us it is terrible . . .'

'You believe in crystal balls?'

Hartmann took out his pipe and sucked at it enviously. There was no question of lighting it. Heljec had shot one of his own men who had started a bonfire to warm his freezing hands when the temperature had dropped after nightfall.

'Crystal balls? Seeing into the future?' Paco cocked her head to one side and peered quizzically at the German. She had come to like Hartmann. 'Can anyone do that?' she asked.

'Maybe in dreams we see what we would give an arm not to see.'

'Now he talks of dreams . . .' Paco spread out both hands towards Lindsay propped against a rock in a gesture of helplessness. 'He is making fun of me, Lindsay . . .'

'I think that when people look back in forty years' time from now,' Hartmann continued, 'they will see what a catastrophe it was to permit Stalin to roll over half, maybe most of, Europe. Generations yet unborn will have their lives blighted by this war.'

'The wise man speaks,' said Paco, pulling his leg.

'Let him go on,' interjected Lindsay.

'Wise man, go on . . .'

'People forget history. Today England fights Germany. England's great enemy was once France, before that Spain. I think England's real ally is Germany, that the day will come when she will realize this. Germany will realize it, too. But how much of the home of civilization – Europe – will have been lost?'

'The whole shooting match,' said Lindsay and fell unconscious.

'Care for a bit of foreign travel, Whelby?' Colonel Browne asked.

'Would it be for long sir?'

Whelby forced himself to maintain his usual offhand manner, to conceal the shock Browne's suggestion had given him. The idea of no longer being Browne's deputy, of being exiled to a distant outpost away from the centre of operations didn't suit him at all.

He had been summoned urgently to Ryder Street and it was close to midnight. So far as he knew the only two occupants of the building now were himself and Browne. And the caretaker downstairs who unlocked the front door and locked it again after he entered the building.

'Cairo,' said the Colonel.

Browne was worried about something. He kept pacing round the office, hands clasped behind his back, shooting glances at his visitor as though trying to make up his mind.

'A permanent posting, sir?' ventured Whelby.

'No. A flying visit. I sense an atmosphere of lethargy out there. Place has become a backwater since Monty cleared Rommel out of North Africa and invaded Sicily and Italy with the Yanks. Their signals reflect that inertia. I need information. Bloody soon.'

'The subject being?'

Again the hesitation, the quick, darting glances. Whelby was, in contrast, imperturbable. Browne, he knew, disliked his deputy being absent. Whelby had made himself indispensable for the day-to-day running of the department.

'It's Lindsay,' Browne said abruptly. 'You don't get on with him too well, the word is.'

'I've only met him on two or three occasions. He struck me as an able enough chap . . .'

'I want you to go out there and raise Cain, find out just what's happened to him. They simply must have some word about Lindsay – good or bad. If not, they'd better get it . . .' Browne paused and then decided to go ahead. 'This comes down from God – who smokes cigars . . .'

It had indeed, which was what had thrown Browne into turmoil. *Where is Lindsay? I want him back. Expense no object. Action this day . . .*

Christ Almighty, Browne thought. . . . *this day*. He'd be lucky to get news next month. And Whelby, sitting relaxed, was careful not to show the triumph he felt at being selected for this mission as the Colonel continued.

'Your father's an Arabist,' Browne recalled. 'Knows the Middle East. Some of it must have rubbed off on you. Your plane leaves tomorrow night from Lyneham, Wiltshire. And this never happened – your trip to Cairo. Sign attendance sheets before you go – showing you were in London . . .'

'I travel under my own name?' Whelby enquired.

Impassive on the surface, underneath his mental turbulence was as great as Browne's. Departure in twenty-four hours – somehow he had to contact Savitsky before he left.

'Like hell you do,' Browne replied. 'You're Peter Standish for the duration – of this mission . . .'

He extracted something from his breast pocket. A British passport landed on the desk together with an envelope. Whelby picked up the passport and examined it, his manner still diffident.

Mr Peter Standish. National Status: British Subject by birth. The usual appalling photograph of himself. They had even weathered the gold seal so it had a well-worn look, a document carried and used for ages.

'Standish is a bit John Buchanish, wouldn't you say?' Whelby remarked as he pocketed the passport.

'Rather suits your personality, we thought,' Browne said and he smiled. 'That envelope contains the name of the chap you contact, Egyptian currency and a letter of introduction. What more could you wish for?'

The American Liberator bomber, *Glenn Miller*, approached Cairo West airfield one hour after dawn. Tim Whelby stretched his aching arms and legs as the huge machine banked prior to landing on Egyptian soil.

It had been a swine of a journey and he hadn't slept a wink. There were no seats inside the great fuselage; each passenger had been provided with a sleeping-bag which rolled and slithered about with the aircraft's movements. Alongside Whelby lay a British major-general with red tabs.

'You're a boffin they've sent out, I suppose?' the general enquired.

Whelby merely smiled, stifling a yawn. His suit was crumpled, he was in need of a shave and he had lain awake all night thinking how paradoxical it would be if they were shot down by a German fighter. Had the Nazis known who was aboard they'd certainly have mustered every fighter available to locate and destroy the plane.

'Shouldn't have asked, should I?' the general remarked. 'Do you realize there are a dozen men aboard this machine and not one of us has a clue as to the identity of his fellow-passengers? You'd think there was a spy aboard . . .'

The Liberator was descending rapidly. The hard ochre of the bleached desert came up to meet them, the wheels touched down, there was a nasty bump, then they slowed into a smooth glide and stopped. The endless engine sound, the vibration ceased. Whelby looked round at the other passengers whose faces wore a blank, washed-out expression.

The exit door was opened from the outside. Fresh air flooded in, displacing the foetid atmosphere of too much carbon dioxide, too little oxygen. The passengers disengaged themselves from their sleeping-bags like insects emerging from cocoons.

'Mr Peter Standish! Sir! You're the first to disembark, if you please . . .'

A brilliant way of covering up my arrival, Whelby thought cynically and avoided curious eyes as he walked stiff-legged along the aircraft, holding his small suitcase.

A metal ladder had been placed below the open doorway. It was the desert's silence which first struck Whelby as he descended. The idiot who had bellowed out his name was standing at the base of the ladder.

'Major Harrington at your service, sir. I'm Security. Care to follow me to that building over there? Oh, and welcome to Egypt! Your first visit? Whoops! Shouldn't have asked that.'

Whelby could hardly believe his eyes. Harrington was faultlessly turned out in khaki drill, neatly-buttoned shirt, well-creased shorts, mahogany-tanned knees and arms to match his face. The moustache! Whelby had seen pictures, caricatures brought back in magazines from the Mid-East, of Flying Officer Kite with his flowing, handle-bar moustache. Harrington actually sported such a moustache.

'Was it wise to broadcast my name to all and sundry?' Whelby enquired as they walked side by side over the hard, arid ground.

'Better than creeping up to you confidential-like. Do it parade-groud style and how many of them back there will even be able to recall your face, let alone the name, by the time they reach Cairo?'

Whelby realized his night's ordeal had loosened the iron grip he normally maintained over his reactions. And Harrington was by no means the chinless wonder he looked. Inside the building his escort checked his passport and then told him the news.

'We're sending in a Dakota to airlift Lindsay out of Jugoslavia. Your arrival could be said to be timely . . .'

'How do you know where he is? He reached the Allied Military Mission, then? You've established radio contact . . .'

Whelby was breaking all his rules, asking a series of direct questions, but he spaced them out, speaking in a sleepy drawl.

'You'll have to let me keep my little secrets, too, sir. No offence meant. Here we are. A very private room. Feel the temperature rising? We have KD outfits in various sizes here for you to change into. You'll fry in that suit – besides looking as conspicuous as a scorpion on a chupatti . . .'

Whelby had to admit this deceptive-looking buffoon was pretty well-organized. Left alone in a sparsely furnished room with a cement floor, he chose from an array of suits in varying sizes spread out across a trestle table. He had just finished changing when someone knocked on the door.

'Do come in,' Whelby called out.

'I say, you look pretty chipper – as to the manner born . . .'

'I noticed the other passengers leave by a bus – taking a *shufti* out of that window. What transport do I get?'

'*Shufti!* Sounds as though you're picking up the lingo out here fast.'

For the first time Whelby studied Harrington more closely as he finished doing up the breast-pocket buttons on his tunic. The foppish moustache was misleading – it drew your attention away from the shrewd grey eyes which seemed to record every tiny movement you made. A dozen years from now, Whelby reflected, you'll know me if I'm dressed up as an Arab.

'Now transport, you said.' Harrington twirled his moustaches like a music-hall comedian. 'One jeep. I drive. You admire the scenery. Monty got rid of all the staff cars before Alamein. He had them dropped into the Med, I think. Too comfortable. Say the word and we're off!'

'I'm supposed to meet a Lieutenant Carson at Shepheard's Hotel.'

'That's the ticket. Just spoke to Jock – that's Carson – on the blower while you were changing. Wanted to know the moment you hit solid sand in one piece. You found the Gents over there? You're settling in nicely, you are. Off we go. Tally-ho!'

There was a little mystery here, thought Whelby, as they drove along a tarmacadam road coated with powderish sand across the desert. *Major* Harrington as escort from Cairo West. *Lieutenant* Carson waiting at Shepheard's. Something told Whelby they had been juggling ranks, like shuffling a pack of cards. He had the distinct impression that 'Jock' was running this show.

'Pyramids coming up,' Harrington chattered on. 'Obvious remark of the year! You can climb that one. Cheops . . .' He pointed, driving with one hand on the wheel. 'The Turks – or somebody – stripped off the marble. Like giant stepping stones – you have to watch it. They're just too big to stride up. Go up at one of the corners. Bit of a scramble. Marvellous view from the top, right out over the Delta . . .'

'I must try it one day.'

'Drive you out here, if you have the time . . .'

The three ancient edifices were grouped close together. They were sharp-edged against the clearest of blue skies. Already the sun was warm on Whelby's back.

They left the desert abruptly, turning a sharp corner left and the road stretched ruler-straight as far as the eye could see. Weird two-storey villas, a mixture of different European architectures, lined the road.

'Mena House Hotel over there,' Harrington continued. 'Looks as though the bloody Russians are going to win the war for us. Don't know about you, I wouldn't like that.'

'I ex . . . pect . . . we'll con . . . tribute . . . our bit when the right moment arrives.'

As he stuttered his reply Whelby was aware Harrington had turned towards him, was studying his profile. He sensed a change in his brief relationship with Harrington – like a cog missing a ratchet.

'All the rich Wogs live in these crazy houses,' Harrington said in the same tone. 'They say a lot of pre-war Italian architects put up these Walt Disney efforts.'

For the rest of the journey they travelled in silence.

'Could you drop me short of Shepheard's? Say a hundred yards?' Whelby requested. 'Better I'm not associated with the military. Nothing personal, of course.'

'Of course. Will do. Room 16 . . .'

'I know.'

Whelby cut him off abruptly. He had retired into his shell, a reaction which intrigued Harrington. They were driving slowly through the streets crowded with Arabs. Dragomen, who earned their living as tourist guides, stared at Whelby.

'You will get noticed,' Harrington warned. 'A stranger from far away – your knees aren't browned. We did our best – giving you trousers instead of shorts. Face and hands will give you away. White as the virgin snow . . .'

Whelby was sniffing the mixture of eastern smells – rubbish rotting in the gutters, the indefinable odour of eastern bodies, eastern bazaars. He found it comforting, familiar. Market stalls overflowing with coloured bead necklaces and other junk narrowed the street. A cacophony of voices arguing in Arabic. Harrington handled the jeep with great skill, weaving nimbly in and out, sliding past a camel with inches to spare.

'There it is, that building in the distance. See it?' he asked. 'Right. You disembark here. Twenty minutes to your appointment. Jock likes people who get there bang on time.'

'Thank you for the lift . . .'

Whelby stepped down on to the crowded pavement, carefully avoiding the foetid gutter. Harrington never looked at him as he drove off while Whelby paused in front of a shop window. The glass was smeared but the reflection was clear enough to act as a mirror, to see if he was being followed.

A horse-drawn gharry pulled in to the kerb. The Arab driver was pointing something out to his passengers, a couple of British officers. Brown as a berry, Whelby noticed, glancing casually over his shoulder. Old hands.

Just the types they'd use if they were tracking him. The ideal shadow would have been an Arab. But they wouldn't use one for him. Wogs couldn't follow him into Shepheard's. Whelby was experiencing two conflicting emotions.

He was revelling in the atmosphere of noisy, alien chaos, which reminded him of his childhood in India. The wary side of his head suppressed the feeling. All his defences were coming down, like the closing of a portcullis. Had he passed muster with Harrington? On balance, he thought so. The gharry moved on and he followed in its wake. The officers inside couldn't see through the back of the raised canopy.

At the foot of the steps leading up to Shepheard's he stopped to mop sweat off his forehead. The warmth of the naked sun beat down. The street was faintly blurred with heat dazzle. As he put his handkerchief away he glanced at his watch. The timing was tricky.

Inside the crowded lobby overhead fans whirred, stirring up turgid air. He strolled up the staircase and paused in an empty corridor, studying the room numbers and waiting to see if anyone followed him. When he was satisfied he continued along the quiet corridor and rapped, an irregular tattoo, on the door of Room 24.

Inside Room 16 the phone rang. A short, burly Scot, his fair hair clipped short, dressed in the uniform of an army Lieutenant, picked up the receiver. His voice was abrupt, very Scots, a bit of a drowned mumble.

'Yes? Who is it?'

'Harrington. The package is about to be delivered to you. And it could be damaged goods. Oh, I had a chat with that new chap in the mess.'

'And?'

'Worries me. Chucked a question at him out of the blue. When he did reply he stuttered. A man does that when you throw him off-balance. Only time he did it. Just a thought. Probably nothing in it . . .'

'Thanks for calling. See you later.'

The man called Jock Carson clasped his hands on the table and gazed out of the window. *Probably nothing in it* . . . Translation: alarm bells screaming like bloody banshees.

In response to Whelby's rapping on the door of Room 24 the door opened immediately and a small man in crumpled khaki drill civvies ushered the Englishman inside. He closed the door and locked it.

'Vlacek?' Whelby murmured. 'The mosquitoes are biting well . . .'

'Malaria is a burden Allah wishes us to bear,' Vlacek replied.

'I've only got minutes,' Whelby said irritably. He looked round the room, noted the mess of discarded clothes on the bed, then he stared at the open French windows.

'The balcony, I think. Room 16 *is* on the other side of the hotel, isn't it? You're quite sure?'

'Quite certain, dear sir. Yes, let us converse together on the balcony.'

Vlacek, nominally a Pole from the Russian border region, had a typical Slav face. High cheekbones, prominent nose and jawline. Everything bony. Brown eyes like glass. Hands long-fingered, fleshless, with a wiry strength. Strangler's hands.

He spoke English carefully, slowly, with a thick accent. He had trouble with his 'r's and his voice was soft. He padded after Whelby onto the balcony in tennis plimsolls, making no sound so the Englishman was startled to find the Pole alongside him. After a quick glance in either direction from the balcony, Whelby began speaking.

'London has sent me to bring back Lindsay. He's apparently alive in Jugoslavia. There's talk of a Dakota airlifting him out. Presumably to here on the first stage of his trip back to London . . .'

'Not here.' The little man shook his head and lit a cheroot. 'And he must never reach London alive. That's my responsibility. Yours is to see the Dakota lands at Lydda Airport. That's in Palestine . . .'

'I know. But why Palestine?'

'I need him kept there two days. That will give me the time to complete my mission. Two days . . .'

'That could be really difficult. They'll want to rush him home. I might manage the switch to Lydda – but two days . . .'

'Tell them you need it for initial debriefing. And Lindsay will be tired. Insist he needs a rest before he completes the journey to London . . .'

'Why Palestine?' Whelby asked for the second time.

It was becoming a duel for control between the two men. Vlacek seemed to be deliberately not answering his questions. Whelby made a great show of looking at his watch. Five minutes more at the outside. Carson might start coming to look for him.

'In Palestine,' Vlacek explained in his slow monotone, 'many English troops and policemen are shot in the back by the Jews. It is not like Egypt. Palestine is a volcano, ready to erupt – one more murder will be put down to another Jewish outrage. If possible, we meet here one hour later tomorrow; if not possible, one hour later the following day, and so forth . . .'

'And supposing I can't get away from them, which is likely?'

'I shall know if you have left for Palestine. Contact me at the Hotel Sharon in Jerusalem. Again, Room 24 . . .'

'And now I really must go. This very minute . . .'

'Lieutenant Carson is a high-ranking officer in Intelligence.'

Whelby left the quiet little man standing on the balcony, gazing into the distance as he smoked the cheroot clamped between tobacco-stained teeth. He thought Vlacek one of the most sinister men he had ever met and tried to recall what he reminded him of.

He had opened the door and glanced into the still-deserted corridor before leaving the room when he remembered. Those eyes like glass. A lizard.

In the corridor Whelby paused before making for Room 16. He had two minutes to kill before his appointment with Carson. Two minutes to regain his normal poise.

What a shit of a rush it had all been in London after his interview with Colonel Browne. And rushes were dangerous. The urgent call from a public phone box to Savitsky. The effort to get over to the Russian in innocent-sounding language the sudden development dropped on him by Browne. Savitsky's instruction for them to meet each other at Beryl's place, '. . . to see how the poor girl is getting on. Eight hours from now suit you?'

God, they must have moved in Moscow! Savitsky's signal would put the cat among the pigeons. But they had managed it – Whelby gave them full marks for trying. He had joined Savitsky for breakfast at the Strand Palace Hotel close to the river. No food coupons needed, thank God.

'We have put a man into the same Cairo hotel where you make your rendezvous with your British contact,' Savitsky had told him.

The Russian, dressed like a British businessman, had even found a corner table where they were invisible to the remainder of the restaurant. He was good on small details.

'His name is Vlacek,' Savitsky had continued. 'He will wait

in Room 24 until you arrive. For days, if necessary. He will live in that room. The password is . . .'

At certain stages in their hurried conversation Savitsky had gone vague on Whelby. At the time the Englishman had put it down to the hellish rush – verging on panic – of the whole operation.

'Who is this Vlacek? Is he underground?' Whelby had asked.

'Good God, no!' Savitsky had been shocked. 'He's a Pole, employed in some capacity by the British with a propaganda unit. He can walk the streets openly in Cairo. Just don't be seen together in public, that's all . . .'

Now, standing in the corridor of Shepheard's, Whelby wondered about Vlacek's real status. He had talked – albeit subtly – as though he were Whelby's superior. The unnerving suspicion crossed the Englishman's mind that he had just conversed with a professional executioner.

Harrington had been jocular, extrovert, affable. Jock Carson was dour, watchful, guarded. There was no shaking of hands. He closed the door and gestured towards a chair on one side of a glass-topped table. As the stockily-built Scot walked round to sit in the facing chair, Whelby studied him.

First the two, full lieutenant's pips on either shoulder. He had thought they might be new, fresh from the store. They were well-worn, like the face with the beaked nose, the heavy-lidded eyes. Carson wasted few words.

'We expect – God and the weather willing – to have Wing Commander Lindsay in Cairo for you to escort him home within one or two weeks. You, of course, have never been here. The passenger manifest of the Liberator bomber which flew you from London shows only the names of eleven passengers. You will maintain a very low profile while you wait . . .'

'Hold on a minute, Lieutenant. I do have some say in how this matter is handled. Your discretion I appreciate. May I ask the proposed route along which Lindsay will travel to reach Cairo?'

'*Proposed?*'

The Scots burr became more pronounced. Inside that stocky body Whelby sensed the power and drive of a locomotive. They were fencing for supremacy, of course. The first encounter – clash – was always vital. It established the pattern of authority from which there would be no deviation.

'That's the word I used,' Whelby said quietly.

'We fix the route. We fix the timing. We deliver the goods. You escort them back to London.'

'These details have been arranged for how long? Hours? Days?'

'Days.'

Carson left it at that. His hands were clasped again, he sat motionless, blue eyes staring at the man opposite.

'And the route?' Whelby insisted.

'Jugoslavia to Benghazi in Libya. Dakota touches down at Benina airfield – isolated, out in the desert. Refuels. Then on to Cairo West . . .'

'No!' Whelby's tone was sharp, inflexible. 'The arrangement has been known for days, so there could have been a leak. Lindsay is a prime target. From Benina I want him flown to Lydda in Palestine. I'll be there to meet him. The chap will be exhausted after his experiences, then the flight. A couple of days in an unexpected place, somewhere in Jerusalem will do nicely. The route change will counter any leak. London isn't happy about the security out here . . .'

'Poor old London . . .'

'They could send someone else out, wielding an axe. A word to the wise. Just between the two of us. Lydda. Please?'

Carson sat like a man carved out of mahogany. Incredible how still he could remain for long periods. Whelby was careful not to add a word. He could sense the Scot weighing up the pros and cons. Whelby knew there was a logic to his argument difficult to refute. He had been careful not to sound threatening, simply a man reporting how things stood, his tone almost sympathetic. *You know how things are, I don't make the rules. A word to the wise . . .*

'Lydda it is,' Carson announced eventually. 'We like to

389

keep our visitors happy. My guess – subject to checking – is you'll fly to Lydda this hour tomorrow. That doesn't tell you anything about when Lindsay lands. Frankly, I don't know that myself yet. A night in Grey Pillars for you . . .'

Grey Pillars was local slang for GHQ, Middle East. It was a residential district of solemn buildings cordoned off from the rest of Cairo by wire fences. Carson had stood up behind his desk as though the interview were over. Whelby, remaining in his chair, recrossed his legs.

'A room here, this one, if available, would suit me better. I didn't come out here to be confined to a POW camp. I do have the freedom to make my own decisions . . .'

It was a statement, not a question. Spoken in the same offhand, amiable manner. Carson half-closed his eyes, adjusted his Sam Browne belt and holster.

'Give me a reason. Just for the record.'

'Security. The opposition has to be keeping Grey Pillars under surveillance. I'm anonymous here, as anonymous as I can get. No guards, please. I can look after myself.'

'Agreed! And you can have this room. Major Harrington will be in touch with you. Incidentally, your flight to Lydda will be from Heliopolis Airport, not Cairo West. You'll be aboard a Yank plane again.'

'For the same reason – the passenger manifests?'

'You're catching on quickly. The RAF just won't fly you over Sinai without a name. Next of kin in case of a crash, and all that red tape. The Yanks don't often pile up a machine, by the way . . .'

Carson put on his peaked cap. He hoisted a slow salute, held it for longer than the regulation period, staring again at Whelby, went to the door and said only one more thing.

'I'll book you in here on my way out. You don't need to go anywhere near the reception desk. You don't exist . . .'

'Lydda!' Harrington exploded in his second-floor office at Grey Pillars. 'Palestine is a minefield! I don't like it one little bit . . .'

'Do it . . .'

390

Carson stood gazing out of the window across the sun-baked garden below, across the wrought-iron railings beyond, across the quiet tree-lined street. He could just see the checkpoint everyone had to pass through before penetrating the holy of holies.

'That last radio signal from Len Reader – tell me what it said again, if you please . . .'

'In a nutshell we have a map-reference for where the Dak is to land in Bosnia. Identification signals agreed prior to the plane landing – Jerry often lights fires marking out a fake strip. It's a straight exchange – a consignment of weapons and ammo for Lindsay. They've O.K.'d it upstairs. Reader's next signal is the go-ahead.'

'And the Dakota is where?'

'Waiting at Benina Airport with the cargo already aboard. The pilot is instructed to fly back to Cairo West afterwards.'

'You're a trier, Harrington – I'll give you that. Lydda I said and Lydda I meant. Inform the pilot of his new instructions.'

'Will do.' Harrington hesitated. 'What did you make of Tim Whelby? Oh, and when does he arrive here . . .'

'He doesn't. He's staying in Room 16 at Shepheard's. That's the way he wanted it.'

'Christ! This is a funny one. He should be *here* . . .'

'I know.' Carson turned away from the window as a whisper of breeze – God knew where from – rustled the heavy net curtains. 'On the other hand it may be a good idea that he doesn't get a *shufti* inside the nerve centre. I have two men who know what he looks like – they observed his arrival from a gharry – posted so they can see if he leaves the hotel.'

'What's the big idea? So he leaves the hotel for a look-see at the delights of Cairo, maybe a visit to a belly-dancers' dive . . .'

'He gets followed well and truly. Said he wanted to stay under cover. His behaviour was very logical. Let's see whether he stays inside the pattern he laid down for himself . . .'

'You still haven't told me what you really think of him,' Harrington commented.

Carson paused, holding the handle of the door. His impassive, erudite features froze into a frown of concentration. He liked to consider what he was going to say before replying.

'I wouldn't go into the jungle with him,' he said and left the room.

Chapter Thirty-Eight

At precisely 8 a.m. the following morning Whelby again rapped on the door of Room 24. One hour later than the previous day. Again the door was opened at once by the small bony man. Whelby thought he looked even more skeletal than on his last visit. Perhaps he was fasting, he thought wryly.

'You have news?' Vlacek asked as soon as they were standing on the balcony.

'I've managed Lydda Airport, God knows how . . .'

'When does he arrive?'

'I don't bloody know. You want it all packed up and tied with pink ribbon?'

'Pink ribbon?' Vlacek continued in the same calm monotone but Whelby shivered inwardly at the little man's next words. 'This is not a joke, I trust? This is a serious matter we find ourselves engaged on. What route?'

'Jugoslavia to Benina airfield outside Benghazi to Lydda after refuelling at Benina. Good enough for you?'

'So you will go to Lydda.'

'Today sometime. From Heliopolis Airport.'

'Then go to Jerusalem to wait. Hotel Sharon. I shall be . . .'

'In Room 24! I can remember a simple fact like that.'

They were firing questions and answers back at each other like ping-pong, neither liking the other, each wishing to make the meeting as short as possible. Whelby put both hands in his tunic pockets, thumbs tucked outside. He didn't look at the little man as he made the statement, brushing aside interruptions.

392

'I have now done all I can so far. Harrington may call to see me at any moment, so please listen. I cannot guarantee I will be staying at the Hotel Sharon. There may be a very short time lapse between my hearing when Lindsay is coming in, his arrival and our subsequent departure . . .'

'I said two days.'

Vlacek hardly seemed to be listening. In his left hand he held a tiny, green-enamelled cup of Turkish coffee; in his right, one of his foul-smelling cheroots. He took alternate sips of coffee and puffs at the cheroot, his brown, glassy eyes staring into the distance.

'I'll do my best.'

'Two days are essential.'

Whelby didn't reply. He deliberately wrinkled his nose to show his distaste for the smell. It had no effect on Vlacek. He had great economy of movement, Whelby noted. He decided to take the offensive and end the interview.

'You can get to Lydda in time? With my flying there today?'

'Of course . . .'

'Then that's it. I must get back to my room. I don't admire this arrangement of our meeting in the same hotel.'

'I am very persona grata in Cairo . . .'

'Not with me, you're not. Now, I'm going . . .'

'Two days, Mr Standish.'

Whelby left the room with the same caution he had displayed the previous day. Walking rapidly along the corridor, turning a corner to his own room, he had a nasty shock. Outside his door stood Harrington, his hand raised to rap on the panel.

'Ah, there you are . . .' The Major carefully omitted any name and waited while Whelby inserted the key, opened the door and gestured for his visitor to precede him. As he closed the door Harrington sniffed and pulled a face.

'A smell of cheap cigar – reek might be a better word. You must be keeping bad company. Are you?'

'The lobby downstairs has all the sweet aromas of the East . . .'

This brief exchange, jocular, penetrating, alerted Whelby.

Harrington was an expert interrogator. He recognized the style. The casual question. Left drifting in mid-air. Then the silence which instilled in the suspect a compulsive urge to reply, to say something.

'Do sit down,' Whelby suggested. 'Something to drink? Coffee? The hard stuff?'

Harrington chose the hard-backed chair at the glass-topped table, forcing Whelby to sit in the other chair so they faced each other. Like an interrogation session.

'Nothing for me,' Harrington said amiably. 'Sun's hardly up over the horizon. Never before the clock strikes twelve. The clock is striking twelve for you . . .'

He paused as Whelby slowly sat down opposite him. There had been an ominous ring to the phraseology. Could Harrington possibly have found out about Vlacek? And just how 'persona grata' was the little man in Cairo? With an effort of will Whelby suppressed his anxieties. The first-class interrogator permitted the suspect to destroy himself with his own fears. He waited, saying nothing.

'Heliopolis at noon,' Harrington continued eventually. 'The plane takes off for Lydda. I've squared it with the Yanks. I drive you out there, point you in the right direction. Then it's up to you. The cover story is you're a pal of mine who's going on sick leave. Exhausted with overwork. You look a bit peaky, come to think of it. Getting you down? The responsibility, I mean?'

'I'll cope. What job do I have? The Yanks are a sociable lot . . .'

'Admin,' Harrington said promptly. 'Covers a multitude of nothings. You're hitching a ride. No one will bother about your identity. Were you in the lobby when I arrived?'

Quite diabolical, the technique, Whelby thought. Just when you think he's given up he comes zooming back at a tangent. Should he lose his temper? He decided against that. He stretched both arms and stifled a yawn.

'We sit around here till noon?' he enquired.

'*You* damned well do. I've been rushed off my feet since we met yesterday. My top informant links the theft of three sten guns and thirty mags from an army depot at Tel-el-Kebir with a coming attempt on the life of Lindsay . . .'

Whelby was startled. He allowed the reaction to show. And his companion's eyes never left his face. Blank. That's how Harrington had gone. Blank in expression, in tone of voice.

'Where's Tel-el-Kebir?' Whelby asked.

'Good question. It's the RAOC depot. Here in Egypt, half-way between Cairo and Ismailia on the Canal.'

'So they must still think he's flying in here. If your information is correct. Excuse me, but it takes some believing.'

'This informant – he's underground, of course – has never been wrong.' Harrington studied Whelby who pulled at a loose button on his cuff. He never bothered much about clothes. Again Whelby remained silent, refusing to jump into the inviting void.

'I'm waiting for you to ask the obvious question, the one anyone in your position would have jumped in with,' Harrington remarked.

The pressure was building up. Harrington was dropping the *I know you won't mind my asking you this, old boy, manner*. He was openly querying the state of Whelby's bank balance. Still, an outburst of temper would be unwise.

'And what question might that be?' Whelby asked.

'Who is behind the assassination attempt . . .'

'The Germans, undoubtedly, I presume . . .' Whelby looked surprised at the turn the conversation had taken. 'That is, if there is anything in this rumour. You must grant me the right to reserve my judgement.'

'Reserve yourself a seat at the opera. It isn't the Germans – and my source is the cat's whiskers. Accept that and we'll go on from there, shall we? The whisper is it's the Russians who don't want Lindsay to go home.'

The American plane took off from Heliopolis at exactly noon. Harrington, shading his eyes with his hand against the glare of the sun, watched it disappear towards Sinai, spewing out a dirt trail in its wake.

From a building behind him Carson, wearing dark glasses,

walked out with his slow, deliberate tread to join him. They stood together in uneasy silence for a moment.

'What do you think?' Carson asked.

He removed his glasses, folded them and tucked them inside a case. His movements were careful, precise.

'He's a funny, I'll swear it,' Harrington replied.

'Prove it.'

'Can't. Know anyone who smokes cheap cigars, maybe cheroots? With a smell like camel dung?'

'No. Why?'

'He carried the stench with him when I met him at Shepheard's. It only lingers a short time – comes from being in the close, repeat close, proximity of someone who smokes the things. But he gave the impression he hadn't spoken to a soul. And he's good at parrying leading questions . . .'

'That's to be expected – considering where he comes from.'

They stood in the heat of the noonday sun, hardly aware of it. They had been out there so long. They were in a backwater now, and both men knew it. The war had gone away from them, far away. The tide had gone out – and would never come back again.

But there were still thin threads linking them to the Balkans. To Greece. To Jugoslavia. They stayed a while longer in the sun because here they could talk in perfect secrecy.

'I've an odd feeling,' Harrington said. 'A very strong feeling that there's something terribly important here – in the palm of our hands. This Wing Commander Lindsay. We've got to get him out alive. I'm horribly afraid . . .'

It was such an uncharacteristic remark that Carson stared at him. Harrington was still gazing into the sky where the plane had now disappeared, as though he'd have given his right arm to be aboard.

'Who did you contact in Jerusalem?' Carson asked.

'Sergeant Terry Mulligan, Palestine Police. He's meeting this Standish off the plane at Lydda. Remember him?'

'Tough as old hickory. Wouldn't trust his own grandmother. But why the Palestine Police instead of the Army?' Carson queried.

'He's used to intrigue, to grappling with thugs in the gutter.'

'That's a good reason?'

'Dealing with Standish, I'd say it is. He smells of intrigue – as well as of cheap cigar smoke. Mulligan will spot that smell the moment Standish steps off the plane.'

Aboard the plane there were no more than half-a-dozen passengers. When they took off from Heliopolis they all occupied isolated seats. Whelby sat by a window, staring out at the hard ochre of the Sinai Desert, flat as the proverbial billiard table. In the distance rose mountains like black cinder cones, trembling in the dazzle of a heat haze. He became aware that someone had paused by the empty seat next to him. Cautiously, he glanced up.

'Do tell me to go away if you want to be alone, but when I'm flying I do like company . . .'

'Please join me – I'm feeling lonely myself.'

For once Whelby was not dissembling. And he had always liked women, had got on with them. She was American, maybe thirty, her well-built figure hugged closely by her tropical, two-piece suit.

'Allow me . . .'

In the most natural manner he reached over and helped her fasten her safety belt. She relaxed and watched him with her large grey eyes, their faces inches apart. Gently, he took hold of her slim, long-fingered hands and clasped them together, much to her amusement.

'There. Relaxed?'

'Very. Thank you. I'm Linda Climber. On vacation from the American Embassy . . .'

'Peter Standish. On vacation from life . . .'

They shook hands. She made a point of re-clasping hers again afterwards. Her hair was very dark, shoulder-length. Whelby was sure she had visited the hairdresser before boarding the aircraft. She had thick, dark eyebrows – not those horrible, plucked slashes. Her nose was long and straight, her mouth wide and full-lipped, her chin firm. She sat quite still while he studied her with a half-smile, something shy in his manner.

'You'll know me again,' she said and smiled with her lips meeting. 'If you're wondering why I'm alone, my husband has had to fly off somewhere. You wouldn't know a quiet hotel in Jerusalem?'

'Now, I just might. Hotel Sharon. But since I've n . . . ot s . . . s . . . tayed there we must inspect it first. A friend told me about the place. Friends are not always reliable. Hotels go up, they go down.'

'But I'd be imposing on you . . .'

'I have official transport waiting for me at Lydda. It would be a pleasure – for me – if we could travel together.'

Whelby had a way with women. Back home other men envied him his gift, but it incurred no dislike – probably because he never seemed a woman-chaser. With his charm, his diffidence, his shyness, they fell into his lap. It was one step from his lap to his bed.

On the surface it was quite out of character for him to mix with strangers while he was on a mission. His action had been partly whim – Linda Climber was an attractive woman with legs that made a normal man's mind move in one direction. But she was also excellent *cover*.

If he could decently park her at the Hotel Sharon it gave an excellent reason for visiting the place when he had to contact Vlacek. It would also neutralize Sergeant Mulligan – ghastly-sounding name – on the drive from Lydda to Jerusalem.

'We'll change places,' he said later, 'then you can see out of the window. There's something to see . . .'

Her hand, surprisingly cool, brushed his as he stood in the corridor while they switched seats. She peered out of the window and he leaned across to see for himself. He had timed it well.

'See that hard division, that line with arid ochre desert on this side and an endless green oasis coming up . . .'

'It's as straight as a ruler.'

'Egypt, the Sinai Desert, this side. Palestine – the fields cultivated by the Jewish people on the other.'

'It's two different worlds, Peter. Alien to each other?'

The remark kept coming back to him later after they landed. *It's two different worlds . . . Alien to each other.* Like the two alien worlds he held inside his own head. Kept always separate from each other. He smiled as she said something, her pale face flushed with pleasure.

By the time they were landing at Lydda he knew she was ready for an adventure. He had done nothing special to lead her on. It was a relationship which the younger Wing Commander Lindsay could never have contrived.

He took an instant dislike to Sergeant Mulligan, a dislike he was careful to conceal. Mulligan, a tall, terse man of about thirty years old with his hair cut very short, reciprocated his attitude, but not his *finesse*.

'I have an American lady with me, a Mrs Climber. I'm going to see her settled in a hotel in Jerusalem.'

'Who is she? Sir . . .' As an afterthought. 'Security here is very tight.'

'I'll take full responsibility, Sergeant. You know the Hotel Sharon? She'll probably want to put up there, subject to seeing the place . . .'

He made it sound as though the suggestion had come from Linda. They waited in blazing sunshine as she alighted from the plane. Lydda Airport was little more than a field with the grass trimmed short – like Sergeant Mulligan's hair.

'She's from the American Embassy in Cairo,' Whelby murmured. 'Nothing to worry about.'

'If you say so . . .'

Disapproval of the whole arrangement was patent in Mulligan's voice and manner. He was courteous when introduced, then led the way towards an armoured car standing close to a building. Beneath dark, bristly brows his eyes darted everywhere, one hand close to the holster at his right side. Whelby noticed the flap was now unbuttoned.

'We travel in this thing?' Whelby called out.

'You must be joking,' Linda Climber whispered. 'I'll snag my stockings.'

Mulligan stopped in the lee of the armoured car, a narrow space between the vehicle and the building. He gave his lecture in short, sharp bursts. A British soldier seated behind the controls stared down at them, frozen-faced.

'This armoured car is a good introduction to what you've come to,' Mulligan began. 'Did you by chance when you flew in see the straight line, desert one side, fields on the other?'

'We did . . .' Whelby replied in a bored tone.

'Both of you listen. It may save your lives. South of that line is Egypt, peace now Monty's put a boot up Rommel's backside. North of that line – here where you're standing – we're in a state of war. Don't go roaming round on your own. If you do go out, avoid back alleys.'

'Is all this really necessary, Sergeant? You're frightening the lady.'

'I'm trying to scare the living daylights out of her . . .' The sergeant regarded Whelby with active dislike. 'I had twenty-four men in my unit. Note the past tense. In the past eight weeks three of them have been killed by the murdering swine in the Jewish underground. Shot in the back. Never had a cat's chance in hell. They're worse than the Germans – at least *they* wore uniform and fought clean. That's it. We travel in that.'

He pointed to a staff car with amber net curtains drawn over the windows and parked in shadow.

'The armoured car?' queried Whelby. The driver had started up the engine. The protective metal plates vibrated.

'This poor bastard leads the way. We follow one hundred yards behind. Then if the Jews have sown any mines he takes the blast. Say thank you to Corporal Wilson up there . . .'

Open hostility now, in Mulligan's speech and manner. Whelby pursed his lips, carefully not looking up at Wilson. The sergeant walked them to the staff car, then turned to Linda Climber, his voice soft and polite.

'I'll take your case. You get inside and make yourself comfortable. It'll be all right. Not far to Jerusalem . . .'

He held open the rear door, took her elbow in his free hand to help her inside, ignoring Whelby. She leaned forward on the edge of the seat and smiled with genuine sympathy.

'Thank you, Sergeant. I'm beginning to understand how awful it must be. Please do say thank you to Corporal Wilson from me, if that isn't ridiculous . . .'

'He likes an attractive lady. It'll make his day . . .'

The road to Jerusalem from Lydda was uphill, a series of steep bends which took them higher and higher above the plain. Ideal ambush country. Sergeant Mulligan drove, a submachine-gun on the empty passenger seat beside him. Drove keeping a good hundred yards clearance from the armoured car grinding ahead up the ascent.

The staff car was a luxurious vehicle with spacious room in the back. A sheet of sliding glass – closed before they started – divided them from Mulligan and gave them privacy to chat. Linda Climber, normally ebullient, was quiet for the early part of the journey. Whelby squeezed her hand once reassuringly and was then careful to say nothing. He always let a woman make the running. At the outset.

They had almost reached the top of their zigzag ascent, could feel the road levelling out, when Whelby leaned forward and slid back the glass panel.

'Could you stop about a hundred yards short of the Sharon? Give me a moment to inspect the place?'

'I think that could be arranged . . .'

'Will that iron monster still be keeping us company?'

'Corporal Wilson will escort us inside Jerusalem and will then go his own way.'

The clipped tone, the distant glance Mulligan shot over his shoulder at Whelby expressed his controlled fury at the reference to 'that monster'. Whelby closed the panel and smiled to himself. It had worked. He had distanced himself from the probing Mulligan.

'I don't think he liked what you just said,' Linda remarked.

'I'm not very good at expressing myself. I think I did put my foot in it. What do you do at the Embassy? Or am I being nosey?'

'I'm an assistant to one of the officials. It sounds very grand but really I just type, take down the odd letter in shorthand – my shorthand's good – and do masses and masses of filing. You must be an important man – to warrant this attention and protection – or am I being nosey?'

'You're being nosey,' he said easily. 'Don't be impressed by my reception. I'm taking a vacation – as you Americans call it – myself. They said to me, "Do us a favour, old chap, carry these papers to Jerusalem for us. They're rather important. We'll lay on transport for you at Lydda." ' He smiled diffidently. 'I'm really nobody . . .'

The lie came out smoothly, convincingly. He had thought it up on the spur of the moment. They didn't speak again until they had arrived in Jerusalem and Corporal Wilson's 'monster' trundled off in a different direction at an intersection.

Whelby returned to where Mulligan had parked the staff car by the kerb a hundred yards from the Hotel Sharon. He opened the front passenger door, dipping his head, checked to see that the divider panel was closed, sealing off the rear where Linda Climber sat waiting, and spoke so quietly Mulligan had to lean over to catch what he said.

'The Hotel Sharon looks reasonable enough for Mrs Climber. I think I'll bunk down there myself.'

'The barracks for you. All laid on.'

'Which is just the place anyone looking for me will watch. I do have freedom of action. I intend to exercise it. This fits the bill nicely – an out-of-the-way hotel. Security, Sergeant Mulligan. I'm not an amateur.'

He was adopting the same tactics he had used with Carson in Cairo when the Lieutenant had tried to incarcerate him in Grey Pillars. He spoke as though there was simply no point in arguing the matter. Mulligan had one more try, keeping his own voice in low key.

'Even at that small hotel you'll have to register, show your passport . . .'

'I'm travelling on false papers . . .'

'Jesus Christ! You people think you're God.'

'Make up your mind which of those exalted gentlemen you

402

want me to be. Meantime, give me a phone number where I can contact you. I'm in Room 6 at the Sharon.'

He took the folded piece of paper on which Mulligan, tight-mouthed, had scribbled the phone number, then opened the rear door. Linda emerged onto the pavement, shook the creases out of her skirt and turned to take her suitcase from Mulligan. A pale hand, Whelby's, grasped the handle, nodded to the sergeant and took her arm.

'I've inspected the Hotel Sharon. It's not the Waldorf, but it's clean and the menu looks edible.' They crossed a paved street. Very few people about. On the opposite pavement Whelby paused and gestured into the distance with his head. 'Amazing, really. As a small boy at Sunday school they gave me coloured pictures of ancient Jerusalem – like large postage stamps to paste into a book. One picture each week. The place looks exactly like those pictures . . .'

In 1943 Jerusalem still had its biblical atmosphere. Set in a bowl, it was encircled by a rim of seven hills. There was a deceptive air of peace, of the stability of centuries.

'It's quite overwhelmingly beautiful,' said Linda. 'You took your case when you went to inspect the hotel. Where is it?'

'In my room . . .' He began walking again. 'I told you I was on my vacation. They have reserved Room 6 for me. They're holding Room 8 for you. The choice is yours. Stay here if you like it. If not, I'll find you somewhere else.'

The Sharon was a long-fronted, two-storey building built at the beginning of time. It had a shallow roof of once-red tiles now mellowed to faded terracotta. Four steps led up to a wooden verandah railed off from the street where small tables sported red-check table-cloths. Dense creeper snaked up the supports and enveloped the walls, peering in at the open windows.

'It's lovely,' said Linda.

'It's up to you,' Whelby replied. Not pressing.

Sitting stiffly behind the wheel of the parked staff car, Mulligan watched them mount the steps. His eyes flicked to the rear-view mirror, his hand whipped to the submachine-gun as he heard footsteps approaching. Then he relaxed. The clatter of hobnail, Army boots. Corporal Wilson, blank-faced as ever, opened the front passenger door. Mulligan gestured for him to get inside.

'Did they spot me bringing up the rear, Sarge?' Wilson asked.

'Quite sure they didn't. Glad to see you in one piece.'

'What's going on? Or shouldn't I ask?'

'On this one, the more you know the better,' Mulligan replied. 'Especially as I'll need you as back-up. Where have you parked the armoured car?'

'In a side street fifty yards back. Nobby Clarke in charge till I take over. I thought we was takin' our pick-up back to the barracks.'

'So did I, Wilson, so did I. Said pick-up has a mind of his own. Nice chap. Swallows his vowels and loses most of his consonants. He's bunking down – his own phrase – at the Sharon. So, I'll need a couple of uniformed men patrolling the front. That makes them targets for the Jew bombers. I want your armoured car with its Lewis gun and all the trimmings in a side street to back up my men. I'll phone your Colonel Payne as soon as I get back, but I'm sure he'll agree.'

'He will after the recent bit of help you gave . . .'

'So Bloody Mr Standish of no vowels and few consonants will be tying up six of my men every twenty-four hours and more of yours. If he'd gone to the barracks no extra man-power would have been needed. *Blast him!*'

'What about the tart? Nice-looking piece. He's gone off with her?'

'Which I think is the attraction about staying at the Sharon.' Mulligan took off his police cap and scratched at his stubble of hair. 'You know something, Wilson? Never assume the obvious in this world. Just before I drive back I'm going in to check that hotel register . . .'

'Our rooms are next to each other,' Linda observed as she held the key without inserting it in the lock. She gave Whelby a sideways glance. 'Room 8 for me, Room 6 for you . . .'

'You heard Mulligan describe the situation out here. I thought you'd feel . . . safer.'

He stood holding both cases. His own, collected from reception where he had left it on his earlier visit to the hotel, hers which he had insisted on carrying up the ancient flight of stairs.

'That was nice of you. Let's inspect it.'

Unlocking the door, she walked into an old-fashioned but well-furnished room. Another door led to the bathroom. She chuckled and put a hand over her mouth.

'My, just look at the bed . . .'

It was very big with great brass rails surmounted with acorn-shaped decorations. The French windows were open and the view looked across to the distant Mount of Olives. Whelby placed her case on a chair and stood beside her. She waited for him to touch her but he remained aloof, an absent-minded expression on his pale face.

'I have to deliver those papers,' he remarked and checked his watch. 'Could you wait till two, and join me downstairs for some lunch?'

'I'd love that. I'm going to take a peek at the shops . . .'

'Be careful how you go. Two o'clock. And keep your door locked at all times.'

'Yes, Sergeant Mulligan . . .'

He closed the door on the outside and waited in the corridor. Only when he heard her lock it did he move quickly. Carrying his case he headed for the staircase and ran lightly up to the next floor. Room 24 was at the far end of a corridor which was deserted and smelt of floor polish.

In response to his knock the door was opened as though the occupant, Vlacek, had been waiting for him.

It was a peacetime scene. The morning sun a warm glow on the fertile green of the polo field. The only sounds the click of polo stick against ball, the gentle thump of horses' hooves.

Jock Carson was in the middle of a chukka when he saw Harrington on the edge of the field, waving a piece of paper to catch his attention. Gezira Sporting Club was on an island in the middle of the Nile, facing Cairo to which it was linked by bridges.

Carson waved his stick to warn the other players. He trotted the horse off the field, dismounted, produced a lump of sugar which his steed dutifully made disappear, then handed the animal over to a waiting Egyptian.

'Trouble?' he asked as he walked alongside Harrington towards the pavilion, reading the message.

'At last!' Harrington sounded excited. 'Signal from Reader in Jugoslavia. Deal clinched. Three hundred sten guns with thirty mags apiece. In exchange we get Lindsay . . .'

'We have to get more weapons to Libya?'

'No! That's the marvellous thing. This bloody Heljec, or whatever his name is, started out wanting twenty-five pounders, a whole armoured division – you name it. Reader has bartered him down to what is already aboard the Dakota waiting at Benina! Fabulous chap!'

'I see the signal confirms a map-reference for a landing zone in Bosnia. For how long?' The turf was springy under their feet, the bedlam of Cairo's daytime existence a thousand miles away. 'We'll have to get moving.'

'I've got the jeep waiting. Bet I break my record back to Grey Pillars.'

Carson was mopping sweat from his brow and neck with the towel handed to him by the Egyptian steward. He frowned as he continued studying the signal.

'I've got the most horrible feeling about this business. Something's wrong. It's going to end badly, very badly . . .'

Chapter Thirty-Nine

The phone was ringing in Harrington's office when they arrived back. He flew in from the doorway, skidded across the highly-polished floor – as he'd done so often before – recovered his balance, laid one hand on the desk and grabbed up the receiver with the other before it stopped ringing.

'Harrington . . .'

'This is Linda Climber. That is the American Embassy? *Embassy* is what I said. You want it a third time?'

'Harrington at your service, as always. A package has arrived for you from New Jersey.'

They had established positive identities. Sliding into his seat, Harrington gestured towards the extension phone with his other hand. Carson, who had closed the door, picked up the instrument.

'I can't be sure one way or the other – about our friend . . .' She sounded unhappy as she went on. 'He seems O.K. Got a pencil and pad? Good. We're staying at the Hotel Sharon. Yes, together, so to speak. Phone number and extension . . .'

Harrington scribbled in the excruciating scrawl only he could decipher. 'Anything more about our friend?'

'He goes off on trips on his own. There could be someone else inside this hotel. He stumbled once. Said he was going out and I watched from an upper floor window overlooking the exit. He never appeared. After ten minutes he came back, said he'd left his wallet in another suit and maybe I would like to come with him for a morning stroll . . .'

'What time was that – the missing ten minutes?'

'Precisely ten o'clock to ten after ten . . .'

'His manner when he came back?' Harrington pressed.

'Normal.' A pause. 'Maybe a little more relaxed, a shade of relief. That's all. I'm phoning from Mulligan's place. He's out at the moment.'

'Take care. Keep trying.'

'I intend to.'

They replaced the receivers at the same moment. Carson picked up an officer's stick and began walking round the room, tapping his teeth lightly with the end of the stick. He paused by the open window. Not even a shiver from the curtain this morning. An airless humidity like a smothering blanket had closed over the Grey Pillars complex.

'Warn the pilot at Benina to be ready for immediate

take-off,' Carson said. 'Don't supply a map reference yet. It may be changed at the last minute. Talking about minutes – that missing ten minutes out of Standish's life keeps niggling at me . . .'

'What can you do in ten minutes?'

'Men have changed history in that time. I don't like any of this, you know.'

'Check urgently with London? Express your doubts.'

'And what will London reply?' Carson demanded savagely. 'Not urgently, for a start. Maybe in a fortnight – when they've cranked up their brain-boxes – a dismissive answer. *Our courier has our full confidence. Wholly reliable* . . .' He spoke the few words in a plummy voice. 'They like "wholly" – probably because it sounds like "holy" . . .'

'So, no signal to London?'

'We have to do it ourselves – as always.' Carson's pace became brisker. 'I'm leaving you in sole charge. Anything crops up, you decide. Right?'

'Of course. You're going somewhere?'

'First available plane to Lydda. Have transport standing by to rush me to Jerusalem. Pray God I spot the niggle which is driving me mad . . .'

With Stalin now placing full confidence in the information from Woodpecker and Lucy, by early winter '43 the Red Army had retaken Kiev. All along the front, at the price of enormous blood-letting, the Russians were advancing.

Snow had fallen on the forests smothering the Wolf's Lair. The branches of the trees were sagging, encased in ice. Frequently inside the dense forest a rifle shot would ring out. *Crack!* But it was not a rifle shot – it was the sound of a branch snapping off.

A lowering sky like a grey sea, heavy with snow, pressed down on the encampment. The atmosphere – as much as the news from the front – was affecting the occupants. Only the Führer maintained an air of optimism.

In his spartan quarters inside a wooden building – he disliked the bunker built for use in an air raid – he was striding back and forth as he lectured Bormann. He wore his usual dark trousers, his tunic with wide lapels, the three buttons fastened down the front, his sole decoration the Iron Cross attached to his breast.

'I need Wing Commander Lindsay brought back here urgently. We must negotiate an arrangement with England. I will guarantee the existence of the British Empire, an important – unique – stabilizing force in the world. If that is ever destroyed there will be chaos. Then we can devote our whole strength to eliminating the Soviets, as much England's enemy as ours. Where is Lindsay now? My lunch is getting cold . . .'

On the table, with a cover to keep it warm, was a bowl of vegetable gruel. Hitler ate sparingly, took little interest in his food. His sole weakness was apple cake which he indulged in at the Berghof.

'I'm worried that Lindsay may have detected your impersonation,' Bormann began tentatively. 'I have read his file. He was once a professional actor. Some of the visitors here look at you with puzzled expressions – Ribbentrop . . .'

'And who has said a word?' Hitler challenged him. 'Even if they suspect anything how dare they voice their doubts? I am the keystone of the arch holding up the Third Reich. Without me they are nothing. They know that . . .'

'Then there is Eva . . .'

'Eva!' The Führer was amused but he spoke with mock ferocity. 'Eva and I get on fine! You keep your lecherous eyes off her or you'll hang from your ankles!'

'My Führer! I did not mean . . .'

'I ask you again. Where is Lindsay?'

It was a typical tactic of the Führer's – to divert someone from an awkward topic they had raised by introducing another subject which threw them off-balance. Eva Braun had told him about this ploy.

'I am expecting a signal at any time from Colonel Jaeger who has made his headquarters in Zagreb. He is still hunting Linday in Jugoslavia. Jaeger has so far successfully kept the Partisan group hiding Lindsay on the move – to stop the English air-lifting him out of the Balkans . . .'

'He is an excellent fellow, this Jaeger. I chose him for the task myself. Remember? But he must move quickly. Alexander now controls southern Italy. Allied Military Missions are in close touch with the Partisans. *Bormann* . . .' Hitler's mood changed suddenly. He hammered the table with his fist. Gruel from the covered bowl slopped over the edge. 'See, you have ruined my lunch. I want results! I want Lindsay!'

'I will go to the signals office and get in touch with Colonel Jaeger at once . . .'

'I'll expect you back by the time I have finished what remains of my gruel.'

'A fresh bowl . . .'

'Go! Bormann, go!'

On his way to the signals office Bormann met Jodl who had just entered Security Ring A after showing the special pass issued by Himmler. Jodl, his face looking drawn, waved with his gloved hand round the compound.

'This claustrophobic place is getting us all down . . .'

'Where have you been, my dear chap?' Bormann asked casually.

'For a walk in the forest – and a think . . .'

'So, apparently, has someone else . . .'

Keitel, his boots clogged with snow, muffled in great-coat and scarf like Jodl, had also just come in through the checkpoint. His manner distant, as always, Keitel raised his baton to them and changed direction to avoid them, stalking at his slow, measured tread towards his quarters.

'Keitel also is going round the bend,' Jodl observed.

'He must have gone a long way into the forest. Did you see his boots?'

'So, he too likes to get away from it all. You seem to be on edge, Bormann,' Jodl teased. 'Trouble with the Führer?' The tall Chief of Staff folded his arms. 'You should take some exercise yourself,' he remarked and smiled cynically. 'The hours you keep, it's all going to get on top of you one of these days.'

'Trouble with the Führer? Of course not! And I took a walk early this morning.'

'I know. I saw you from my window . . .'

He watched Bormann hurrying away, a small, stumpy figure scurring through the snow. Jodl shrugged, clapped his gloves together to warm his frozen hands.

'Servile little creep.'

In the depths of the forest the transceiver operated by Woodpecker still rested in its log hide. Thick snow was packed hard where gloved hands had that morning concealed it after usage.

'Colonel Jaeger has just come through on the 'phone direct from Zagreb . . .'

In the signals office Bormann, short of breath, settled his ample buttocks in a chair. Without a word of thanks he took the instrument from the duty officer and jerked his head. *Get out and leave me alone . . .*

'Bormann here . . . I was just going to call you . . . The Führer . . .'

'Kindly listen to me. I am short of time . . .'

Jaeger's deep, booming voice cut off the Reichsleiter in mid-sentence. The Colonel was speaking in his barrack-room voice. He had finally run out of patience with the whole gang at headquarters. What the hell did they know about what was going on in the outside world?

'I am phoning so you can tell the Führer we have the Partisan group holding Lindsay cornered. Time and again they have slipped away from us after a battle involving appalling casualties. I am launching an airborne attack – using paratroopers. This should give us the element of surprise which has hitherto been lacking. Put the Führer on the line and I'll tell him myself.'

'I have understood you so far . . .'

'So far! Good God, man, I've just given you the most precise military appreciation of the situation possible. That's all.'

'But the timing of the operation . . .'

'Not settled. Depends on weather conditions.'

'And Lindsay is definitely with this group?'

'Are you listening to me? Has your memory gone? I've just used the phrase "the Partisan group holding Lindsay".'

All traces of patience had vanished from Jaeger's voice. By his side Schmidt looked anxious, wagged a warning finger. The Colonel lifted a threatening hand, holding the earpiece like a club, then smiled and winked.

'What was that?' he snapped into the 'phone.

'When may I expect news of developments?' Bormann repeated.

'When they develop.'

He slammed the earpiece back onto the cradle and walked to the first-floor window of the ancient stone villa on the outskirts of Zagreb. It was snowing, but only lightly, the flakes drifting in the windless air.

'What do the Met geniuses predict this time?'

'A complete clearing of the weather in twenty-four hours from now. A cloudless day tomorrow. Positively no snow. No "if's" or "buts" and their report is in writing,' Schmidt replied.

'You twisted their arms, you must have done! Are Stoerner's paratroopers standing by?'

'Men and machines are ready for the air-drop when you give the word . . .'

'What would I do without you, my dear Schmidt?'

'Have a nervous breakdown . . .'

Jaeger threw back his head and roared with laughter. This rapport between senior officer and subordinate had been built up slowly, in the great campaign of '40 in France; during the terrible ordeals on the Eastern Front. The Colonel's expression became grave again.

'It's going to be a race against time, you realize that?'

'I don't quite follow you, sir . . .'

'That fine weather, if it materializes. Perfect for our parachute drop, but perfect also for the British to land a plane on that plateau to take out Lindsay. And God knows we have had enough rumours of an imminent airlift. From inside

412

Fitzroy Maclean's headquarters, from other sources. Oh, I've decided to go in with the paratroopers myself. Long time ago since I dangled from a 'chute . . .'

'For God's sake, sir. After Kursk you were going to be invalided out of the Army. You remember what that doctor told you in Munich.'

'That I should only do what I felt like doing. I feel like dropping in on Wing Commander Lindsay. Inform Stoerner one more parachute will be required.'

'Two more. I took the same course with you at Langheim.'

'Now listen to me, Schmidt.' Jaeger's tone was grave. 'I've a premonition about this operation. You have a wife and two children . . .'

'Like yourself. I've carried out every order you've ever given me. Don't make me guilty of insubordination now . . .'

'Oh, hell – have it your own way,' Jaeger growled.

As Schmidt left the room to 'phone Stoerner, he sat down at a desk and took a sheet of notepaper from a drawer. It took him some time to compose the letter to his wife. He had always hated correspondence.

Dear Magda, We've had a marvellous life together. And all thanks to you, for your infinite kindness and consideration. I am writing on the eve of a somewhat difficult business we have to undertake. I wouldn't like you to suffer a shock if they send one of those bald official communications . . .

'Signal just came in,' Reader told Lindsay. 'It's the green light. Plane lands tomorrow at 1100 hours, subject always to the ruddy weather changing . . .'

'Christ, it's snowing. Are they mad?'

'Clear day forecast for tomorrow. And our weather's coming in from the west – over the Adriatic from Italy, so they should know.' Reader sounded buoyant. 'My God, inside twenty-four hours we could be out of the bloody Balkans forever. Promise myself one thing. I'm never coming back to this hell-hole.'

He looked up as Paco strolled over to join them. She wore a camouflage jacket, a heavy woollen skirt and knee-length boots. Her blonde hair was neatly brushed and she carried Reader's sten gun in her right hand. He had shown her how to use it.

'Care to come for a walk, lady?' Reader suggested chirpily. 'Get the old circulation moving.'

'All right. How are you feeling this morning, Lindsay?'

'I'm O.K.'

He watched her walk away across the plateau with Reader, so close together they were almost touching. His expression was bleak, bitter. He had been standing, holding his stick. He was mobile now, his temperature was back to normal. Under the ministrations of Dr Macek the glandular fever had been brought under control.

Their relationship with the Partisans had radically altered over the months they had fought with the group, constantly fleeing from the Germans, evading Jaeger's attempts to trap them. Often by the skin of their teeth.

Reader, still playing the role of Cockney sergeant, still wisely concealing his real rank and Intelligence background, was largely responsible for the change. He no longer hid his transmitter, which he lugged from place to place. He had engaged the aggressive Heljec in a number of verbal battles and had won.

'If you want the guns and the ammo,' he had persisted time and again, 'you must co-operate with my people. Lindsay, myself, Paco — if she wants to leave — have to be flown out. Hartmann, too. The plane that takes us out brings in the guns.'

Reader had lost track of the weeks, months, the argument had raged in the quiet times. Haggle, haggle. It was the way of life in the Balkans. He had thrown in Hartmann as a bargaining counter, intending to sacrifice the German at the right moment. That had precipitated a violent struggle with both Lindsay and Paco.

'Hartmann has been very kind to me,' Paco told Reader. 'He must have a place on the plane.'

'He's a Jerry,' Reader told her. 'Heljec won't wear it — and what's all the fuss about, anyway . . .'

'Gustav Hartmann is coming with us,' Lindsay intervened. 'And that's an order. Don't forget I outrank you, Major . . .'

'And who's organizing this how's-your-father?' Reader had exploded. 'Spendin' 'arf me bloody life arguing the toss with this bandit. You know what his latest demand is? Mortars and bombs, for Christ's sake. He'll be lucky . . .'

'Hartmann is Abwehr,' Lindsay said quietly. 'Your people are going to be very interested in grilling him . . .'

'It's not on! It's not part of my instructions . . .'

'It's part of mine.' Lindsay's tone was clipped. 'I don't have to give you a reason. It just so happens that he's anti-Nazi. I've been talking to him . . .'

'Anti-Nazi!' Reader snorted. 'All the bleeders will be when the chips are down.'

'That's enough. I'm giving you a direct order. Hartmann is part of the deal. It's up to you to fix it. That's why you were sent here. Make Heljec give way or I'll take over the negotiations myself.'

'If you say so. *Wing Commander!*'

Lindsay had deliberately concealed the fact that Hartmann also was an invaluable witness to the extraordinary conditions prevailing at the Wolf's Lair. On the morning before the plane was expected, as Paco wandered off with Reader, Hartmann appeared and joined Lindsay.

'Those two seem to be developing a relationship,' Hartmann observed as he perched on a rock next to Lindsay.

'I'm not blind . . .'

'Get her out of your system,' the German advised. 'A woman is an unpredictable creature. Falling in love with someone who will never love you is worse than Gestapo torture. It lasts longer . . .'

'She's got into my bloodstream . . .'

'Then I'm very sorry for you.'

Hartmann tamped tobacco from his pouch into his pipe and lit it with enormous satisfaction. He rationed himself to one pipe a day now. Paco had brought him a fresh supply taken by a Partisan off a dead German. At the time Hartmann had

415

thought, what things we'll do to satisfy our cravings!

'The plane is due tomorrow,' Lindsay said suddenly.

'I rather thought so. I saw them clearing rocks from the airstrip over there. It doesn't seem possible. In this weather.'

He brushed flakes from the shoulder of his jacket. Snow fell gently, flecking the ground cleared for the airstrip. It was cold – but the raw, biting wind of recent days had dropped.

'A clear, sunny day is forecast for tomorrow,' Lindsay said.

'Which might coincide with a fresh attack by Jaeger. Our persistent Colonel has been too quiet recently.'

'Heljec has made all his dispositions. All approaches to the plateau up the ravines are guarded. Heljec may not be worried about us but he does want those sten guns.'

'I saw you writing again in your diary, huddled under a rock before Reader spoilt your day."

Lindsay produced his black, leather-bound book from inside his jacket, keeping it closed to protect it from the drifting flakes. He balanced it in his hand and looked at Hartmann with a grim expression.

'I've been scribbling away for weeks, as you know. Everything's there. Our suspicions about the second Hitler at the Wolf's Lair. Your conclusions as to the identity of the Soviet spy. Then if anything happens to me this simply has to get to London and they will know . . .'

'Don't sound so doomed . . .'

'It really doesn't matter whether I get through or not. That's being realistic. The diary must get through. And it would help if you got through with it. There is a first-class seat booked on the plane for you . . .'

'Thank you . . .'

Hartmann puffed at his pipe which no longer tasted so good. He was disturbed by Lindsay's attitude, the sense of fatalism in the RAF officer he detected. And all the time they had talked, Lindsay had been watching the two small silhouettes walking slowly round the plateau. Paco and Reader.

NDA OK QSR5 . . . NDA OK QSR5 . . .

Seconds later Meyer, listening at the Dresden Monitoring

Centre with Walter Schellenberg opposite him, recorded a series of five letters and five figures. They provided the agreed code.

'Now,' said Meyer, 'we switch from the 43-metre band, which *The Ghost* uses only for the call sign, to the 39-metre band. That's the wavelength on which they transmit the main signal . . .'

Meyer had cracked Lucy's system.

It had taken months of patient experimentation but the peacetime watchmaker had persisted. Schellenberg's shrewd eyes gleamed with triumph as he leaned forward, a pair of headphones over his ears.

Ten minutes later the transmission Meyer was recording ended. It was the night before Jaeger was due to launch his airborne attack on the plateau in Bosnia. Schellenberg removed his headphones, stood up, reached an arm across the table and shook hands with Meyer.

'You are a genius. You will go down in history. You know that, I hope?'

'I have just done my job.'

'And the mobile monitoring station at Strasbourg . . .'

The 'phone inside the glass cubicle rang. Meyer reached for the instrument and nodded to Schellenberg.

'This will be them, I suspect. They're very quick . . .'

He identified himself, nodded again to Schellenberg, listening with only the occasional comment.

'Again? As on previous occasions. You're quite sure?'

He thanked the caller profusely, a point Schellenberg did not miss. The chief of the SD – SS Intelligence – never did miss a point. Meyer, always so modest, had trouble concealing his satisfaction.

'Strasbourg has pinpointed the location of *The Ghost* for the fourth time. It is Switzerland. It is Lucerne.'

'I've got him! Masson of the Swiss Intelligence.' Schellenberg shook his head in reluctant awe at the audacity of his Swiss opposite number. 'He is permitting a secret transmitter to send signals to the Soviets. We know it's the Soviets . . .'

'Because they always use five letters and five figures for the code,' Meyer interjected.

'Exactly! After all these months!' Schellenberg couldn't keep still. It was this uninhibited and infectious enthusiasm he displayed which partly explained his popularity with subordinates. 'Now I can break Masson! Compel him to reveal the identity of the Soviet spy at the Wolf's Lair! We may be in time to change the outcome of the whole war.'

It was typical of Schellenberg that he talked openly to Meyer about the most closely-guarded state secrets. Meyer was complete trustworthy. By sharing his confidence Schellenberg gained his subordinate's total loyalty, his incredible application to his task.

'I gambled on this fourth confirmation,' Schellenberg continued. 'I have already made an appointment to meet Masson within hours inside Switzerland . . .'

'They will let you across the border?'

Meyer was astounded. Technically it was a gross violation of Switzerland's precious neutrality which that country preserved in a way a girl protects her virginity.

'I travel incognito,' Schellenberg explained with a flamboyant flourish. 'There have been previous visits. Now, I must leave Dresden immediately. Brigadier Roger Masson, I am coming . . .' Snow was falling heavily as he hurried from the building.

It was ten o'clock at night in Zagreb when Jaeger heard from the guard-room downstairs in the old villa that Karl Gruber of the Gestapo was waiting to see him.

'Tell him to wait!' Jaeger slammed down the 'phone and turned to Schmidt who sat at another desk, poring over a map of Bosnia. 'We need every minute to check over the details of Operation Raven, we'll be damned lucky to get an hour's sleep and who do you think lands on our doorstep? Gruber of the Gestapo!'

'He must smell profitable pickings – to risk his precious skin even in Zagreb. You'd better see him. Get to know what he's up to and we can sidetrack him.'

'You're right, of course.' Jaeger's admission was reluctant. 'You always are,' he added drily.

'Shall I go down and bring him up myself? I could twist his tail first. Tell him how busy you are. Is it really that important? Better get some sleep and leave it till morning. I might just pull it off! We'll be gone by morning.'

'You'll be lucky! Not a word about Operation Raven,' he warned.

'Do I look thick?' Schmidt enquired.

'Ask an embarrassing question, expect an embarrassing reply.'

On the eve of the parachute drop the two men had, if possible, drawn even closer together. I'm born lucky to have Schmidt, Jaeger reflected as he waited alone. I should have stopped him coming on this thing . . .

He only had to wait a few minutes. There was a knock on the door. He called out *Enter!* And framed in the doorway stood Gruber accompanied by Willy Maisel. The whole bloody clown act had arrived. Behind the two Gestapo agents Schmidt threw up a mock salute.

Jaeger sat behind his desk like a man of stone, offering no greeting. He noted Schmidt had rolled up the map on his desk before going downstairs. Trust him to attend, unbidden, to the small details.

The two Gestapo officials sat in chairs Schmidt placed some distance from the desk. Gruber promptly shifted his closer to the desk. He extended a pudgy hand which Jaeger, glancing down at his papers, pretended not to notice. He thought Willy Maisel looked unhappy about the whole business.

Gruber swivelled round in his chair. He stared at Schmidt, now seated behind his desk. He turned back to stare at Jaeger from under pouched eyes. There were signs of fatigue about both men.

'This is highly confidential,' Gruber began. 'It would be better if we were alone, if you please.'

'I don't please. And your suggestion is an insult to Schmidt who would automatically assume my command if anything happened to me.'

'Is something going to happen to you, Colonel?' Gruber asked.

'Something could happen to any of us. The Croat rebels like to place time-bombs in the most unexpected places. You would be a prime target if they gain knowledge of your presence . . .'

He had the satisfaction of seeing the dough-faced Gestapo officer wince. Again he said nothing more, forcing Gruber to make all the running.

'We understand you may soon have Wing Commander Lindsay in your hands. He is to be handed over to us for questioning at Gestapo headquarters in Graz.'

'Thumb-screws and pliers for a little amateur nail-varnishing?' Jaeger shook his head. 'Not a chance. If we ever apprehend Lindsay again I shall personally escort him into the presence of the Führer at the Wolf's Lair.'

Gruber lost his temper. Maisel lifted his eyes to the ceiling as his companion snatched a folded document from his pocket and threw it on the desk. He raised a clenched fist to crash it on the desk as he opened his mouth to speak. Then he caught Jaeger's expression. The fist dissolved in mid-air.

'My instructions,' he said in a normal tone, 'are by order of the Führer.'

Jaeger unfolded the sheet, watching Gruber all the time. Then he read the document carefully, refolded it and handed it back politely. Sitting back in his chair, he folded his arms.

'That bit of bumf is signed by Bormann. I have a document granting me full powers – signed by the Führer himself. Go back to your headquarters and get some sleep. Better still, go to the airfield and fly back to Germany. I cannot guarantee your safety any longer in this part of the world. It's up to you . . .' He stood up, clasping his hands out of the way behind his back. 'A safe journey, gentlemen . . .'

'Open the van yourself, Moshe. See what is within your grasp after you have carried out the assignment,' said Vlacek.

He handed his small, heavily-built companion a key. The van stood inside a secluded courtyard in a remote part of

420

Jerusalem. Moshe – it was not his real name – was a commander of the Stern Gang, one of the most active and violent of the Jewish underground groups.

Moshe took the key, looked again swiftly round the cobbled yard and inserted the key in the lock. He opened the left-hand door and stared at the pile of freshly-greased Lee Enfield .303 rifles. At the back of the van was a pile of ammunition boxes.

'Hurry up,' urged Vlacek. 'This is sight of the goods only. Delivery only after the job is done.'

'This Lindsay you want liquidating. When is he coming in?'

'Soon. Soon. He will be flown into Lydda Airport.'

'Too well-guarded.'

'Wait till I've finished,' Vlacek snapped. 'He will stay in Jerusalem for one day, possibly two. You will be told where he is being kept. You will know immediately he arrives . . .'

Dark-haired with a sun-tanned complexion, the skin pitted with old pock-marks, Moshe nodded dubiously, climbed inside the van and picked up a rifle at random.

Testing the mechanism after checking to make sure it was unloaded, he released the safety catch, squinted along the sight under cover of the van and pressed the trigger. Laying down the rifle, he walked over to one of the boxes, produced a tool from under his shabby jacket and levered the top off the box.

He picked up a handful of cartridges, selected one, took it back to the rifle and inserted the cartridge in the breech. First, he had put back on the safety catch, much to Vlacek's relief. Extracting the cartridge he threw it back into the box and dropped the rifle. With an agile movement he jumped out of the van and left Vlacek to close and lock it.

'Your Lindsay is dead,' he said.

It was a bitter irony. At the starting point of Lindsay's journey Reader bartered guns to save the RAF officer's life, to fly him to the safety of the Middle East.

In Palestine Vlacek used guns stolen from a British army depot to pay the Stern Gang to end Lindsay's life. In the vicious turmoil of war it was not money – not gold – which was the universal currency. It was guns.

As soon as Moshe had driven away on his motor-cycle, Vlacek made a signal. The double doors of one of the buildings enclosing the abandoned courtyard were opened. Inside stood a larger van without markings, its rear doors open. Two heavy planks formed a ramp leading up to its interior.

Vlacek himself took the wheel of the smaller van loaded with the guns and ammo. He drove it with great skill across the yard, up the improvised ramp and inside the larger van. The other man closed the doors and hurried to the cab.

Within minutes of Moshe's departure the larger van moved under the archway leading into the deserted street beyond. Keeping well within the speed limit, it followed a devious route to another courtyard a couple of miles away where it was parked inside a similar building.

Vlacek emerged from the larger vehicle, brushing dust off his clothes. He had no intention of risking the Stern Gang mounting a raid to seize the rifles before they completed their side of the arrangement. As in Jugoslavia, there was no trust anywhere.

'1100 hours tomorrow,' said Reader as he closed the telescopic aerial of his transceiver. 'They're sending a Dakota, God help us. Let's hope they send us one with wings on . . .'

'That's really positive?' asked Paco. 'No reservations?'

'Gospel. I've given them the map reference. Lady, you want a ticket to convince you.'

'You know bloody well we've had enough false alarms before . . .'

'They're coming. They want Lindsay. Some geezer has flown out specially to meet him.'

'What geezer?' Lindsay demanded, suddenly alert.

It was well after dark. Huddled together in a cave, Lindsay, Paco and Hartmann had waited for Reader to come back after operating the transceiver from an eminence at the edge of the plateau. It had stopped snowing, one hopeful sign. But it was bitingly cold. No fires could be lit. Heljec had banned them.

'Can't tell you more till we're aboard the plane and away,' Reader replied laconically. 'Instructions.' He slipped inside his makeshift sleeping bag.

'Whose instructions? What is our destination? Why all this mystery?'

Lindsay was uneasy. He couldn't have said exactly why, but he felt something was wrong. Reader snuggled down, made no effort to conceal his irritation.

'Security, I suppose. Now, mate, do I get some shut-eye or are you going to yammer on the whole bleedin' night? You've a long day ahead of you tomorrow. Haven't we all?'

'H-Hour is 1100,' Schmidt informed Jaeger as he put down the 'phone. 'Just came through from Stoerner himself.'

'I know.' The Colonel initialled the last operational order and pushed the sheet across his desk, then stretched and yawned. 'I decided on the time for the attack myself. Not dawn as usual, they'll be alert for trouble then. By eleven they will have relaxed, decided it's just another peaceful day. I'm so tired I could fall asleep in this chair . . .'

'On your feet,' said Schmidt. 'I didn't have these camp beds brought in here to decorate the room.'

Jaeger stood up, stripped off his tunic, sat on the camp bed and took off his jump boots. He had put them on in the morning to get used to them. Supple, comfortable jump boots can make the difference between life and death to a paratrooper.

Lying full-length on the bed, he pulled the army blanket over him. Turning his head on the pillow, he looked at Schmidt before closing his eyes.

'1100 hours tomorrow. Sleep well.'

Chapter Forty

General Walter Schellenberg was driven across the Swiss border at Konstanz. He would have never known he was moving into another country had he not passed through a frontier control post. Konstanz is one of Europe's geographical oddities.

The town is literally split in two. The northern district is German, the southern Swiss. Seated in the back of the Mercedes, its windows masked with net curtains, he wore a smart civilian suit. The pause at the post lasted no longer than one minute. Brigadier Masson had sent an aide who brushed aside all normal formalities.

It was late evening, very dark – the night was moonless – as the Mercedes proceeded to a small place called Frauenfeld. Brigadier Masson awaited his guest in an upper room of the Gasthof Winkelreid.

A table was laid for dinner. Solid silver cutlery. Superbly polished glass which gleamed in the candlelight. Schellenberg's favourite wine in an ice bucket cradled in a tripod. The panelled walls reflected the faint shiver of the candles.

'My dear Brigadier Masson! What a pleasure to meet you again! If you knew how relaxing it is for me each time I visit Switzerland! For a few hours I forget all my cares and worries.'

Schellenberg was at his most charming and ebullient, so cordial that his manner would have disarmed a man less wary than the Swiss Intelligence chief.

Masson's mood was quite different. He greeted the German with courtesy but his expression was cool and aloof, almost cold. A sensitive man, Schellenberg spotted the change in atmosphere from his previous visit but pretended not to notice.

They had dinner.

'I came across a Rubens recently . . . quite by chance . . . a supreme example of his genius.'

Schellenberg ate and drank with enjoyment and appreciation. He talked intelligently. Old master paintings. Goethe's work. A new French novel. Beethoven's music. Masson simply listened, his blue eyes studying the German's mobile expressions.

It was only when dinner was over, when they had retired to two arm chairs drawn up in front of a fireplace where half a tree trunk blazed, crackled and spat, that something snapped.

No servants would enter the room again unless summoned by Masson. Schellenberg held his balloon-shaped glass of fine old Napoleon brandy up to the light. He was gazing contentedly at the glass when he spoke.

'The Führer's life is in danger. You are responsible. You are harbouring a Soviet spy transmitting our top secrets to Moscow. Immediately the Führer knows this he will order an invasion of Switzerland. Who is the spy at the Führer's headquarters? I have come for his name.'

Jock Carson was sitting at the bare wooden table in the office placed at his disposal in the police barracks by Sergeant Mulligan. Through the open window he could see the lights of Jerusalem, there was no black-out here.

A faint stench of cordite, which he always associated with death, drifted in with the cloying night air. It was uncomfortably humid. He stared at the table, its well-scrubbed surface disfigured with old ink stains. He had been waiting for a call from Cairo for over an hour. The 'phone rang twice only before he whipped up the receiver.

'Carson here. That you, Harrington? We're on a direct army line so get on with it. Any gen?'

'We may have panned a little gold.' Harrington's voice was faint but clear, clear enough for Carson to detect triumph.

'I said get on with it, for Christ's sake . . .'

'You know that list of names you gave me of people staying at the Hotel Sharon? Well, I've checked it with the register at

Shepheard's. Apart from Standish there is one common denominator. Man called Vlacek. V. Vlacek. V. for Victor.'

'How long was he at Shepheard's?'

'Two nights. The night before Standish arrived – and the night Standish was there.'

'Pity we don't know when Standish knew he was flying out. Who is this Vlacek?' Carson asked.

'A perfectly respectable Pole working for that funny propaganda outfit near Abassia Barracks. Come out from Russia with the Polish Army . . .'

'From Russia!'

'What's up, Chief?' Harrington sounded perplexed. 'It's the Nazis we're fighting, not the Russians.'

'Sometimes I wonder. This Vlacek seems to have a licence to roam . . .'

'I checked that, too. Discreetly. Gather he had overdue leave. Decided to take it on the spur of the moment . . .'

'That's it! What I've been looking for. That really is stretching the long arm of coincidence to breaking point. An interview with Mr Vlacek is overdue. And we've damn-all time left.'

'That's why I called you as soon as I knew. Does Standish know Lindsay is coming in?'

'He had to . . .' Carson sounded regretful. 'Also that he's flying out on a Dakota. I couldn't sit on everything. What he does not know is the timing. Nothing else? I've got an appointment – with Mr Victor Vlacek . . .'

Linda Climber had gone to bed early. She turned on her side and with her index finger explored Whelby's face, starting with a thick eyebrow and drawing the finger along his cheek-bone and down the bridge of his fleshy nose.

'You are a very mysterious person, Peter. For a man on vacation you seem to have so much to do. You're always flitting off somewhere.'

'I've always liked walking alone. I've walked alone since I was a child in India.'

He cradled her nude back with his arm and pulled her

426

closer. She persisted talking as he turned his wrist and glanced at the time.

'You're a very deep man, Peter. I can sense it. You lock so much away inside you.'

'And now I'm going to flit off again for a few minutes.' He kissed her and got out of her bed. 'I've forgotten to 'phone an old friend I promised to meet tomorrow.' He put on his dressing gown and slippers. 'I'll be back in a few minutes. Don't run away . . .'

'Dressed like this? With nothing on? You can 'phone your friend from here . . .'

'The number is in my room. Never could remember numbers . . .'

He glanced in a wall mirror, combed his hair, and looked back at her as she sat up in bed, clutching the sheets to her bare breasts. Whelby had never understood this curious aspect of feminine modesty. He nodded reassuringly as he left.

Linda swore under her breath. What perfect timing. She was hardly in a position to follow him to see where he was going. Which might mean nothing. But there had been too many such nothings.

'Definite news at last,' Whelby told Vlacek inside Room 24. 'Lindsay is being flown in sometime tomorrow to Lydda Airport. The machine will be a Dakota. It could land after dark, but it will be tomorrow.'

'I need more than that . . .' The bony-faced man made an impatient gesture. 'Surely they gave *some* idea of the time of arrival, where the plane is coming from?'

'They didn't. I asked. Mulligan went vague. I didn't press. It would have looked suspicious. I showed you Lindsay's photograph, so identification should be no problem.'

'I would like to keep that photograph. May I have it?'

'No. It has to go back into the file I pinched it from in London. Overlooking a tiny detail like that can lead to disaster. When do I see you again? What method will you employ to s . . . s . . . solve the problem?'

'You won't see me again. The method is not your affair. I am leaving this hotel tonight. Are you enjoying yourself with Mrs Climber?'

A sharp look, assessing Whelby's reaction. A waste of time. The Englishman's bland, diffident manner gave away nothing as he wandered round the room, hands in dressing gown pockets.

'She worries me. She asks a lot of questions. She is clever but I get the sensation of being interrogated . . .'

'You met her how?'

'A chance meeting on the plane flying in from Cairo. She came over to me . . .'

'*She* approached *you*?'

Something in Vlacek's voice made Whelby turn and study the little man's expression. He didn't like what he saw. It had been a mistake to talk about the American woman.

'Why? What are you getting at?' Whelby demanded.

'Get dressed immediately. Go straight to the barracks . . .' Vlacek checked his watch. 'Stay till midnight and be sure people know you are there all the time. Say you are waiting for a 'phone call from Cairo. Anything. Establish your whereabouts.'

'I don't like this . . .'

'Will your fingerprints be present in Mrs Climber's room?'

'No. That's why I keep my hands in my pockets. It's become second nature . . .'

'Have you left anything in that room which belongs to you?'

Vlacek's cross-examination was remorseless, spoken in a monotone Whelby found unnerving.

'No,' he said abruptly.

'Don't go back there. Go straight to your own room, dress quickly and leave. You have ten minutes . . .'

'I don't like this,' Whelby repeated. 'What are you planning? The woman doesn't know a thing . . .'

'That is your assumption. Do as I say. From now on I am in full control. You are under orders.' Vlacek smiled unpleasantly. 'You always have been . . .'

Jock Carson parked the Vauxhall by the kerb, got out, locked the car and strolled towards the Hotel Sharon he could see in the distance as a glow of lights. A lot of lights for that hour. He saw the two empty police cars parked carefully in the shadows as he drew closer. He quickened his pace.

One of the night duty guards intercepted him as he was about to mount the steps to the terrace. There seemed to be unusual activity inside the place.

'You've heard about the murder, sir?'

'What murder?'

God, he thought, they've got Whelby.

'Some American woman staying here. Apparently she . . .'

Carson never did hear the end of his sentence. He bounded up the steps, pushed open the door and walked into the reception lobby. A blue-uniformed Palestine policeman stopped him.

'Excuse me, sir, could I have a word? You're staying here?'

Carson produced his special identity folder, handed it to the man and stared around as though searching for a clue. The policeman handed back the folder and looked uncomfortable.

'Sorry, sir. You're part of the investigation?'

'Where do I go?'

'Room 8, first floor . . .'

Carson strode across to the reception counter, his stocky legs moving like pistons. Ignoring the clerk, he turned the hotel register through a hundred and eighty degrees and ran his finger down the list of names. Mrs L. Climber, Room 8. Mr P. Standish, Room 6. V. Vlacek, Room 24 . . .

'Can I help you . . .?' the clerk began.

Carson ran up the stairs, paused at the top to check his watch. A quarter past midnight. Another uniformed policeman stood on guard outside Room 8. The same routine of showing his folder. Inside, the room was crowded with policemen. A middle-aged man in civilian clothes carrying a bag was on the verge of leaving. They were checking for fingerprints, taking photographs with a flash-bulb. Sergeant Mulligan came forward.

'Nasty business this . . .'

'May I see her?'

Not from choice. But a feeling of more than duty. Carson had sanctioned Linda Climber's mission to Palestine. He had had doubts but Linda had persuaded him. They had a quid pro quo arrangement with the Yanks. An American girl worked for British Intelligence; he had provided an English Wren to work for them. It had seemed like an original idea. At the time. He approached the bed, Mulligan at his heels.

'She was garrotted,' Mulligan warned. 'A piece of wire like they cut cheese with, so the doctor here says. Not a palatable sight . . .'

She was lying back on the pillow which was stained red. Her throat was cut from ear to ear, her expression one of terror. Stony-faced, Carson observed the bed-clothes were crumpled and pulled free of the mattress. All the signs that she had fought for her life.

The room was a bigger mess. Drawers pulled out, the contents spilled on the floor. A jewel case lay on the floor, the lid ripped from the hinges. Carson felt a twinge of nausea. When he spoke it was with unusual harshness.

'Room 6 is next door. Occupied by Standish. I suggest you check it for his fingerprints. Was she raped?'

His mind was flitting all over the bloody place.

'No,' Mulligan replied. 'By the way, this is Dr Thomas . . .'

'Not raped,' Thomas said in a professional, dry voice, heavily Welsh. *I have seen all this before, I just want to go home and get back to bed*. 'But sexual intercourse had taken place very recently. This evening.'

'Definitely not rape?' Carson persisted. The point was more important than probably anyone else in the room realized.

'I've just said so,' Thomas told him. 'She was willing . . .'

Carson turned to Mulligan who was looking at him curiously. 'I'd like you to get on with checking Room 6 for fingerprints, for comparison in here. It doesn't matter if Standish is in bed. Get him up.'

'He's not in bed. He's not even in the hotel. And my men

are dusting his room for prints now. They used the manager's pass-key. Standish has been at the barracks for the past two hours. Waiting for a call from Cairo, I gather . . .'

'When did it happen?'

Carson avoided looking at the bed. He didn't even look at Thomas who was replying to his question. He disliked doctors.

'Until the post-mortem . . .'

'I know all that!' Carson was at his most dictatorial. 'I don't want the reservations. Give me what you'll qualify as an educated guess . . .'

'You always write other people's dialogue for them?' Carson had got under Thomas's skin. He continued not looking at him as the doctor went on. 'Some time between ten and midnight, closer to midnight as far as I can judge . . .'

'Which exonerates Standish of any suspicion,' Mulligan observed. 'The check on Room 6 is pure routine. I think Dr Thomas wants to get off – if you have no more questions . . .'

Carson shook his head and waited until the doctor had gone. 'What's the verdict about how it happened? Place looks as though a hurricane hit it.'

'Robbery with extreme violence. Her jewel case was jemmied open. Nothing left. Signs that a ring was forced off the finger of her left hand. That suggests a professional burglar. The murder doesn't, particularly the method employed.'

'Room 24,' Carson said. He unbuttoned the flap of his holster. 'Better bring a couple of men with us, with their weapons at the ready. A Mr Victor Vlacek occupies that room.'

Mulligan didn't argue the point, ask any questions. Calling to a couple of his men, he followed Carson out of the room. They arrived outside Room 24 and Mulligan looked to Carson for a lead.

'Pass-key,' Carson whispered. Ambidextrous, he held his .38 Smith & Wesson in his left hand, took the pass-key with his right, inserted the key carefully in the lock and turned it with equal care. Then he took hold of the handle, revolved it quickly and threw open the door.

431

They stood just inside the doorway, caught off balance. The room was empty and in a state of chaos. Clothes half-ripped off the bed. Pillows on the floor. Drawers pulled out and left upside down on the floor. Wardrobe doors open, a mess of clothes hauled off the hangers lying on the floor.

Carson tiptoed across to the bathroom where the door was open. He peered inside, shook his head, them a wisp of night breeze fluttered the curtain drawn across the window. He walked across and looked out. Only then did he holster his revolver and turn to face the others.

'Bloody repeat performance,' said Mulligan. 'How many rooms has he turned over tonight?'

'Just these two, I imagine . . .'

'I don't get it . . .'

'Probably that's the idea.' Carson gestured towards the open window. 'There's a fire escape out there. Any way out at the back of the hotel?'

'Easy as falling off a horse. There's a courtyard, garages, a low wall a kid could climb over, an open space of waste ground and beyond that he's on a quiet road. And there's a fire escape outside Mrs Climber's window, which was also open. When you brought us here I thought it was Vlacek but . . .' Mulligan made a helpless gesture. 'Same thing happened here. Where's his body?'

'I don't think you're ever going to find that, Sergeant. It was a very professional job. All round. I really am worried now . . .'

'About this?'

'I think this is just the beginning. Just for openers . . .'

Outside the Gasthof Winkelreid in Frauenfeld it was snowing heavily as Masson faced Schellenberg in the first-floor room. They could hear the rumble of a snow-plough the Swiss Intelligence chief had summoned to keep the road open. On no account must his German guest stay in Switzerland overnight.

'I insist that you reveal to me the name of the Soviet spy in Germany,' Schellenberg repeated. 'Otherwise I cannot be responsible for the consequences.'

'There will be no invasion of my country by the Wehrmacht,' Masson interrupted coldly. 'You are using blackmail but you are bluffing . . .'

'I do not bluff. There is a map in existence . . .'

'I have had a copy of that map for over two years . . .'

Masson was speaking the truth. The map Schellenberg alluded to had been printed in Germany. It showed the future frontiers of the Greater Reich which embraced all German-speaking peoples, including German-speaking Switzerland – seventy per cent of the entire country.

Despite the glowing heat from the great log fire the warmth had gone out of the conversation between the two men who now faced each other openly as adversaries. In all earlier encounters Schellenberg had alternately coaxed and threatened; Masson had been compliant and co-operative. It was Schellenberg who was in a state of shock. Masson was impassive but obdurate, refusing to give an inch.

'The Wehrmacht cannot cope with what it has on its plate already,' Masson continued bluntly. 'Opening up a new front is beyond it. Or haven't you heard that the Red Army is advancing beyond Kiev? The Wehrmacht is retreating everywhere. The Allies are in Italy. In '44 we all know they will open the Second Front in France . . .'

'We have our problems,' Schellenberg agreed.

'*You* may soon have your problems,' Masson said mercilessly. 'Supposing – I am only supposing – that Germany loses the war? You will need a bolt-hole to run to – to escape capture by the Russians. On your way to meet the Allies your route to freedom may well be via Switzerland.'

Nothing demonstrated more dramatically the changed relationship between the two men than their postures. While Schellenberg sagged in his arm chair, one hand holding his empty glass of brandy, Masson sat erect like a judge, his expression stern.

'We know,' Masson pounded on, 'that with the encouragement and full backing of Himmler, you have made already fruitless overtures to the Allies – trying to come to an arrangement with them which would close out the Soviets . . .'

It was true. Archives which have since come to light prove that as early as the end of '43 Himmler authorized Schellenberg to put out tentative peace feelers to the British. Himmler was taking no risks. If by chance the Führer had ferreted out this treachery, Reichsführer Himmler could have disowned all knowledge of what his deputy was up to.

'That bloody Casablanca announcement. Unconditional surrender,' growled Schellenberg. 'It stiffens the resistance of our people. Crazy! Crazy! Doesn't Churchill know the menace the West faces from the Bolsheviks?'

'Churchill knows,' Masson replied. 'Three thousand five hundred miles away from Europe, Roosevelt does not know. You will need your bolt-hole, my friend. One of these days. This part of our conversation I shall not report to my Commander-in-Chief, General Guisan . . .'

'I am grateful . . .' Schellenberg was reduced to gratitude. He made one last effort. 'You refuse to name the Soviet spy? Soon I must leave . . .'

'In that, I cannot help you.'

And although Schellenberg never believed it, Masson spoke the truth. He hadn't a cat's idea in hell as to the true identity of Woodpecker.

In Jerusalem, Sergeant Mulligan drove Carson back to the barracks at high speed through the darkened streets. The jeep did not slacken pace at corners. To Carson they seemed to skid round them on two wheels.

'You always drive like this?' he asked mildly.

'At night, yes. You don't want a grenade lobbed at us, do you? Corners are dangerous.'

'As bad as that?'

'Worse. Here we are, thank God.'

Mulligan's first action at two in the morning was to put out a full alert for Victor Vlacek. He had a complete description, obtained from Harrington in Cairo. Slamming down the 'phone, he looked across the table at Carson who was looking round the bare room.

'I can't guarantee anything,' he warned. 'He could slip over the border into Syria just like that. They'll warn the Free French, but why should they care?'

'Indeed, why should they?' Carson agreed wearily.

Vlacek was, in fact, never seen again. It was assumed he had crossed into Syria. From there he could so easily have travelled north, crossed the long Turkish frontier and made his way into the Soviet republic of Armenia.

As dawn cast its first ominous light over Palestine, the man called Moshe – who many years later occupied a high position in the Israeli government – was in position concealed behind a cluster of rocks above the road from Lydda to Palestine. He adjusted his field-glasses, and Lydda Airport jumped forward in the twin lenses. Moshe settled down for a long wait. This was the day.

Chapter Forty-One

Squadron-Leader Murray-Smith, a small, compact man who sported a small, dark, neat moustache sat behind the controls as he flew the Dakota across the Mediterranean towards Jugoslavia. A conceited bastard – in the opinion of his colleagues – he was also endowed with guts.

At Benina airfield in Libya he had sprung his decision in the mess at the last moment. Normally, an officer of his rank would not have undertaken the mission.

'Is that wise?' the station commander had enquired.

'And who is interested in your wisdom?' Murray-Smith had rapped back. 'I'm in charge of this show. I'm taking the Dak myself,' he repeated. 'God knows they've been trying to get this poor swine, Lindsay, out of the shit long enough.'

'It's your decision.'

'Nice to know you've grasped the situation so rapidly.

Conway can be my co-pilot. All right, Conway? Happy? Then smile, blast you.'

'Whisky' Conway, nick-named for an obvious liking, had been anything but happy and suspected he had been chosen out of sheer malice. Murray-Smith had recently overheard himself referred to in one of Conway's more inebriated moments as 'that pocket Führer'.

As the plane flew on at ten thousand feet Conway, acting as map-reader, had a large-scale map spread out over his lap. He didn't know it but this was the reason Murray-Smith had press-ganged him into the job; he was probably the most brilliant navigator between Algiers and Cairo.

'Looks as though the Met stupes got it right for once,' remarked Murray-Smith. 'Sheer bloody fluke, of course . . .'

The sky was an empty sea of pale blue without a wisp of cloud in sight. Below them the Med was another equally deserted and calm sea of deeper blue. Murray-Smith checked his watch. He never trusted the flaming instrument panel when there were alternative aids at his disposal. He was a terror with the ground staff.

'I have to pilot this flying coffin,' was his favourite phrase. 'You keep both bloody feet safely on *terra firma*, Corporal,' he had told the mechanic before take-off. 'One screw loose, up here . . .' He had tapped his head. '. . . Or inside here . . .' He had slapped his hand against the fuselage. '. . . And I'm a goner.'

Oh, Squadron-Leader Murray-Smith was the cherry on the cake in his world. People ran when they saw him coming – in the opposite direction.

'Be there in sixty min. Agreed, Conway?' he asked as he banked the machine a sliver to maintain course.

'Sixty minutes, sir, and we land in The Cauldron . . .'

'Heljec, or whatever your bloody name is, here we come!' Murray-Smith shouted. 'We've got the guns, you've got the man, so no frigging about . . .'

Oh, Christ, thought Conway, he's enjoying himself.

Hartmann and Paco had walked slowly along the full length of the makeshift airstrip, followed by a rebellious Heljec while they examined every inch of the ground. The German had imposed his personality on the Partisan leader, stopping every now and again to insist on the removal of a rock projecting a few centimetres above the surface. Paco acted as interpreter. Afterwards the defective patch had to be filled in with grit and hard-packed soil from a large wicker basket two Partisans carried.

'No wonder they never get anywhere in this benighted country,' Hartmann grumbled. 'Sloppy. I'm sorry, I'm talking about your home . . .'

'I'm half-English,' she reminded him. 'And I don't think I'm going to want to come back here. Ever. I can't get out of my mind what the Amazon Brigade did.'

'Go and cheer up Lindsay . . .'

'When we've finished this job. The plane should be here soon. It's nearly eleven o'clock.'

Lindsay, aware that Hartmann was doing the job he should have attended to, sat on a rock feeling exhausted. The glandular fever was sapping him again. He cursed the timing. Dr Macek appeared from behind a boulder and felt his forehead.

'We are not feeling in love with the world?' he enquired.

'Not too bad. I should be over there, with Hartmann and Paco.'

'No temperature. A period of convalescence is needed. It is good that the plane is coming after so many months . . .'

'I want to thank you for all you have done . . .'

'But it is my profession. Thank me by resting when you arrive at your destination. Maybe we shall meet again one day.'

'Somehow I don't think so . . .'

Macek nodded, a smile on his gentle face, and walked away. The whole plateau was deserted in the brilliant morning light apart from the group checking and putting finishing touches to the airstrip. Heljec had cleared the plateau of men and weapons, concentrating them on the rim at the head of ravines – inside the ravines – leading up to the plateau. He was convinced he had sealed off all approaches to his temporary stronghold.

Lindsay made the effort, forced himself up off the rock and trod step by dragging step towards the airstrip. He used the stick Milic had fashioned for him. Poor Milic, killed in the German mortar attack a hundred years ago. Milic who was never mentioned, whose existence most of the Partisans had forgotten.

'How's it going, Hartmann?' he called out. 'Plane's due soon now, isn't it?'

'The airstrip is level, my friend,' the German replied. 'As level as it ever will be. And yes, the Dakota should arrive any moment if it's on time.'

'If it ever finds us, you mean.'

'Surely you have faith in the RAF?' Hartmann spoke jocularly, realizing what the walk was costing Lindsay. He deliberately made no attempt to help the Englishman: Lindsay wouldn't welcome being treated as a cripple. 'He will come in from the south, so that is the direction we should watch . . .'

'I'm as nervous as a girl about to have her first baby,' Paco said. 'Isn't it ridiculous?'

'We're all a bit on edge,' Lindsay reassured her as he halted and lifted a hand to scan the sky.

Was it old instincts returning? A throwback to the days when, behind the controls of a Spitfire over the glorious green fields of Kent, he had learned to look everywhere. Constantly . . .

He looked to the south, as Hartmann had suggested, then continued searching the sky slowly in a three-sixty degree radius. Not a cloud anywhere. Incredible after yesterday's snow. The jagged peaks of mountains silhouetted against the blue. Nothing to the east. East-north-east. Nothing. He turned slowly, circumscribing the points of the compass. He had always been noted for his exceptional far-sighted vision. Soon he would be facing due north. He turned through a few more degrees. *Oh, my God! No!*

'All aboard for the Clipper! See it coming over that ridge – there, to the south . . .'

It was Reader joining them with his transceiver carried inside his back-pack. He had been to the high point of the plateau, attempting a last-minute contact. The elevation had given him the first sighting of the approaching Dakota.

'Look to the north, you stupid sods!' shouted Lindsay. 'The Germans are coming – a whole armada of troop transports . . .'

Aboard the Dakota Conway was hammering his clenched fish on his lap with excitement. He smashed a hole in the map.

'There's the plateau! There's the marker – the Communist star, five-pointed, laid out with rocks. God, there's not a helluva lot of margin for error . . .'

'Calm down, man,' Murray-Smith reprimanded. 'I can land this on a bee's bum . . .'

'And that's about what it is!'

Conway snatched up a pair of field-glasses and focused on the tiny figures staring up towards the Dakota. One of them waved a stick with one hand, elevated the other in the thumbs up sign. Then he began gesturing madly with the stick.

'I think that's Lindsay down there, the one with the stick. He's waving the thing about like a lunatic. Understandable, I suppose . . .'

'Considering the whole bloody Luftwaffe is coming in from the north, it is understandable,' said Murray-Smith in a tone of biting sarcasm. 'We're much closer, we might just make it . . .'

'God Almighty . . .!'

For the first time Conway saw what Murray-Smith had spotted seconds earlier. A fleet of dark blips growing larger as he watched them. Jerry troop transports. At a fairish height. Well spread out and stepped in layers, no one aircraft above another.

'A parachute drop is my bet,' said Murray-Smith. 'A major operation. Down we go. Let's just hope they've dug all the

439

rocks out of that airstrip. We'll know soon enough, won't we?'

Jaeger, with Schmidt alongside, equipped with their chutes ready for the drop, sat in the command plane. The flight from Zagreb had been uneventful, the first off-key occurrence being when Colonel Stoerner, the paratroop commander, had been urgently summoned to go and see the pilot.

'We must be bloody near the target,' said Schmidt. 'And I'm sweating . . .'

'Who isn't?'

The paratroopers sat in two rows, facing each other along the full length of the aircraft. The drop controller stood by the door now. Jaeger glanced along the rows of faces frozen in rigidity, beads of perspiration on their foreheads. No one was speaking. Jaeger could *smell* the tension, the raw fear.

The men stared straight ahead. Unnaturally still. The only sound the steady purr of the plane's motors, the creak of a harness. It never got any easier with each drop. With every operation there was a ten per cent ratio of nervous breakdowns. Among those who did survive.

'Funny,' Schmidt whispered, 'our last time was Maleme airfield in Crete. I can't even recall which year that was. I can't think . . .'

Jaeger looked up as Stoerner came back from the pilot's cabin and grasped his arm. A bullet-headed veteran, he looked odd; he had hardly any eye-lashes. He tugged at Jaeger's arm.

'A word with you. Up front . . .'

Which meant a crisis had arisen before the operation had even started. Jaeger puzzled over possibilities as he followed the paratrooper down the centre of the aircraft. An hour earlier a small plane had flown towards the target, keeping well clear of the plateau. The pilot had reported back that the Partisans were still in position. So . . .

He entered the cabin, crouching to ease his parachute through the narrow opening. Stoerner, able – but impetuous – in Jaeger's opinion, closed the door. He pointed ahead with a stubby finger. Jaeger could see the Dakota clearly.

'We're just in time,' Stoerner said throatily. 'Watch that English pilot run for it . . .'

'He isn't going to,' Jaeger replied. 'He's landing – he's got guts . . .'

'He's a maniac!' Stoerner stared ahead. 'He hasn't the time . . .'

'Don't count on it. I'm going back. Send me out of the aircraft first. Then Schmidt and the rest.'

'You want to be brave? Be brave . . .'

Stoerner made a gesture as much as to say you wish to commit suicide it's O.K. by me. The gesture was wasted. Jaeger had left the cabin. This time he did not return to his seat. He waved to Schmidt to join him and stood by the drop controller.

The red light was on. Jaeger attached his snap catch to the overhead wire as the door was opened. A blast of chilly air dispersed the sweat-laden atmosphere inside the fuselage within seconds. Schmidt attached his own snap catch.

'Trouble?' he asked, his mouth close to Jaeger's ear.

'The British are taking Lindsay out. At this very moment a Dakota is landing on top of the plateau. It will all hinge on minutes. When we hit the ground shoot up the Dakota – stop it taking off. That's the first priority.'

As he spoke Jaeger double-checked his machine-pistol. Satisfied that it was in working order, he took off the magazine and thrust the weapon, butt first, into the breast of his jacket.

There was a stirring of systematic activity inside the aircraft as men made their way to join the queue. The usual mix of relief and apprehension on their faces, Jaeger noted. Relief that the waiting period was over. Apprehension as to what was going to greet them on the plateau – if their 'chutes opened. Stoerner had earlier told Jaeger that over half of them had only made one practice drop. Germany was running out of time – and trained men. Jaeger waited for the green light.

'A bee's bum it is,' Squadron-Leader Murray-Smith said cheerfully as the plateau rushed up to meet them.

'God! They were told the minimum length,' Conway gasped.

The landing wheels touched down, bumped, the wingtips hardly wobbled. Murray-Smith slowed the machine at the extreme limits of safety. He pouched his lower lip, a sign of intense concentration as the Dakota swept on towards the northern rim where the plateau fell into eternity.

He had almost stopped when he performed a manoeuvre that almost gave Conway a nervous breakdown. He circled the machine through one hundred and eighty degrees, ending up on the airstrip – facing south, ready for immediate takeoff. Against all regulations he did not switch off the engines.

'Open the cargo door,' he snapped at Conway. 'We've got to get this gang of Wogs moving.'

He opened the cabin door and jumped to the ground, an absurdly small figure among the Partisans crowding towards him. He spotted the man limping forward with a stick, the stained and worn RAF jacket, the smashing blonde by his side.

'Lindsay?'

'Yes. I . . .'

'Which wallah is in charge of this show?'

'Heljec here. Paco can interpret for you . . .'

'No time for flaming interpreters. They'll understand me. Just watch . . .'

'They won't let me board the plane till they have the guns and ammo . . .'

'Won't they, by God! We'll see about that . . .'

He ran to the cargo door where Conway had already lowered several wooden boxes with rope handles into the hands of the waiting Partisans. Flicking open the catches on one box, he threw back the lid, gathered up a random collection of sten guns and thrust them into Heljec's arms. Grabbing hold of Lindsay with one hand he gestured into the aircraft with a stabbing thumb, talking non-stop to Heljec.

'You've got your bloody guns! I've risked my life to bring

442

you this frigging lot! Lindsay goes aboard now! In case you haven't noticed, you've got visitors – not the sort I'd ask to my mess . . .'

He was miming madly. Pointing to the aircraft. Making more stabbing gestures towards the Luftwaffe armada which was almost on top of the plateau, shouting at Heljec as though he were dressing down some useless mechanic.

It was comic, if the situation hadn't been so desperate. The small man standing up to the six foot two Heljec. And he had been right, he needed no interpreter. Heljec stared at him in amazement, then began distributing the sten guns and magazines.

'Well, get aboard, for Christ's sake!' Murray-Smith told Lindsay. 'Conway, give him a hand – he's got a gammy leg. Expect me to do every flaming thing? As usual . . .'

The exchange took place very rapidly. The cargo hold was emptied. Lindsay was hauled aboard, Conway helping from above, Hartmann from below. Next the German hoisted Paco aboard and Reader climbed inside by himself.

'What about Hartmann?' Paco snapped.

She reached down and helped him inside. Conway closed the door as Murray-Smith appeared from the direction of the cabin. His manner was abrupt and urgent.

'Come on through here! We've got seats. This isn't one of those Yank Liberators where you roll about like peas out of a pod. Sit down in the bloody seats! Strap yourselves in with the bloody belts! This is going to be a rough takeoff – a very rough takeoff. Turbulence won't be the word for it . . .'

'And turbulence isn't the word for you, mate,' Reader said as he sagged into a seat.

He was talking into a void. Murray-Smith was already back in his cabin, seated behind the controls. He peered out at the umbrella-like objects blossoming above in increasing numbers.

'Here they come, Conway. Whole flaming army of them. Time we used our return ticket . . .'

The Dakota seemed to commence take-off with incredible slowness as Paco watched from her window seat. They were

443

crawling when she saw the first German land, roll over, detach himself from his harness and crouch, aiming his machine-pistol.

'Oh, my God, Lindsay . . .!'

She clearly recognized Jaeger. He was aiming the muzzle of his weapon at the pilot's cabin. More paratroopers landed. Heljec, armed with one of the new stens, rose up from behind a rock and fired half a magazine in one lethal burst.

Jaeger was pushed forward by the shock of the bullets, his face distorted with agony. What does a man think in his last moments? *Dear Magda, We've had a marvellous life . . .* He was dead before his body hit the ground. Paco felt physically sick. A vivid image came into her mind. The Four Seasons Hotel in Munich. Dining with Jaeger, so smart in his uniform, so courteous, so . . . Oh, hell!

The aircraft picked up speed as Murray-Smith, looking neither to right nor left, headed for take-off. He could hear above the engines the rattle of machine-pistol fire, the spatter of bullets entering the fuselage, the *crack!* of grenades detonating. He ignored it all.

Lindsay saw the so familiar figure of gentle Dr Macek rise up behind a rock, holding something as though about to hurl it. A burst of rapid fire threw him backwards out of sight. Lindsay had no doubt Macek had just died.

'They just got Macek,' he said to Paco who was sitting beside him. 'Poor sod . . .'

'Christ, what is it all about?'

'I've been wondering that ever since I first flew to Berchtesgaden,' Lindsay replied.

After months of pain, endless trudging and ever-present fear in the winter of the Balkans, their first sight of North Africa was unforgettable. Peering from the windows of the Dakota, the warm ochre of the flat Libyan desert spread out to the horizon.

Still over the intense blue of the Med, they saw the white ribbon of surf separating sea from shore. The plane began its descent. Ten minutes later Murray-Smith touched down at

444

Benina. The door was opened by Conway and glorious heat flooded inside the machine.

'Half an hour's wait here while we refuel,' Conway told them. 'You have to disembark so you can stretch your legs but don't wander out of sight of the plane. Dr Macleod is waiting for anyone who requires medical attention . . .'

'I'd like to thank the pilot,' said Lindsay.

'Wouldn't advise that, Wing Commander, if I may say so. He's a bit of a character, is Squadron-Leader Murray-Smith. Never can tell how he's going to react. In any case, a fresh pilot is taking you on to your final destination.'

'Which is?'

'Haven't a clue. Sorry, sir . . .'

They strolled about in the glowing heat with an odd sense of disorientation. Lindsay decided it was caused by the feeling of vast space after the claustrophobic atmosphere of Bosnia. He also decided it was time to extract information from Reader. Paco and Hartmann followed him.

'I believe I outrank you, Major Reader,' Lindsay began. 'I wouldn't normally give a tinker's cuss on that score but now I need to know. What *is* our destination? Cairo? Tunis?'

'Lydda, Palestine . . .'

'That's crazy . . .' Lindsay's tone expressed sheer disbelief.

'Could we have a little chat on our own? Maybe stroll over to the airfield building in case you'd like to take the weight off your feet . . .'

Lindsay made his apologies to Paco and Hartmann and headed away from the building. He was soaking up the heat like a sponge after the chilling cold of Jugoslavia. When they were out of hearing he stopped and faced Reader.

'How much do you know? I want all of it. Something smells rotten. We're flying in the wrong direction – my destination is London.'

'The planes for London fly from Cairo West.'

'Crazier still! Why fly me to Lydda first?'

'Security I understand. And someone is waiting for you at Lydda, a chap flown out specially from London. So you are enjoying five-star treatment.'

'What chap?'

'A Peter Standish . . .' Reader hesitated. 'You'll meet him by the end of the day so I may as well tell you. Standish is a cover name. I'm talking about Tim Whelby.'

'I see.'

Lindsay started his dot-and-carry tread across the hard rock of the desert. You couldn't see Benghazi at all – it was over the far side of a low ridge, on the edge of the sea. Nothing but desert and heat dazzle and one building and one Dakota and a fuel truck alongside. He heard Reader following him, then quicken his pace to catch up.

'So,' Reader said, 'you've had a minute to think about it – I'd appreciate hearing what's wrong. Tim Whelby is harmless enough. Never going to set the world on fire, likes to keep on the right side of everybody . . .'

'Oh, you've spotted that intriguing trait?'

'Intriguing?'

'Have you ever noticed . . .' Lindsay continued walking while he talked – he was feeling better than he had for months – '. . . that he takes great pains to get on with the Indians *and* the university crowd?'

The 'Indians' were those members of SIS recruited from the Indian Civil Service. They tended to be hard-nosed men, wedded to tradition, inflexible where change was concerned but loyal to the Crown.

The 'university' men were dons from Oxford, intellectuals who approached every problem with an open mind. They formed a second clique, apart from the traditionalists. You belonged to one club or the other. It was rare for a man to span both worlds.

'Well,' Reader agreed, 'come to think of it, I suppose you are right. Isn't that one up to Whelby?'

'Another thing – I always got the feeling he was acting a part, that no one ever met the real man . . .'

'I can't change the route now. It's all laid on.'

'Laid on by who?'

'Whelby, I suppose . . .' Reader gave way to a burst of irritation. 'Damnit, I've been out of touch, marooned in

446

bloody Jugoslavia like you. Take it up with Whelby – when we get to Lydda. If anyone is after your hide – if that's what's bothering you – who's going to dream of your turning up at a one-eyed dump like Lydda?'

'Whelby.'

When they boarded the Dakota for the second leg of their flight Lindsay was surprised. He had chosen a window seat by himself, expecting Paco to sit with Reader. She sat in the adjoining seat next to him without a word and proceeded to fasten her seat belt.

'You're not bored with my company I hope?' she murmured as the new pilot taxied for take-off. 'I can always move, there's any amount of room . . .'

'No, you're welcome. I had thought . . .'

'That I'd choose Len Reader as a travelling companion? I can see the answer in your expression. You still haven't caught on, have you?'

'Am I being a bit slow . . .?'

He was still unsure of himself where women were concerned. A rebuff was something he always feared. He might have shot down six Germans over Kent and the Channel but in some ways he was still immature, shy of coming out of his shell.

'*Yes!*' Her voice was low, vehement. 'You are just a little bit slow and a girl doesn't like to have to make all the running . . .'

'But you said . . .'

'I know what I said back in Jugoslavia – but what chance did there seem to be that any of us would ever get out alive? And I said also that I was suspicious of Reader. I *was*. I wanted to be sure we hadn't a dummy slipped in amongst us . . .'

'A dummy?'

'A German masquerading as an Englishman, for Christ's sake. It's a technique they've used before – with hellish consequences. Remember I was educated in England, so I know quite a lot about the place. I used every bit of knowledge I could drag back to test Reader, to try and catch him

447

out. The easiest way for a girl to test a man is to pretend to be keen on him – in the hope that he'll let down his defences. God, Lindsay, sometimes I think you're thick . . .'

She slipped her small hand over his, just resting it there. He jerked his head round and stared at her. She had that marvellous half-smile on her face. Her greenish eyes, half-closed, were smiling, too. She rested her head on his shoulder.

'Oh, Lindsay, Lindsay, you stupid man . . .'

'Bloody thick,' he agreed. 'Thick as three pit-props . . .'

He was choked with emotion, found it difficult to form the words. He took her hand, it really seemed so very small, and squeezed it as he swallowed. She understood.

'Lindsay, will you take me to London? I want to see the Green Park again . . .'

'Green Park, just Green Park . . .'

'They have those big birds by the pool, the funny ones with great pouches . . .'

'Pelicans. That's St James's Park. I'll show you the whole of London. Then we'll go out into the countryside . . .'

'I'd like that.' She turned her head on his shoulder and her hair brushed his cheek. 'I know a little village in Surrey, near Guildford. All huddled down in the folds of the hills . . .'

'Peaslake?'

'You know it, too!' She sat up and her face glowed. 'Oh, this is wonderful. I'm never going back to Jugoslavia. I've got dual nationality, you know – a British passport . . .'

'I didn't know – you never told me. It will make things so much easier. Haven't you got any people back in Jugoslavia?'

'No ties. I'm an only child – so after both my parents were killed in the Belgrade bombing I was completely on my own.' She slipped her arm inside his. 'I'm not going to let you out of my sight until we get to London. Does that make me a forward hussy? I don't care. I don't care . . .!'

For that short time, as the Dakota droned steadily on towards Palestine, they must have been very happy. Across the gangway in the window seat Reader, who had exceptionally acute hearing, listened to most of their conversation without wishing to.

He kept his eyes turned towards the window, gazing at the sea they crossed for most of the flight. He was convinced that neither Lindsay nor Paco had any idea they were over the Med. As she repeated *I don't care . . .!* Paco clasped her free hand over her mouth.

'God, was I shouting? The whole aircraft must have heard . . .'

'You were. It must have done. And I don't care either. One thing, we may not travel together all the way until we arrive in London . . .'

'And why not?'

'Security. I have a job to complete. Which reminds me – I'd like a quick word with Reader over there. Won't be long – and don't get up. I can squeeze past . . .' He put a hand on her leg to support himself and held it there for a moment.

Settling himself in the seat next to Reader, he turned away from Paco so she couldn't catch even a snatch of his conversation with the Intelligence Major. He took out the leather-bound diary from his pocket.

'This is strictly between you and me, Reader. This diary is vital. The information is what I'm carrying inside my head – so if my head never reaches London I need a safe place for the diary. Otherwise everything that's happened becomes pointless. That I wouldn't like . . .'

'What exactly are you asking me to do?'

'You're not fireproof either. Do you know someone in Palestine you can trust, really trust – someone you could deposit this diary with until I send for it?'

'Only a civilian. Chap called Stein. He's a diamond broker. Their careers hinge on their integrity. And he's not mixed up with any of the Jewish gangs. You could trust him with your life . . .'

'Maybe that's how it's going to turn out . . .'

Leaving Reader, he was standing in the gangway when Hartmann approached him. The German asked if they could have a quiet word together. They chose two isolated seats and

449

Hartmann began speaking in English.

'Now we are over Allied territory I can reveal my secret.
I've been sent on a special mission by Admiral Canaris, chief
of the Abwehr as you know. He instructed me to escape from
Germany – which is why I seized on the opportunity to follow
you. Rather a nerve-racking business. I had to fool so many
people – Gruber, Jaeger, Schmidt, Maisel – the most dangerous adversary. And, of course, Bormann himself . . .'

'I always sensed there was something odd about you . . .'

'I thought you did,' Hartmann commented. 'I know the
names of the entire anti-Nazi opposition. We tried to pass on
our peace proposals to Allied agents in Spain but someone
road-blocked us. A man called Whelby was in charge . . .'

'I know him,' Lindsay replied and left it at that.

'I have to be escorted safely through to London. In return
for assassinating Hitler and establishing a civilian, non-Nazi
government we are prepared to negotiate a peace settlement.
I can only give you names after I have arrived in London.
Until then I ask that you alone should know about this
matter . . .'

'That is your only passport to safety,' Lindsay told him.

It was still daylight when Moshe, crouched behind the rocks
overlooking Lydda airfield, first spotted the Dakota coming
in to land. He was aching in every limb from his long vigil but
he possessed quite abnormal powers of endurance.

In the canvas satchel by his side was his water-bottle, his
few remaining cheese sandwiches and a pair of night-glasses.
Dusk would soon spread its dark pall over the silent land and
he had no way of knowing whether the aircraft bringing
Lindsay might arrive after dark.

He adjusted the binoculars looped round his neck and
focused them on the grassy runway. The Dakota flew straight
in, touched down and reduced speed as it headed for the
reception building. Moshe knew that on the far side of the
building beyond his view were parked a staff car and an
armoured vehicle.

The man who had been pointed out to him by Vlacek in

Jerusalem as Tim Whelby strolled towards the aircraft, hat-less and wearing only a tropical drill suit despite the chill of the evening. Moshe locked his lenses on Whelby, waiting for the signal which would identify Wing Commander Lindsay for him.

A metal ladder was placed against the side of the machine by one of the ground staff. Two British soldiers armed with sten guns began patrolling the area round the Dakota. A man appeared at the top of the ladder, a man holding a stick.

Moshe pressed the glasses hard against his eyes as the passenger slowly descended the ladder rung by rung. Reaching the ground, he turned and in the twin lenses Moshe saw his face close up. No doubt about it. This was Lindsay! Then Moshe got his final confirmation of the RAF man's identity.

As Whelby shook hands with Lindsay he casually reached up with his left hand and gripped the lobe of his ear, the signal Vlacek had arranged. Other people were emerging from the aircraft. To Moshe's surprise one of them was a blonde-haired girl – followed in rapid succession by two other men.

Moshe continued his watch. He wanted to observe the system of protection employed, because when Lindsay re-turned from Jerusalem to fly on to Cairo they would un-doubtedly employ the same technique. It was this British habit of clinging to routine which had been the death of them – literally – on so many other occasions.

Chapter Forty-Two

'My dear chap, welcome back to civilization after all these months . . .' Whelby extended his hand, shaking Lindsay's as he fingered the lobe of his left ear. 'I must s-s-say you look a bit p-p-peaky.' He lowered his voice. 'I'm known to the locals as Peter Standish . . .'

'What brings you out here?' asked Lindsay, his expression unsmiling.

'To escort you home, of course.'

'To London, you mean?'

'That's right.'

'By what route?'

'Well, if you must know now.'

'I must.'

'Back to Cairo in a couple of days, after you've rested up. Then on to dear old London . . .'

A uniformed sergeant of the Palestine Police had joined them and was showing obvious signs of restlessness. He butted in on the conversation, ignoring Whelby, addressing Lindsay.

'Excuse me, my chaps are getting a bit trigger happy. We're exposed standing about here – and I'd like to get you safely to Jerusalem before nightfall . . .'

'Sergeant Mulligan – Wing Commander Lindsay,' Whelby introduced. 'I suppose you're transporting us to the Hotel Sharon in that old tin can . . .'

'Better not let Corporal Wilson hear you,' Mulligan snapped. 'Last time you referred to it as "that iron monster". Now it's become an old tin can. Maybe you'd like to know Wilson has survived three bomb attacks and has grown rather fond of his mode of transport. There are five of you, so four of you travel in the back, two on the flap seats. I'll be driving.'

'I don't mind sitting beside you, Sergeant,' Paco offered.

'Much as I'd enjoy the pleasure of your company you're taking a back seat, if you'll pardon the phraseology. The front passenger is the dead man's seat. You've just entered a war zone.'

'I've just left one,' Paco replied pleasantly.

'So,' Mulligan informed her, 'you're entitled to all the safety you can get. Now, Mr Standish, I'm sure you won't blench at the idea of sitting alongside me? Shall we go . . .?'

Lindsay was beginning to get the distinct impression that Standish was not Sergeant Mulligan's favourite person. Interesting in view of his own feelings.

Moshe watched the convoy leave the airfield and turn onto the curving road which climbed the hillside leading to Jerusalem. The armoured car first. The trail-blazer in case the road had been mined.

One hundred metres behind, the staff car followed. All five passengers aboard. The Palestine Police sergeant driving at a pace which maintained the gap. Headlights on because dusk was falling. Moshe had switched to his night glasses.

One hundred metres behind the staff car, two British Army motor-cyclists protecting the rear. They could prove to be a bit of a problem. Behind them at a reasonable distance a vegetable truck took the road to Jerusalem. The driver would check the convoy's route and report later to Moshe. Halfway to the city at a turn-off the vegetable truck would disappear – to be replaced by a grocery van – driven by another member of the Stern Gang. Moshe stood up, hoisted the pack on his back and walked to the spot where he had hidden his own motor-cycle.

They were driven to the barracks. There had been a brief confrontation about their destination before they left Lydda. It was Sergeant Mulligan who bluntly contradicted Whelby's idea of putting up at the Hotel Sharon.

'We've already had one murder there. The place is wide open. I can't guarantee anyone's safety.'

'Where would you suggest?' broke in Lindsay.

'Police barracks.' Mulligan had glanced at Paco. 'We can provide a separate room for the lady . . .'

'A hotel is a damned foolish suggestion, conditions being what they are here . . .'

It was Hartmann who had made the surprising intervention. He had been studying Whelby ever since they landed. Mulligan, who still didn't understand the German's presence, looked at him.

'How do you know about conditions out here?'

'We have our sources . . .' Hartmann left it at that.

'The barracks it is,' Lindsay had said decisively. He saw no reason even to consult Whelby over the decision. The man from London had merely shrugged. Better not to press the point.

Inside the barracks they met Jock Carson who didn't ask them a single question – he could see the new arrivals were tired out after their long trip. They had a meal together, eating in silence, leaving half the food on their plates. Fatigue and the long months of short rations had contracted their stomachs. They dropped into their beds – another experience their bodies were not used to – and after tossing and turning for a while fell into a deep sleep from sheer exhaustion.

The following morning after breakfast Lindsay took Reader aside. To avoid being overheard they walked in the enclosed parade ground. Surrounded by two-storey buildings, they relaxed in the novel feeling of being safe once again.

'This Stein chap,' Lindsay began. 'Could we see him today? I want to off-load this diary. Mulligan says we take off for Cairo tomorrow . . .'

'I was stationed in Jerusalem two years ago for a few months,' replied Reader, 'so I know the place. Stein's office is only a short walk from the barracks. Mulligan's preoccupied with organizing tomorrow's flight. We might slip past the guard-post now . . .'

'Let's get on with it.'

'Leave me to do the talking. I know how these chaps react . . .'

It proved surprisingly easy. Reader marched into the office alongside the exit barrier, his manner confident and firm. He already held his Army paybook showing his rank as Major, arm of service Intelligence – in his hand.

'We're going out to keep an appointment,' Reader said briskly to the guard sitting behind a desk. 'Urgent Army business. I expect we'll be back within an hour, two at the most.'

They waited while the guard laboriously copied their names in a ruled register. Their ranks. Time of leaving the barracks. Then he gestured to the guard outside who raised the pole.

'Isn't their security a bit lax?' Lindsay commented as they walked away from the barracks.

'We were *going out*,' Reader explained. 'So we must have been checked in properly earlier. *Entering* that place is a different kettle of fish altogether . . .'

'Mulligan will go spare if he finds out . . .'

'Let's hope we get back before he even knows we're gone . . .'

Aaron Stein's office was on the first floor of an old stone, two-storey building in a side street. There was no indication on the door outside of who occupied the place. In response to Reader's rapping on the panels a Judas window was opened in the door, a pair of dark, shrewd eyes stared out and then Lindsay realized how much security Stein employed.

He counted eight locks and bolts being unfastened before the door swung open. The same performance was repeated after they were inside. Stein's appearance surprised Lindsay. He didn't look a day over twenty. His complexion was smooth and pale, his hair dark, he was of average height and heavy build.

'Aaron, this is Wing Commander Lindsay,' Reader introduced. 'He wants to leave something in your safekeeping. I can vouch for him personally.'

Lindsay was careful to extend his hand quickly. Aaron Stein shook it with old world formality, his dark eyes studying his visitor. He seemed satisfied with what he saw.

'I am pleased to meet you, Wing Commander. This way, please, to my office.'

Inside the office a second youngster was standing waiting for them. Again Lindsay shook hands as Aaron made introductions.

'This is my brother, David. No matter how confidential your business you may talk freely in front of him. We are partners. Also, it is a precaution in your own interests. In case something happens to me.'

'I hope not . . .' Lindsay began.

Aaron made a deprecating gesture with his hand. As he spoke he ushered them to chairs. David Stein looked remarkably like his brother. One could easily be mistaken for the other. Lindsay thought for a brief moment of the scene he had witnessed when he had first arrived at the Berghof. The second Adolf Hitler practising gestures and speech, reflected a dozen times in the circle of mirrors. They said every man had his double somewhere . . .

'These are dangerous times,' Aaron explained. 'My brother and I fled from Roumania when Antonescu and the Iron Guard took power. The Roumanian version of the Nazis . . .'

'My brother is talking about the local situation when he speaks of danger,' David interjected. 'We believe in a homeland for the Jewish people but we do not believe in violence . . .'

'We left Roumania for that reason,' Aaron continued. 'We do not like the Irgun Zvai Leumi, the Stern Gang . . .'

'Or even the Haganah – the Jewish Home Army,' David interjected. 'We are not liked by many of our own people because we reject violence. After the war, when Germany has lost, we may go to Antwerp – or even London . . .'

'Just so long as Russia does not win,' broke in Aaron. 'That is the terrible danger . . .'

The words poured out from both brothers. Lindsay had the impression they were glad to be able to speak freely, that normally they had to watch every word they said. Aaron made an apologetic gesture.

'We talk too much of ourselves. What can we do for you, Wing Commander?'

Lindsay showed them the diary and asked for a stout envelope. Aaron produced a very thick envelope of the type used by lawyers. Lindsay sat down at a side table, put the diary inside and sealed the envelope. Borrowing a fountain pen, he thought for a few minutes. Then he wrote with careful legibility.

Account of my visit to the Third Reich in the year 1943 and my subsequent sojourn in Jugoslavia. In the event of my death to be handed to Lieutenant Jock Carson, Section 3, Grey Pillars, Cairo, Egypt. Ian Lindsay, Wing Commander.

He handed the envelope to Aaron, returned the pen to David and sighed. He felt as though a great weight had been lifted from his shoulders.

'I will keep this in our safe,' said Aaron. 'Is that acceptable? Good. I see from the wording that you also feel we live in dangerous times, even here . . .'

'Thank you, that will be fine. Incidentally, could you give me something so if I write, asking you to hand that envelope to a courier, you will know the request does come from me?'

'My business card? I will draw on it the Star of David . . .'

'Good idea . . .' Lindsay fitted the card inside his wallet. 'If I write you a letter, as an added safeguard, I will make brief reference to the blue fountain pen I used when writing on your envelope . . .'

Aaron was already turning the combination on the lock of the wall-safe. Opening the door, he held up the envelope and stood aside so Lindsay could watch him place it inside. He closed the door, revolved the combination with a random twist.

'Thank you very much,' said Lindsay.

He shook hands with both brothers who regarded him closely, with a certain sadness Reader thought. Nothing more was said as they left the office. Lindsay paused in the passage. They could hear Aaron turning the locks, shooting the bolts back into place. He smiled wryly at Reader.

'There was something awfully final about that envelope going into the safe. Come on – back to the barracks . . .'

Chapter Forty-Three

They left the barracks the following morning to drive back to Lydda Airport where the Dakota was waiting to fly them on to Cairo. The convoy was assembled in the compound. First the armoured car, Corporal Wilson perched in his turret.

Behind waited the staff car which Sergeant Mulligan would

again drive. The time of departure had been advanced at the last minute by one hour so there was a last-minute rush.

The two motor-cyclists who would bring up the rear waited behind the staff car. The riders smoked a final cigarette in the morning sun. It was going to be another beautiful crisp day.

There had been an argument, almost a stand-up verbal confrontation, between Mulligan and Whelby. Standing in Mulligan's office, hands tucked inside his jacket pockets with his thumbs protruding, he was stubborn as a mule.

'As you know, Sergeant, I've phoned Cairo. I'm expecting an urgent reply from London via Grey Pillars. I must wait for that call to come through, so I'll catch you up. I need transport and a driver. Now don't fuss, I'll be there in time for the plane to take off. You don't make all that speed with an armoured car in the convoy . . .'

'You'll get a jeep – an open jeep with no protection,' Reader had snapped. 'It's all the transport I can spare. And a driver . . .'

'A jeep will be fine. That way we're bound to catch you up . . .'

'Please yourself. The plane departs on schedule. It's not waiting for anyone – not even you . . .'

Whelby had waited in the office, watching the four passengers climb into the staff car. Lindsay, Paco, Reader and Hartmann in the back, two again on the flap seats. No one beside Mulligan in the 'dead man's' seat. He saw the armoured car trundle away through the exit.

There were other watchers. From windows in the buildings enclosing the compound, men off-duty stood staring as the convoy left. Officially no one except Mulligan and the participants in the convoy knew its destination. But the grapevine inside a barracks is sensitive. The staring faces were quite motionless and there was an air of depression.

After waiting for the hundred yard gap to open up, Mulligan drove the staff car forward. Whelby stood perfectly still, aware of the clerk sitting at a desk behind him. The staff car disappeared beyond the gateway and Whelby forced himself to maintain his cool stance.

The motor-cyclists had just left when a jeep drove at speed through the still-open gateway, braked savagely and turned a half-circle in the middle of the compound, sending up a cloud of dust. The driver dismounted and came over to where Whelby waited.

'Corporal Haskins reporting for duty. Mr Standish?'

'That's correct . . .'

The jeep Mulligan had summoned over the 'phone had arrived far more swiftly than Whelby had anticipated. He glanced towards the silent 'phone on the desk for effect.

'Ready when you are, sir!' the freckle-faced Haskins said cheerfully. 'And I know your destination.'

'Better take the weight off your feet, Corporal. Don't hesitate to smoke a cigarette while you wait. I'm hanging on for a call from Cairo.'

'That's good of you, sir,' Haskins replied and winked at the clerk as he sat down and took out his pack. Mulligan banned smoking anywhere in his vicinity. He thought Standish seemed a good sort, but this was always the impression Whelby created on subordinates. He was thinking of Vlacek's warning.

'Whatever you do, don't travel back with them to Lydda . . .'

'At last we're on our way to London,' said Paco joyfully. 'I can't wait to get there. I'm in seventh heaven . . .'

Her mood did something to lighten the rather quiet atmosphere inside the staff car. She occupied one of the rear seats facing Hartmann perched on a flap. Beside her Lindsay sat silent with Reader opposite. He was suffering from a mild relapse of the glandular fever. Hartmann put a hand towards his side pocket, withdrew it. The gesture was very familiar to Paco by now.

'Go on,' she encouraged him cheerfully. 'Light up your pipe.'

'There's not much air . . .'

'You are allowed one pipe before we get to Lydda. It's such a lovely morning . . .'

She lowered the window on her side. The sun was shining out of a clear blue sky. Not a cloud in sight. Hartmann smiled his gratitude, took out the pipe and began filling it . . .

'Where's Whelby?' Lindsay said suddenly.

He sat bolt upright. In the rush of their departure he had not realized the Englishman was missing. Alarm showed in his expression. He slid back the glass partition separating them from Mulligan and repeated the question.

'Following us in a jeep,' the sergeant called back laconically. 'Something about expecting a call from Cairo. Told him I'm not holding the flight so it's up to him . . .'

'I see . . .' Lindsay replied slowly.

'Stop fretting, do!'

Paco clasped her arm inside his and hugged him. Hartmann watched her with pleasure. She had never looked younger, her eyes sparkling, her manner displaying that extraordinary animation which had manifested itself ever since they had landed at Benina. He sucked contentedly at his pipe as the staff car began the long, winding descent to Lydda.

The nondescript civilian mending an apparent puncture to his cycle near the barracks had watched the staff car leave. He waited a few more minutes and then cycled off a short distance to a 'phone box. The number he asked for answered immediately.

'Danny here,' said the cyclist.

'Moshe speaking. Well?'

'The consignment is on its way.'

'Did they pack everything? Nothing missing?' Moshe asked.

'Nothing. I counted the items myself.'

'Good. So now you can arrange the next delivery . . .'

The cyclist put down the phone. The next delivery was planned for tomorrow. Danny would cycle back to his hideout and wait for the 'phone call the following morning, the call which would tell him where to pick up the secret hoard of guns – and that would only come when the news appeared in the papers and over the radio.

460

Inside an old house on the edge of the city close by the road to Lydda, Moshe hurried to his motor-cycle concealed in a shed. He had to hide the machine again after he arrived before he got into position.

In the turret of his armoured car Corporal Wilson's eyes were everywhere as his vehicle continued the descent. He was searching for the slightest sign of movement. The armoured car moved at the head of the convoy as protection against mines being laid in the road overnight. The weight of the vehicle would detonate any impact mine, guaranteeing safe passage for the staff car driving one hundred yards behind.

If the road were safe for the armoured car, then it was safe for the lighter-weight staff car. No other form of attack would be risked with the armoured car equipped with its machine-gun so close. The convoy proceeded on down the hill. Another two miles and they would reach Lydda Airport.

Moshe was concealed behind the same group of rocks he had used to watch the Dakota landing the previous day. But this time he was facing in the opposite direction, his field-glasses aimed uphill at a point where the road turned sharply.

Moshe considered himself a patriot. All that mattered was the establishment of the state of Israel. The British were enemies as were the Arabs. And the most valuable currency in his eyes to help buy them their homeland was guns. He would do anything to obtain more guns – whatever the source.

He saw the armoured car come into view, the soldier perched in his turret swivelling his head from side to side. Moshe froze. The armoured car continued on down the hill. The staff car came into view.

Through his powerful glasses Moshe was able to see the passengers inside the car. Lindsay was in the back close to the window on his wide. Beyond he had a glimpse of a girl with blonde hair. He mentally shrugged. How many Jewish girls had died in Europe?

Carefully removing his glasses which had been looped round his neck, he shoved them into his pocket. Without taking his eyes off the staff car, he felt for the plunger handle,

461

grasped it with both gloved hands. A stunted tree by the roadside showed where the huge mine had been buried overnight. They had even re-surfaced the road, covering the new section by smearing dust over it. A cable led from the mine up the hill-slope to the detonating mechanism. The armoured car had ruled out the use of an impact mine.

The staff car reached the stunted tree. Moshe rammed down the plunger with all his strength. The road erupted.

The framework of the staff car was shattered. They heard the tremendous roar of the mine detonating down at Lydda Airport. Appalled, Corporal Wilson jerked his head round. He took a split-second look, lowered his head and pulled down the lid.

Relics of the car were hurled into the sunlit air, showered on the closed lid of the armoured car like shrapnel. Later a twisted, burned-out remnant of the staff car's chassis was found in a nearby field. The diameter of the huge crater torn in the road was nine feet across. There were no survivors.

Once the shrapnel-like clatter ceased Wilson whipped back the lid and gazed backwards. The staff car had vanished, disintegrated in the terrible explosion. There are no graves for Lindsay, Paco, Major Len Reader, Major Gustav Hartmann or Sergeant Mulligan. They never found enough of the bodies to make burial worthwhile. A quiet memorial service was later held inside the privacy of the police barracks.

Arriving half an hour later in the jeep, Whelby was driven off the road to avoid the cratered zone. Ambulance men gazed helplessly at the carnage. Whelby spoke briefly to Wilson who was still in a state of shock.

'Obviously another Jewish outrage. The fortunes of war. Tell the press that when they get here. I've got a plane waiting for me at Lydda, so I'll push off . . .'

At the airfield Jock Carson, who had gone ahead to check the plane, was waiting for him. Whelby shook his head and boarded the Dakota without a word. Carson, who would have given anything to drive back to the scene of the disaster, followed him. He had just received an urgent signal from Grey Pillars ordering him to return to Egypt at the earliest possible moment. Within minutes the machine was airborne for Cairo.

After hearing the news over the radio the following morning, a brief reference to a military staff car being blown to pieces on the road to Lydda, Aaron Stein called the number at Grey Pillars given to him by Lindsay. He asked to speak to Lieutenant Jock Carson of Section 3.

'There is no one here of that name,' the operator informed him. 'Who is calling . . .'

'But there must be,' Stein insisted. 'Lieutenant Jock . . .'

'I said we have no one here of that name. *Who* is calling . . .?'

Stein, frightened by this strange development, put down the 'phone and looked at his brother, then glanced towards the wall-safe.

'What are we going to do with the envelope? Carson doesn't exist . . .'

'Leave it there and mind our own business. These are troubled days,' answered David.

They had no way of knowing that as soon as he reached GHQ the previous day Carson had found waiting for him an urgent, immediate posting to Burma. When Stein called, he was already aboard a plane half-way to India. Army Records show a Colonel Carson of Military Intelligence was later killed in Burma.

PART FOUR

WOODPECKER:
Der Specht

Chapter Forty-Four

Christ-Rose.

Watch on the Rhine.

These were the first two code-names which Hitler chose for the secret offensive to be launched against the Western Allies through the defiles and forests of the Ardennes.

But this was not May 1940 when the massive Ardennes breakthrough at Sedan across the Meuse had heralded the defeat of the BEF and the destruction of the great French Army – all based on a plan the Führer of those days had worked on and approved himself.

Autumn Fog.

This was the final code-name chosen for the new Ardennes operation by the German Army. And the date was 11 December 1944. The Allies had landed in Western Europe on 6 June and were now close to the Rhine. In the East the Red Army was sweeping ever westward across the Balkans and central Europe. And always the advances had been made with prior knowledge of just where the opposing German troops were, on information supplied by Woodpecker and transmitted via Lucy in Lucerne to Stalin.

'Autumn Fog is crazy,' Jodl confided to Keitel in the dining-car as the Führer's train, *Amerika*, approached Hitler's temporary headquarters in the West.

'Possibly, but why?' enquired the stiff-necked Keitel.

'I remember his exact words in April 1940 when he rejected the idea of reviving the First World War strategy. He said, "This is just the old Schlieffen Plan – you won't get away with that twice running . . ." Now he's committing the same error himself. Autumn Fog is a repeat performance of his brilliant strategic plan when we were here in 1940 . . .'

'Maybe you'd like to voice your objections to this chap,' suggested Keitel as Martin Bormann entered the coach.

The Reichsleiter, self-confident as always, despite his dwarf-like stature, strutted through the coach, his eyes flickering over every passenger in the dining-car as though he might still detect the traitor Hitler was always convinced was buried among those closest to him.

His eyes met Jodl's, who stared back at him ironically until he had passed their table. The Chief of Staff picked up the conversation where he had left off.

'I find the whole business very strange – as though the Führer of 1940 was a different man from the Führer of 1944 . . .'

'He is ill. He was subjected to the bomb explosion at the Wolf's Lair . . .'

Keitel stopped speaking and began eating some more bread. It was a trait Jodl had noticed often in Keitel – he issued broad statements but if you listened carefully he never really said anything, anything that could be quoted against him.

'We're even going to the same headquarters – Felsennest – as Hitler used in 1940,' Jodl continued. 'The Eagle's Eyrie. I find that an unsettling omen for Autumn Fog . . .'

'*Gentlemen!*' It was Bormann calling out from the end of the coach. 'Conference in the Führer's quarters. At once, if you please. Breakfast will wait.'

'Breakfast will get cold,' Keitel muttered.

Autumn Fog dissipated. Literally. While fog shrouded the forests of the Ardennes the Panzer divisions advanced, breaking through towards the vital bridges over the river Meuse, as they had in May 1940.

Then the weather changed. The skies cleared and the overwhelming might of the Allied air forces pounded the Panzers, forcing the German Panthers and Tigers to retreat. Hitler seemed to have lost his military flair.

Hitler arrived at Felsennest on 11 December 1944. He left the place for Berlin on 15 January 1945 with his entourage – including the inevitable trio; Bormann, Jodl and Keitel. He was never to leave Berlin alive.

30 April 1945. Berlin was in flames. Smoke and falling ashes mingled with the red glare of the inferno. The Red Army was advancing into the centre of the city, was very near the underground bunker where Hitler and Eva Braun had committed suicide.

Their bodies, carried up into the courtyard outside the bunker, had been liberally soused with petrol and set alight. Nothing was now left except their bones.

Panic gripped the remaining members of his entourage as they tried to find a route to escape from the Russians, to surrender to the Allies. In the early hours of 1 May Martin Bormann joined a group of fellow-escapers.

They planned to make their way along the underground rail track from the station below the Wilhelmplatz. Out of sight of any Russian patrols in the streets above, they would emerge again above ground at the Friedrichstrasse station. From there they would cross the river Spree and slip through the Russian lines.

The plan went wrong from the beginning. The city, bombarded by Soviet guns, was in ruins, the streets littered with giant pieces of masonry; there was hardly a single intact building in sight. Dust from powdered masonry was everywhere, coating their clothes, polluting their mouths.

'We must keep moving,' Bormann told Artur Axmann, a Hitler Youth leader. 'Get behind that tank – it will shield us from Russian small arms fire . . .'

They stumbled on through the night, using the German tank as a mobile wall as it fired repeatedly into the enemy lines. Night was turning into day by the incessant blood-red flares drifting down from above. The noise was an assault on the ear-drums. The detonation of Russian shells exploding. The crash of one of the few remaining buildings collapsing, walls heaving outwards, crumbling in the streets. The Asiatic hordes had now over-run one of the West's greatest capitals.

'Get down!' Bormann warned.

There was a sinister hissing noise. Something struck the tank they had been following. It stopped, bursting into a searing flame. Bormann's uniform was blackened with

469

smoke, smeared with filth. Leaving Axmann crouched behind a pile of rubble Bormann pressed on.

The last Western witness who saw Bormann alive was an SS Major Joachim Tiburtius who was close to the Reichsleiter and his companion when the tank was destroyed. He couldn't see Bormann after the explosion and made his way towards the German lines which were still holding.

Fifteen minutes later Tiburtius, alone in the hell Berlin had become, saw one building still intact among its neighbours which were silhouetted against the flaming glare like jagged teeth. The Hotel Atlas. He entered the building. In the lobby he paused in sheer astonishment.

Martin Bormann was walking across the lobby towards the exit. That he should have survived was a miracle. But he was no longer wearing his uniform. Somewhere he had found a suit of civilian clothes. Major Tiburtius waited eight years before he reported what he saw that night. His story was printed in the Berne newspaper *Der Bund* in the issue of 17 February 1953.

He (Bormann) had by then changed into civilian clothes. We pushed on together towards the Schiffbauerdamm and the Albrechtstrasse. Then I finally lost sight of him . . .

Stalin himself had despatched to Berlin the special, highly secret unit of the Red Army charged with a dual task. An unusual aspect of the unit of eleven, heavily-armed men, was the fact that an interpreter was attached to it – and that this individual was a woman, Yelena Rzhevskaya.

Even stranger was the fact that the real commander of this unit was Yelena. For her first task she had been personally instructed by Stalin to find Hitler 'alive or dead . . .'

Barely one kilometre from the Hotel Atlas, Bormann walked straight into the arms of this unit. He stood quite still as the unit surrounded him, aiming their machine-pistols. He was astounded when Yelena appeared and addressed him in fluent German.

'You are Martin Bormann?'

'That is so.'

'And where shall we find Hitler?' she asked.

'Outside the underground bunker by the ruins of the new Chancellery. I can tell you how to get there . . .'

'It will not be necessary,' Yelena interjected, 'we have our map of the whole of Berlin.'

'Only his bones are left,' Bormann continued. 'They poured petrol over the bodies . . .'

'Bodies?'

'Eva Braun was burnt beside him. They got married just before . . .'

'You can tell us the details later,' she said brusquely. She gave brief orders in Russian to the unit and seven of the eleven men in Red Army uniform disappeared. 'Now, Mr Martin Bormann,' continued Yelena, 'you will come with us. A plane is waiting to fly you to Moscow.'

The Russian aircraft carrying Yelena, Bormann and the four other members of the special unit landed at a military airfield outside Moscow. Two large black limousines were waiting, their windows masked with amber-coloured net curtains.

'You sit in the back with me,' Yelena informed Bormann.

It was still dark, the gloomy dark of early morning with a sky full of snow, when the first limousine entered the Kremlin. The Reichsleiter peered curiously out, remembering Ribbentrop's description of this strange place after his return from signing the Nazi-Soviet Pact in August 1939 which triggered off the outbreak of the Second World War.

The limousine, which had moved at nerve-racking speed on the drive from the airfield, now barely crawled as it moved slowly into the mysterious inner city. Bormann had the odd feeling he was leaving life itself behind.

The limousine drove across a courtyard past the largest cannon of its day – so enormous that no one had ever dared fire it. He stared at the little wooden houses and cathedrals which formed a world all their own. Finally the limousine pulled up outside a modern administration block. Yelena ushered him inside. Stalin was waiting for them. The only other occupant of the small room was Laventri Beria. The

Soviet chief, dressed in his full uniform of Generalissimo, waited until Yelena had left before he spoke, his tone quite casual, a malicious glint in his yellowish eyes.

'This,' said Stalin, pointing at Bormann, 'is Woodpecker.'

Beria was speechless. Word that a special unit had been sent to Berlin had reached his all-hearing ears and he had wondered why the NKVD had not been used. Now he began to understand. He fiddled with his pince-nez before he reacted, staring at Martin Bormann who no longer looked like a dwarf. Stalin and the German were of approximately the same height and build.

'So you had a pipeline right into Hitler's headquarters . . .'

'From the moment he launched his attack on us . . .'

'But it seemed to take you a long time to believe me,' Bormann remarked petulantly.

Beria's normally impassive face froze. No one interrupted Stalin. The Generalissimo seemed unperturbed by the gross impertinence. He pulled at the end of his moustache and his expression was crafty.

'You were planted many years ago. I had to be certain your role as spy had not been penetrated, that you were not being forced to supply disinformation.'

'I dealt with the new Hitler rather well,' Bormann preened himself.

'Ah! The second Hitler . . .' Stalin was amused. 'He never existed. It was always the same old Hitler. That is our version of history, is it not, Beria?'

'Of course.'

'You can rely on my discretion,' Bormann assured them.

Stalin chuckled. 'I am sure we can! You will be taken to another place for interrogation, naturally . . .'

'In a way,' Beria interjected slyly, 'we might even say that Woodpecker won the war . . .'

'I would not go so far as to say that,' Bormann replied with unconvincing modesty.

'It is time for your formal interrogation,' Stalin said abruptly. 'The car is waiting for you at the main entrance . . .'

He pressed a bell and three men in civilian clothes appeared as though awaiting the summons. The three NKVD men escorted the bewildered Bormann back to the limousine which had brought him to the Kremlin. The same driver drove him the short distance to the notorious No 2, Dzerzhinsky Square, the anonymous grey stone building which was NKVD headquarters. Oddly enough, before the Revolution, it had been the property of the All-Russian Insurance Company.

There was a weird atmosphere as the limousine drove inside the courtyard surrounded by buildings which closed it off from the outside world. All the staff who normally worked there had been given a day's holiday. 'To celebrate the capture of Berlin.'

Two more NKVD officers in civilian clothes joined the three men accompanying Bormann as he alighted from the car. He was immediately hand-cuffed and stood against a wall. Armed with rifles, the five NKVD men formed a firing squad. Bormann sagged against the wall in horrific disbelief as the rifles were aimed at him.

'Fire . . .!'

Following the precedent set by Hitler's death, the body was soaked in petrol and set alight. The ashes of the Reichsleiter were later scattered from the air over Lake Peipus.

Once the ashes were collected, a much larger contingent of NKVD officers, totally ignorant of what had taken place, arrived. They had been told that certain of their colleagues had been found guilty of treachery against the state. The five men who had formed the firing squad together with the driver of the limousine and the pilot who had flown Bormann to Moscow were shot. There was now only one person left besides Stalin and Beria who knew that Martin Bormann had ever reached Moscow.

In his office at the Kremlin Stalin waited with Beria for the first 'phone call. The Generalissimo was relaxed. He chatted with his Minister of State Security, smoking his pipe.

He picked up the 'phone himself when it rang. He listened

473

for less than a minute and ended the call. He took a few more puffs at his pipe before he spoke to Beria.

'Bormann is dead. You can start the campaign of rumours. I might even give a hand myself . . .'

'And the bones of the second Hitler . . .?' Beria ventured.

'Already collected by the special team Yelena took to Berlin. They have been scattered over the Baltic. So they will never be found. It was a necessary conclusion to this war. We cannot risk a cult growing up of new Nazis worshipping the grave of the Führer, can we?'

'Of course not. It was well done.'

Beria wisely said no more. He knew there were a dozen other reasons why the faithful Woodpecker, recruited so many years earlier, must disappear. Generalissimo Stalin was posing as the military genius who had won the war. The myth would be destroyed if it was ever revealed that he had known the German order of battle as the Red Army, a five-million strong horde reinforced from the Far East, swept across Europe.

It was equally essential that no one should ever know of the existence of the second Hitler. If this were exposed there were the makings of a second myth. The real Hitler had been a military genius.

He had over-ruled his generals by sanctioning the audacious invasion of Denmark and Norway in 1940. He had shown the same insight when he tore up the Schlieffen Plan for the invasion of the West, backing Manstein and Guderian with their operation for a blitzkrieg through Sedan against France and Great Britain.

Had Western Intelligence agents found the remains of Hitler's burnt-out corpse – and under Trevor-Roper's guidance they looked hard enough for it – pathologists could well have proved it was the wrong body.

The savage irony of the story is that it started with blood. When the Führer's plane returning from Smolensk was blown up in mid-air, just before landing at the Wolf's Lair, it triggered off a bloodbath.

It ended in a similar bloodbath. For similar motives Stalin

474

liquidated everyone – with two exceptions – who knew Bormann had been brought to Moscow. The men who shot Bormann in their turn were killed by men who knew nothing of Bormann's journey to Moscow.

Yelena Rzhevskaya, the woman who commanded the special squad flown to Berlin, was one exception. Even dictators can act inconsistently. There is evidence that Stalin had a soft spot for this remarkable woman who led her team into the raging inferno of Berlin.

'Yelena, apart from myself and Beria, you are the only person alive who knows what really happened. So, if anything should ever leak out I will know where to look, wouldn't you agree?'

It was probably something like that. It is a fact that in 1965, twelve years after the death of Stalin in 1953, Yelena contributed an article to the Russian journal, *Znamya*, which she called Berlinskie Stranitsky – Berlin Notes. In this she alluded to her special mission to the German capital 'to find Hitler, alive or dead . . .' The article was vague and no reference was made to Martin Bormann. This was in the days of the 'great thaw'. Two years later in 1967 Yuri Andropov took over the post as Chairman of the Ministry of State Security and revived the sinister power of the KGB.

As he had said he would to Beria, Stalin did take the opportunity to do his bit in fuelling the rumours Beria's Soviet agents in South America were spreading that Bormann had escaped to that continent.

He was talking to Harry Hopkins, President Roosevelt's special representative. He inserted the remark casually into their conversation.

'I have serious doubts as to whether the Führer is dead. He surely escaped and is in hiding in Argentina with Martin Bormann.'

This was Stalin's only epitaph for Woodpecker.

Epilogue

Returning from abroad a few years ago, the author met David Stein (that is not his real name), a diamond broker living in Hampstead. He was shown an opened envelope containing a black, leather-bound diary. On the outside of the envelope were the following words.

Account of my visit to the Third Reich in the year 1943 and my subsequent sojourn in Jugoslavia. In the event of my death to be handed to Lieutenant Jock Carson, Section 3, Grey Pillars, Cairo, Egypt. Ian Lindsay, Wing Commander.

He was not permitted to take away the diary, so he read it as he sat in Stein's study. When he returned it, he gained the impression the diary would shortly be destroyed. Stein explained that the thought of his home being invaded by security men was abhorrent. In any case, his brother, Aaron, had died in a car crash recently.

The fate of certain leading characters in this story is now a matter of record. All the facts can be found in historical archives.

Colonel-General Alfred Jodl. Tried for war crimes at Nuremberg. Condemned. Hanged.

Field Marshal Wilhelm Keitel. Tried for war crimes at Nuremberg. Condemned. Hanged.

Brigadier Roger Masson. The head of Swiss Intelligence survived the war. The man who protected Lucy (and therefore, without realizing it, Woodpecker) retired at the end of World War Two. Accused of collaboration with the Nazis, because of his dealings with Schellenberg, he had to endure a government enquiry which completely exonerated him. Nevertheless, it was an embittered man who took up residence in his home overlooking Vevey on Lake Geneva.

Rudolf Roessler. The asthmatic German code-named Lucy, who played one of the strangest roles in history, lost all sense of purpose when peace came. He had devoted himself with such dedication to his task of defeating Hitler that he felt like a fish stranded on a beach when it all came to an end. Tired out and disillusioned, he died in October 1958. His grave may be seen in the cemetery at Kriens near Lucerne. The small marble plaque bears a brief inscription. *Rudolf Roessler. 1897–1958.*

Walter Schellenberg. The chief of SS Intelligence reached the Allied lines at the war's end. He spent the next three years in Great Britain as the guest of the Secret Service. He undoubtedly provided invaluable information. Tried at Nuremberg, he should have been acquitted, but the Russian judge insisted on a verdict of 'Guilty'. Sentenced to four years' imprisonment, he was released after serving three years because of ill-health. He died a few years later.

Tim Whelby. During 1944 Whelby was promoted to run a new department formed by SIS. Its purpose: counter-espionage. Its sphere of operations: Soviet-occupied Eastern Europe.

It all happened a long time ago.

Colin Forbes
Target Five £2.95

No quarter is asked or given when a top Russian oceanographer defects across the Arctic icefields with plans of their submarine network. The Americans send in dog teams and an unconventional trio under Anglo-Canadian agent Keith Beaumont. The Russians use everything they have in an increasingly bloody life-or-death struggle to win him back . . .

Tramp in Armour £2.95

The time is that fateful spring of 1940 when the Panzers rolled across Northern France with nothing to stop them. Stranded behind the German lines, a solitary Matilda tank and its crew, led by the resourceful Sergeant Barnes, scheme, smash and manoeuvre their way towards Dunkirk.

'A caterpillar-tracked cliff-hanger' DAILY TELEGRAPH

Year of the Golden Ape £2.50

Racing at Concorde speed from the Middle East through Europe to California, a ruthless battle of wits reaches unparalleled tension as mercenaries hijack a giant British tanker, arm her with a plutonium bomb and sail into San Francisco harbour.

Jack Higgins
Touch the Devil £2.50

'Touch the Devil and you can't let go' – an old Irish saying which fits Frank Barry, 100-per-cent a terrorist; his ideology is money and his track record is the best. When the Russians want review copies of the latest NATO missile system, Barry's the man to deliver them. The only man who can stop him is Martin Brosnan, poet and scholar, a killer trained in Vietnam and polished in the service of the IRA, currently a convict rotting in the French prison fortress of Belle Isle. To get him out of there and working for British Intelligence is a job for his oldest friend, Liam Devlin . . .

'Higgins . . . knows what he's about and does his job with skill, speed, sang-froid' NEW YORK TIMES

Day of Judgement £2.50

1963: on the eve of Kennedy's historic visit to Berlin, Ulbricht's commissars plan their propaganda counter-strike from the red side of the Wall. Father Sean Conlin, survivor of Dachau and apostle of human freedom, is held captive in the impregnable fortress of Schloss Neustadt, his gaolers determined to make him admit to being a CIA hireling. The West must save Conlin, and a small band of intrepid men take on a rescue mission that could sway the course of history.

'Fast moving, meticulously organized, relentlessly demanding' SUNDAY TIMES

Storm Warning £2.50

Across 5,000 miles of wild Atlantic dominated by Allied navies – twenty-two men and five nuns aboard the barquentine *Deutschland* battling home to Kiel . . .

A U-boat ace captured in a desperate raid on Falmouth . . . an American girl doctor caught in the nightmare of the Flying Bombs . . . a gunboat commander who's fought from the Solomons to the Channel . . . a Rear Admiral who itches to get back into action . . . all drawn inexorably into the eye of the storm . . .

'Stunning . . . the work of a superb storyteller' DAILY MAIL

Gavin Lyall
The Secret Servant £2.50

A suicide at the Ministry of Defence. A hand grenade through the door of Number ten. A Czech defector with a file worth killing for. The whole sequence of grisly incidents points the finger at Professor John Tyler, nuclear strategist and insatiable lecher. The man who will state Britain's case when Europe's think tank on armageddon gathers in Luxembourg.

Harry Maxim – SAS major on special assignment to Downing Street – is under orders to watch Tyler. The professor is a flawed man. Maxim knows how flawed . . .

'Splendid . . . all the fascination of a le Carré plot' THE TIMES

The Conduct of Major Maxim £2.50

When Corporal Ron Blagg shot down a German registrar of births and deaths, the Secret Service chose to forget he'd been working for them at the time. Now Corporal Blagg's AWOL and running scared. If anyone can help him it'll have to be another soldier, one who can survive in the world of pinstriped cloak and old-school dagger – a soldier like Harry Maxim. It's not long before the conduct of Major Maxim in places as diverse as Billy Dann's boxing gym and a German garrison town is causing concern in the more sensitive corridors of Whitehall.

'Lyall saunters down the corridors of power . . . with laconic grace and steady aim' SUNDAY TIMES

All these books are available at your local bookshop or newsagent, or can be ordered direct from the publisher. Indicate the number of copies required and fill in the form below
....

Name _____
(Block letters please)

Address _____
_____

Send to CS Department, Pan Books Ltd, PO Box 40, Basingstoke, Hants
Please enclose remittance to the value of the cover price plus:
35p for the first book plus 15p per copy for each additional book ordered
to a maximum charge of £1.25 to cover postage and packing
Applicable only in the UK

While every effort is made to keep prices low, it is sometimes necessary to increase prices at short notice. Pan books reserve the right to show on covers and charge new retail prices which may differ from those advertised in the text or elsewhere

HIGH PRAISE FOR CAROLINE GRAHAM
AND
FAITHFUL UNTO DEATH

"Intricate and shocking . . . The conclusion of this excellent novel is truly surprising—plausible and satisfying. . . . Lovers of British mysteries who haven't yet sampled Graham's work will find this an excellent place to start."   —*Booklist*

"Graham makes her characters humanly believable in her witty and tragic novel, a real winner . . . An uncommonly appealing novel."   —*Publishers Weekly*

"Graham writes in an old-fashioned way with leisurely grace, ironic wit, real-seeming characters, ongoing suspense, and a corker of a plot. The result: top-flight entertainment."   —*Kirkus Reviews* (starred review)

"Graham expertly balances low-key style of detection with a rich variety of disparate characters."   —*San Francisco Chronicle*

"Fawcett Green: an ideal setting for a comfortable English cozy, you'd think. For only about a page or so, until Caroline Graham's incisive, almost savage take on village quaintness opens your eyes. And then come the surprises."   —*Philadelphia Inquirer*

"Fans of English writer Caroline Graham's Chief Inspector Barnaby mysteries will want to queue up to read FAITHFUL UNTO DEATH. Graham's dry wit is on full display in this seemingly cozy tale."   —*Orlando Sentinel*

"Great stuff for British procedural fans."   —*Library Journal*

"Terrific . . . with an ingenious plot and excellent characters and characterizations."   —*The Guardian* (UK)

"Graham is probably the most underrated British crime writer. Her talent is rare, combining wit, pathos, and an entertaining narrative. Here she takes the 'mayhem parva' so beloved by Christie fans and weaves her own magic into it. Brilliant."
—*Yorkshire Post* (UK)

"Her books are not just great whodunnits but great novels in their own right."   —*The Sunday Times of London*